THE HIGH SEER

DARKLING SOULS BOOK ONE

ALEX BREE

DARKLING SOULS ONE

THE HIGH SEER

ALEX BREE

CONTENT WARNING

This is a dark fantasy story about monsters with content that may not be suitable for all readers. For a complete content list, please visit the author's website at www.alexbreewrites.com.

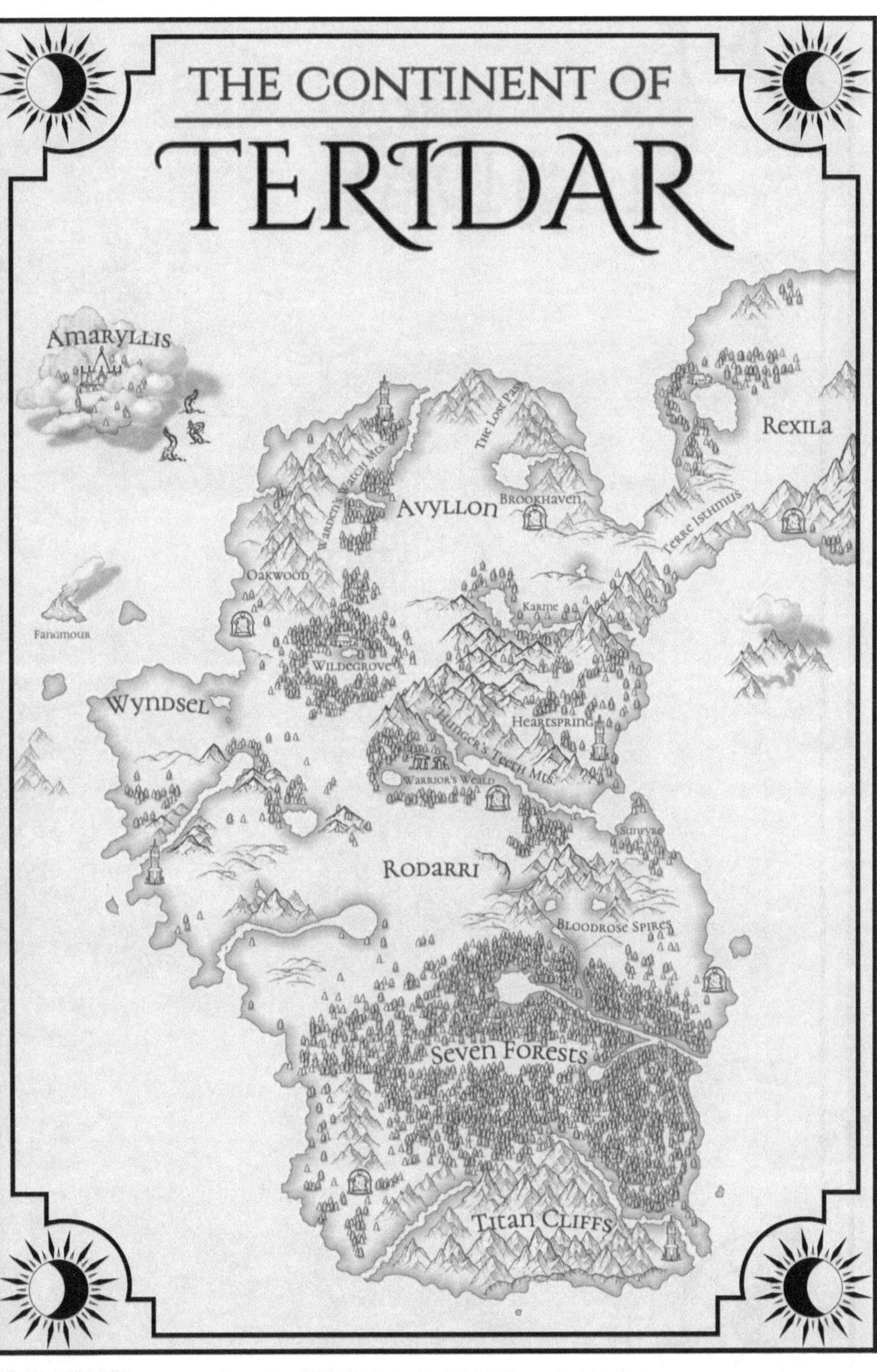

THE CONTINENT OF
TERIDAR
Amaryllis
Rexila
The Lost Pass
Avyllon
Brookhaven
Warden's Watch Mts.
Oakwood
Karme
Terre Isthmus
Fangmour
Wildegrove
Heartspring
Wyndsel
Thunder's Teeth Mts.
Warrior's Weald
Sunfyre
Rodarri
Bloodrose Spires
Seven Forests
Titan Cliffs

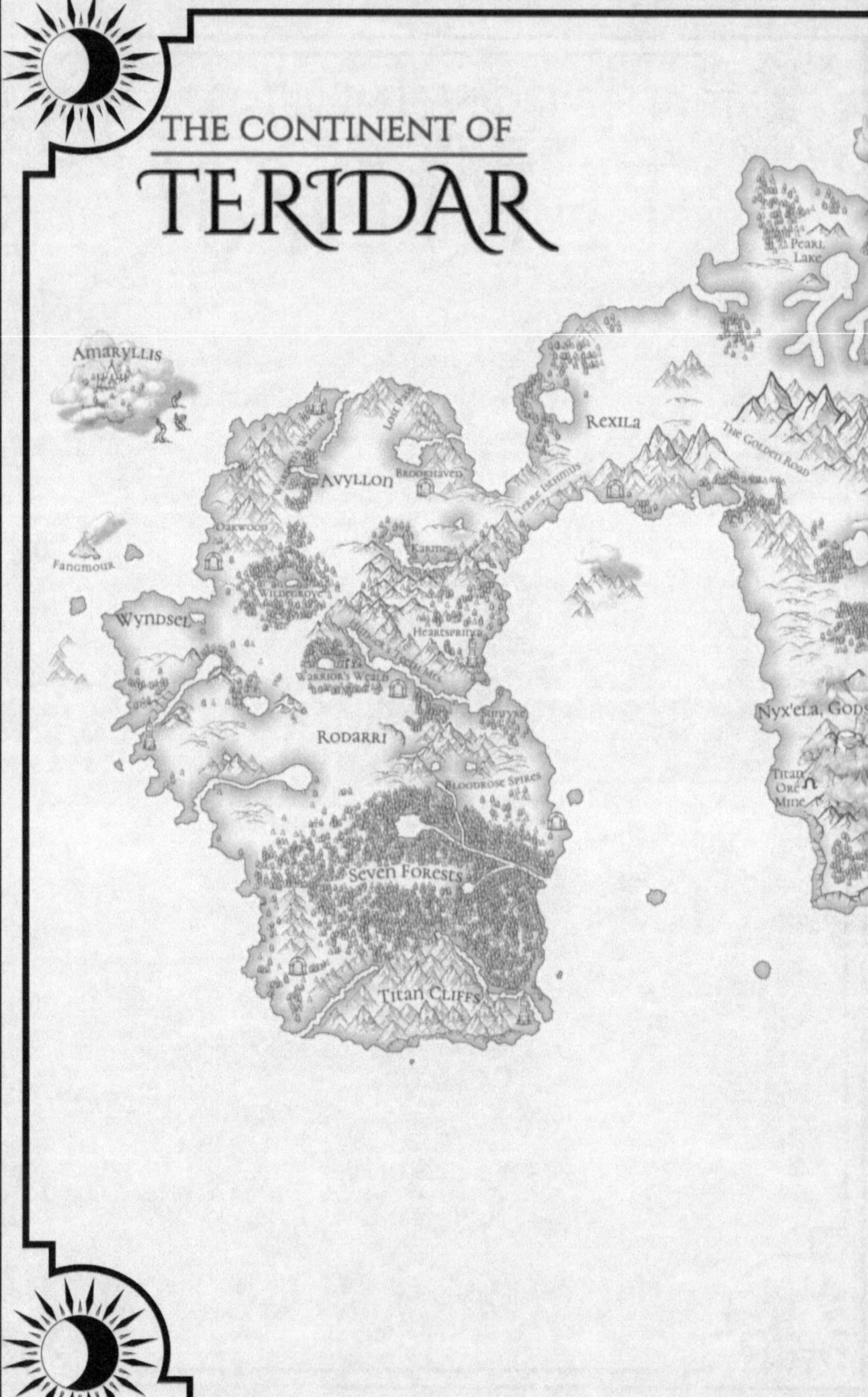

THE CONTINENT OF
TERIDAR
Amaryllis
Fangmoux
Wyndsel
Oakwood
Avyllon
Brookhaven
Karine
Wildegrove
Heartspring
Warrior's Weald
Rodarri
Suvyar
Bloodrose Spires
Seven Forests
Titan Cliffs
Rexila
The Golden Road
Pearl Lake
Nyx'ela, Gods
Titan Ore Mine
Lost Pass
Teethe Isthmus

Moon Wilds
Stone Tongue
Revarie
Dreamfruit Orchards
Wolf Run
Sharktooth Islands
Sun Peach Orchards
Midnight Apple Orchards
Eternal Orchards
Twisting Sands
Dragon's Egg Lake
Kraken's Hook Villages
Khesross
Dragon's Spine
The Golden Road
The Golden Road
Nucifera
Ala'end
Lotus Lake
Bonewealh Wood
Dragon's Eye Lake
Bottomless Lake
Meili'de
Enzhu
Giant's Stair
Whale Tail Cove
Cutting Shoal
Isle
THE CONTINENT OF
DEMORRA

DARKLING SOULS

This is not a story of heroes saving the world from evil. Here the champions are just as dark as the villains they fight, and their deeds as terrible. Curses, sacrifices, and hellsdamned souls losing the fight against corruption yet refusing to give up the last of their humanity.

This is the story of how monsters saved their corner of the world. Whether they deserved to be saved is another story.

PART ONE

THE LAST OMEN
CHAPTER ONE

One thousand stars fly as souls unearthed.
The monsters of old roam the earth.
Four pillars lost and the fifth lost by Fate.
Darkened skies fill with howling hate.
The fate of the world hangs by moon's light.
Darkling souls fight, darkling souls die.

— BIRTH PROPHECY FOR THE HIGH SEER
AURIENNE AZARRAH.

1152 N.T.C. Lunahain Festival. The namesake capital city of Avyllon.

With a sweeping arc of her hand, the High Seer summoned her divination deck from its spelled box on her altar. Enchanted cards soared through the air, coming to rest in a perfect fan at Aurienne's feet. Dark prophecies whispered at the corners of her mind as she studied her cards, which changed as the magic of her own blood, sweat, and tears granted them life.

Four dozen cloudy-eyed seers in ornamental gowns waited silently for her reading, still as the dead. A hundred candle flames flickered as their melted wax dripped to the intricately carved stone floors in her chambers. Colored scrying crystals and glass orbs reflected the light into dazzling patterns on the pearlescent quartzite walls. Carved skulls and ancient cursed tomes adorned her altar beside bone runes and delicate glass bottles filled with swirling liquids and florae.

Aurienne knelt, taking care not to wrinkle her ceremonial gown of white semi-translucent spider silk; delicate as dragonfly wings, and spun with gold thread stitching. Her tattooed skin was painstakingly painted with celestial designs in ink as dark as a moonless sky. As her decorated hands traced across the cards, the delicate golden chains connecting her fingers to her wrists clinked.

She paused at the Death card.

"You're still here," Aurienne murmured. "I haven't seen you all year. I wondered if you had left."

Sixty-three cards in three suits watched her. The figure on one card blinked. Aurienne paused, noticing a new design.

"The Traveler," she said as she skimmed over the deck. "You replaced...the King."

Aurienne resisted the urge to chew her gold-painted lip or rub her kohl-lined eyes. The rest of the cards remained unchanged. With a wave of her hand, Aurienne collected them. She breathed on the deck before raising it to her forehead, lips, and heart, touching lightly enough to not disturb the paint on her skin.

"I offer my blood to the cards for the annual eclipse foretelling."

She sliced her fingertip with a ceremonial blade, adding a new layer of scars. The cut burned, and she had to force herself not to flinch or let the hiss escape her painted lips—not in front of the others. She gritted her teeth behind a false smile, or what she thought a smile ought to look like. Blood welled, and precious droplets dripped onto the back of the deck, which devoured it eagerly.

"Triple Goddess—maiden's hope, mother's love, crone's

wisdom," she prayed. "Seer of all. The great eye. Open my Sight to See our salvation. Tell me what I must do to avoid our horrible fate. Show me how to save our people."

In her mind, her prayer was different and full of guarded secrets.

Please help me save them. I'll do anything. I'll bear any cost, but please don't let me fail them.

She shuffled the deck, letting them go where they willed while holding three questions in mind. The deck warmed, whispering it was time.

"I ask for guidance this coming year for our people."

Aurienne flipped the first.

The Traveler.

The seers leaned forward, murmuring to one another as their serene masks slipped and revealed their excitement. They never missed a chance to observe their High Seer read fates, but especially not on this most important day of the year. Not when this much was at stake, and there was so much to lose. Aurienne was the youngest High Seer in history, gifted with the power of the Goddess herself and ascending at over twelve years ago at the age of thirteen. Her birth prophecy haunted her tirelessly, and she saw danger in every shadow. She glanced at the seers, studying their reactions for the slightest hint of doubt. The Goddess would not tolerate it. *Aurienne* would not tolerate it.

"The Traveler signifies great change and new knowledge," Aurienne said.

She paused, staring at the card. Newly changing and being drawn first held great importance. The dread in the pit of her stomach promised she would soon know the full meaning of it.

The second question struck fear into her heart. Though snippets of visions came to her daily, sought or not, the foretelling ceremony opened her Sight to all Avyllon's fate for an entire year. Such a feat could only be accomplished on this day when the veil between worlds thinned, and her own soul was close to death. It required a Rite.

"I ask whether the Rite of Earth, Sky, Flame, or Water will open my eyes to the knowledge of the eclipse."

Aurienne prepared herself for the next question. *Please be Sky. Please be Sky.*

"The Rite today shall be…"

She turned the next card.

The River.

"The Rite of Water," Aurienne said.

Dread rose in her throat like floodwaters. She could almost taste the water at the bottom of that accursed pool again and feel its deadly, silky caress on her skin. Weight pressed down on her, dragging her to the depths—lungs screaming for air that would not come. Her lips pulled taut, and bile rose in her throat. She clenched her hands to keep them from shaking.

No. The others couldn't see her fear.

While nearly drowning was not a pleasant Rite, her ankles still bore scars of the Rite of Flame, and nightmares of being buried alive plagued her. She *should* be thankful she did not draw either of those, but if she were honest, she was angry—furious—that she had to do *any* Rite. She let anger overtake her dread as she schooled her features flat.

I've given too much, and still, the specter of that accursed prophecy remains. When will I be free of it?

Against her better judgment, and it being too late to turn back now, she took a steadying breath and asked her final question.

"I ask for Avyllon's fate in the coming Darkling War."

The other seers exchanged dark looks. This question had not been asked since the first reading at her birth, and their lips quivered as though they wanted to beg her to retract. Only they knew her secret.

The Eye's Sight shall betray her. Avyllon will fall. Her visions will cause them to lose the Darkling War and doom all of Teridar.

Aurienne's fate. The thought of failure made her want to disappear into the floor stones. Under their respect and adoration remained an unspoken doubt that she'd bring ruin upon them all. Her expression hardened.

That would not happen.

Though the people of Avyllon knew about the impending threat of the Darkling War, if they knew *her* visions would be their downfall, there would be widespread panic. The city, nay, the nation, would fall to chaos. As it was, the other seers were terrified because Aurienne's visions and readings always came true.

She took a steadying breath. The others were waiting.

"Tell me our fate this year."

Show me our foe.

Every seer in the room, young and old, from every corner of Avyllon, held their breath. The only sounds in the still room were the crackling of candle wicks and the rubbing of oiled skin from seers wringing their hands. Serene masks froze in pained grimaces.

Aurienne flipped the final card.

Death.

The figure on the card winked at her deviously. She stifled a soft gasp. For a long and terrible moment, her heart stilled. War. Destruction. Death. Every dark vision haunting her waking and dreaming hours, whispering to her that her birth prophecy would soon consume them all was *here*. *Now*. Their time was up, and she had no path to save them.

A bolt of terror struck it beating again, and blood pounded in her ears. She quickly covered the card with her ring-encrusted fingers and painted her best soft, reassuring smile on her face for the other seers.

"The Triple Goddess card," Aurienne lied. "Our fate rests with her. She will guide us. Our salvation lies in our faith."

The other seers released a collective breath and exchanged nods, the tensions in the room dissipating.

Saryll, one of the younger and more powerful seers, stepped forward, her long skirts sweeping the floor. "We will prepare the pool for the Rite and let the public know. It will be ready at midday, just before the eclipse."

"Thank you, Saryll."

The other seers filed out of the room, leaving Aurienne alone with Death hidden under her fingers. Aurienne lifted her hand. She had only drawn it three times in her life, and calamity followed. Drawing it today was a terrible omen; it meant that the foretold war would come *this* year. By the next eclipse, Avyllon might be gone. She had to figure out what to do before the others learned of their fate.

I'm doing everything I can.

Aurienne forced back the tears welling at the corners of her eyes. She would not cry. She would not. No tears spilled when her mother left her on the temple steps at the age of five and never came back. She would not cry now. Anger took the place of hopelessness.

She studied the three cards, tapping a gold-painted nail on the Traveler. Death turned its head toward the Traveler. A shudder traveled down her spine, and she blinked and looked again.

Goddess' breath.

She returned Death and the River to the deck but held the Traveler. "Who are you?"

The card remained silent. With a final glance, she placed it down. Standing, she smoothed her gold-adorned gown before placing her cards inside the spelled box with reverence. Then, the seer prepared herself to drown.

Her instincts screamed at her to run, prickling her skin with dread. Her lungs contracted in anticipation of what was to come, and she forced herself to take measured breaths. The fear roiled her blood in waves, crushing her under the weight of a furious tempest. She fought back with wrath amassed from a life lived chained by fate, duty, and desperation until her body reached its limit. Until the dread numbed, and she felt nothing at all.

Retreating into her soul, she slipped into the world of spirits and pressed her fingers against the veil separating the worlds and times. The veil parted, and she stepped into the domain of futures and fates.

"We're ready for you," Saryll said moments later, clasping her painted hands in front of her.

Aurienne blinked and noticed the stiffness in her bones. She glanced out the window. The sun was at its height. Once more, hours had passed while Aurienne was lost in thought. It was already time. Any peace she found fled. She took a slow deep breath, and another, and though her throat was thick, she would *not* cry. She painted on the expected expression.

"Thank you," Aurienne said absently.

She followed her sister seer through the empty temple. Soon, it would fill with thousands of supplicants asking for readings and omens. The seers would be busy for days, ensuring every last one of them had their fate read. But for now, her footsteps echoed against stone walls, and shadows filled every room. They passed the giant unopened wooden doors at the front of the temple, between the columns carved from a single ancient tree.

Aurienne paused as the other seers filed outside between the columns and through the veils. Saryll gave her a long and quiet glance —one she never would have risked in front of the others. Saryll squeezed her hand and stepped outside.

Should I have smiled at Saryll? Squeezed back? Nodded?

The temple's speaker began to announce her. She took a steadying breath. It was not the Rite of Flame. It was not Earth. Sky would have been best, but Water would end within minutes. Her brain betrayed her and threatened to panic, but she repeated calming words.

It will be fine. Drowning comes quickly, in just minutes, unless something goes wrong. No. I've done this before. It will be fine.

The Death card meant it was critical she receive visions or every person in Avyllon would perish. Aurienne narrowed her eyes. She'd do whatever it took to prevent that. She let anger fill her chest and clung to it for dear life.

She stepped into the light. The crowd roared and cheered, though she barely noticed. Flower petals danced in the air and kissed her skin, but she hardly saw them. Her gaze panned across the crowd, coming to rest upon one young man who stared at her with his mouth open. He stood taller than most, covered in the dust of a long journey, with wide, bright green eyes following her as she stepped into the sun. She concealed a smile.

Her mind drifted again. She knew the other seers hovered behind her in a semi-circle. She knew her brother Adonis and his sorcerer mentor would be standing to the side. She knew there were temple guards, and the Commander of Avyllon's armies, General Kane, would be in a place of great import. She Saw this in her mind's eye, so there was no reason to look.

She spoke the ceremonial words. "Today, we celebrate the eclipse and honor the Goddess who guides us. The solar eclipse comes every year…"

The familiar words were so etched into her mind that she hardly paid attention. The cards from the reading flashed into her thoughts.

Traveler.

River.

Death.

Aurienne winced. She had no idea what they meant, and worse, she had lied to her sisters. Having finished with her speech, she prepared for what came next.

She silently prayed under her breath to the Goddess. "Please show me. I have served you my whole life. I'll serve you until my last day. Help me save them."

Aurienne dipped a painted foot into the pool. The water lapped gently against the golden anklets on her flame-scarred ankles. Ink twirled in the water in tiny eddies. With a deep breath, she stepped off the ledge and sank. Her head went under, and she tried to force away the fear building in her chest. The eclipse darkened the skies, turning the water around her to shadows. The sun disappeared, and the world was enveloped in darkness.

The surface faded away as her heavy gown pulled her down, dragging her toward darkness and causing her heart to beat wildly. She fought the urge to rip off the gown and kick toward the surface as her throat gasped for air.

Goddess be with me.

Sinking quickly, she thrashed until fear darkened the edges of her eyesight, threatening to take her. She searched for the magic that allowed her to slip between worlds, but the fear walled her in.

A voice whispered, "You were born for this."

She stilled.

The Death card told her there was no time left, no room for failure. This was her last chance—surrounded by the faith and belief of Avyllon and so close to death. If she failed now, she wouldn't have another chance. She found that familiar quiet place in her mind. The second her toes touched the bottom, she opened her second Sight. The veil between worlds thinned, and she parted it with otherworldly fingers. Her Sight opened to the city, the mountains, hills, forests, villages, and beyond. Her head threatened to explode as a nation's future besieged her crumbling mind. Visions consumed her.

> *Dusty roads meandering through dark forests.*
> *Bonfires and pentagrams, cauldrons and grimoires.*
> *Blood-drenched golden coins.*
> *Glittering dresses, twirling, twirling, twirling, and*
>   *never stopping.*
> *Footsteps hammering like a heartbeat.*

Untethered, her incorporeal form floated through the realm beyond the veil. Dark pools, clouds of fog, and mirrors surrounded her—each showing her new images in disconnected flashes. Somewhere far away, her skin grew cold. Aurienne's hands came up to her neck as she struggled to breathe. Her spirit form coughed up blood, golden fragments of soul, and cursed water. The visions assailed her.

> *A young woman wailing silently as fangs pierced her*
>   *neck.*

A warrior standing alone beside a river of blood.
A dark ravine with whispering angry spirits.
A man wearing the skulls of wolves as a crown.

Aurienne recoiled. She knew each vision hinted at their future. She stretched her mind for more, absorbing as much as she could handle.

I'm so close.

A few more and she could understand how the pieces of the puzzle fit. Far away, the last bubbles escaped her blue lips.

An immortal hunter wielding a blade forged of
*   starlight.*
Giants standing as tall as trees, and stone men
*   escaping a mountain.*
A blind priestess encircled by rings and rings of light.
A cloaked magician catching pouring sparks from a
*   book.*
A castle swallowed by the sea.
Knots of rope and forged chains slithering into a noose.

The visions started to fade. She clawed for them, but they slipped through her grasp like sand in an hourglass.

No!

It was too soon. This was more than she had ever Seen. The answers were there, finally. It was all right there, just out of grasp. She could save them. Their deaths would not be her fault.

I need more.

A woman's voice whispered to her, *The Eye's Sight shall betray her. Avyllon will fall. Her visions will lose the Darkling War and doom all Teridar.* Her back was to Aurienne. She turned and wore three distinct faces. The Triple Goddess. A whisper of gooseflesh prickled her arms even in the spirit realm. The Goddess vanished.

The visions began slipping away as she was dragged back to her body. She was running out of air—and time. She pushed forward. She Saw too much and understood too little. She was dying. Not that it mattered. No one would care. She had no one to miss or mourn her.

This was more important. Through the mist of her suffocating mind, she Saw glimpses of visions. Just a little longer, she demanded of herself. She would die before she would fail.

Please.

The final visions heeded her call. She opened her mind, feeling part of her spirit tear and veins in her brain pop. She didn't care. Her spirit slipped away from her body as only a final tether lingered.

Aurienne stood on a battlefield under a burning crimson sun. A biting wind raked her spine and stirred the layers of her gown. Bloody mud squelched underneath her bare feet. The valley was littered with screaming corpses. A hand gripped her ankle.

A soldier whose face she didn't recognize croaked, "Aurienne, help."

She knelt, giving in to the urge to stroke the dark hair from his cheek as the life flicked out of his eyes. By the way her stomach twisted, she knew him. But that couldn't be right. She'd never seen this man before. She stood.

Fires burned beyond the distant mountains as steel clanged against steel. Soldiers wearing the purple griffin of Avyllon fell to the black swords of their foe. A howling wolf crest was carved into every enemy chestplate, yellow eyes burning in their helms. Armies poured into the valley. Hundreds of thousands of soldiers raced toward the broken forces defending her city. They came from the northeast, united.

"Demorra," she whispered.

The continent of Demorra was comprised of several dozen warring tribes and twenty-one nations littered with great, ancient cities. But now they were all united under a howling wolf banner. *How?* A chilling realization dawned upon her; the entire sprawling continent was now a unified empire seeking to wash over the nations of Teridar. Five small nations could never stand against these forces.

We'll all die.

Screams from her city called to her, and she started to run. Slipping in the scarlet mud, she fell to her knees again and again. The mud clung to her skirts and wrapped around her legs. She made it to her temple and froze.

Shadows clung to towering beasts with glowing eyes. Metal claws and broken fangs cut down the seers. Their footsteps cracked the tiles, and their roars shattered glass.

"No," she screamed.

"Help," Saryll called, blood bubbling from her lips.

Aurienne fell to the floor beside Saryll, her dearest and perhaps only friend. Her hands shook as she peeled back the white gown to reveal deep gashes that spurted blood across Aurienne's face. White bone from Saryll's ribcage gleamed in the candlelight. Aurienne pressed her hands to the wound, knowing it wouldn't be enough.

"Goddess, help me," Aurienne begged.

Saryll coughed up black blood, and then her soul stepped out of her body. A silver, wispy form hovered above her cooling corpse.

Aurienne stood, hands caked in dripping blood. "I'm sorry."

Saryll gave her a pitiful look. "You could have stopped this. You still can."

The wisp darted away, leaving Aurienne alone with the broken bodies of her sisters.

"I don't know how!" Aurienne's screams echoed off the carved ceilings of the lonely temple.

She stumbled into the streets to find her city burning. Towers fell. People screamed. A mountain aqueduct burst and poured an endless sea down upon the lower portion of the city, drowning the cries in a torrent of icy water.

Demorran troops and the shadowy monsters were everywhere.

Enemies with swords or axes instead of arms cut down any who stood in their way. Wolves so tall they blocked out the sun raced through the valley, trampling homes and villages.

A yellow-eyed Demorran lifted his sword to cut down a child. Aurienne intervened, knocking his arm away at the last moment. The child ran screaming into the wreckage of the once beautiful city. The soldier lifted his sword again. She squeezed her eyes shut, waiting for the end.

Clang.

Another sword made of dark starlight intercepted the blow. It arced up and cut into the Demorran's neck. Blood sprayed across Aurienne's arm.

A man wearing the griffin of Avyllon held out his hand to her. She took it without question, her soul recognizing his at once—though she'd never seen him before. He led them outside the crumbling walls of the city. Turning to face her, he pushed his blond hair out of his face.

Her heel struck a sharp edge, sending barbs of pain up her leg. She moved her ceremonial skirts—a human skull. The field was littered with thousands of them, sinking into the crimson mud. She gasped and reached for the green-eyed man.

"Are you okay?" His green eyes held a love for her she'd never known possible.

She didn't have time to answer before a monstrous wolf bit off the man's head. She screamed as his body fell to the skulls and bones littering the valley. Her heart shattered and the pieces writhed inside her chest. It throbbed as waves of anguish brought her to her knees. She reached for him, brushing her fingers against his chest. Tears spilled from her eyes, though she never cried. He was gone. Dead. Her will to live shriveled to dust. Why was she suddenly heartbroken? She didn't know him.

The wolf stalked forward—eyes black with an ancient rage.

A woman's voice hissed from the wolf's maw. "You can't stop

what's coming. Neither can your Goddess. Not even Fate can save you."

Aurienne screamed. "No!"

The future slipped away as she fell through the world between worlds, falling and falling—her soul unable to find its way back. As her mind darkened, a few final images burned themselves into her memory.

> *Her own reflection watching her with eyes gouged out,*
>   *seeping liquid gold.*
> *An empress wearing a crown of demon horns.*
> *Four stone pillars crumbling to rubble.*
> *Half-buried crowns sinking into the earth.*
> *Hordes of unnatural creatures oozing dark magic,*
>   *pouring over the mountains.*
> *So. Many. Monsters.*

Then nothing.

THE RITE OF WATER
CHAPTER TWO

Terrible secrets sold and bought.
Remember me once, forget me not.
Empires rise, and empires fall.
Death to one, death to all.

— CHILDREN'S RHYME FROM LORE AND LEGENDS.

1152 N.T.C. Lunahain Festival. The namesake capital city of Avyllon.

A golden dawn illuminated a dusty road packed with travelers journeying to the capital for the eclipse foretelling and readings from the seers. Twenty-six-year-old Theo Thatcher and his aging parents were among them. Even at a distance, the strum of the guitar, boom of the drums, and peal of the tambourine mixed with the city's clamor to echo across the surrounding fields. Around the next turn, Avyllon came into view, making him feel dizzyingly small. The flat, white sandstone walls reached for the sky, as tall as one hundred houses stacked atop one another. It looked like the home of gods, not mortals.

Theo whistled long and low, pushing his blond, cropped hair out of his face. He scratched his stubble, not looking forward to the next few days. The city was spectacular, but he far preferred the quiet of the farm and wildness of the mountains. Late harvest would arrive soon, and there was much to do. Eager to get this over with, he nudged his horse forward, and his parents followed.

The long caravan passed beneath the towering city gates. They entered on white stone roads to meet crushing throngs of people. The Festival of Fates was in full force. Plays and music filled the air, as scents of simmering spiced fish and beef along with sugared pastries wafted from vendor's booths. Theo dismounted and let the city wash over him. Colored dust exploded around him, tasting of sugar. Fabric streamers decorated the buildings and walls.

Festival goers milled in the streets with faces painted in the likeness of characters from the stories of old. Older children wearing painted masks of heroes and monsters dueled with wooden swords under a cascade of flowers. Theo brushed the petals from his shoulders.

He led his parents to a moderately well-maintained inn with a stable. Pa walked behind, limping from an accident some years ago, but he still had a straight back and strong shoulders. Ma's arm was looped around Pa's, and she wore a clean green apron with small wobbly flowers embroidered on it—Theo's handiwork from many years ago. Her graying hair was neatly pulled back into a bun, and her eyes were lined with proof of a life spent smiling.

The stablemaster reached for the reins, but Theo pulled them back.

"Our horses will be here when we return, well cared for and fed," Theo said, knowing how city-dwellers would take advantage of rural villagers.

The stablemaster sized Theo up. Apparently deciding that the tall, broad man before him, who spent his life tilling farms and forging metal, was not an argument worth picking, the stablemaster nodded and filled out the parchment proving ownership. Theo handed over the reins.

Outside, Pa stopped a merchant and asked, "What Rite is it?"

"It was just announced. Water," the man answered.

Theo's boot brushed against a gold coin, a week's wage, face down in the dirt. Crouching, he flipped it over so that the eye of the Goddess was face up. It was bad luck to pick up a face down coin, but if he flipped it, then it'd be good fortune for the next passerby. Before Theo hardly walked three paces, someone behind him exclaimed at their good luck. He grinned. It was hard to abandon such a coin, but the gravely poor luck a face-down coin brought was not worth it.

Pa clapped him on the shoulder. "I promised your Ma we'd go find herb plants, as well as some dried spices, before going for wild-flower seeds. Why don't you go on without us and explore? We'll meet you at the temple for the Rite and your reading."

"We wouldn't miss it for the world," Ma said.

"Let's hope I didn't spend seven years apprenticing to be turned away at the end." Theo laughed nervously. "With the blessing of the seers, I can begin building my own forge as soon as we return home."

"If you get a good spot at the Rite, you may be able to see the High Seer," Ma said, nudging him.

A passerby, the Guild Master of the masons by the sigil on his cloak, grumbled, "The High Seer has done nothing to help us avoid the Darkling War."

Ma wagged her finger at him. "The High Seer and those before her have guided us through crop failures, drought, and winter storms. You ought to be more thankful."

More than a handful in the small crowd agreed with her, and one man threw a handful of colored dust at the Guild Master, staining his blond hair. He stormed off in a cloud of sugar, causing Theo to chuckle.

"Without a king, the High Seer must guide us," another merchant said.

The nearby crowd nodded reverently. The last of the kings died childless when Theo's parents were young. Avyllon had been without a king for just over forty-seven years. In that time, Avyllon had known only peace and prosperity, with the seers guiding them past hardship.

"We'll see you later, dear." His parents waved goodbye.

Theo wandered alone for some time. Boisterous crowds surrounded him, and though he knew no one, he didn't mind. Unlike at home, no one in the city knew how at four years old Theo ran naked and giggling through the neighboring livestock pens whenever his mother was too slow to catch him. That at ten, he ate candied plums 'til he was sick all over the Hallohaim holiday banquet table in front of the whole village, or that at seventeen he broke Emyla's heart and she refused to come out of her house for a month. He loved his quiet life, but anonymity could be welcome. Here, he could be anyone.

Theo passed a group of children playing near a training dummy in a wide, enclosed alleyway. Several tossed a leather ball back and forth, while others skipped a woven rope. The group skipping led a sing-song chorus while all the boys and girls joined in. Theo stopped to listen.

> *Terrible secrets sold and bought.*
> *Remember me once, forget me not.*
> *Blood shall fly. Screams to sky.*
> *Empires rise, and empires fall,*
> *Death to one, death to all.*
>
> *Debts of blood and bone are paid.*
> *Immortal oaths forever made.*
> *Out of sight, evil hides.*
> *Shadows rise as grim falls.*

Death to one, death to all.

Smiling skulls and blood-soaked stones.
Darkling dreams and blood-soaked bones.
Evil hides, and darkness dies.
Empires rise, and empires fall,
Death to one, death to all.

Stars light in cursed blade.
Souls of beasts and monsters weighed.
Evil hides, and darkness dies.
Shadows rise as grim falls.
Death to one, death to all.

The song chilled Theo's bones. It continued, switching verses, adding in new lines but keeping to the same pattern. The children giggled. Theo recognized pieces of their song from fairytales and monster stories he'd heard when he was young.

A leather ball flew from the alley, and Theo sprang to catch it. With a smile, he tossed it back to a wide-eyed girl. "Here you go."

A chorus of apologies met him. He waved and was immediately bombarded with invitations to fight swords or skip rope. At home in his village, Theo would have been powerless to resist, but here in a strange city, he thought it prudent to avoid frightening their parents by having a large, muscled man skipping rope with their young ones.

Theo shook his head. "Sorry!"

He tossed the closest boy a red acorn from his pocket. "We plant these in our farms for a good harvest. Bury it in your family's garden, and it will bring you luck."

The boy eagerly darted away, clutching the red acorn to his chest. Other children gave chase, laughing loudly, but the boy disappeared into a doorway.

Theo smiled again and waved as he passed by. As he rounded the corner, the children resumed their singing.

Shadows rise as grim falls.
Death to one, death to all.
Empires rise, and empires fall.
Death to one, death to all.

The dark fairytale faded as Theo toured the market. He stopped at several blacksmith shops, surveying daggers and swords.

Standing in a shop with wickedly curved daggers, Theo asked, "How do you cool your metal?"

"In the quench of ice water, it makes the strongest blades," a guild craftsman answered.

"What lies are you peddling," the craftsman across the street hollered.

"None of your business," the first smith shouted.

Theo concealed a knowing smile and asked the second blacksmith, "Do you quench your blades?"

The smith beckoned him over and leaned in conspiratorially, glancing over his shoulder. "You only quench if you want a brittle blade. Aye, it'll be hard, but it'll shatter. No, we slow cool the blades. These are the ones you want."

Theo inclined his head respectfully. "I'll keep that in mind."

He walked not ten paces before he arrived at the next shop, where he asked, "And what metals do you use?"

"Bog-iron steel. By hagsteeth, it's the strongest there is."

Excellent. Another competing answer.

Theo forced a smile. "My mentor was a master craftsman and told me about titan ore. Do you have any?"

"Psh," the craftsman guffawed. "No one has any titan ore since the Titan Cliffs closed its borders half a century ago. But bog-iron is as hard as you can get nowadays. My forge is vented so the metal doesn't burn up, and we quench in warm water. It gives you the flexibility and strength you need."

Three smiths and three wildly different answers, but Theo absorbed every drop of knowledge, excited to soon experiment with his own forge. None of the smiths agreed on the best methods, including his mentor, opening the door wide for Theo to crack the code himself. He grinned and flexed his fingers.

The sun had nearly reached its zenith when Theo arrived at the city's heart. The Eye, the sigil of the Triple Goddess, was painted everywhere, along with Avyllon's crest—the griffon and Sword of Souls. He peered up. Crystals and mirrors reflected dancing motes of light, illuminating the murals across the sacred walls. They depicted epic battles of the past and terrifying glimpses of the future. Armies charged across the bulwarks while gargoyles and stars sparkled at the spires. Bits of crushed colored glass captured light and infused it into the building.

More impressive than the stonework were the fountains and pools nestled between stark white buildings. The crystalline water sparkled like polished diamonds. Fresh mountain runoff poured down from the aqueducts, providing running water to every house and building. Beneath his feet, hardened glass tiles revealed rivers running underneath the city itself. Truly—a home for the gods.

"It's almost time for the eclipse. We need to make it to the foretelling Rite in time," a passing child called.

"We're going to miss it," another child exclaimed.

Theo clicked his tongue and glanced skyward, raising his hand to keep the yellow light from blinding him. Nearly noon. He followed the crowds to the temple's spacious public courtyard, then inched his way to the front row and claimed a prime spot. People leaned from every window of the tall buildings around the temple and perched on walls to see over the crowd.

In the center of the courtyard were a deep pool and a raised stone platform that might have once held a pyre. People jostled for spots nearest the steel railings that kept them back, but Theo refused to move. He'd finally grown to his full height, and seven years apprenticing at the forge had filled him out such that no one could push him from his spot—and never having seen a Rite, he felt no guilt.

Theo found himself studying the guard's swords—each different from the last. If today went as planned, he'd soon be making swords like these. He noticed that one dark-haired guard with a long scar across his jaw wore an ornamental short sword at his hip that wobbled as he patrolled. The hilt was nearly detached from the blade —suggesting it was not meant to be used. The guard's uniform announced he was a captain. His scar suggested he had considerable experience. The guard turned away to reveal a sturdy, long sword strapped to his back.

Ah. There's his combat blade.

Drums thundered over the crowd's clamor. Seers emerged from the temple in pairs, crossing the raised veranda to form a crescent moon around the platform. Hands clasped serenely , they waited, expressionless. After the eclipse foretelling, it would be one of these seers who would read his fate. With their blessing, he'd complete his apprenticeship and build his own forge back at the family farm. He would be a member of the blacksmith's guild. Theo couldn't help grinning. Everything he had worked toward for seven long years led up to this day.

"Aurienne Celestina Azarrah, High Seer of Avyllon, Regent and Guardian to the Crown Throne..." a bard announced.

The rest of her many titles faded away.

There was only *her*.

The High Seer stepped from the smoky veils of the temple and into the blinding sunlight. She was young, vibrant, and terrifying. Dripping in gold jewelry from head to toe, she was an impossible sight. White wispy fabric and gold adornments reflected the light making her glow brighter than the sun and deepening the black paint she wore into abysmal shadows.

Theo's jaw dropped, stealing the smile from his enraptured gaze. As she emerged, the crowd roared and fought for a view. White flower petals rained down from tall windows, but all Theo could see was her. He thought her gaze lingered on him, but he must have imagined it.

She couldn't have noticed me in this crowd.

In his mind, the High Seer must be a faceless, nameless entity. Perhaps a wise crone or homely sage. Who else could be trusted to rule a nation? He hadn't expected someone his age. Theo wracked his brain. Aurienne Azarrah had been High Seer for...twelve or thirteen years? Had she become High Seer at thirteen? How could one so young carry the weight of so much? He hadn't even opened his own forge yet. One glimpse at this prowling vision in gold, and Theo knew why Guild Masters and commanders alike bowed down. She walked with the grace of a queen and the intention of a general. He would happily run into an inferno if she commanded. At a single word, he would cut out his own tongue or gouge out his eyes.

Hellsdamn me.

The seer crossed the veranda toward the crystal pool. She was barefoot, and the ethereal garb revealed her arms, which were painted with eyes and moons and stars. High slits showed off curving painted thighs. Her skin was fair with a light kiss of color from the sun, and a deep plunging neckline revealed more paint and a hint of perfectly shaped breasts. Theo swallowed and forced his gaze to her face. Her full lips were painted gold, her eyes darkened by kohl and dusted with gold leaf. A third eye, painted in crossed crescent moons on her forehead, signified the second Sight of the seers.

Her eyes, almost entirely white, roved the crowd as she approached the pool, seeing everything. When they glinted across him, his heart clenched, and his breath hitched. He was sure she Saw into the depths of his soul like some cursed soul-stealing wraith.

Theo swallowed and shut his mouth, realizing that it had been hanging open the whole time, and he immediately felt like a gawking country simpleton. Shame tickled his cheeks. He raised his gaze again, attempting to listen to the temple's announcer.

"...we do not interfere in the Goddess' will..."

One glance at the seer, and he failed miserably in his attempt to listen as a lopsided grin escaped his control.

Moonless night, keep it together, man.

The High Seer lifted a hand, and the crowd silenced. The tiny chains attaching her rings to her bracelet clinked together. Her hands dropped to her sides, palms out in supplication.

"Today, we celebrate the eclipse and honor the Goddess who guides us," she declared. "The eclipse comes every year across this exact place. The moon and sun and earth align. It opens the Second Sight if the Goddess wills it. For those who brave death, Sight will be yours."

Theo's brows pulled together.

"The Fates have chosen the Rite of Water," she finished.

She tilted her head back to pray, bathing in the sunlight. Beneath the gilded skin, under the glistening gown, sorrow smoldered. And anger burned. He saw a woman too young to be so tired, so desperate, so furious. But then, it was gone, and Theo wasn't even sure he'd seen it.

To the sky, she said, "Triple Goddess. I come to the water. I call on you to guide us. Open my Eye, open my Sight. Let me See your will. What is the fate of Avyllon?"

The seer paused. She took a deep breath and exhaled slowly. She stepped a painted foot into the water. And another.

Terror spiked through him. She said she'd risk death and was descending into the pool. Did she mean she'd drown? He glanced around, but no one else seemed concerned.

She couldn't possibly mean...

Another step off the ledge, and she was gone.

Without thinking, Theo scrambled onto the balcony to peer into the pool from behind the guarded railing. A dozen others did the same—except they cheered. A guard shoved Theo back, but he ignored him and leaned over the railing. The pool's edge was only three large steps away and wide enough that he could easily see to the bottom.

Her cloudy eyes peered at the surface as she sank. For an instant, they locked with his, then closed. Bubbles escaped her lips as her gilded limbs and beaded dress dragged her down.

As the water enveloped her jeweled hair, the sun darkened. It turned orange, then gray, and finally black as the moon passed through it. With the eclipse upon them, Theo watched the seer with intensity under torch haze and starlight.

Down, she sank. Five paces. Eight. Ten. Twelve. The pool was much deeper than it first appeared. The water was so clear he could see her resting at the bottom, a flash of white and gold, dark hair billowing around her like a halo. Theo held his breath and started counting. Twenty seconds. Spending his summers as a child in the nearby lake, he was a decent swimmer, and though his lungs already burned, she still had time.

The moon passed, and the sun returned to its glorious yellow. The darkness retreated as quickly as it appeared. Though the eclipse passed, the seer had not yet surfaced. He watched her, relieved to see her hands move weakly. She was still conscious.

What was she doing?

Theo motioned to a man next to him and, while still trying not to inhale, asked, "How long will she stay down there?"

"Until she gets the vision," the man said. "One year she remained buried in a box for two days. The feast fires burned out before she rang the bell to let her up. But she foresaw good wheat and maize harvests!"

His stomach turned at the thought of her buried alive while the people feasted. Disgust slithered through his gut and up his throat like a poisoned serpent.

Another said, "She's dedicated. Last year, she remained in the flames until her skin blistered. But she knew to save water for the drought. She saved our farm 'cause of that. We owe her our lives."

Theo counted the seconds to sixty. The cheering subsided to eager anticipation. Though people leaned this way and that to get a glimpse, nobody batted an eye. The lack of concern made Theo angry. No one cared what she endured as long as she provided her visions.

A minute and a half. His lungs were screaming now. His brain told him a hundred things, anything to convince him to take a gulp of air, but he refused. Knowing he could hold his breath as long as she did was soothing. It meant she was alright.

A hand on his jacket tried to pull him off the railing. Distantly, someone said, "You've had more than your turn, friend. Move on."

Theo shoved them away and held the railing tightly. Another hand on his shoulder tapped him, which he batted away. Grunts of protest sounded, and if he had been thinking clearly, he'd have realized he batted a little too hard from years hammering steel. Two minutes.

Between the patrolling sentinels, Theo focused on her distant limbs. They stopped moving. His eyes struggled to focus from the absence of air, but he was sure of it now. She had not moved for thirty seconds. A large bubble of air broke the surface. He tapped his trembling hand on his leg to count the seconds.

Tap. Tap. Tap.

Black dots lined Theo's vision, and his throat made weird gulps without his consent. People nearby glanced at him and leaned away, but he ignored them.

Tap. Tap. Tap.

He tapped out the seconds.

Two and a half minutes gone.

She started convulsing.

One older teen near the veranda wall shifted uncomfortably. He made to step forward, but an older man with a crazed beard beside him grabbed his arm, and the captain with dark hair blocked his path. The teen was the only one to appear even mildly concerned.

If Theo was angry before, he was snarling now as she writhed at the bottom of the pool. Air deprivation might have contributed to the rage, but this was unbearable. This was wrong. He knew it in his bones. It was wasteful. And unnecessary. And idiotic. And cruel. Torture... Archaic. And... Ridiculous. And... And... Words and air left him.

Tap... Tap... Tap...

He could no longer see, and his lungs were filled with fire hotter than his forge. Three minutes.

Theo's mouth burst open. He sucked in air through his nose and mouth like a dying man. He sputtered and coughed as his vision returned. His throat burned, and he made terrible choking noises. His fists clenched around the railing until his knuckles turned white.

"Are you okay?" someone asked.

Not. At. All.

The water remained entirely still. Not a bubble, not a ripple, nothing disturbed the eerily serene surface. Unmoving, she lay like a corpse. Theo realized she would never return. They were watching her die. That divine being gifted to them by the Goddess. That *person* at the bottom of a pool that everyone watched drown. That woman who would sacrifice her life for a chance at saving them, without hesitation, without fear, without complaint. She knew she might die and still stepped into those waters. These were her final moments.

Coldforge that.

"Here goes nothing," Theo whispered to himself.

Theo waited for the next sentinel to pass and leapt over the railing. He crossed the veranda and dove into the pool before anyone could notice or react.

"Stop him!"

"We can't interfere!"

"What are you doing!"

"Stop!"

It was too late. Theo was already several powerful strokes into the pool and too far down to catch. He kicked and clawed at the water, diving lower and lower.

The seer's lips were parted, her eyes half closed, and she was still. Another few strokes and he reached her. He carefully wrapped his arms underneath her and pushed off the rocky sand, holding her tightly to his chest as he kicked upward.

His shoes filled with water and pulled them down. He kicked

them off. The water was deep enough that the pressure compressed his head and lungs. He fought for the surface, carrying the High Seer's lifeless body with him. Finally, the surface neared.

Another stroke and he burst from the water. He kicked and paddled with one arm toward the edge, taking care to keep her head lifted. He dragged her up onto the dais.

Theo gently laid her on the platform, but she didn't move. He placed a hand against her chest, smearing the watery paint. Nothing. He bent to listen for breath, but there was none.

Sentinels gripped Theo's arms and tried to tear him away from her.

"She's not breathing," he yelled, but their grasp only tightened.

Theo shoved the captain backward into the pool, causing his combat sword to tumble into the water. He spun his arm free of the other sentinel's grasp and sent him toppling backward too. Theo refused to leave, not until she had taken a breath. If she dove back into the water and tried to kill herself again afterward, that was her problem.

She was going to breathe, hellsdamn it.

Theo stacked his hands and started to press on her chest as he had been taught by the trading fishermen. Two per second, right over her heart.

The captain clawed his way out of the water and drew the ornamental sword at his hip. The one that Theo had noticed earlier with the inferior hilt. Theo instinctively dodged the strike and slammed his elbow against the wobbly hilt over the sentinel's hand, causing him to howl as the blade flew free of the hilt and went clanging across the polished stone.

"She isn't breathing!" Theo yelled.

Theo kept up the rhythmic compressions. He could never remember if it was one breath or two or none, as it seemed to change with every person he talked to. Theo leaned down, pinched her nose, hoping her piercings would not interfere, and breathed into her mouth.

Please. Please. Please.

She stirred.

Three sentinels grabbed his arms and dragged him away as the seer choked up what seemed to be half the water in the pool.

"No...no...no..." she mumbled.

Water poured from the seer's mouth and nose as she sat up. Her translucent eyes appeared clearer than before, with hints of blue that he hadn't seen earlier. Her hair was a sopping mass, tangling over her nose and getting into her mouth. Paint dripped off her in multi-colored droplets, and her dress lay askew. Bewildered, she glanced around before her eyes settled upon him.

Relief flooded him, and he sat backward onto the white sandstone, exhausted and drenched. He took a deep breath, but the sky caught his attention.

Above them, the sun and moon both turned to floating crimson orbs, coating the skies and entire city in blood-red light. A second blood eclipse filled the sky as a burning star passed in front of the sun.

The cheering multitudes quieted and stilled.

No horse nickered.

No child cried.

Everything was bathed in a horrible, unearthly red light. Every head lifted, watching the sun burn and bleed. A slow and quiet terror spread through the crowd as no one moved. A weight descended, pinning Theo to the ground. He'd heard the stories but had never seen a bleeding eclipse; there hadn't been one in twenty-six years. The crowds were right to be afraid. A red eclipse was a dark and terrible omen. Everyone knew it meant death. His heart expanded until it filled his chest cavity, and his ears rushed with blood. Fingers itching, he clenched his fists.

"What have you done?" the seer whispered.

Her eyes narrowed. Anger poured off her like heat from a forge, and he pushed away from her.

"The visions...are gone..." she said.

Theo had no words. He had saved her life. Why was she angry?

Long moments stretched on. Then the red star passed, and the sun returned to normal. The eclipse was over. People shared quiet murmurs, but Theo couldn't speak. His mouth moved but no words came out. Four sentinels hauled him to his feet.

"What have you done?" the seer demanded as Theo was dragged into the shadows.

"You're under arrest by law of Avyllon," a sentinel said.

Theo's temper exploded, and his lip curled into a snarl. He wrenched his arm from the captain's grasp, seeing red.

"The visions aren't worth your life!" Theo snapped. "You'll see nothing if you're dead, you lunatic."

"You know nothing," she snapped.

A fist caught him in the stomach and doubled him over just as he opened his mouth. He coughed and struggled to breathe, lungs burning. Losing sight of *her* and the crowd, the sentinels hauled him away to a dark dungeon cell. Shouting, he managed to free an arm and knock the captain down. He was hefted through the air by the sentinels and smashed into a wall.

His head hit stone, and darkness descended.

THE OLD WAYS
CHAPTER THREE

Now we enter the realm of dreams and nightmares, and each as terrifying.

— HIGH SEER AURIENNE AZARRAH, PROPHETIC VISION.

1152 N.T.C. The namesake capital city of Avyllon.

Dripping wet and freshly drowned, Aurienne possessed only incomplete visions of destruction and war to offer the fearful crowd, and the bleeding eclipse announced it more clearly than any vision or reading could. The words tasted like ash in her mouth. Her lie to her sisters now seemed futile.

"You have seen the omen, and I Saw the meaning in the Rite. The Darkling War comes, but the Goddess will guide us. Prepare for a hard winter and gird your homes against storms. Prepare the woodpiles and cellars. The tax shall be reduced by ten percent to account for the coming winters and to prepare to provide aid to those who need it."

She studied the crowd as she spoke. Too long had the people lived under the specter of death, making them complacent. Their trust in her would wane as their panic sprouted like a seed given the water of darkling omens, sunlight of the dreaded red eclipse, and fertile soil of fear. It would grow and grow. Aurienne tasted the fearful revolts, riots, and dark days to come.

Touching her chest, feeling the giant stone beneath her breastbone from drowning, she reached for the stone dais to remain standing. Her thoughts were fuzzy, distant. Her limbs were heavy, her throat raw. A fleeting glimpse of a vision showed any of her attempts at quelling the crowd ending in full-blown riots. Her presence would not pacify their fears until emotions dulled, but food and drink would eventually placate the crowd.

"The Goddess has shown us war so we may survive," she announced. "She protects us. I'll pray for answers and will make an announcement soon. Until then, the feast shall begin!"

Furious, Aurienne stumbled to her rooms, leaving the other seers far behind. With a scream, she slammed her stout wooden doors hard enough that unseen dust sprung from the hinges. Her painted feet tangled upon one of the plush rugs, and she kicked it into a ball against the wall. She knew in her bones that the Darkling War was upon them this year.

One year.

That was all the time they had left. Perhaps less. From before she could remember, she knew her fate. It had been read at her birth when she first opened her accursed eyes, and her parents saw the seer's cloud signifying her Sight. Seers read her fate until she was old enough to conduct her own readings. Every year, every reading, it was the same. It did not make it any easier to face now that it was truly upon them.

Another scream ripped from her lips, tearing into her burning throat. It echoed through the rooms of her chambers and spilled out onto her balcony. Falling to the floor, she coughed up more water and was left shaking.

A concerned knock echoed off her door. "Seer? Are you okay?"

"Go away, Kolten," she hissed, wrapping her arms around her aching ribs and bruised chest.

There was nothing she could do, no paths to salvation. She didn't even know what she was saving them *from* until moments ago. Demorra—a united empire descending upon them with the might of twenty-one nations. Now her one chance to find answers was gone, foiled by a foolish young man with a bleeding heart.

Aurienne ripped off her soaking dress, crumpling it on the cold travertine. She tore off the gems and chains adorning her body, flinging them onto her gilded dressing counter and causing carefully organized jewelry and glass containers to tumble to the floor.

Taking a deep breath, she stepped into a shallow, steaming hot bath and furiously scrubbed the paint from her skin, leaving only the tattoos running down her back and limbs of the third eye, stars, and the phases of the moon connected by lines and runes. After drying her skin, she donned a simple gown.

The answer would be hers today. Her visions would condemn no one. She would force this elusive vision identifying their foe to come to her. Any method, any power, any magic at her disposal. If she must, she'd rip this vision from all the hells. Aurienne knelt in front of the small stone altar and prayed until her knees ached. She squeezed her palms together until the tips of her fingers turned white. With every fiber of her being, she prayed.

"Goddess, wise Fates, please grant me your understanding. Give me the sight to see clearly and to avoid this destiny. Protect me in what I must do."

From the bowl on the altar, she collected the worn bone runes and pressed them into her palms. She rolled them along her hands, looking out the window to the reddish, autumn daylight. As she breathed on the runes, the carvings illuminated.

"Reveal the future," she whispered.

Twirling the runes between her fingers, she released them onto the surface of the altar, carved with circles and shapes, with time, calendars, and celestial events. The runes across lay on a variety of symbols and in a pattern that meant—nothing specific. All general warnings of drought, famine, fire, sickness, war, and curses. The last rune caught Aurienne's attention... The death rune. It rested over the third eye symbol. The third eye typically represented a witch or seer. Was she predicting her own death?

Aurienne's breath caught in her throat. Too many possibilities. This was why she preferred cards to runes. She swept up the fragments of bone and returned them to the bowl, forcing herself to breathe.

"If you won't tell me how to stop them, I'll make you," she said. "I'll force the answers from your fated teeth if that's what it takes."

Time for the Old Ways.

They cost Aurienne much, magically sapping her strength, sometimes dulling her vision for days. She feared they stole time from her life. None of that mattered.

Reverently, Aurienne lifted her hand to call the cards from the surface of the altar, and they flew to her. Closing her eyes, she imbued as much focus as she could into the cards then licked the back of the deck. She exhaled against the cards, then took the ceremonial blade and sliced into her arm. Her magic stirred in her chest, whispering and clawing at her mind as the cards eagerly soaked up her blood. She began to shuffle.

The cards remained cool, and she discerned even the Old Ways would fall short. She stopped shuffling. Her answer was beyond the power of the cards. A growl escaped her lips. Peering into the candlelight, she asked a hundred questions in her visions, watched a hundred futures, and failed in all. She squeezed her deck until her own blood seeped out of the parchment.

There must be another way.

A large black candle, painstakingly crafted from sacred materials for enhanced Sight rested at the back of the shelf. She reached for it, but as the air cooled, she hesitated. Her gaze fell upon her journal of visions, a small leather-bound book with silver moons and eyes stamped on the cover.

Beside the journal was an unadorned tome: Rheia's journal, a seer from year 1 N.T.C., if the inscription was believed. The book detailed the forbidden necromancy-powered Sight. Aurienne gripped the folds of her gown and swallowed. It was forbidden for good reason. She clutched the book, then pressed her finger into the corner of her eye, collecting the precious seer's tears necessary to open it.

As the High-Seer-in-waiting, Aurienne's education had been comprehensive. While she knew how to perform necromancy-fueled Sight, she'd never done it. No living soul had. The ancient text nearly fell apart under her touch, but Aurienne had learned, and she remembered.

Be warned: the cost of spiritual necromancy is your own soul. Extensive damage to the soul may prevent the user from finding peace beyond the veil. You may be forced to haunt this world as a wraith in eternal misery.

A shaky breath escaped her lips. Barred from heavenly peace, an eternity of torment might await her for what she did, but it was the only way to obtain the answer she sought.

"I'll accept that cost," Aurienne said.

She closed her eyes, her spirit fading from this world and reappearing into the next. With spectral hands, she reached for the ball of light of her Second Sight. She grasped it, held it, and pulled it into her soul. It slipped into her chest like oil on wet skin. Spirit necromancy was dangerous. Anything might be trying to hitch a ride on the practitioner's soul. It was forbidden by the first High Seer many years ago after a young seer died in the clutches of an angry spirit. If Fate denied Aurienne, she would risk corruption. She drew into her soul more power lingering beyond the veil of reality.

Lost, angry spirits reached for her with long, frigid fingers, but she held her ground. She grasped for them and dragged them into her mindscape, binding them in unbreakable chains of magic—their own memories. With a snap, the chains tightened, and the spirits howled as they relived their worst sins. Then Aurienne opened her mouth and consumed them fully, depleting their clinging lifeforce to fuel her Sight. They burned up, leaving a black smudge on her aura, a deep stain upon her soul.

With a deft flick of her wrist, Aurienne threw the divination cards into the air. They hung there for five long moments, deciding how to fall before dropping to the stone surface before her. A handful looked at her while the rest lay face down. Hearing phantom footsteps echo in her mind, Aurienne read the face-up cards.

The Third Eye, for the Goddess.

The Wolf, for betrayal.

The Devil, for violence and deception.

The Mirror, for self-reflection.

The Knot, for unbreakable bonds.

The Owl, for wisdom.

It doesn't make sense. This doesn't reveal anything.

Aurienne returned the cards to the spelled box and slammed her hand onto the altar. She closed her weary eyes and massaged her aching temples—but she was not yet done.

"You will tell me."

When she opened her eyes, she noticed that the Traveler card had found its way out of the spelled box and was standing on edge. She nearly cried out in surprise, and the card tipped backward. Tentatively, she picked it up. The figure now resembled the man who saved her life and stole her visions. He blew her a kiss.

Hagsteeth bastard.

She clutched the card in her hand, skin still blanched from drowning. The Fates threw that man into her path. Perhaps he was the key to unlocking everything. She glared at the card a final time and slammed her hand back onto the carved runes on her altar.

"Bring him to me."

THREADS OF FATE
CHAPTER FOUR

You will fall deeply in love and lose it, three great loves. You will save lives and take them. You shall live on for centuries, though your death looms near. All of it and none of it. Your fate is sealed.

— HIGH SEER AURIENNE AZARRAH, READING FOR ATHEODOREN WILLEM THATCHER.

1152 N.T.C. The namesake capital city of Avyllon.

A bucket of stale water roused Theo to consciousness. He lurched up with a sharp inhale but the immediate pounding in his head made him regret it.

Bleeding hagsteeth.

Hissing, he gingerly touched his swelling eye and lip. He pushed his fingers against his ribs, feeling for broken bones but found only a bruise. A chuckle escaped his lips. The soldiers could hit, but they were nothing compared to the cranky mare, aptly named "Mischief," at their farm. *Those* kicks were serious.

Theo gasped and quickly patted around for the unsigned guild certificate in his pocket. He pulled it out, but it was soaking wet and limp.

"No," he groaned.

He tried to press the water from it and keep it flat, but it had lost all its shape. The ink ran and smudged. His heart sank. He squeezed the water from his shirt and carefully placed the paper back in his pocket with shaking hands, watching his dreams puddle on the floor.

"Get up," ordered the dark-haired captain, now swordless and looking none too keen about it.

You're going to have to make me, you rat-loving bastard.

Theo leaned against the stone wall and closed his eyes. "If you're going to torture me, you could at least give a man some rest."

"She asked to see you."

Theo's eyes snapped open. *She* asked. There was only one...*her.* The seer asked to see *him.* He scrambled up and looked himself over.

Oh, moonless skies.

"Could I get some shoes? Boots, preferably."

The look the sentinel gave him did not require words.

"Can I get a shower?" Theo asked. "I don't want to meet her smelling of stale dungeon hay, sewage, and rat droppings."

The sentinels made to ignore Theo until he finished with, "I don't think she'd appreciate that either."

He was tossed into a shower and given five minutes. The warm water was welcome on his chilled damp skin. Grabbing soap, he made quick work of scrubbing himself clean. Sentinels provided dry clothes while his were taken away—probably to be burned. No boots, though, so he remained barefoot.

The sentinels escorted him—which was far nicer than being *accidentally* slammed into everything—up the uneven basement stairs and through the several hallways of uneven stone. Leaving the basement dungeon behind, Theo stepped into the temple for the first time, and his bare feet slowed.

Carved niches shone with candlelight, mirrors, and sunlight. Moons and stars were painted along the walls of windows. The white floors, polished and gleaming, swirled with their own intricate designs of gold. Breathtaking and impossible. If he put together every single house and building in his village side by side, it would not be as big as this one temple.

At the top level, they stopped before wide double doors carved from a single massive tree. The sentinels opened them, and Theo stepped inside. He first noticed several other spacious rooms attached. Through another set of double doors, he glimpsed a large bed full of pillows and blankets. There was a small library, a balcony, and an altar. He realized at once he was in private quarters. He peered imploringly at the sentinels, who scowled before closing the doors and leaving him alone.

The High Seer emerged from a doorway, and he forgot how to breathe. Her black, simple gown exposed more arm, thigh, and chest than Theo was accustomed to. She wore no jewelry. The paint had been freshly scrubbed from her skin, though he noticed some of the designs were tattoos. Her feet were bare, and her hair was still damp.

Theo stared. It was so intimate, so familiar. Here he was in her personal chambers, barefoot, with her barely out of the bath. She was all at once nothing like that divine figure from earlier, and yet every inch the same.

She crossed the room and stopped inches away. She smelled of vanilla and something lightly floral that could only be described as moonlight. Her eyes were once more clouded, translucent, and now that he was closer, he could see a faint glow from within. With an expression as hard as stone, a hint of ire crossed her face. Any humanity he'd seen when he dragged her limp body from that horrible pool was now gone. She was cold, calculating, untouchable, divine, and beneath all of that, he now saw ruthlessness. She was happy to die if it meant she got what she wanted. And he had stopped her.

Theo swallowed. Her eyes darted to his throat and back to his own eyes, catching the movement. There was no hiding anything from her.

Theo was tall for his village, tall for Avyllon. Seven years of working the forge as an apprentice steeled his muscles hard and strong. The seer's head came up to his chin, and yet she looked down at him. She studied him in a way that made him want to hide in a corner.

"What is your name?" she asked.

"Theo Thatcher, High Seer," he answered clumsily.

"Where do you come from?"

"I traveled from Karme for a reading to complete my apprenticeship and become a blacksmith."

"You're a traveler," she said as if it meant something. She cast a quick look back at the stone altar behind her.

He knew his expression contorted into a bewildered look and tried to shake it but couldn't find the strength. He settled for simply staring. She must have been under the water too long, and it had addled her brain. That or seers simply made no sense.

Both?

"Come, sit. I'll do your reading." She gestured to two chairs near the altar.

He must have hit his head harder than he realized. The High Seer never did readings for the public. Ever. She did the omens and the foretelling, and she read fates only if it was important—for kings and queens...not him.

"My...reading? You don't do readings for...people," he said.

"Now you deign to tell me what I do and don't do?" Her brow rose.

"No. I-I just heard. I mean. I thought..."

Just stop talking.

The High Seer sat and gestured for him to do the same. "You're right," she said as Theo took a seat across from her. "I typically save my strength for the larger readings. I See too much for everyday readings. Most people don't want to know all I can See in any case. However, I'll make an exception for the man who saved my life. It seems the Fates placed you in my path, and I am not one to ignore omens."

"You didn't seem so happy about me saving your life earlier," he mumbled to himself.

"I didn't appreciate the Rite being interrupted."

Theo's eyes widened.

She folded her hands. "I owe you thanks. I would have drowned had you not interfered. The Triple Goddess showed me all she was willing to, and you ensured I could bring it back to the people. Thank you," she said, but her tone made it sound like it hurt to admit.

Theo pursed his lips. Her eyes darted to them.

"What?"

Theo shrugged.

"Tell me," she said.

He stared at the floor. "You weren't thankful earlier. I get the impression you don't put much value on your own life."

She paused before removing the deck from a carved wooden box and shuffled as she tilted her chin. The cards were a deep and layered, watercolor black. Gold foil lines created figures and shapes, and though he didn't hold them—he could tell they held great weight in Aurienne's hands. Flashes of brilliant reds, blues, and purples emanated from the parchment like forest sprites.

As she spoke, the cloudiness lifted from her eyes for a moment before returning. "I suppose you're right. My life's purpose is to save the people from a reading I had as a baby. Every waking moment, I cannot forget about the impending war. I sometimes forget there is more to life than that."

What do you say to that?

She looked up. "Why did you save me?"

Theo wracked his brain. Why did he save her? Injustice? Fate? Something more?

"I had to."

It was the closest to the truth.

"Why?"

"You don't realize how you look to people. Like a story character. Like a goddess. They forget you're a person. But when you were speaking, before you went into the pool, I saw you were sad and angry. And you went into the pool without hesitation and stayed down, and no one helped you. It didn't even occur to anyone you might need or want help because all they see is the High Seer, but your life matters."

Her brows rose, and she said quietly, "Thank you."

"You're welcome, High Seer."

"You may call me Aurienne."

Theo beamed. "I might have ignored the instructions about interfering."

"Why?"

"You...were... I was watching... I mean... You're beautiful. Sorry." He supposed that she already Saw all the rambling he felt coming, so he allowed himself the small dignity of falling quiet.

Aurienne smiled, and *gods* did he love that sight.

She lifted the deck to his lips, "Breathe on it."

Theo swallowed but complied. As he leaned in, he became painfully aware of how close they were.

"You may ask three questions," she said. "Choose them well and keep them in your mind now."

"And they'll come true?"

"I See futures that may happen and fates that will. I'll tell you which I See for you."

She drew a small ceremonial dagger. Offering his hand, he was unsure of what to expect but trusted her. She made a small slice, and he barely even noticed. Three drops splashed onto her deck.

The seer lifted the cards to her head, lips, and heart before she shuffled once more. "Cut the deck."

He cut it, the cards nearly burning his skin.

"Ask your first question."

"Will I become a blacksmith and make beautiful blades?"

She turned the first card. The Sword reversed.

"You will make the finest swords," she said with a frown. "Ask your second question."

Theo frowned. Never having experienced a reading, he couldn't be sure, but this didn't seem at all like how they were supposed to go.

"Will I fall in love?"

She turned the next card. The Lovers. She chewed her lip.

"That's odd," she said.

"Doesn't the Lovers mean I'll fall in love?"

"Ask your third question."

"Will I live a long, happy, good life?"

She turned the final card. Life.

"What in the—"

"What?"

"It makes no sense."

Aurienne held the deck up to her lips and whispered something that sounded suspiciously like, "If you do not knock it off, I will burn you, bury you, and start again with new cards that behave."

Theo shook his head, clearly having misheard her. "What do you mean?"

"You asked your question. The affirmative card for each was drawn. Each was reversed. Upside-down," she added at his puzzled look.

"So?"

"If you asked if you would make swords and the Farm card was drawn, the answer would be negative. If you ask to make swords and the Sword card comes up, it usually means yes. But the reverse means —I don't know what it means," she admitted.

Her eyes snapped to him as her painted nails tapped on the table. He saw her draw a card from the deck and glare at it. He leaned forward to see the Traveler. She stacked her deck and then looked back at him. The look in her eye was positively predatory.

"Very well. We'll do it the Old Way."

A stillness settled over her, sending chills across his skin. Her eyes were unfocused, becoming so cloudy her pupils completely disappeared. The energy of a divine, unworldly presence crackled under her skin—lifting the hairs on his arms at her touch. Her lips parted, and she drew in a slow breath. The sun dimmed as clouds coalesced in the sky. Wind rustled the tree canopy outside her high balcony. Time became murky and slow. She took his hand palm up and looked deep into his eyes. Chills raced down his skin as everything but Aurienne faded away.

"What do you want in this life? What are your deepest desires?" she asked distantly.

"I want to become a blacksmith. I want love and family. I want a good life," he said.

Her laugh was no longer her own, but the voice of another that sent frigid spears of fear into Theo. "Is that truly all? With the Fates all around us, I am asking you your deepest desires. They could make it so if they desired. You could be a king or a hero. Ask."

"I don't want to be a king, and I'm no hero."

"You could ask to wed a princess or a girl back home who holds your heart."

"I've never met a princess, and I've never been in love."

Gods, though, he wanted to fall in love with Aurienne.

"Ask. You can ask for anything, and I'll know if you are lying. Tell me your wish."

Theo looked down. They *were* his deepest desires. "I want to be a blacksmith, the best in the world one day. I want to make the most beautiful blades. I would like to fall deeply in love. I just want to live a good and long life."

The seer leaned back. "You ask for so much and so little."

Instinctively, somewhere deep in Theo's core, he recognized was not only speaking to Aurienne. Her Goddess was here, peering out from Aurienne's eyes. This was more than a reading. She was testing him, measuring him. Theo braced himself and raised his chin.

Let her see his mettle.

"What do you see in my future?"

She took his hand, wrapping her thin fingers around his palms. Faster than he could blink, she sliced his hand with her ceremonial blade. Blood poured from the cut, but her firm grip did not let him pull it away. It stung horribly, but Theo was determined not to let her see his pain. He hissed and clenched his other fist, but that was all.

The High Seer met his eyes with her own and held his gaze as she licked the blood from his palm in one long motion. It stained her lips. His heart hammered at her touch, sending bolts of lightning from his core to his limbs. She placed her other hand on the side of his face, and her gaze deepened. Theo couldn't have looked away if he tried. Not that he wanted to.

Time slowed to a near stop. The only sounds were his own breath and heartbeats. All he felt was her warm hand on his face. His chest pounded as if his ribs split from the inside, and he felt completely exposed, naked. All his secret thoughts exploded behind his eyes—his regrets, mistakes, and secret desires.

She spoke in a voice not her own. "You want to make the most beautiful blades, to fall in love, and live a good life. All of that will happen. And it won't. You shall make the most powerful blade in the world, but it will break. Or it shall break, and then you make it. You will fall deeply in love and lose it, three great loves. You will save lives and take them. You shall live on for centuries, though your death looms near. All of it and none of it. Your fate is sealed."

He must have imagined the golden threads of fate sinking into his flesh. Seconds later, they vanished, but the crackling sensation remained. A sinking feeling took root in the pit of his stomach as the chains slithered into his flesh. *Fate stung like hellsteeth.*

Theo stammered, "Wait. No, I don't understand."

Broken glimpses of visions assailed him. Her visions. He saw monsters, magic, swords, shadows, curses, and war. Terrible images of death and pain. Crowns.

She whispered, "You will understand. But before all of that—you have a different fate."

Her eyes went dark for an impossibly long moment. She inhaled sharply as her eyes returned to white. She recoiled and released his hand as if it were fire or poison. The world came crashing back.

He was suddenly aware that the clouds had parted, and the light was again shining through the window. Once more, he felt the sting of his hand and his warm blood oozing to the floor. The stone tiles chilled his bare feet.

Aurienne stared at him. A strange look settled upon her face. Hope? Fear? Surprise? Anger? Something else?

Coldforges and bonedust. What was my fate?

How terrible must it be? Frigid chills locked his limbs, and he hardly dared breathe.

"What did you see?" Theo leaned in.

Aurienne's hands shook, and her breath was shallow. "Everything."

Haunted

Chapter Five

— Journal of Queen Rosalindt Daniella Lenore, 579 N.T.C.

1152 N.T.C. Castle Rodarr, Rodarri.

In Rodarri, more often than not, the title and trappings of royalty were an unbreakable, inescapable cage. Queensblood Rianne Lenore, the eldest daughter of the eldest daughter going back forty-four generations to their first queen, knew this better than most. In this court, position did not mean power. Not when there were dozens of queens, and their deaths were worth more than their lives.

Rianne stood outside under the night sky, caught in a trance or perhaps a dream. She couldn't recall waking up or sneaking out here. Suddenly, she was *here*, in the cruelest place in the entire kingdom, and she was alone.

Or so she hoped.

Not a single star twinkled in the layers of black, velvet sky. The wind bit into Rianne's arms and legs underneath her silky nightdress. Gusts howled high overhead as they wound their way over the tall walls of the abandoned and forbidden courtyard. Faraway snarling of hounds from the kennels lingered in the night. But even the wind stilled to silence near the executioner's block and the cursed ravine.

She should *not* be here.

Decrepit stones older than Rodarri itself lined the courtyard. Crimson bloodroses with black vines and lethal thorns wound between the gaps in the wall. High walls and amphitheater seating spanned the entire length of the castle, large enough to fit nearly all the inhabitants of the city of Rodarr proper. Thousands. Other than the perimeter stadium seating, the courtyard was nearly empty. Only a worn wooden block upon a raised dais beside the ravine's maw graced the center.

This was the Courtyard of Queens, where queens were crowned, executed, and ascended. Here, they sometimes returned to life, so the stories said. Standing in this horrible place without the roaring crowds, Rianne wondered whether those stories were true. She dragged her hand across the dirty stone dais, shuffling on the cobblestones.

Rianne had never been here without blood-drunk crowds watching the annual ascension. The ceremony by which queens were executed and their bodies were thrown in the ravine.

The ravine was endless, and who could live without their head?

Queens, something whispered.

In that moment, Rianne nearly laughed at the title. Queens lived, bore more queens, and died so their blood would replenish Rodarri's magic and protect the land. They might be called queens, but they were little more than sacrificial lambs. A thousand queens died for Rodarri. Their bodies lay at the bottom of a cursed chasm in this forbidden courtyard. She was honored to one day join them.

Right?

Rianne was happy to protect the people. Her body was frail from the withering sickness. There was nothing she could do for them alive, but in death she could protect them.

Couldn't she?

Rianne believed this.

Didn't she?

It was hazy and hard to think.

Rianne suppressed a shudder. Her eyes were drawn into the seemingly bottomless pit. Harsh and grating whispers broke the silence, and an overwhelming sense of dread washed over her. She forced herself to breathe. It would be a while yet before her own head was freed from her shoulders and sent tumbling down into that terrible, dark ravine. She had time. A thousand rasping voices whispered terrible secrets and bitter truths.

> *Death is only the beginning.*
> *Save us. Save us. Save us. Save us.*
> *Saveussaveussaveussaveus.*
> *Die. Die. Die. Die. Come to us. Come. Come to us.*
> *Come. Die. Come die.*
> *A thousand queens, dead for nothing. A thousand*
> *more to die.*
> *Lies and lies and lies. Don't believe their lies.*
> *Let us out.*

"Don't you hear them? All those queens, dead for nothing," Rianne repeated, half-awake, half-dreaming, and not sure of what it meant.

Looking around at the empty courtyard, Rianne swallowed, fingers reaching for her neck. Biting wind like the edge of a sword brushed against her skin. So many voices spoke over one another, calling out such horrible things. She wanted to scream, pressing her hands against her skull in an attempt to ignore the whispers. They would not be ignored.

> *We see only darkness. We are only darkness. Come to*
> *the dark.*
> *Creature of chaos, creature of war. Ancestral crimes to*
> *answer for.*
> *Run, child, run. Yes, runrunrunrunrunrunrunrun-*
> *runrunrun.*
> *Come closer, dear. Let me look at you.*
> *Run before they never let you leave.*
> *The screams never stop. The smiles never end. The*
> *screams never stop.*

A thousand pairs of silver eyes opened from the darkness of the ravine, unblinking and angry. They floated upward as the whispers grew louder. She tried to back away, but her limbs would not move.

Rianne's voice was small in the midst of these nightmares, and it trembled. "Please stop. I don't know what you're saying. Please. Please. Don't hurt me."

> *Rising queens and falling kings, truth unseen and*
> *ghostly rings.*
> *Skulls, bones, blood, death. The cycle never ends. Skulls,*
> *bones, blood, death.*
> *The worst is yet to come.*
> *Rianne. Wake up. Rianne.*
> *When I am freed, my vengeance will have no bounds.*
> *The kings will die.*
> *Grimfall. Grimfall. Grimfall. Grim falls on us all.*
> *Grimfall murderer.*
> *Let us out!*

"Don't you hear them? All those queens, dead for nothing," Rianne screamed again.

Dark shadowy hands reached for her from the edge of the ravine. The icy fingers were cold on her ankles. Tears streamed down her face, unbidden. She screwed her eyes shut. She must be dreaming. This couldn't be real. Ravines didn't whisper, and angry spirits didn't shout.

It must be a dream.

It must be.

This wasn't real.

Rianne awoke in her bed, heart hammering as though she'd run a mile through the gardens. She wiped a hand over the sweat pooling on the clammy skin of her face and neck. A thousand eyes seemed to be watching her from the darkness, but nothing was there. Nothing was there.

She exhaled in relief and forced herself to breathe deeply and slowly. It was a dream. It had just been a terrible dream. The ascension was a noble sacrifice of the Queensblood bloodline that protected Rodarri against foreign invaders and drought. It had worked for over a thousand years. Never had Rodarri been invaded while ascensions protected them. Never had the rivers run dry. A sacrifice once a year was worth the lives of millions.

Rianne was honored to be chosen, she told herself. They all were. The ascended queens were at peace, looking down and protecting them. Rianne had never questioned her duty before. She would not now. The Courtyard of Queens was not full of angry dead spirits clawing to escape. Rianne had been there every year for the ascension, and she'd never heard whispers.

Just a terrible dream. Just a nightmare.

She placed her hands over her face, but her skin was strangely rough. She froze, horror rising once more in her chest. She slowly lowered her hands.

They were covered in dark crimson and black dirt.

She ripped the blankets off.

Her feet were coated in gritty filth.

Rianne screamed.

PROPHECY
CHAPTER SIX

Smiling skulls and blood-soaked stones.
Darkling dreams and blood-soaked bones.

— JOURNAL OF THE SEER RHEIA, DATE UNKNOWN.

1152 N.T.C. The namesake capital city of Avyllon.

The unwilling universe finally relented, providing Aurienne the answer she sought—it had come in the form of a blacksmith, and cost her more than she was willing to admit. Already, a darkness crept into her soul. In the hours since the Rite, she'd twice turned to the Old Ways and performed forbidden necromancy that still stained her soul. The answer she had sought so desperately all this while was locked in the blood of this man.

In her vision, the crowns and sigils of every country in Teridar came together in the summit room at Avyllon's forsaken palace under a full moon. Theo stood in the throne room, a blazing sun, holding invisible strands of fate that spooled around each nation. The Avyllon crown slipped from Aurienne's head and bounced off the floor. A faceless figure grasped her crown and set it upon their own brow. Echoing sounds of footsteps and claws clicking on the floor filled the room.

The summit from her visions must occur in one month, on the next full moon. One month until the fate of the continent would be decided. This must come to pass, or all Teridar would fall. Theo's reading showed her the thousands and thousands of outcomes, like leaves on the river. So many sealed fates and possible futures.

All of it tied to him, to her—and the summit.

It all began with a gilded letter dripping foul bubbling poison, offering peace but seeking destruction. The Demorran emperor would come—the source of their prophesized war. They would be here soon, and Theo—he was the key to it all. Those phantom footsteps filled her head again, an omen of something more terrible than war. She shook the footsteps from her mind. She'd figure that out later.

A drop of his blood remained on her lips, and she pressed it into her mouth with her finger before realizing what she had done. She glanced at him to check whether he had noticed. His elevated brow confirmed he had. The edges of her lips curved into a wicked smile.

Pacing like a caged wild animal, she tried to make sense of it. The blacksmith watched her warily, but she paid him no heed. Since he appeared, time moved too fast, sensations crashed into her, and nothing made any sense. He made everything feel too sharp, too bright, too real. The tang of his blood lingered on her tongue, all forests and fires and sunsets. She pushed open her doors and stormed to the grand receiving room, Theo hot on her heels.

"Aurienne?" he called.

The visions replayed in her mind as the Old Ways opened Theo's soul to hers. In the visions, she Saw Theo. His past. His futures. His heart. Barriers fell away to reveal his soul. So many simple, precious, beautiful moments.

At night watch, he laughed with farmers and friends, telling old stories of shared adventures. Long days, sweating in the baking sun, his back aching from tilling the fields, and still, he came home to find his mother mending socks, her fingers shaking with the day's effort. He took the needle from her, staying up past midnight to have them ready for her clients in the morning. Upon the livestock, his hands were gentle and kind, but at the forge, they were unyielding.

Reaching the receiving room, she rang a bell connected to a rope, summoning an attendant.

"Bring General Kane, every seer in the temple, the one without a name, my brother Adonis, and the sorcerer Mathis here at once," she directed the attendant.

She winced, pressed her fist against the spreading bruise on her breastbone. Theo'd brought her back to life, but her ribs were paying the price. She swallowed and winced. Her throat still raw.

"What's going on?" Theo asked carefully.

She scowled. "We're about to have unwelcome guests."

Demorra.

The seers came first on hastened steps, flooding the grand, white stone room with a flurry of ceremonial gowns. Saryll led them inside, fear on her young, painted face. She pressed her damp palms against her gown, glancing from Theo to Aurienne. The nameless spy, a plain man in a simple gray cloak, slipped in from a side room and situated himself in the corner. Aurienne's brother, Adonis, soon twenty and in the midst of his apprenticeship to join the guild of sorcerers, entered the room. He was trailed by his mentor, Mathis. Both wore the purple robes of Avyllon University.

Aurienne's brother raced up to her and gave her a tight hug. "You scared me," he said, releasing her. "Don't do that again."

Aurienne ruffled his hair. "I'm sorry. I nearly had the vision I needed."

"It doesn't do us any good if you drown," Adonis said.

"That's what I said," Theo muttered.

Adonis strode up to him, grabbed his arms while looking Theo over, and then locked Theo in a tight hug hard enough to make the blacksmith cough. Although Theo was taller and much broader, he looked around for help like a cornered feral cat. Adonis gave him another squeeze and let go.

"Thanks for dragging her out. I wanted to help, but *Captain Laurier* got in my way. Good on you for knocking him on his rear, though," Adonis said.

Aurienne fought the urge to roll her eyes at Adonis.

General Kane, Commander of the Royal Armies of Avyllon, entered her room last. "High Seer, can you please explain the appearance of the red eclipse? Our sentinels are trying to keep the peace, but people are uneasy," he said as if she had painted the sky red herself.

Boots sounded in the hall. Her stomach dropped at the inkling of what came next. The Demorran Empire. They were already here.

She looked to the door. "We receive our invitation to war now."

Five hulking soldiers in shining black armor, stamped with the gold wolf crest of the Demorran Empire, strode into the room, following a temple attendant and five surly Avyllon sentinels. The Demorran soldiers still wore their helms, not even offering her the respect to remove them.

Theo stepped forward, angling himself between the soldiers. Theo was unarmed, barefoot, beaten, and he still stepped in front of her. A small crack of warmth filled her chest, and her eyes dragged to the blacksmith, his stance, arms, and back. She tore her gaze back to the soldiers.

Amber eyes surveyed her from behind the helms. Long black cloaks draped over the black bog-iron steel armor. She noticed the glimmer of diamond and flecks of gold and nearly gasped. Not bog-iron steel, *titan ore*. They wore full sets of titan ore armor, an element long thought lost. Magical relics were made with the fabled substance —she'd recognize it anywhere.

Leather and fur peeked from gaps in the plating, and a collection of gilded onyx swords, axes, bows, and knives glinted cruelly. One of the soldiers stood hunched slightly forward, his shoulders so muscled they were nearly deformed. Another shifted from foot to foot in boots twice as large as they ought to be. One was missing an arm. All five were breathing too deeply and slowly. It was hard to tell behind the helms, but somewhere around the shape of the eyes or mouth, something was off with them.

"An imperial demand for the High Seer of Avyllon." The middle soldier, wearing gold stripes painted along his pauldron marking him as a commander of some level, thrust a gold-plated missive to her.

Her sentinels shifted and tensed, gripping their swords, and Aurienne's personal guard, Sentinel Kolten, stepped forward.

Aurienne reached for it, but Theo beat her to it, snatching the missive from the Demorran's fingers, which were stained yellow and black. Theo never broke eye contact with the scowling soldier but handed Aurienne the missive.

The commander released a low, rumbling growl at Theo. Aurienne's sentinels took a small step forward, hands on their weapons.

Aurienne carefully took the letter with the howling wolf wax seal. Something about it wasn't right. The paper was cold in her hand, and visions of wolves tearing through the forest raced across the grand receiving room. It felt...enchanted, imbued with magic.

"Emperor Rexil sends his regards," the commander said, voice low and rough—as if there were too many teeth in his mouth.

Years of searching for threats, decades of waiting, and now they were out of time. How she answered this missive would change everything—and she'd been shown the way out. The summit of leaders was the only way to withstand the might of the emperor and his afflicted soldiers in titan ore armor.

One month to accomplish so much.

Aurienne swallowed but lifted her chin. "We have received your missive and shall send an answer by the next full moon."

The commander leaned in, but Theo stepped forward, keeping him away from her.

"He demands an answer now," the commander growled.

"Sentinel Kolten, please escort our guests out of the city," Aurienne said curtly. "We shall send an answer in one month's time. It is the will of the Goddess."

The commander snarled, and his soldiers stalked forward. Kolten and the other sentinels flanked the Demorran soldiers. Theo remained blocking Aurienne, and General Kane gripped his sword. A low chuckle grated in the commander's throat.

The sorcerer Mathis stepped forward, chanting and tracing his hands in a complicated pattern. He broke a purple vial on his palm, and a blazing fireball appeared in his hand.

The soldiers whipped their heads toward him as one, eyes burning almost yellow inside the helms.

"The High Seer has received your message and asked you to leave," Mathis said, his menacing tone in contrast with his wild hair and the happy bells chiming in his beard.

The commander growled, low and deep in his throat like a wolf. He gripped the hilt of his axe, but Mathis' purple fireball flared. Aurienne held her breath as futures of violence and bloodshed overlaid her reality.

The commander glanced between Aurienne and Mathis. "We'll see you again," the commander finally said, leaving the room with booming footsteps.

The Demorran soldiers and Avyllon sentinels followed him out, and Mathis extinguished the fireball. A collective breath was released from those remaining in the grand room.

Footsteps echoed in the prison of Aurienne's mind.

Step.

Step.

Step.

Every day, those accursed footsteps from the Rite were coming closer and closer.

"What does it say?" General Kane asked.

Without opening the letter, Aurienne said, "It invites us to join the Demorran Empire. Our choices are a pledge of fealty and a promise of tax and troops yearly to Emperor Rexil, or he invades and burns Avyllon to the ground."

General Kane's jaw dropped, and his arms fell to his sides. Aurienne handed it to General Kane. He cracked the wax seal and read the letter aloud.

To the High Seer Aurienne Celestina Azarrah of Avyllon, Regent and Guardian to the Avyllon Crown Throne,

This letter invites the High Seer of Avyllon to join the Empire of Demorra. The Imperial Throne requires one hundred thousand able-bodied men to serve in Imperial Majesties armies, and an additional ten thousand men be brought to the all-wise emperor each year thereafter. The Imperial Throne requires one million gold pieces; two hundred thousand swords; one hundred thousand cattle; fifty thousand sheep, horses, and chickens; forty thousand bushels of grain, barrels of butter, barrels of ground wheat; and twenty percent of the vegetable harvest. Half the seers, sorcerers, and healers with copies of all major works must travel to the empire within the year to reside.

Response is required imminently, or the emperor shall force your decision.

— EMPEROR JHAMES EDWYRD ALEXANDIR REXIL, HIS IMPERIAL MAJESTY, THE WOLF EMPEROR OF THE DEMORRAN EMPIRE, AND ALL PROTECTORATE NATIONS THEREUNDER, THE MOON-BLESSED, CONQUEROR OF SEVENTEEN KINGDOMS, AND FAVORITE SON OF THE LUNAR GODDESS NIAMH.

"One hundred thousand men," General Kane spat.

"And ten thousand more each year," the spy said.

"That's more than half of our standing army," General Kane said.

"And one quarter of all taxes brought in," Aurienne said.

"Does the emperor have an army?" General Kane asked.

In visions past, Aurienne had Seen previously unidentified hundreds of thousands, millions, of troops crossing continents and burning cities, and she now knew to whom they belonged. She nodded grimly.

"*Hagsteeth*, he demands enough that our city and farms would struggle to provide it. The people would hardly be able to pay any taxes to the crown and to the empire," General Kane said.

"This is the beginning of the Darkling War," Aurienne said quietly, feeling chills run down her arms.

Every seer gasped, shifting in place, while Theo backed away, leaning against the wall.

"The red eclipse signaled this?" Saryll breathed.

"No one returns home," Aurienne whispered. "I see blood and bones and screaming. Cities burning. The emperor will begin with these demands but take and take and take until there is nothing and no one left."

The magical cords of Fate wrapped around her chest and throat, threatening to strangle them all.

"Our only choice is whether our destruction is slow and compliant or if we fight like hells," she said.

"Seventeen nations," the nameless one said quietly. "There should be twenty-one in Demorra. Not counting Rexila, there should be three more. If he's not counting them, it means he destroyed them. I was just there before my time in Arryn, not five years ago. He conquered the entire continent in that time."

The room fell silent. General Kane stared at the letter in his hands like it was made of poison. Theo shifted at the edge of the room, eyes darting from one person to the next.

"I Saw a single chance at our salvation," Aurienne said. "There is one path out of the darkness. The cost is great, but a chance at saving a continent is worth the cost."

"What is it?" Saryll asked.

"There shall be a summit of all five of Teridar's leaders in one month on the day of the next full moon, or it will be too late."

Everyone stared.

"The summit will decide the fate of the world," she said. "Wyndsel and Demorra have no love lost for Avyllon or each other, and the Seven Forests and Titan Cliffs closed their borders decades ago. The journey to gather the allies may very well kill us. It *will* kill some of us. The path to gathering our allies is fraught with monsters, gods, corrupted magic, and nightmares coming to life."

A heavy weight filled the room. Dark expressions crossed their faces as her words hung in the silence. Fear bloomed in the corners of their eyes.

Some of them would die. The only question is who.

She folded her tattooed hands. "Death hangs over this future, but it is the only path that gives us a chance to survive the Darkling War. Its cost is blood."

Taking a steadying breath, she glanced out the window. Birds sang, and fountains bubbled. The clouds were lined with golden sunlight. Children laughed. The breeze smelled of roses. She looked back at the fearful room.

"There is only one person who can save us," she said.

Aurienne looked at Theo, and the rest of the room followed her gaze. The blacksmith stood quietly at the edge of the room, trying to blend into the wall. Aurienne felt another pang of guilt as he tugged at his borrowed clothes and shifted on bare feet under their scrutiny.

Her forthcoming words would change his life forever. There was no going back, of that she was certain. These were the final moments of a life he was about to leave behind. She wished she knew how to break the news and ease him into his new destiny, but that was not the sort of thing a heartless creature like her knew.

"You will bring together the armies that fight the Darkling War."

"Me?" Theo stumbled as he uncrossed his legs from where he leaned stiffly against the wall. "What? You must be mistaken. You must have seen someone else. I have no idea how to do that, even if I wanted to. Are...are you sure?" His face paled.

"It has been Seen, and it shall come to pass."

"I have no idea how to gather armies. No one will follow me." He tucked his hands under his arms, but she glimpsed how they shook.

"Your heart beats true without wanting power," she said. "Maybe that is exactly the kind of person we need."

"None of this makes sense. I can't... I'm just..."

"It is. Trust me. You cannot fight your fate," she said quietly.

Theo's shoulders sagged.

General Kane interrupted, "High Seer, the borders of the Free Peoples and Titan Cliffs have both been closed to outsiders for many years. We won't be welcome."

"We first visit Wyndsel and Rodarri. Hopefully, I'll learn more once events have solidified," Aurienne said.

"You're going? With the unrest and fear, now is not the time to leave. They will think you are running away—"

Aurienne interrupted, "Your words are well-taken, and I understand the risks. But I have Seen this. I'll travel to Wyndsel and Rodarri with Theo—that I know. Your men shall protect me, and you shall protect Avyllon while I'm away. It is safe in your hands."

General Kane snapped his mouth shut and grimaced.

"There is no one better to protect our beloved city," she added.

General Kane pursed his lips but finally nodded.

"Prepare a full official caravan of one hundred soldiers, the necessary staff, and supplies for them and me, Theo, Adonis, Mathis, and Saryll. Bring two extra horses. We leave in the morning. I must send word to Wyndsel and Rodarri that we plan to visit. Do not speak of this vision to anyone until the summit." She found the spy, already blending into the shadows of the columns. "Nameless, travel to the empire of Demorra. See what you can learn about this emperor. Write me just before the month is out."

The general bowed and stomped out of her chambers, already shouting orders to the sentinels waiting outside. The one without a name slipped away.

"I get to go?" Adonis exclaimed.

"Yes, you can visit the royal universities while we are there," Aurienne said.

The sorcerer Mathis pulled his mismatched, blue cloak around himself. His graying hair stuck out at all odd angles, as if he had been struck by lightning once too many times and permanently fried the follicles. He shuffled forward.

"Would you mind accompanying us? I wouldn't ask you to leave your other students and classes if it was not important," Aurienne asked the sorcerer.

"What can we bring to be of service?" Mathis asked.

She cast a soft smile. "Everything you have."

"Shall we be using the Ways? I should like to demonstrate to Adonis."

"Our first host might take it as an act of aggression," she said. "But perhaps after that."

"Come along, Adonis. We'll continue your studies on the road," Mathis said to the teen as they exited the room.

"You can't possibly think much studying will be accomplished while we're riding horses..." Adonis' voice faded away.

Aurienne and Theo were alone once more. The silence was deafening.

Theo looked down as his face fell. "But I... My guild certificate. I finished seven years of training. I completed the tests. I-I saved up to build a forge."

"I know," Aurienne said sadly.

Her vision had shown her the long years he toiled. All he ever wanted was right there, just out of reach. Aurienne tried to be patient, knowing it would take time for him to come to terms with the news, but it was difficult for her to be patient when she knew how it would end. He wouldn't have a choice.

He shook his head. "I don't... I just want to go home with my family. I don't want to travel to see kings and attend summits. You have the wrong person."

She crossed the room and took his hand gently. He met her gaze.

"We will get through one day at a time. Together. I See your family is in Avyllon. You must bid them goodbye and prepare to travel."

Theo said nothing. She squeezed his hand, wishing she could tell him everything would be alright, wishing she could make it so, but her words fell utterly short.

"If you don't go, every single person that you love will die," she whispered. "I'm sorry. I would not ask if there was any other way."

"Can't your visions change?"

"Not this one. There are fates and futures, and this is a fate."

"This isn't what I want."

It wasn't what she wanted for him. She didn't want her fate either, but it wouldn't change it. Her heart seized in agony for him, and she completely failed to comfort him.

"Those who want a great destiny rarely deserve it."

Theo shook his head and glared at the ground, but he didn't pull his hand from hers.

She said, "I'm sorry. I'm not good at this."

"What? Threats?" he said lightly.

She winced. "Talking to people. So often, I live in the world of unreal things that I forget what it is to be...human. I don't know how to tell you about what I have seen. What I do know more certainly than anything else is that you can save the people you care about. And everyone else."

"You're sure?" He let out a heavy breath.

"I don't know that we will succeed," she said. "But I know that it is the only chance we have."

He shook his head. "I saw glimpses of terrible things. Dreams fading with morning light. Did you show me those?"

She swallowed a gasp. The Old Ways were unpredictable, dangerous. Sharing blood with magic held incredible power. She hadn't realized he'd shared her visions. It shouldn't be possible.

"The Goddess showed you the truths you needed to see," she said. "Will you do it?"

Theo stared at the floor for long moments, eyes full of thoughts. He flexed and unflexed his fists before releasing a long breath full of doubt. He lifted his chin and locked eyes with her. "You know I will."

Theo paced as he waited for his parents to respond to Aurienne's summons. Aurienne watched the door with a bemused smile, and he wondered what she found humorous. He eyed her suspiciously, but she gave nothing away. Sentinels escorted his parents into the large temple receiving room. Pa was wringing his hat while Ma fisted her dress pockets.

"Theo!" Ma broke away from their escort and crashed into him with a surprisingly firm hug for a small woman, driving the wind from his lungs. She touched his slightly bruised face and checked him over.

"I saw you arrested and have been so worried!" Ma smacked him on the back of the head. "What is wrong with you?"

Keener than the impact of her scolding was the love that prompted it. Theo unsuccessfully tried hiding his smile. She batted at his chest with her hand, suggesting an oncoming tirade.

"What were you doing diving into the ceremonial pool?" Ma threw up her hands. "I've been trying to get you to take a wife for nearly four years now, and every time I bring it up, it's 'No, Ma, I need my own forge first,' and 'No, Ma, there's no one in town I fancy,' and 'No, Ma, after I join the guild first.'"

That's what Aurienne found amusing.

"...but then you see a fancy woman jump into a pool, and suddenly she's the one you need to dive in after," Ma scolded.

Then Ma noticed Aurienne standing at the edge of the room with folded hands. Both recognition and embarrassment flooded her face, but Ma always refused to back down. That was how she loved—fully and aggressively.

"No offense, High Seer. Not questioning you," Ma said with a slight bow.

Aurienne inclined her head, and the corners of her lips rose slightly. "I told him he should not dive into pools when unwanted as well, but he refuses to see the prudence of my counsel."

Ma smiled broadly enough that the corners of her eyes crinkled with mirth. "She's a smart one."

"Is he in trouble?" Pa asked.

"No, I have pardoned his desecration of the ceremonial pool in light of his heroic actions. And in exchange for a favor I must ask of him," Aurienne said.

"Favor?" Pa asked.

Theo swallowed. He'd have to get used to explaining things and might as well try now. His tongue grew sandy, and his mouth filled with cotton.

"Ma—Aurienne, the High Seer, I mean—has Seen that I will assist her. The bleeding eclipse foretold the Darkling War. She Sees that I'll...visit the...kingdoms. I'll ask them to join the war as our allies so that we might beat the...Emperor Rexil," Theo stammered.

Aurienne politely strained to hide a wince, but Theo noticed. His parents stared like he had failed to speak intelligible words. He cleared his throat and tried again.

"The bleeding eclipse signified the prophesized Darkling War, and Emperor Rexil has demanded all nations of Teridar join his Empire. We believe... Aurienne believes...this is the threat foretold. She had a vision that I'd be the one to gather the armies to fight him if we are to stand a chance. She's asked me to accompany her to the nations of Teridar to make the pleas."

His parents both turned to Aurienne as one.

"Is this true?" Pa asked.

"I Saw a summit of the five nations of Teridar gathering in one month's time, and that Theo would be the only one able to get them there. If there is no summit, then Teridar will fall. With the summit, we have a chance. I do not know why, but the vision was clear. It must be Theo," Aurienne said.

"When are you leaving?" Ma asked.

"Tomorrow," Aurienne said.

"Ma, it's okay. I can do this," Theo said gently.

Ma drew herself up as tall as she could and pressed her shoulders back. A person who did not know her would have missed the nervous twitch of her hands or the way she wrung them in her pockets, but Theo noticed.

"Well, of course you can," Ma said. "I'm just surprised. And I'll miss you. But if you have to go help our High Seer, then that's that."

Ma then grabbed his arms and began babbling all manner of advice.

"Remember to avoid a black feather in the road."

"I know, Ma," he said fondly.

"Purple moss means danger."

"I know..."

"Don't cross dark water."

"Thank you, I..."

"A black line across the road means a sinkhole."

"I know, Ma."

"And beware of curses."

"Curses don't exist, Ma."

"Of course they do."

"What—"

"This is the most important. Remember, if you hear a long low whistle, so low your ears bleed, the stars fade, and the fire goes out, run. It doesn't matter which way, just run," Ma said.

"I know, Ma," Theo said.

"And..." Before Ma could finish, he wrapped her in a tight hug and enveloped her. He kissed the top of her head.

"I love you too," he said.

She squeezed him back.

"The land will protect those who remember its ways," Pa said, clapping him fondly on the shoulder.

Theo pulled Pa into a hug, and smiling, Pa hugged him and patted his back again.

Theo noticed Aurienne walk to a desk and begin writing.

"Did you get your guild certificate signed?" his Pa asked.

Theo stammered, remembering the drowned certificate in his pocket.

Aurienne appeared between them. "I have signed a paper that shall be sealed and delivered to the blacksmith guild upon our departure. When Theo returns, he'll be a full member of the guild upon my personal signature and recommendation." She held up a signed paper.

Theo stared. Even with all that he had yet to do for Aurienne's vision, a hundred tons lifted from him as though rods of steel binding his chest had been severed. He swallowed and met her clouded gaze.

"Thank you." He wet his lips.

Aurienne smiled softly at him and nodded.

"No, thank you," he repeated.

"I know," she whispered.

"When will Theo be returning home?" Ma asked.

Aurienne looked at his mother with an expression Theo did not recognize but Ma seemed to understand. The two women shared a long look. A silent conversation passed between them, leaving Theo and Pa scrubbing their jaws. Aurienne tilted her chin, and Ma took a deep breath. Aurienne looked down, and Ma wrapped her arms around herself.

"I see," Ma finally said.

Aurienne took Ma's hands gently in her own. "His fate showed me a long, good, and happy life. The journey to get there may be fraught, and there will be darkness, but in almost all his futures he has a great destiny. He will change the world."

Ma nodded and quickly wiped away a tear.

"Will you protect him?"

"We will have sentinels on the journey..."

"No, will *you* protect him?" Ma interrupted.

Aurienne twisted her lips and creased her brows deeply. Her eyes glazed, perhaps searching for a promise that she could truthfully make. Theo wondered what she Saw to make her pause. Maybe he didn't want to know.

Aurienne whispered, "I'll do everything in my power."

Ma removed an eyestone looped around her neck on a long leather cord.

"Take this," she said to Theo.

"Ma, this is yours," he said.

She held his hands firmly. "You're going on an adventure to meet kings and warriors and the like, and they have a tendency to deceive. It will help you see into a person's heart."

"Thank you," Theo said.

She looped it over his neck and tucked it into his shirt, then patted it and gave him a final hug, pulling Pa into the embrace.

Ma said, "The eyestone will help you find your way home."

CHANGING FATE
CHAPTER SEVEN

We all must die sometime. Every story has an end. What matters is what you do with the time you have.

— HIGH SEER AURIENNE AZARRAH, PROPHETIC VISION.

1152 N.T.C. Outside the city of Avyllon, at the fork of the main road.

The traveling party waited outside the city gates of Avyllon, facing the dense forests and towering mountains of the valley. Taking a deep breath, Aurienne settled her mind and drew upon her gift. Theo waited beside her, and she tried to ignore the draw. He was a catalyst—making things go faster, burn brighter, and feel deeper. Prophecies decades in the making twisted and changed like quicksand underneath her feet. He set her life on fire even as she was drowning. It made her brow sweat, her skin itch, and her heart beat a little too fast.

So much had changed since yesterday. With this new knowledge, it would be prudent to check her cards before deciding which route to take—the main southwest road or the smaller west-southwest path. She flipped through the deck and froze.

"They've changed," she whispered.

The cards slipped from Aurienne's shaking hands. She quickly knelt in the dirt to retrieve them.

Theo crouched beside her. "What's wrong?"

"The arcane suit. They're all different." Aurienne frantically flipped card after card and finally sat back on her heels. "Life, Death, and the new Traveler card are here. The virtue and lore suits are unchanged, but the rest of the arcane suit has changed itself overnight. Every. Single. One."

Bringing the cards to her lips, she whispered to them, "What have you done?"

She stared at her cards like seeing a lover who had become a stranger. New faces looked back at her keenly. One blinked. Another unsheathed her blade. A third grinned.

"Do they do that often?" Theo stammered. "Do they move?"

She pursed her lips. "Of the twenty-one cards in the arcane suit, in the past year, only one card has changed. Since yesterday, nineteen have changed."

"What does it mean?" Theo asked.

Saryll neared. "What's wrong?"

Aurienne gestured to the cards.

Saryll pressed her fingers to her forehead, lips, and heart and muttered, "Goddess protect us."

"We have taken steps toward our future," Aurienne said, "and it has changed everything. Everyone will bear the costs of transformation."

Aurienne studied her new cards. Every seer's or witch's deck was unique, and even the number of cards or suits varied. Since childhood, she had seen hundreds of past and current decks recorded in the temple library. The rituals, meanings, combinations, numerology, suits, and cards were carved firmly in her mind. Yet, she had never seen a single one of these named cards before.

Aurienne glowered at the new cards. She could guess which changed into which new card for... most of them. Several sharp words sprang into her mind, and she'd be repeating them to her deck later.

"Which way?" Theo interrupted her thoughts.

Aurienne didn't know how long she'd been sitting in the middle of the dusty road staring at her traitorous cards while well over one hundred soldiers, her brother and his mentor, her sister seer, the cooks, and royal attendants, and all their horses and supplies waited in the morning sun. Sweat rolled down her neck, and she became aware of the scent of wildflower fields.

"Which way should we take to Wyndsel?" she asked the cards.

She shuffled her changed deck until it warmed and faced the wide western road before flipping the top card. The Emperor. Endings, mistakes, lies—she shuddered the slithering feeling from between her shoulder blades. She faced the narrower road and flipped the card. The Witch. Crackling cabin hearths, warm tea, homey thick blankets, and welcome poured into her soul.

She smiled and pointed to the road winding south. "That way."

"That road winds through the forest and is longer. It will add days to our trip to Wyndsel, seer," Sentinel Kolten, answered.

"It is the right way," she said. "It might be the less expected way, as well."

She pocketed her cards and mounted her white spotted mare. Nudging her heels against the horse's ribs, she led the caravan into the shadows of the chosen road.

"Wait." Theo knelt to inspect a long dark line across the path. "We should go around."

"Why?" she asked.

"Lore says that these signify places where the land swallows people."

"Quicksand?"

Theo shrugged. "The land protects those who remember its ways."

The words struck Aurienne as singularly true, and she glanced at Theo. In her core, she knew those words held greater power than Theo or his parents realized. They were ancient words, a promise passed down in legend.

"The land protects those who remember its ways," she echoed.

The caravan skirted the dark line and rode for some time.

Aurienne studied the path, trying to discern why the Goddess chose it for her. It was narrow enough that the tree canopy parted only occasionally, and patches of sunlight bathed the dirt. The road curved one way and another. At times she couldn't even see the end of their caravan. Aurienne watched the dark and curling vines climbing the tree trunks through the shadows. She shifted in the saddle, each bump sending flaming spears of pain through her chest.

"Do you travel much?" Theo asked.

Aurienne blinked, noticing Theo had ridden up beside her. She looked up and tried to determine the sun's place in the sky. It was nearly above them. Hours had passed while she stared at leaves and trees.

Shifting in the saddle, she was suddenly very aware of the time she'd lost. "Not much. I visited Wyndsel and Rodarri once when I traveled to the major universities for study—and I did meet the royal families enough to know not to trust either of them. However, I have not left the capital in..." She chewed her lip. How long had it been? "I suppose it's been five years now."

"My apprenticeship kept me from traveling much," he said. "I mainly stayed in Karme or in Riverlim where my blacksmith mentor lived. We trade with nearby villages several times a year, most often Tache and Goldenfern, but sometimes we go farther. Other than that, I haven't traveled much either."

Aurienne inclined her chin. "You traveled to your apprenticeship every day?"

"Five days of the week," he said. "It was about an hour ride from our farm. I helped tend and feed the animals in the morning, did my apprenticeship, and came back to help with fences and watering fields. Of course, during harvest, I stayed home for a few weeks."

"Had you been to our capital before?"

"Just a few times to trade or sell. Ma is a skilled weaver, and my mentor let me keep a few tools I made to sell."

A beautifully simple life.

"This was your first foretelling?" she asked.

Theo snorted and nodded. "I was unprepared. I won't admit this to Ma, but I should have listened better when they were talking about the ceremony. I was not expecting the Rite."

A chuckle escaped her lips. "I'm glad you didn't listen."

Theo blushed and shifted in the saddle.

She grinned, giving him the mercy of changing the subject. "I can tell you love your parents dearly."

Theo smiled, and a tiny ember warmed her heart. Aurienne soaked in his smile and the bright forest day as birds chirped and leaves rustled. A red and black fox peered out at the group from the undergrowth with yellow eyes. It'd been tracking them for quite a while now. She tossed a piece of dried meat to the fox, and it gobbled the offering eagerly before stalking the group through the shadows.

"Where are your parents?" Theo asked. "Your brother is here, but where are they?"

Aurienne's smile faded. "I was born with the seer's cloud in my eyes. They traveled to the temple and received my birth reading."

"The one that says there will be a war?"

Aurienne found herself answering, unsure why she was telling him her secret. She hardly knew Theo, and yet felt like she'd known him all her life. Just another unintended consequence of the Old Ways. There was more than one reason it was discouraged. The cost to the soul being the greatest, but also the bonds it formed for seeing so much of a person. She shouldn't say more. Yet, her heart burst to know him better and share her truths.

"That's not all it said," she said. "Few know this, but the reading said that *my* visions would be the downfall of Teridar."

"I don't believe that for a second," Theo scoffed. "They heard wrong."

Aurienne's heart swelled, and a smile spread across her face. Relief washed over her like a warm summer breeze. She had to remember that she did *not* permit herself to cry, but she needed to hear that. His words snapped a link in the chain of a thousand guarded memories of fear and guilt squeezing the life from her heart. She now breathed a little easier. The words were a salve to many painful sharp jabs from seers and whispers from temple attendants, which bored into her heart.

"No one but the seers know," she said. "I would appreciate it if you kept my secret."

"To my grave." He crossed his heart.

"To answer your question, I haven't seen my parents in years," she said. "They did what was expected. When I turned three, they brought me to the temple for training. They left me there, and I did not see them again for years. They came back to the temple with Adonis. He was about three years old and had begun to manifest magic as well. Sorcery. My mother stayed with him at the temple on and off for a few years until one day, she left him there as well. I understand that my parents and Adonis exchange letters from time to time."

"They just left you? A child?"

"They were afraid of my fate." Aurienne paused. She had never told anyone this next truth either but found it slipping from her lips, desperately wanting someone, anyone, to know her. "They had the chance to end me early." Bile rose in Aurienne's throat at the remembered vision. "They nearly took it, but couldn't."

Theo's face turned crimson around the edges and pulled tight. "Who could do that to a baby?"

"People who believed that it was the right thing to do. I understood. I know what it means to be terrified of possible fates. Though I couldn't blame them, in that moment, I no longer loved them. Seeing my mother dote over Adonis made it worse. She wiped his mouth and caressed his head, pressing kisses against his brow, and yet when she noticed me watching from the shadows, an eight-year-old child starving for any love, she refused to meet my gaze. Adonis visited them once a few years ago, and we have siblings that they adore. Apparently, it is a house full of love and care," she said bitterly.

Aurienne recalled a vision from when Adonis had told her of their siblings. Strawberry juice dribbled down the lips of dirty-footed squealing children. Their mother, a plump woman wearing a clean apron, stepped outside wielding a broom and suppressed a chuckle while shouting, "Are you stealing berries again!"

The children stuffed the berries in their mouths, giggling with shining eyes as they raced across the garden, running from their mother, who caught them in a hug and covered them all in kisses. The lance of resentment hurt today just as badly as it did then.

"They're good people. If they thought about drowning me, something the High Seer Syaoran Amydeo told them about my birth prophecy made them believe that killing me was a kindness." Aurienne looked away. "The fact that they didn't go through with it showed the depth of their love. That I never saw them again showed their guilt. When the seers realized the extent of my gift, my magic, they believed I was the only one who could stop the prophecy. I suppose it's good that I didn't die."

The fox pounced from a bush and made a chirpy barking noise. It turned a circle with its fluffy tail darting about. Aurienne tossed it another bit of meat. A vision flashed in front of her of this fox following the caravan for miles, begging for strips of meat the whole way. She ignored the warning, handing it another bite of fruit. The fox barked again happily.

Another fleeting vision appeared. Aurienne Saw Theo's horse step into an unseen vermin hole and throw him to the dust. The other sentinels snickered, and Theo's face turned beet red while Captain Laurier called out veiled insults. Dejected, Theo rode sullenly for the rest of the day, staring at the ground.

"Theo," Aurienne called.

Theo maneuvered his horse closer to her with expectant eyes. Aurienne spotted the vermin hole as they passed it by. The vision fizzled away, having been avoided. Theo waited for her to speak.

Aurienne took a swig of water from her canteen and offered it to him, thinking of something to say without admitting she saved him from embarrassment. He had his own water, but he accepted hers with a bright smile and took a matching swig before handing it back.

Finally, she said, "Tell me about your farm."

The smile he gave sparked warmth straight into her soul.

MONSTER STORIES
CHAPTER EIGHT

A thousand years ago, a great darkness fell over the land... Five bound the monsters in chains.

— LEGEND OF THE SHADOW WAR AND THE SHADOWS OF HEARTSPRING. CIRCA 11 N.T.C.

1152 N.T.C. The southern road between Avyllon and Wyndsel.

Nine hours in the saddle was a long time when the most that person had spent in the saddle was an hour or two. Theo rubbed his back, rear, and legs. He stretched all manner of ways and promised himself tomorrow he'd spend time walking to avoid this wretched stiffness. His pants and shirt were damp from sweat yet also stiff. This was a different sort of hell than a long day at the smithy. He rubbed down his horse and brushed it, led it to water, and left it in a meadow to graze with the others.

After an exhilarating dunk in the stream that left him shivering, Theo surveyed the caravan. Adonis and Mathis stirred a bubbling concoction in a copper pot. Adonis squinted at a large leather book, at the pot, and then back at the book. Saryll was perched on a log, watching them hawkishly.

"Dreamsmoke can blind and disorient your enemies," Mathis said. "Careful, don't get the vapors in your eyes, or you'll be blind for an hour."

"I know," Adonis retorted.

The sorcerer watched silently. His hair did not take well to travel. It stuck out in all manner of directions, and a twig and a leaf had found their way into the mess. His long gray beard hung down to his waist and clinked with silver orbs as he corrected Adonis' stirring. Mathis glanced toward Theo.

"Adonis will be stirring for some time," Mathis said, eliciting a groan from his apprentice. "Did you have a question?"

Theo kicked the dirt. "What do you know about royal etiquette?"

Mathis smiled. "Let's discuss what to do when you meet the king."

An hour later, with Theo's brain set to burst, he glanced around, but Aurienne was nowhere to be seen. "Have you seen Aurienne?"

"The High Seer is meditating just beyond those trees," Saryll replied, her eyes glued to the bubbling green liquid in the pot, which now emitted small blue sparks and yellow smoke rings.

"You don't want to disturb her when she's meditating. Once as a child, I did that, and she stabbed me," Adonis said with a chuckle before returning to his work.

Theo couldn't tell whether he was kidding. "Thanks."

Theo stepped through the bushes toward the clearing Saryll gestured to. Thorny vines snagged his arms as he pushed through the branches and jumped over a stream. He climbed stones and wove his way through trees until he reached her.

Like a malevolent enchantress, Aurienne kneeled alone in the middle of the woods beside the stream, surrounded by flickering candles arranged in a pentagram in front of a small carved bowl of water. She chanted softly and dipped her fingers into the bowl.

Theo paused in the darkness of a tree, away from the waning moonlight. Starlight softly illuminated the curves of her shoulders, arms, and hips. Beautiful. Brilliant. Determined. Slightly terrifying. He was drawn to her in ways he couldn't explain and didn't understand.

Goddess, she was beautiful and terrifying—and why was it so intriguing?

Without turning, she said, "Hi, Theo."

He froze, not having caused so much as a leaf to rustle. His skin prickled, but he stepped into the meadow. "What are you doing out here alone?"

"Gathering moonwater to cleanse my runes and cards," she said. "Also, praying to the Goddess for visions, as I sense peril at our destination and am trying to See it."

Aurienne splashed water over her runes. She dribbled it onto the back of her cards. Lifting the bowl, she poured the rest over her face. It soaked her skin and neckline, and her gown and tunic clung to her. Wet tresses of hair curled around her face, just like the foretelling— just like in her room.

His heart clenched and his stomach flipped as attraction and apprehension warred beneath his skin. He searched for words. "What's moonwater?"

"Fresh stream water gathered under the moonlight." Her eyes glimmered, and a smile curled her rosy lips.

He took another few steps closer, just outside of her candle circle. "Is it magic?"

Aurienne laughed. Theo's cheeks grew warm, but she explained, "Water purified in the moon possesses special properties if you know how to use it. It can cleanse runes or a divination deck. Bathing in it can dispel bad luck. It can aid healing from infection and work in alchemical reactions. In fact, if I do not bring Mathis back a vial, he will be cross."

She flashed him an amused smile and raised the small glass vial. She tucked it away into the folds of her traveling tunic.

He wondered whether the seer possessed a library in her head for all that she seemed to know. "I had no idea there were so many...types of Seeing."

"There are many ways to use Sight," she said. "My studies at the temple and universities taught the more accepted and reliable ways. Some methods work better for certain questions or certain people. Some people are more gifted in one or another. Certain days give access to stronger Sight: the eclipse foretelling, Lunahain, Hallohaim, or the night of a full moon. These days lower the veil between reality and Sight. Mainly, it is about having the most open mental state. Meditating in the dark or alone, listening to music, or prayer can aid in this. Or, like the foretelling—pain, or near-death experiences. Even sex-fueled readings." She winked.

The blush crept higher into his face and down his neck. He tried to dispel his curiosity about the sex readings before she Saw his thoughts.

"Why do you need the cards if you have visions?" he asked, desperate to change the subject.

"Some visions come unbidden, and you never know what they will show you," she trailed off.

Theo took a few steps closer, his boots crushing the long grass. "What about the cards and runes and blood?"

"The deck answers questions, but you must ask the right ones," she said. "Knowing which questions to ask, how to ask them, and how many cards to draw is an art form all on its own. Bone runes are one of the oldest forms of Seeing using objects but are less precise, which is why many seers no longer use them. The oldest and most archaic is the blood, as I did for you. The Old Ways. There are darker forms too, but they're forbidden."

Theo tripped on a large ivory-colored rock and froze when it rolled over. A human skull.

"What..." he said slowly.

Her gaze swept the clearing. "Ancient battles were fought here in the time of the Shadow Wars. I sense the wandering spirits of the dead, those with unfinished business refusing to cross into the land of death. I fear the Shadow War and our Darkling War are connected, and one day our bones shall litter some unknown grove." She blinked and shook her head. "That's why we go to Wyndsel and Rodarri."

The seer began to clean up her unnerving ritual site, and Theo rushed to help her, gathering about a dozen candles while she carried the bowl and a few other objects. They picked their way back to camp.

"Do you always do what the Fates say?" he asked.

"Yes."

"Do you ever do anything just because you want to?"

Her lips parted as her head tilted. "What do you mean?"

He shrugged. "You want to eat something or kiss someone or go somewhere. Do you only do it if the Fates tell you to?"

Aurienne fell quiet. They wove through the trees in the darkness, finding patches of moonlight to guide their steps. Ahead, the camp-fires crackled and beckoned. Laughing and singing echoed through the trees.

Finally, she said, "I do things without asking the Fates. Mostly small things. I practice my gift often, though. I sometimes even ask what I should have for breakfast."

Theo snorted.

"What?"

He said, "That's... I'm sorry, that's funny. And sad."

Aurienne joined in with a small laugh. "It helps keep my gift sharp."

"I've never met someone with so much freedom and yet so little."

She tilted her head. "What do you mean?"

"You can do whatever you want if you get a good omen," he said. "You Saw you were supposed to come on this trip, so you did. There was no one to tell you that you couldn't. You just came. You can meet kings and emperors, and you travel to other cities. It's freedom I never dreamed of. You might be bound by omens, but there are so many more things you can do than I ever could. Even if you don't know what to have for breakfast."

Aurienne was quiet. She shifted the candles and bowl in her arms and stepped over a small stream.

"You do want things, don't you?" Theo asked with a frown.

"I... sometimes."

"When was the last time you did something just because you felt like it? No visions or readings, no prophecies?"

"I don't remember," she admitted. "I never really want anything. Sometimes, I follow a distraction, but I don't really want... I don't know. I guess no one has asked me that before."

Theo held up a branch for her, and she walked under it.

"Tonight, for instance. You're done meditating in the woods alone like a lunatic," he said and caught sight of her curving grin. "What are you going to do with the rest of the night? If you could do anything tonight just because you wanted to, what would you do?"

Aurienne froze. Theo nearly crashed into her and had to dance around her and a thorny-looking shrub to avoid knocking her down. Aurienne turned and faced him, just inches away. She gazed up into his eyes.

Theo held his breath, aware of her proximity and consumed by her unearthly eyes and full lips. His eyes traced the curve of her shoulder and clavicle. Heat radiated off her body—which he felt through his linen shirt. He glanced into her hazy eyes, and she studied him.

She bit her lip, and he nearly leaned forward to kiss her but refrained. His heart hammered. What was wrong with him? He swallowed.

"I want to sit in front of the fire telling stories," she said. "I want to hear fairytales and monster myths, drink wine until I can't see straight, and sing filthy campfire songs. I want to forget about tomorrow for just one night."

Theo's heart melted as a firestorm of empathy rose in his chest. He took those moments for granted. Countless nights he had watched livestock before a fire and shared stories and songs with the other villagers. Recalling those nights, they were some of his favorite memories, and he had a sneaking suspicion that Aurienne had never had the pleasure.

"I can make that happen," Theo said.

Theo stepped past her and hooked his arm about her shoulder. A part of him screamed that it was improper, that she was the High Seer, the regent and ruler of Avyllon, and not to forget his place. But in that moment, he was just taking his friend to the fire to share stories, to drink and sing.

They returned to camp and took their places before the fire. Theo motioned for a wineskin, and a sentinel passed it. He took a long swig of the wine-filled canteen and passed it to Aurienne. She hesitated before taking a matching draught and passing it on.

"Who wants to hear a monster story?" Theo asked.

Laughs and encouraging calls rose from the lounging sentinels. Even the sentinels on watch lifted their spears in cheer.

Theo cleared his throat and began the story. "This is the tale of the 'Shadow of Heartspring.'"

Words held power, and if told right, stories swept the listeners away.

"A thousand years ago, a great darkness fell over the land," he said. "Ten thousand villages banded together to form an army, but they were losing. Villages and farms burned. The darkness spread across the land, consuming all in its path and leaving only destruction behind. One man saw the shadow fall over his family home with his wife and children within. He carved a heart necklace from heartwood and left it with his wife, with a promise to save them."

Theo scanned each face, pausing for emphasis. Aurienne wrapped a blanket around her shoulders and watched with a wide, enraptured expression. Her lips parted, and Theo had to look away or risk being distracted.

"He went into the forest to implore the spirits there. A devilish phantom answered, promising to help. The devil asked what he was willing to give for such a boon. The man answered, 'Anything.' The devil smiled, granted his wish, and was gone. The man and his warriors didn't realize what they asked for. They pushed back the darkness and saved their families as promised."

The canteen circled back to Theo. He took another draught, leaned toward the group, and continued the tale just as his parents recited it to him. A pang of homesickness washed over him, unaware of how much he missed them until he heard their voices in his mind as he told the story he had heard a hundred times.

"Five bound the darkness in chains," he said. "Once they returned, they learned the cost of their actions. Bloodlust consumed them, and the more blood they drank, the more powerful they became. Their fangs grew until they no longer fit in their mouths. Their hands turned into claws as long as a grown man's arm. Bat wings sprouted out of their backs. Their eyes glowed scarlet."

Theo paused for effect and swept his gaze across the group. Aurienne pulled the blanket over her head with her little fox friend curled up in the shadows beside her. Saryll covered her face in her hands and peeked out from between her fingers. Adonis was wide-eyed and hanging on every word. Even Mathis listened with interest. Good—they hadn't heard the tale.

Captain Laurier and Sentinel Kolten exchanged knowing grins with Theo, and the two crept away into the darkness in opposite directions.

"At nightfall, they tore apart the very families they swore to protect," Theo said. "In the morning, heartbroken, furious, and possessed, they shed their mortal forms and fully became monsters. They ravaged the countryside for centuries, devouring and destroying all in their paths. No one knows how, but rumor says they were imprisoned in the heart of a mountain outside of a heartspring. They have remained there for almost a thousand years, waiting for their release, waiting to inflict their hunger upon the world again."

Right on cue, a branch snapped. Aurienne, Adonis, Saryll, and Mathis jumped and stared at the forest. Leaves rustled from the other direction, and a metallic dragging echoed in the trees, causing their heads to whip that way. All was silent except the wind.

Behind them, Captain Laurier burst out and roared. Sentinel Kolten jumped out of the trees on the other side, growling.

Saryll screamed. Adonis fell off the log backward into the undergrowth. Mathis started with a squeal. Even Aurienne even stood straight up with a yelp. Several sentinels yelled in alarm as well.

Laurier and Kolten burst out laughing, and Theo joined them. This was a common prank pulled on first-time listeners.

Aurienne whirled on Theo. "That was not funny!"

Theo tried to respond but was laughing too hard to defend himself properly. "I-I'm...sorry," he said between laughs. His ribs ached.

"How did I not See your prank?" she demanded, stifling a laugh. "What trickery was this?"

Theo wiped tears of mirth away, "I'm sorry. It's a thing we do in the villages to children who've never heard the story before."

Surprise overtook anger in her tone. Theo wondered whether she'd ever been surprised like that.

"You all knew about this!" Aurienne exclaimed.

"I was hoping someone here knew to scare you," Theo said.

Across lonely mountains, a wolf howl cut the night, long and low and far too loud for the distance it echoed across. Clouds swirled before the moon, darkening the campsite. The caravan stilled, listening to the melancholy sound of a predator—a warning. No one spoke until the howls faded into the night.

Adonis righted himself, regained his seat on the log, and brushed himself off. "Well, you right did that, and that wolf conspired with you. Scared me half to death. I nearly soiled myself. Touch and go there for a moment."

Everyone slowly turned to stare at him. The sentinels' eyes bulged, trying desperately not to laugh at their charge, but Aurienne's crystal-sharp laugh pierced the night sky. Her laugh broke the dam of self-control, and immediately everyone began hollering and laughing.

"If a Shadow monster came out of those trees," Saryll said between breathless giggles, "I was going to leave all of you here and run."

The admission received roaring cheers and laughs from the sentinels and attendants.

"I've never been so afraid in my life," Adonis said.

"Good show," Mathis called out merrily.

"Just wait 'til you hear the story about the sunlight hunter that hunts the shadows," Theo chuckled.

It took several minutes for the laughing to die down, for the people to resettle into their bedrolls, and for the canteen to continue around the fire.

"You're full of surprises," Aurienne said to Theo.

He winked and said, "You have no idea."

I hope I get to show you.

Then he proceeded to sing the dirtiest ditty he knew. As the night stretched on, Theo sang every single working song he knew and loudly sang the dirtiest ones in exchange for Aurienne attempting to embarrass him earlier with talk of sex rituals. At first, she blushed, and then she joined in. By the end of the night, Aurienne led the chorus, much to the delight of many.

Apparently, years of reading rhyming prophecies had given her quite the gift of lyric, and her imagination was obscene. Most importantly to Theo, not once did Aurienne stare off into the nothingness with clouded eyes and an empty expression. Her eyes were sharp, and in the campfire's glow, Theo thought for just a second that they saturated into a sparkling blue. Sleep came eventually under glimmering stars and a waning, expectant moon—while Fate made other plans.

Witches and Wild Magic

Chapter Nine

She tasted like moonlight, magic, and delicious heartbreak he would forever crave.

— *Curse of heartbreak.*

1152 N.T.C. The southern road between Avyllon and Wyndsel.

The path forked, and before Aurienne drew her cards, the one to the right drew her attention. She sensed the same crackling cabin hearths, warm tea, homey thick blankets, purring cats, and soft music.

"We go that way," Aurienne pointed.

"That way is the village of Wildegrove," Captain Laurier said with a look of puzzlement. "There are stories—of the witches..."

"We go to Wildegrove."

Arriving at sunset, Aurienne led them to a small cottage on the outskirts of town. The feeling of warmth pooled around this haven. Aurienne dismounted and approached.

The cottage was made of ancient, stacked stones and covered in leafy vines. Cobblestones forged paths between wildflower clusters to raised gardens. The shutters and door were painted with bright floral designs. Several black cats meandered around the low stone wall encircling the home.

A woman, nearly sixty, emerged. Her skin was a beautifully dark onyx, with curly hair twisting down her back with flowers woven through. She wore a green dress and a green apron with pockets full of plant stems. As Aurienne approached, the women flashed a welcoming smile.

"It is good to meet you, High Seer. I am glad you came," the woman said. "The forest whispered you might choose this path, and I hoped you would. Please have your companions make camp in that meadow and come in."

Aurienne relaxed. She'd chosen right, and her cards led her to this wise witch who could help them on their journey. She followed the woman into the cabin. Saryll, Theo, Adonis, and Mathis trailed close behind.

Aurienne perched on a wooden chair and surveyed the cabin. Homey did not adequately describe the atmosphere. Bookcases and shelves were packed with labeled apothecary bottles, vials, potions, and candles. Knives, paper, and all manner of witchy things were tucked between bottles and books. Drying herbs and plants hung in bunches from the ceiling. The windows were open, and the smell of the lush wildflowers wafted in.

Everything was lived in, well cared for, and well-loved. Aurienne's heart, for the first time that she could remember, was at peace. If Aurienne was not bound up in prophecy and destiny, she'd have wanted to live in a place exactly like this one.

The witch smiled softly, as if reading her mind. "You would have had a home like this, wouldn't you, High Seer? Had your gift not called you to a different duty."

Aurienne met her gaze. "Please, call me Aurienne."

"Aurienne Azarrah, High Seer of Avyllon," the older woman said, "it is good to meet you. Stories of your power have made their way here over the years. When I turned a card with the Goddess on it, I had a feeling that you might be coming here. I'm Lorayne Guara. This is my granddaughter Kassia Guara. We are the witches of Wildegrove."

She gestured to a younger woman in her early twenties with skin equally dark and smooth. Her black hair was wavy and bound in a long braid that hung to her hips. It, too, was braided with flowers. The warmth, welcome, and general peaceful feeling of this place were contagious.

"I felt you all the way back at the city gates to Avyllon," Aurienne said. "I knew we were meant to come here."

Lorayne's smile never seemed to fade. "We are glad you arrived safely. The roads are dangerous."

Aurienne placed her hand on Theo's shoulder, causing him to shift on his chair. "This is my traveling companion, Theo Thatcher. The Goddess showed me he is destined to bring together the five leaders of Teridar for a summit."

"A heavy fate," Lorayne said.

The tension fell from Theo's shoulders. The welcome of this magical cottage reached him as well.

His eyes glistened. "I'll try to live up to it."

"This is Saryll, another seer, my blood brother Adonis, and his sorcerer mentor, Mathis," Aurienne said.

"Welcome to all," Lorayne said. "Please stay with us tonight. There is a wildecraft festival. It is a bit early, seeing as how Hallohaim is in a few weeks, but I had a feeling we would have visitors."

Aurienne inclined her head, already feeling more comfortable than she had in months—years. "We would be honored, thank you."

"Please sit. We have tea ready," Kassia said.

The party sat on the collection of mismatched chairs and accepted the steaming clay mugs. They sipped the piping tea, and the wearies of travel fell away.

"I have heard stories of your gift. May I see your cards?" Lorayne asked.

Aurienne produced the deck from the spelled box in her pack and reached across Theo to hand them to the older witch.

"That box is one of mine," Lorayne said.

The Goddess worked in powerful ways.

"I did not know," Aurienne said. "Thank you. I came across it in the market as a child and felt it was the right one to protect my deck from ill omens."

"I felt a special call to carve that box. I'm glad it ended up with you." Lorayne flipped through the deck, examining the cards. With a frown, she said, "I have not seen some of these cards before."

"Me either. I have three suits. Arcane represents people. Lore represents the land. Virtue represents emotions, principals. There are twenty-one cards in each suit. Overnight, all but Life, Death, and The Traveler in the arcane suit changed," Aurienne said.

Lorayne handed the deck back to Aurienne, and she returned them to the spelled box.

"Your deck is impressive. I have not seen many who carry more than one suit, much less three. My own deck only has lore and virtue, with thirteen cards in each," Lorayne said.

Saryll piped up, "Most temple seers have only two decks with approximately thirteen to seventeen cards in each, as well. My own deck only has fourteen cards in each."

"We have no need for an arcane suit," Lorayne said. "We only want to help the people here. We have no need of kings, champions, and monsters. The cards in the arcane deck have the influence to change the world. We don't need that."

"May I see your cards?" Aurienne asked and then turned to Kassia. "And yours?"

Both women handed Aurienne their decks one by one. Aurienne carefully flipped through each.

"I have worked up to fifteen cards in one suit. Soon I hope to add a second. Though the cards are not my specialty, not like wildecraft," Kassia said.

Aurienne fingered the thick paper. They were covered in flower drawings around the borders and stained with flower petals and berry juices. Aurienne lifted the cards and could smell the distinct aroma of wild roses. Power dwelled in them.

"They're beautiful," Aurienne said.

"We have pressed certain plants into the face of each to draw certain meanings," Kassia explained.

"That's different from our method. Could you teach me?" Aurienne asked.

"Of course," Lorayne said.

Over tea, Lorayne explained the properties of certain plants and how they imbued the cards. Aurienne took meticulous notes, and she noticed that Saryll, Mathis, and Adonis were doing the same.

"May I ask how your cards were made?" Lorayne asked.

"I made every part of them," Aurienne said. "It was imperative that they be imbued with as much of my essence as possible to be fully tied to me. I went into the forest and cut down the tree with an axe in my own hand. I boiled the bark, crushed it, and flattened it. I cut the paper with silver scissors then gathered the nightrose myself and mixed it with moonwater to make the ink. I stained the cards with the ink so they would be dark as the night sky they were stained under. I shaved gold from a coin earned by the sweat of my brow to make the paint and drew the designs."

"They're tied to your essence?" Kassia asked.

Lorayne answered, "Our gift is not the same as hers. The seers are gifted Sight from the Triple Goddess, Aurienne most of all. *Our* gifts are rooted in nature."

Aurienne exhaled. It was such a relief to be around someone with such wisdom. For just a moment, she released the burdens of responsibility and always being the one to have the answer. It slipped away, and she relaxed.

"I imbue my deck with my sweat and blood," Aurienne said. "I cleanse it with white smoke and moonwater from time to time, but it has been taking my blood and breath since I was a child."

"That is quite dangerous," Lorayne said.

"I know," Aurienne replied gravely.

With a wide smile, Lorayne said to Kassia, "That deck is one of the most powerful objects in existence as long as Aurienne lives." Lorayne winked at Aurienne. "I would imagine it has a will of its own."

Goddess—that was true.

"What do you mean?" Kassia asked.

"My deck does not stay the same. Sometimes cards appear. Sometimes cards disappear. Sometimes I'm inspired to make a new one. Sometimes they change on their own," Aurienne explained.

"They just change?" Kassia asked.

"The ink shifts, and a new design will emerge. Sometimes the designs are minor, but the card name remains the same. Other times the entire card changes, or a new card appears out of nowhere."

Theo looked up from the plates of food on the worn, round table. "I saw one of the figures turn and look at me once."

"Really?" Kassia asked.

Theo nodded solemnly.

"Does your deck do that?" Kassia asked Saryll.

"No," Saryll said. "None of ours do. Aurienne's deck is the largest of any in history and has a mind of its own. She has never been wrong when she's read a Fate." She looked to Theo. "What she read for you was a Fate."

Lorayne glanced at Aurienne. "You've been reading many fates? Your visions are frequent then, even unassisted by cards and ceremonies?"

Aurienne shifted in her chair.

"Ah. Have the headaches started then?" Lorayne asked.

Aurienne studied the floor and nodded. "The long travel and frequent readings have been difficult."

Theo's and Saryll's eyes snapped to her.

"I see," Lorayne said, and Aurienne thought she could see through the lies.

"The tea will help. I'll send more with you tomorrow. Until then, enjoy yourselves and rest. The festival will begin at nightfall." Lorayne studied Aurienne carefully.

"Thank you," Aurienne said.

Adonis and Mathis eventually left the cottage and returned to where Captain Laurier and the others were setting up camp.

Theo nudged Aurienne's arm. "You didn't tell me that you were having headaches," he said.

"It's nothing a good tea can't fix," Aurienne lied.

Theo's brows tugged together. "I'll help rub down our mounts."

Aurienne and Saryll remained in the cabin with the witches. Kassia spread out a collection of herbs to prepare for the new deck cards and healing salves. Aurienne started peeling a bulb of vetiver root.

Out the window, Theo walked toward the camp, lifted a saddle from one of the horses, and set it carefully on the ground. Leaning in close, he whispered something to the stalwart mount and patted its salty side, then scratched it behind the ears and rubbed its nose before slipping it an apple bite.

"Would you take some well-intentioned advice from an old woman?" Lorayne asked Aurienne.

"Of course," Aurienne said, dragging her attention away from Theo.

"I don't have your gift. I'm not sure anyone living or dead has had your gift. I don't have your training, but I've lived a rather long life."

Aurienne smiled. "I don't doubt it."

"You're used to telling the Fates what you want, not the other way around," she said.

Aurienne remembered herself slicing her arm for thick heart's blood to feed the deck, drawing the Sight into herself and consuming the life force of lingering spirits to force Fate into giving her answers. Drinking Theo's blood from his palm, taking more from him than he knew. She watched herself drown under an eclipse.

"Yes," was all she said.

"From time to time, you may try being open to the messages Fate wants to send you," Lorayne said gently. "Sometimes, it will tell you the things you need to know instead of the things you want to know."

"I'll try," Aurienne promised.

"I see what you've done and what it cost you. You've got a strong heart. Don't forget that."

Aurienne forced the tears away. She didn't cry when she was a child receiving her readings. She didn't cry when her parents left her at the temple and never returned. She didn't cry at the Rites when she was burned, drowned, and buried alive. She wouldn't cry now.

"It was just the once, and it gave me what I needed." Aurienne shuddered, remembering the slick oily feel of those spirits against her aura and the ashy mark they left behind.

Lorayne squeezed her hand. "There's still a cost, and once that path is started it is terribly difficult to leave."

They worked in comfortable silence. Kassia stained her new cards while Saryll painstakingly wrote notes about wildecraft. Lorayne prepared medicinal poultices, and Aurienne considered the witch's words, wondering where this path she'd chosen would lead.

Witches' magic hung heavy in the night air, glimmering with possibility. As nightfall darkened, crowds arrived in a nearby sprawling meadow of wildflowers and lit bonfires in stone wells. Theo felt incredibly underdressed in his traveling clothes compared to the others. Or in some cases, he was overdressed compared to the sheer garb woven from grass and leaves. This wildecraft festival was nothing like the harvest festivals back home.

Lorayne and Kassia emerged in thigh-length dresses woven of freshly picked flowers and vines, while Aurienne and Saryll donned lightweight sheer ceremonial gowns that showed every curve and pooled in the wildflowers at their feet. The seers and witches conversed as Adonis seamlessly inserted himself into another group sharing wineskins. Theo hesitated before joining Aurienne and Saryll, unlacing his shirt and rolling up his sleeves.

"Theo, dear," Lorayne said in a grandmotherly way, "Aurienne tells me that your Ma enjoys wildflowers and herbs. I have put together a pack of seeds for her."

Theo clutched the small leather bag carefully. "Thank you, she will love these."

He beamed at Aurienne, mouthing his thanks for her thinking of him. The cloud in Aurienne's eyes made her expressions difficult to read.

"Aurienne, would you like to come gathering with us early tomorrow?" Kassia asked.

"Of course," Aurienne said. "I'd love to see what naturally grows in Wildegrove."

A grin warmed Theo's face watching Aurienne offer to help the others so freely. She ought to be bitter and cold with what she'd endured, but underneath the stoic exterior—she was kind and caring. Even if she pretended not to be.

Aurienne waved to the other women and took Theo's offered arm. They strolled toward the bonfires with Saryll and the witches following a little way back, chatting about teas and runes.

"Do you get visions often?" he asked, wanting to keep her talking.

"A dozen per day, mostly fleeting. More since the Rite, and it's taxing." She stared off at the trail once more, a far-off look in her eye.

Over the past few days, Theo had seen that look more often than not. She was lost to her visions as if her mind, even her soul, seemed faraway. Theo wondered when she'd forgotten to be a person. How young must she have been, burdened with so much that she no longer saw the need to interact? She hardly lived in their world anymore.

He caught her attention, determined to drag her back. "You read everyone else's fate, Avyllon's fate. What questions have you asked about your own future?"

She chuckled quietly. "More than I can count."

"Like what?"

"Everything. If there's a question, I've asked it."

"Did you ask the same questions you answered for me?"

Aurienne tilted her head, finally nodded, and said, "Some."

"You Saw that I lived a long life, or at least there were many futures where I did. Do you know when you die?"

The grass and wildflowers flattened under their feet in explosions of petals. The chill of the wind brushed against Theo's skin, mixed with heat from the fires. Aurienne shivered and drifted closer to him.

"There are too many potential futures. There is a darkness in my Sight after the Darkling War. Too much is at stake. Too much can go wrong. I do not see my future beyond that yet."

"Do you know if you will find love?"

Blushing again, Theo immediately avoided her gaze. Embarrassment flooded him as soon as the words left his lips. He knew he shouldn't ask, but poor sense compelled him.

"When reading true love, I select three cards. I drew the Eye for the past, Death for the present, and the Lovers for the future. How can death precede love? Either I'll die before I find true love, or my loving someone is a death sentence. I don't know. I know I am not fated to fall in love." Her tone remained constant, and her face stone —as if it no longer bothered her.

Her words bruised Theo's heart, and worse than her fate was her acceptance. His face and heart were weighed with empathy for her. This explained so much.

She glanced at him and grinned. "It does not keep me from seeking passionate moments. The feeling might not last, the love might not be meant to be, but I won't live a dull life just because I don't get to keep my love."

"I'm sorry," he said.

"I've learned that there are some questions that should not be asked. It can be a curse to know your fate." Her lips pressed together.

"You told me about my fate for love."

"I did not ask it. I asked to see your life, and that is one answer I received. Once received, I share the truth. It is not mine to hide. But I avoid asking, if I can."

Theo nodded, unsure of what to say.

Aurienne nudged his arm. "I'm curious to see how you have three true loves. People are lucky to have one. You'll have thrice that."

He tried to smile, but it died on his lips.

"Are you alright?" Aurienne asked.

"I'm not sure," he admitted. "Everything is moving and changing so quickly. I haven't had a chance to catch my breath."

"I wish everything didn't have to change for you," she said. "I Saw the life you would have had, and it was a good life. If it helps, the new future could be better."

"If the summit goes to plan?"

"Yes."

Theo nodded. Everything rode on the summit, and they were only a few days away from the city of Wynds. Soon they would pass the border of Avyllon and ride for the city, which he tried to push from his mind.

He glanced at her. "Do you remember when I asked you what you wanted to do the other night if you could do anything?"

"Yes."

"Tonight, I want to forget about prophecies and fates."

Aurienne smiled. "I can do that."

They stopped near a flickering bonfire, their arms touching. Theo's skin prickled at her touch, causing his neck and chest to grow warm.

The crowd grew as the moon rose and the sky deepened. The large meadow filled with bonfire after bonfire until they numbered in the dozens. Jars of honey mead, golden beer, and spiced cider passed from hand to hand. Laughter, shared food, and drink increased until the crowd numbered in the hundreds. Candles covered tree stumps until their light rivaled the stars.

Musicians found a shared rhythm between the fires, and their instruments called to one another from across the field. Drums, strings, and flutes filled the skies with energy. Theo couldn't help but sway with the beat as he swallowed cup after cup of the sweetened drink. Pairs turned into groups, which turned into throngs dancing in wide circles around the fires.

"Join us," dancers called.

Theo and Aurienne were drawn into the groups and separated, swirling and twirling with nameless strangers. From time to time, Theo glimpsed Aurienne moving from partner to partner, from fire to fire, drink to drink. Finally, Theo spun in front of her and took her partner's place. They caught hands and weaved around the fire. Her fingers grazed his arms and chest, and fireworks erupted at her touch.

A soft smile settled upon her mouth, and lyrical laughter poured from her wine-stained lips. Theo twirled her, and her translucent skirts spun outward like moonlight. She spun off to the next partner and returned once more before she was off again.

Kassia and Saryll, along with Adonis and their armed escort, joined in. They changed partners, spinning between campfires, laughing, joking, and sharing the drink. Theo found himself doing a turn with Captain Laurier, old resentments buried.

"I'll forge you the strongest, grandest sword that you've ever seen!" Theo promised heartily.

"You owe me one!" the captain called with a chuckle.

Saryll and Adonis linked arms and were spinning and spinning and spinning until they both fell into the grass, giggling. Saryll's bronzed brown skin reflected the firelight. Even Lorayne and Mathis lounged together on a stump, calling out encouragement to the youths, laughing loudly and throwing back drinks. Kassia danced and sprinkled flower petals on Adonis and Saryll, giggling luminously.

Kassia took Theo's arm and whirled around. Her green eyes

seemed to nearly glow from the rising magic. A crown of flowers and ribbons was braided into her midnight hair. She disappeared into the tall grass with another beautiful young witch garbed in only flower petals, and Aurienne was back in Theo's arms.

The festivity lasted long into the night. Midnight passed, and people discarded layers of clothing until little remained. Clothing and wine lay in piles atop blankets around the fires. Theo's eyes were lidded from drink and revelry, and he peeled off his shirt, boots, and socks. The drink, music, and undeniable power strumming the air chased away his hesitance.

The music slowed, taking on a darker, deeper tone. Theo's heartbeats matched the beat of the music, and it made a home in his soul. Magic drifted about like glittering, sparkling dots of light.

The music darkened as the witching hour neared. Drumbeats grew louder but slower—sensual and dark. Then it arrived. All at once, couples paired up to share moonlit kisses. Mathis and Lorayne shared a quick and friendly kiss. Adonis kissed a young witch garbed only in vines underneath the boughs of a tree. Kassia pressed her lips to Saryll's and wrapped her fingers in her hair.

Theo hardly realized everyone else had paired up until Aurienne twirled toward him.

Their lips crashed into one another under the cool air, the glimmering stars, and the warmth of the fire. The sounds of music and people dancing and breathing and laughing and living. She tasted like moonlight, magic, and delicious heartbreak that he would forever crave.

Her fingers wound into his hair, and his hands found her waist. He tugged her against his bare chest. She smelled of vanilla and dark night skies, and he breathed her in like she was glorious air and he was suffocating. The kiss deepened, and he devoured her. She kissed him back with abandon, wild and dangerous. Her teeth grazed his lip, sharp and wolfish. He could kiss her forever, and it wouldn't be enough. The kiss lasted a single minute under moonlit skies and forest trees at the witching hour. A minute that could have been a lifetime.

The music picked up, the minute over, and she spun away from him dreamily, dancing in wide circles, hands lifted, worshiping the stars. Time all but stopped. Her jewelry clinked between the nearly frozen music notes. She had stolen his soul, and he didn't want it back. His heart thundered in his chest harder than a blacksmith's hammer, each beat so patiently taking its time that in between he wondered if it would ever start again.

Aurienne was in slow motion, spinning in the firelight and wildflowers. Her sure-footed steps moved in time with the impossibly slow music. Her bare feet slid through the leafy mist, her skin reflecting the stars. The swaying of her hips hypnotized him. Theo could taste her on his lips, which painfully suffered her absence. He caught her gaze for half a second, her eyes brilliantly blue, the seer's cloud almost gone. Her gaze, full of shared secrets and forgotten memories, laid bare his soul.

Theo knew the exact moment he fell in love with Aurienne. He should have been terrified, but all he could see was *her*. Time sped up. Theo found himself taking a turn around the bonfire with another nameless partner, his mind catching up to reality.

The memory of Aurienne's voice echoed in Theo's mind. *"How can death precede love? Either I'll die before I find true love, or my loving someone is a death sentence. I don't know. I know I am not fated to fall in love."*

Theo's heart exploded in pain. She would never love him back. His senses were taken by love and drink and magic. He closed his eyes and took another turn, losing himself to the night.

Betrayal
Chapter Ten

1152 N.T.C. The southern road between Avyllon and Wyndsel.

Early the next morning, drunk on heartbreak, Theo stirred to the sounds of waking revelers departing the meadow. Blanketed rolls littered the grass around the still-crackling bonfires. Theo propped himself up in a blue and gray woven wool blanket, searching for Aurienne and finding her, to his surprise, just within arm's reach.

She stirred and slowly sat, wrapping her blanket around her bare shoulders. The golds, purples, and blues of the blanket blurred into the celestial tattoos on her bare skin. She rubbed her face, and he studied the dreams slipping from her eyes. What he would give to watch one of those dreams. Could she share her visions? She caught him watching her and smiled. A blush climbed up his neck and settled on his cheeks.

He pulled on his boots and went to find breakfast. He gathered two bowls and brought Aurienne one.

He leaned down and mischievously said, "While we're forgetting about fate, you don't have to do a reading this morning to know what breakfast would be."

Aurienne's dazzling smile caught Theo off-guard and quickened his pulse. His heart ached, but he smiled back, feeling anything but happy. Adonis, Mathis, and Saryll joined them, as did Captain Laurier. They discussed the upcoming travel plans between bites of egg and bread.

"We might reach Wynds in two days if we hurry," the captain said. "We've been making good time, even with the longer route."

Theo stared off into the distant sky with Aurienne's reading of his fate playing in his mind. He would find love three times. There was no promise it would be requited. Now he was sure Aurienne was the first. She was destined never to return it, and the thought made him sick.

Lorayne and Kassia strolled up, Kassia's arm looped into her grandmother's to keep her steady. Kassia's eyes were bright green and sharp, and she still wore a crown of ribbons and flowers.

"Good morning," Lorayne said.

Kassia helped Lorayne sit on an overturned log. Kassia then handed Theo and Aurienne a cup.

"Drink it. It will clear your heads," Kassia encouraged.

Aurienne took a long sip, face expressionless. She passed it along. Theo sniffed it and found it pleasantly aromatic. It was a nice surprise seeing as how most hangover cures tasted like raw egg, sawdust, and spoiled vegetables. To be fair, those were the likely ingredients at home. He emptied the cup.

"Would you still like to join us gathering supplies?" Kassia asked Aurienne.

"That'd be lovely," Aurienne said.

"Me as well," Saryll said.

Aurienne looped her arm through Lorayne's. The witches and seers entered the woods with baskets.

Adonis nudged Theo after the women had left. "You too, eh?"

Theo blinked. "What?"

"You fell in love with my sister?"

Hellsdamn it, was it already so obvious?

Theo said nothing.

"It's alright," Adonis clapped him on the back. "They all do. I should warn you, though. She never loves them back."

Theo stared into his bowl. "I know."

An hour later, Aurienne heard the caravan packing up outside. She could stay in this cottage, braiding flowers and picking the leaves from gathered plants, knitting, and petting the stray cats and dogs forever, but it was not the life she was called to lead.

"It is time I go," Aurienne said.

Lorayne and Kassia walked Aurienne and Saryll to the horses. Theo had already saddled and packed her horse for her. She noticed his eyes lit up when he saw her, and she could not help but return a bright smile even if she knew better.

"Thank you, Theo," Aurienne said.

"It's no problem," he said, flushing.

Images of their kiss filled her mind. What could she say to him? She'd told him the fate she'd been given. Loving her was a death sentence, one she couldn't risk on someone so good. She'd never minded the reading before; it made some things easier. But now...

"Aurienne." Kassia ripped her attention from Theo.

Aurienne noticed that Kassia had brought a large bag with her. She looked at the two witches questioningly.

Kassia said, "I've been meaning to refill my herbs and plants stash for some time. I've wanted to travel, expand my practice, and learn. What better way than with an armed escort?"

"You are welcome to travel with us," Aurienne said. "We're heading to Wynds and then to Rodarr, the capital of Rodarri. We won't be coming back this way, though. Are you sure you can find your way home?"

"I know I'm meant to come with you. My cards told me." Kassia shrugged.

Lorayne simply nodded.

"We have an extra horse," Aurienne said. "I had a feeling we might need one."

"I'll be back soon." Kassia hugged her grandmother.

Lorayne pushed a tendril of hair from her face. "Follow your heart."

Lorayne turned to Aurienne and gave her a tight hug as well. "And you do the same."

"Be safe," Aurienne bid Lorayne farewell.

The caravan left the cottage behind, and more than one of them gave it long, last look. It was peace, tranquility, and safety wrapped in happiness, family, and love—all things that the journey ahead lacked. After another day of travel, the road meandered out of the forest.

They traveled for another day, avoiding sinkholes and downed bridges. Altogether, around one hundred and sixty people traveled the roads—causing a constant rhythm of hooves pounding the dirt and stones. Saryll and Kassia took turns predicting the delays and dangers with their new cards, which was a welcome break for Aurienne. Her head throbbed, and her ribs still ached from Theo saving her life.

The road meandered out of the forest. Gnarled trees strangled by dark vines opened to rolling golden wheat-filled knolls. In the distance, jagged snow-capped mountains reached for the sky and colossal aqueducts brought water down from the mountains to the city behind them. Aurienne inhaled deeply and savored the scents of farming. Soon, the road brought them back to the forest, spearing deep into the dark foliage. They left behind the open skies for moss-covered ruins and foreboding trees.

The caravan crossed over the border into Wyndsel. They'd just returned to the road from midday meal when Aurienne sensed a trace of danger. Beside her, Saryll and Kassia looked around anxiously. The horses shifted as they walked. The forest quieted.

"Something is wrong," Aurienne said.

Stabbing pain slammed into Aurienne's stomach nearly hard enough to make her retch. She doubled over and heard someone cry out, probably herself. Her vision blurred and her head swam. Disoriented, she felt herself slipping from horseback. She heard distant and distorted shouts of alarm, but strong arms caught her before she plummeted to the packed dirt.

"Aurienne?" Theo was saying from miles away.

Visions slipped over her unbidden.

> *A winding forest road with their traveling party.*
> *Titan ore armor of soldiers clinking together and boots*
>   *marching.*
> *Wolves howling under a daylight moon, prowling*
>   *amongst the trees.*
> *Screams. Blood. Shattered skulls.*
> *Bone dust so thick she choked.*

The visions released her. Her eyes were damp, and when she reached up, her fingertips were smeared in tears of blood. She felt pale, bloodless, and sick. Theo's expression twisted—she must have looked nightmarish. Visions did not often come to her so forcefully and immediately. It was a warning from the Goddess herself.

"Something is coming." Aurienne wheezed. "We need to hide. Now."

"We're on the road. There is nowhere to hide," Captain Laurier said.

Theo pointed. "That should be a thicket. We should be able to get the wagons through there."

Theo dismounted and guided his horse behind the brush and into the clearing. He returned and said, "There's space, hurry."

"Everyone in. Something is coming," Captain Laurier said loudly.

Captain Laurier directed and helped everyone into the thicket and far off the path. They pulled branches across the thicket's opening, hiding them. Theo gathered the horses.

Aurienne's legs were woozy, and Adonis wrapped her arm around his neck to help hold her up. His face was etched with concern.

"Are you okay?" Adonis asked, though Aurienne's head was spinning.

"Just an intense vision, no need to worry." Aurienne patted his arm.

"Your nose is bleeding," he said.

Aurienne quickly wiped the blood away onto her dark tunic.

Hellsdamn it.

"I'm fine. The Fates have been sending me more visions than usual. I'll be fine with a little rest," Aurienne said and tried to crack a smile.

Adonis grimaced.

Abruptly, Saryll was running so quickly she was tripping over her own feet back toward the road. "We need to hide our tracks! Hurry, help."

Saryll dragged fallen branches across the evidence of the wagon wheels and hoofprints. Kassia scrambled to grab her own fallen branch and disturb the dirt down the path and where they exited into the thicket. The pair tossed their branches into the brush and ran back to the caravan.

"Hide the wagons." Captain Laurier tossed branches and shrubs over the wagons.

"Dig a circle around the caravan," Kassia murmured.

Kassia bent down and started digging a shallow groove in the dirt with her hands. Saryll knelt beside her and scooped dirt out frantically. Theo dropped down and threw dirt like a hunting dog on the trail of a varmint. The sentinels, chefs, and other travelers raced to help. Even Mathis hunched over to complete the circle. Kassia sprinkled crushed vetiver root, red salt, and white dust into the channel. She struck a match, and the whole circle lit. Within seconds it burned out.

"Pray to every god and goddess you know," Kassia whispered.

Kassia knelt in front of the ashes and pressed her fingers into the ash. She chanted softly and rocked back and forth. Saryll knelt next to her and closed her eyes.

The air around them popped like a glass canning jar sealing fruit preserve, hiding their scent and sound. A thick haze clouded up from the circle, obscuring them from view. Kassia prayed.

The rest of the caravan crouched in the dirt, silent. Theo kneeled next to several of the horses and whispered to them while patting their necks. The horses tossed their heads.

Aurienne was still woozy and feeling like she'd been run over by one of the wagons. Sweat poured off her brow, and time drew to a standstill. Peering out from the witchshield through the thicket, she waited.

"They're here," Aurienne whispered.

The caravan froze.

Men in dark armor on all-black horses rode past. More than fifty of them in precise, straight lines with sharp eyes scanning the road and the trees—looking for something, and she knew exactly what. Fifty more stalked through the undergrowth, pausing to pick at the ground or sniff the air—like dogs. Some were hunched, others with too-large limbs. They moved more like beasts than men. Their eyes were gold like the Demorran soldiers they'd met. The horses' eyes were gold as well, and they stamped metal hooves against the road. They, too, moved unnaturally. They were more lithe, more aware, more erratic.

Aurienne studied the men through the haze. She leaned forward, trying to get a better look. One of their horses whinnied. Aurienne froze.

A helmed face appeared at the thicket's entrance, and Aurienne clapped her hand to her mouth to keep from screaming. Her shoulders and hands shook, and icy rivulets of terror slipped down her spine. He lifted his face and sniffed, inches from her, just on the other side of the witchshield. A low growl escaped his jaw.

She glanced at Theo, who stood stiffly, wearing a tight, anxious expression. He took a step forward, boot snapping a twig, and she held up her hand to stop him. He froze, and she swallowed. She slowly turned back to the soldier. The soldier's amber eyes, too large to be fully human, scanned the thicket. He leaned closer to the shield, and Aurienne's heart hammered so loudly she wondered if he could hear it.

In a blur, he was gone, and she exhaled. The soldiers passed by and marched down the dusty road. In silence, the caravan waited for over an hour after the Demorrans passed, peering every few minutes down the road.

Finally, Kassia broke the circle, and they escaped the thicket to continue their journey. They hurried down the road, glancing over their shoulder the entire way.

"Who were they looking for?" Saryll whispered, eyes wide with terror.

"Us," Aurienne replied, chewing her lip.

"How did they find us?" Captain Laurier hissed.

Aurienne wrapped one arm around her stomach to steady herself, blinking against the pain. "Someone told them."

Theo urged his horse to trot beside her. "Who?"

"The only people who knew they were leaving were General

Kane, the other seers, King Jaekob Juri of Wyndsel, and King Edmunton Cavendar of Rodarri," Mathis answered.

Aurienne replied, "General Kane may fancy himself the uncrowned king of Avyllon as the Commander of the Armies, but I have read him, and he wouldn't betray his country. The Goddess would strike down any seers that did not follow Her will. That leaves one possibility for who may have betrayed us to the emperor—one of the very kings we are traveling to meet."

INTERLUDE

501 N.T.C. Hunger's Teeth Mountains, Avyllon.

A mountain tomb—*fitting for monsters such as us.* Monsters with soulless eyes blacker than a moonless midnight in hell, wings that darkened the sun, and fangs that tore the life from their prey waited inside. A thousand pairs of claws raked against the rune-sealed titan ore, and teeth gnashed the stale air. Though some still raged against this final resting place, there was no escape from their eternal prison.

Just as well. The monster's mind filled with images of beasts fighting shadows, cursed creatures warring new gods, and ancient powers defending hellsdamned souls.

Rivers of blood.

Mountains of bones.

Shadows twisting the continent into a hellscape.

Even now, with a throat burning for lifeblood, nearly lost to madness, the monster relished the silence of the prison. Finally, the screams had stopped. The innocent would be safe from the twisted creatures they had become. They'd not always been this way. Once they had been mortals, warriors. Heroes. No longer.

No price was too steep to save the ones they loved—even if it cost their souls—and they had paid the price willingly. Eventually, their families were sundered, the bloodlust more than they could overcome. Their intentions did not matter, simply what followed. Only hunger, rage, and darkness remained, and the wretched sins they committed over the next century were unforgivable. Insatiable appetites destroyed all they sacrificed for, and the army of darkness was unstoppable.

Not even the sunlight hunter could destroy us.

Until Grimfall. Icy fear sluiced down the monster's spine, freezing the beast's blood. If *they* were monsters, what was Grimfall? Powerful. Deadly. Ancient. An otherworldly being that even the gods would not look upon directly. Imprisonment was better than facing hell itself.

Perhaps, this army of monsters locked away in the heart of a lonely mountain range would wither and turn to dust as the centuries turned.

We did not deserve to be saved, and none would free us.

PART TWO

Seafaring Wynds

Chapter Eleven

Poisoned treasure called to the ocean king crowned.
He dove into the faceless waters and drowned.

— *High Seer Aurienne Azarrah, prophetic*
vision.

1152 N.T.C. The city of Wynds, Wyndsel.

Wynds stood on the edge of a cliff overlooking the stormy ocean. Hundreds of feet in the air, even the highest waves couldn't reach the soaring walls surrounding the city. Hexagonal redstone buildings were decorated with flat tile roofs, arched open-air windows, and twisted iron adornments.

Orange blossoms filled Aurienne's senses as the salty breeze danced with the sea glass windchimes and tickled her skin. Crashing waves echoed through the streets—so different from her home with the softly bubbling fountains. Deep within the city, the royal castle perched on the very edge of the cliff, overlooking the floating armada in the bay she'd glimpsed on the road in.

The caravan tiredly wound through the city. Above their heads, ornately carved balconies hung over the roads. Colorful tiles swirled in brilliant geometric designs on the walls.

Aurienne dismounted on wobbly legs and stepped up into the back of a creaking, still-moving wagon to change clothes. They would not be afforded the opportunity to freshen up before the audience with the king. A typical tactic to put them off-balance. She shook the creases from a gown and stepped into it. She fastened the gold jewelry on her body that felt more like chains than decorations. Carefully, she drew lines of kohl across her eyes—Seeing the bumps before they jostled her hand and holding the stick away from her face until they passed. As she was dusting gold across her cheeks, Saryll and Kassia entered.

"I Saw that Kassia and I wouldn't be permitted to attend the banquet this evening, so I'm going to shop the market. Kassia would like to find some trinkets to bring back to Wildegrove," Saryll said.

"From what I've Seen, I'd rather go with you two," Aurienne said dryly.

Her cards knocked against the inside of the spelled box in agreement.

"Is the king in league with the emperor?" Saryll asked.

"I'm not sure." Sighing, Aurienne placed the gold-dusted brush into the makeup case and closed it with a click, eyeing the vendor carts wistfully. "Enjoy yourselves in the market. Keep an eye out for anything you think I'd like."

The wagon rolled to a stop. Pushing the curtain aside, Aurienne stepped onto the rickety wooden step. Theo's hand found hers, and she glanced up. He'd donned one of the emissary suits and slicked his hair back with water. His thumb brushed the top of her knuckles, and her skin warmed.

"Thank you," she murmured, stepping onto the hexagonal red cobblestones.

The witch and the seer wandered toward the vendor carts arm in arm.

"Kolten, would you send a handful of sentinels with them?" Looking back into Theo's eyes, Aurienne asked, "Are you ready? They're going to test us, search for any weakness. We can't show any."

"I hope I'm ready," Theo replied, tugging on his starched collar and sleeves.

A company of Wyndsel guards emerged from the castle, and Aurienne released Theo's hand. The guards wore steel armor across their shoulders and chests with blue rivets and spiraled parallel lines resembling waves. Leather gauntlets were thrice wrapped by braided cords. Long sashes fluttered from their wickedly gleaming curved swords, reminding Aurienne of serpent fangs.

"The king will see you now."

Aurienne nodded as the guards escorted her, Theo, Mathis, and Adonis to the throne room. Their own sentinels, led by Aurienne's personal guard Sentinel Kolten, formed a wall around them. The palace halls were wide, covered in murals and painted tiles, and revealed open-air windows to the coast.

They turned a corner to enter the throne room through tall copper doors. Glass chandeliers shaped like crashing waves hung from vaulted ceilings three stories high. The walls were a subtle red, but everything else in the room sparkled in shades of blue. The king and queen, crown princess and her fiancé, as well as the Council of Wynds were waiting for them on the raised stone dais sitting on thrones made of twisted iron and sea glass. Several dozen guards lined the perimeter.

Aurienne glanced at Theo.

Theo stood stiffly, and the collar of his shirt had a thin line of perspiration. His expression was flat end nearly unreadable, but the serious tilt of his brows hinted at his determination.

An attendant introduced the royals, but Aurienne only half listened. She knew their names and titles well from her previous visit, all but Donovan, he was not yet betrothed to Princess Arissabett yet. Instead, she studied the people.

King Jaekob glowered at her while she held his gaze. He was fifty-five years old and did not bear the belly of age but instead remained fit with a dark beard peppered with more gray than when she had visited a few years ago. His wrinkles carved a permanent frown into his severe features. Finally, he glanced away.

A smile tugged at Aurienne's lips. She had timed their arrival, clothing, and position of guards down to the minute for a chance at the best outcome. The king was no match for her Goddess. So far, things were going well.

The attendant began listing the council members, but her gaze crossed the airy room with its open curved arches letting in the salty sea breeze that softly clinked sea glass chimes to the rhythm of the waves. Colorful tiles adorned the walls and floors in dazzling geometric patterns. The reflections of sunlight on glass reminded her of flashing wolf fangs. She blinked. It reminded her of the Demorran fangs *from her foretelling visions.* Icy fingers ran down her spine.

The attendant finished introducing Aurienne and her party. Aurienne inclined her chin respectfully while Theo, Adonis, and Mathis bowed deeply and held it for a pause before rising.

"Welcome," King Jaekob said in a tone anything but welcoming. "We were not expecting you."

"Yes, welcome, dear," Queen Elissa said.

His wife was just under fifty, though her youthful face did not match her age. She was particularly beautiful with deep olive skin, a thin face, and a willowy form. Thick brows framed her sharp features, and her long dark lashes were as dense as fans. Her dark hair was half-pulled back into a braid that prominently displayed her crown.

Interestingly, the queen lacked the wrinkles around the corners of her eyes, and Aurienne wondered whether it was from a life with too few smiles. Then she wondered whether she'd have any smile lines herself if she reached that age. She pursed her lips.

Probably not.

Beside her, the princess's gaze was fastened upon her fiancé, Prince Donovan Elsher, the second son of the king of Arryn. If Aurienne had divination cards for that pair, they would be the doe-eyed beauty and the smug prick.

"Your Majesties, it is good to see you again," Aurienne replied. "It has been many years since I visited your library. I apologize for the short notice. I did write as soon as I learned of the trip myself. The Goddess did not give me much warning either."

"I see," the king said. "It is…unusual for a reigning monarch or regent to visit another, especially on short notice. Should I be concerned?"

"No need to be concerned, but we do have a request to make at the formal audience," Aurienne said.

"You did not bring many soldiers." Prince Donovan smirked.

"I did not," Aurienne said.

"Tell me, seer," King Jaekob cut in, "you are here unprotected and uninvited. Your country is without a proper king. I could ransom you back, or give you to the emperor."

Sentinel Kolten took a small step forward, hand on his hilt.

Aurienne met the king's gaze and held it. She had been expecting this question. "There are no futures where you succeed at either. There was one future where you succeeded at kidnapping me. However, I just planted doubts. That future has evaporated like the morning mist."

A vein in the king's forehead bulged, and his face turned redder than the walls. He glared at her through partially lidded eyes. Aurienne watched him calculating and deciding which response to employ. She narrowed her gaze.

Time to roll the bone dice.

"I would not have come if I would have been in danger, but your hospitality and honor are beyond dispute," Aurienne finished.

The Council of Wynds exchanged nervous glances. She waited, so many futures fluttering at the edges of her mind like butterfly wings. The king's mouth soured into a thin line. It was difficult to contradict flattery, and he knew she'd trapped him.

"I, of course, was joking. A little ribbing between monarchs is customary," the king said sarcastically.

"Of course," Aurienne said in her most gracious tone.

This was going as well as it could have so far.

She inclined her chin. "Please allow me to offer a reading, as is our custom?"

"I could not accept," the king replied. "You have traveled a long way. I'm sure you are tired. I would be a poor host for taxing you."

Aurienne forced herself to smile, having guessed he'd refuse, but it was worth asking to obtain precious information.

"You are a gracious host," she said tightly. "You should know better than anyone how time changes all things. Friends become enemies, become allies as circumstances demand. I hope to leave here allies."

King Jaekob's mouth tightened.

King Jaekob's father and King Cavendar's father plotted to take Avyllon when the last Avyllon king died, but the first High Seer stopped them. Not too long after, Jaekob and Edmunton nearly went to war. Jaekob had personally killed the current king's older brother in a duel to keep Jaekob's sister from marrying him. His sister threw herself from the high castle walls and died. Then, Edmunton had returned the favor by killing Jaekob's younger brother in a tournament. In a twist of fate, they were allies again, each sharing in the loss of their siblings.

Aurienne wanted him to remember the past to sow the seeds of discord between him and King Cavendar of Rodarri—their next destination. It might help their cause.

Or piss him off.

She'd already pushed it this far. She might as well dig the knife a little deeper.

"I recently had a vision of your sister; may the gods protect her soul and guide it to peace. It has been some time since her passing, but I Saw it like it was yesterday," Aurienne finished, forcing her expression as grieved as she could.

The king said nothing, but his mouth twitched with the unspoken words. His eyes filled with long-buried anger.

Tight-lipped, Prince Donovan stood from his seat beside the princess and strode toward the party. He looked somewhat like the Juri family. His hair was a dark brown, and his skin a shade even deeper. His face was squarer as opposed to long, and his eyebrows rested lower on his face as if he intended to perpetually frown. Taller than the princess, he was not as tall as the king but far more heavily muscled. Though the people of Wyndsel were brave adventurers who once left Arryn to settle Wyndsel, centuries had slowly changed their features. He strode forward, skipping down from the dais.

Hellsdamn it, Aurienne thought, *not this future.*

"Who else has joined you?" Prince Donovan asked, circling Aurienne and the sorcerers.

"My brother Adonis Azarrah and his mentor, the famed sorcerer Mathis Kaster from the Avyllon University," Aurienne said.

The prince stopped in front of Theo. Theo did stand out from the group—he was taller than most of her sentinels and built like the forge he worked in. Long years of smithing left him with the build of a warrior.

"Why does one of your guards stand with you as an equal?" Prince Donovan scowled.

"I'm Theo. Her emissary for the trip." Theo looked down at the prince.

Prince Donovan drew a jeweled dagger and pointed it at Theo's throat. Theo grimaced but did not move. He stared down the prince, prompting the prince to press it until the point broke skin. The smallest bead of blood welled on the blade's point. Aurienne knew Donovan would likely not hurt Theo in this future, but prickles of anxiety filled her anyways. It was physically painful to stay still.

The prince tapped the blade against Theo's neck. "I could slit your throat. I could kill you, and no one would be able to do anything about it."

Theo didn't move. His face flushed, and every inch of him tensed. He clenched his jaw as the prince's smirk deepened. The prince pressed the blade harder against Theo's skin, but Theo remained motionless. He stared the prince down, and the prince snarled. A dark gleam flashed in Donovan's eye, and Aurienne Saw terrible things in that look.

Her fingers itched toward the gilded dagger at her thigh as rage bubbled along the back of her neck. Gaze narrowing on Donovan's dagger, if he moved it even a fraction, she'd drive hers through his eye before he could blink.

"If you harmed my advisor and emissary, I would personally count that as an act of war against the state of Avyllon. The Goddess would give me Sight to ensure that within the month, you would walk off the edge of the castle walls and crash against the rocks below. I have Seen it," Aurienne warned.

She also Saw Theo lose his temper and toss Donovan out the window, but she'd keep that to herself.

Prince Donovan lowered the dagger and glared at her. Her stony and clouded gaze must have made him think better of it. He lifted his hands placatingly and backed away.

"I was joking, too, of course," the prince said, returning to his fiancé, Princess Arissabett, who fawned over him.

The king gave Aurienne an appraising look. "You are indeed a worthy adversary."

She worked her jaw. "I hope to be a worthier ally."

"Please join us tonight for a banquet held in your honor. Tomorrow, we will have a formal audience. Please see them to their rooms." The king gestured to the staff.

Aurienne bowed and backed out of the room. They followed the attendants into a quiet wing of the castle, where she reached and touched Theo's hand. He un-balled his fist and gave her a gentle squeeze.

"I'm sorry for Donovan," she whispered.

"Knowing that you will See terrible ways to kill him if he murders me does make me feel a bit better," Theo said.

"I Saw that his cruelty has ensured a dark fate for himself," she said.

"Good."

She wracked her brain for any way to make it up to him, and an idea struck her. "After you change, I have something for you to see."

A knock at the door sent excited sparks down Aurienne's neck for the surprise she had for him. She opened the door, wearing a simple and demure gown, perfect for where they were going. She took Theo's hand and led him through the castle and outside.

"Where are we going?" he asked.

"You'll see."

Dodging castle staff, they made it outside. They crossed the courtyard between the round redstone buildings, underneath chiming sea glass, and finally entered a doorway. Striding down the hallway, she froze. Hellsdamned Donovan was coming.

"In here," she whispered and pulled Theo in after her.

She pressed her fingers to her lips and waited until Donovan passed—aware of how close she was to Theo. Her hands grazed his rock-solid chest. She looked up and saw him gazing at her with eyes of molten green. He pushed hair out of her face and glanced down at her lips. His fingers brushed her cheek. She could almost feel his lips against hers again as his hot breath tickled her neck.

The stomping of Donovan's boots faded. She laughed nervously and pulled Theo out behind her.

They crept down the hall until they reached a thick wooden door. It opened into a blacksmith's workshop. The forge was lit, and blacksmiths were hammering away.

"This is amazing," Theo said.

"Tell them we're royal guests, and they'll answer all of your questions," she said.

Theo strode away and excitedly engaged one of the smiths. The smith glanced at Aurienne in her High Seer garb and stepped away to let Theo hammer out the sword.

Aurienne claimed an oak stool in the corner and watched Theo hammering out the blade, asking questions and adjusting accordingly. He was beaming wider than she'd ever seen. Worry dripped off his body with the sweat. He settled into a familiar *ting-ting-ting* of hammer on hot metal.

Unable to tear her gaze from him, happiness eddied in her heart. In his element, Theo came alive. His eyes sparkled, and he had an easy swagger to his motions. Already laughing with the smiths, he already had a casual camaraderie with strangers she'd never known with anyone. These few moments of reprieve were the least she could do. Her happiness faded. *This* was what she was stealing from him—the life he should have had, and never would. For there was much she did not know, but she knew with clarity his life would never be the same. His great destiny would cost him all of this.

An hour passed, and she finally managed to drag Theo from the forge. They walked up a little used stairwell and down a hall to their wing of the castle when Aurienne stopped. A vision. Aurienne grinned, opened her water skin, and dumped the contents on the stone floor.

Theo cocked an eyebrow, but she only shrugged. He escorted her to her room and stopped at the door. He pressed his lips to the back of her hand and stole her breath as his stubble scraped her skin and breath warmed her knuckles. She swallowed, reminding herself he was not hers to keep. No one was.

"Your clothes will be laid out for you. You have about an hour to clean up." Aurienne allowed her eyes to roam over his sooty clothes.

He had rolled up his sleeves, and his arms were covered in smoke and coal. Aurienne wanted to drag her nails across those arms. Sweat beaded on his brow, dripping down his neck, chest, and back. Aurienne blinked. She shook her head, clearing the indecent images she was conjuring.

"See you at the banquet," Aurienne said.

"Thank you for showing me the forge and armory." He hesitated before turning toward his own room. "You don't know what it means to me."

She knew.

It would also be his last moment of peace for some time.

Dinner Knives & Poison

Chapter Twelve

The thrill will never come again,
Of dinner knives and poison.

— *Folksong of Karme.*

1152 N.T.C. The city of Wynds, Wyndsel.

Ribbons, flowers, and predatory expressions filled the royal ballroom, and Theo tried his hardest not to look like prey. The guests were gathering in a stifling sea of blue fabrics as the king and queen arrived. Adonis and Mathis mingled with guests, and Avyllon's protection escort surrounded the room in full armor carved with a golden griffin. Theo adjusted his suit. It was soft but stretched tight across the shoulders and backside. He had to place his feet on the polished travertine floors carefully or else his new, formal boots would squeak.

Aurienne emerged from the entry and paused at the balcony high above the room. Theo froze. She looked every bit the Goddess that people believed she was. Breathtaking. Her eyes scanned the room, and divine tattoos peeked out from beneath the gossamer fabric of the sleeves. Studs filled her ears and rings covered her fingers, connected to bracelets by tiny chains.

Theo whistled long and low under his breath. Instinctively, he knew what Aurienne would be thinking. She'd be reading every possible future to see which could give her the best leverage and would have chosen this exact moment to enter, wearing exactly those clothes and descending the stairs at the exact moment. She'd do anything to give them an edge. He wondered whether she made any of those choices for his reaction.

Her alluring gown increased the illusion of divinity—indigo by her neck, brightening to lavender near her feet, like a dark midnight sky lightening before dawn. Thousands of golden and silver stars glistened from the layers of thin fairy-wing fabric. The material was so fluid and light that it looked like she wore only colored mist, catching the air and floating impossibly. A high slit revealed glimpses of thigh as she descended the stairs.

How good would that dress look on the floor?

Theo shook the thought from his head, as he caught Aurienne grinning. He pushed to the front of the crowd and offered her his hand at the bottom stairs. She took it gently and let him guide her off the staircase. Releasing her hand, he extended the crook of his arm, which she accepted. They approached the refreshment table.

"You look stunning," Theo whispered.

A small smile played with the edges of Aurienne's painted lips, and it took considerable self-control for Theo not to drop to his knees and beg to kiss her there in the ballroom.

"Thank you," she whispered. "You look handsome. I'm glad the suit fit."

Her eyes roved over Theo's chest, and he thought he saw her bite her lip. It made him stand prouder and straighter.

Hellsdamn it.

"You knew it would," he whispered.

She chuckled. Theo reminded himself of her fate, knowing that falling for her promised heartbreak, and craving every moment of it. He offered her a crystal glass full of golden sparkling liquid, brushing his fingers against her soft skin and trailing up to her wrist. She accepted and took a small sip.

Next to a tall glass aquarium, Adonis chatted with a group of young noblemen and from the looks of it, was making plans to get into trouble later. Theo was suddenly very appreciative of Adonis' advice on the road, as Adonis looked quite at home here. Mathis conversed with a group of elderly, equally wizened men. He had combed his hair flat and everything.

"Do you think he magicked his hair like that?" Theo whispered to Aurienne.

She hid her grin behind a sip of the bubbly wine. Mathis' conversation quickly turned animated with excited hand gestures and sharp head nods and shakes.

Theo studied the room, seeking out the royals and council members. Princess Arissabett was ringed by a large group of other young noblewomen. The princess's dark hair, dark lashes, and soft olive skin contrasted against her full-skirted, pale pink dress. Giggling and blushing, they watched the men across the room. She had her father's dark eyes, though hers were naïve, and her mother's lips, though hers wore a smile.

Prince Donovan skulked in an alcove on the other side of the grand staircase, away from the princess' view, inappropriately close to another young lady. He played with her red hair as she giggled. Theo rolled his eyes. The princess was clearly infatuated with him, and he was brazenly flirting with one of her ladies in public.

What a prick.

Aurienne nudged Theo, drawing his attention to an approaching King Jaekob. Theo's heart sank into his gut.

Aurienne murmured, "We have about twenty seconds before you need to start convincing his council to ally with us. Are you ready?"

Theo straightened his shoulders. "Whatever it takes, right?"

The king and queen approached with the princess. Donovan appeared behind the princess, straightening his jacket.

"Dinner shall be served. May I escort you to the table?" King Jaekob asked Aurienne.

It was not a question, but Aurienne answered graciously with an incline of her head and took his arm. The prince stepped forward to offer his arm to his future mother-in-law. She accepted, and they followed the king. The princess glanced at Theo. He swallowed and wracked his brain, hoping he could remember what to do. This was not what he practiced. Immediately, sweat pooled under his arms.

Theo bowed low to the princess and said, "Your Highness, it would be my greatest honor to escort you to the table while your betrothed escorts the queen."

Theo hoped he had said everything right. He called her the right title, and he tried to bow low enough but not too low. He offered his arm but allowed one of a higher station to approach first. Respectful and humble, he made sure to let her know he knew she was engaged and, therefore, unavailable.

She smiled politely and took the offered arm. Theo nearly sighed in relief. He must have gotten at least close to the proper protocol. She did not look offended, so Theo counted that in his favor. In fact, she looked appreciative not to have been left without an escort. His head already ached at the many rules. It would be a painfully long night.

Theo escorted Princess Arissabett into the dining room. He kept his back spear-straight, and his chest puffed like Adonis had told him to. He held his chin level with the floor but avoided eye contact with his betters, as Mathis had told him.

The dining room was three stories tall but open, decorated with painted stone and carved inlaid wood paneled designs. Rounded arches near the ceiling allowed a view of the night sky. In the center of the room sat a single imposing dining table that could seat Theo's whole village. In the center of the table, the tallest chair signaled the king's seat.

Theo's stomach flipped. The layout was nothing like the diagram Mathis showed him. He trailed the other royals and Aurienne, hoping it would become apparent.

It did not.

Theo cleared his throat. "Your Highness, where shall you be seated tonight?" he asked quietly.

Princess Arissabett offered him a sympathetic smile and nodded to a tall chair off to the side of the king's. Theo whispered his thanks. Perhaps he'd have one ally at Wyndsel already. Theo pulled out the chair for the princess.

Prince Donovan stepped in rudely and said, "I'll get my future wife's chair."

Theo bowed and stepped back. "Of course, your Highness."

Theo made sure not to glance back at the princess for it to be misinterpreted as interest, as Adonis instructed.

"Let's be seated," the king said tightly and sat.

Theo slid carefully in front of the chair beside Aurienne. She gave him an encouraging smile. Theo nearly let out a deep, anxious breath. Aurienne's personal sentinels stood behind them, eyes roving across the dining hall.

King Jaekob gripped the table. "That chair was reserved for one of my advisors. I'm sure Mr. Thatcher would be more comfortable at one of the other tables. Perhaps with the rest of the staff."

Theo's throat tightened as shame covered him like a hot blanket.

When Aurienne spoke, Theo wanted to kiss her even more. "As I told you upon my arrival, Mr. Thatcher is my personal advisor, and part of the royal caravan. He shall sit next to me."

"The *regent* caravan," the king corrected. "You're not royal blood."

Aurienne simply smiled demurely but firmly. "I'm regent and High Seer. Mr. Thatcher is a member of my advisory council. The Goddess showed me he was imperative to the outcome of this visit."

"We were unaware, and so the seating is simply full," the king said. He spoke quietly enough that only the closest could hear, but the whole room was peeking over and gossiping.

Theo felt the size of a mouse with them arguing over him. He felt useless and helpless that Aurienne had to fight for him, and there was nothing he could do or say. He took Adonis' advice: if you don't know what to do or say, keep your mouth shut. Pretending not to listen, he reached for his glass.

"No matter. I Saw that Lord Farghall would be absent today due to a fall he took on spilled water in the hall. Those old stone floors can be treacherous," she said sweetly.

Theo choked on wine. He'd seen her spill the water, and it was *entirely* intentional. Aurienne sabotaged the lord. Her tone and posture were the definition of regal. She walked a tightrope of politeness and insults and yet had no qualms about using her gift to maim. It was mildly terrifying.

Theo leaned over to Aurienne and whispered, "Spilled water?"

"If I had been clumsy on the stairs, he'd have broken his leg, not his wrist," she whispered. "He will be fine before Hallohaim, and it freed up a seat."

Had they not been seated at a terrifying dinner table, Theo would have whistled; Aurienne had ice in her veins. An army of waiters appeared behind each chair and served the first course of many.

Everything Theo learned about etiquette rushed out of his head as the food was set before him. He was hot and cold and jittery. Glancing at Aurienne, she was dabbing her nose with a napkin. Blood. She pushed herself too hard again.

If he did better, she wouldn't need to. He tapped his hand on the table and sat tall in his plush chair, trying to keep all the rules in his head. Staring at a horde of silverware, he knew he had to get it together. Breathing shallowly, he prepared himself. He could not let her down.

Aurienne dragged her painted fingertip across the top of her glass. Wolf claws clicked inside of her mind, followed by a constant drumbeat of footsteps. Always wolves and always those footsteps bringing something closer, *someone* closer, every day. Only three and a half weeks before the summit from her vision. Theo just had to convince these cowardly and foolish kings of the danger.

"How were your travels?" The king had a glint in his eye. "I did not receive word of you coming up the main road."

It confirmed what Aurienne already suspected about who had shared their location with the emperor's scouting party. A future where she stabbed him in the hand floated across her vision, and she smiled softly to herself.

"We made excellent time," she replied. "The Goddess showed us the way."

King Jaekob leaned closer. "Which route did you take?"

"We followed the Goddess' will. I'm not acquainted with the names of each road and village we passed through, but I'm sure we could piece it together."

"That won't be necessary. I was just curious how you avoided all notice. It seems as if you were sneaking here." He glared at her as he took a long drink of wine.

She tapped her glass. "If we meant to ambush you, Your Majesty, we would not have written ahead. We do have a sorcerer traveling with us who is able to open the Ways, but out of respect, we took the roads."

"You are, of course, welcome to visit at any time as *regent* of Avyllon. I have heard rumors of the people calling for a king. It seems forty-seven years without a true ruler is long enough," King Jaekob said.

He spoke the truth. Many were loyal to the Goddess and the High Seers, but there were those among the Guild Masters who wished to return to the times of kings. Kings could be bought. The Goddess could not. It was concerning that he was so well-versed in Avyllon politics.

"I never wished for this role," she said. "None of us did. If a king shall be selected, then the Goddess will find one. If the Goddess willed a monarch to reclaim the throne, I would follow her will and support them."

Aurienne glanced at Theo who was staring at the assortment of cutlery beside the plate like he was trying to solve a riddle in another language while holding his breath. Some of the council members and other nobles watched him, jeering and motioning to one another discreetly. Aurienne ground her teeth. She Saw a future where she defended him, but it ended with amplified embarrassment. Aurienne snapped her mouth shut.

Some of the younger noblemen waited for Theo to select a fork. They waited to make a comment. Even without her Sight, their disdain for an untitled commoner to sit with them tainted the air. They hardly tolerated her.

Theo scratched his jaw and caught Aurienne watching. He pasted a reassuring but false smile on his face and straightened his back. Theo confidently grabbed a fork, the wrong one, but you would never have known by his ease. She hid a small smile with her hand.

Goddess, the man was endearing.

The nobles chuckled, and she Saw they were going to say something. Quickly, she cycled through her options of potential futures. Aurienne could drop her own fork, but it wouldn't stop the brown-haired noble's comment. She could make a polite comment to the king or queen, but it left Theo alone to the rudeness of the black-haired one. A surprising future slipped into Aurienne's thoughts, where she turned and kissed Theo. It *would* silence all comments. She blushed, then Saw another future that quieted the nobles.

Aurienne stopped a waitstaff and said, "I'm sorry, but my emissary seems to have been served with soiled cutlery and has been forced to use his dinner fork for salad. Would you be so kind as to bring him new ones?"

The waitstaff bowed and immediately took Theo's forks back to the kitchen. The nobles quieted and returned to their meal, scowling.

Aurienne whispered to Theo, "Go from the outside cutlery to inside. Just watch me."

As the meal continued, Theo was slowly assuming a princely air. He engaged in polite conversation with a couple across the table, watching everyone else carefully and inconspicuously.

One young man addressed Theo. "We haven't been introduced. I'm Bryand, son of Henriel, the master of ships and lord of Vizca estate, a direct descendent of Etham the Conqueror."

Theo placed the fork and knife carefully on his plate and dabbed his napkin deftly on the corner of his lip. Over the last weeks, his stubble had grown and made him look more a man. A future vision of kissing him at the dinner table slipped back into Aurienne's head, and she had to banish the urge. She forced her gaze from that enticingly strong jawline. It had just been one kiss. Why was it suddenly all she could think about?

What Theo said next snapped her back to reality.

"I'm honored to make your acquaintance. I'm Atheodoren Willem Thatcher of Karme, son of Willem and Anna Thatcher. When I return home from accompanying Aurienne Celestina Azarrah, High Seer of Avyllon, Regent and Guardian to the Crown Throne, Chosen Eye and Vassal of the Triple Goddess, Steward of the Temple at Avyllon, Flamekeeper and Historian, then I'll serve as our town blacksmith."

Aurienne stared, unsure if she was more surprised Theo's given name was Atheodoren or that he knew her full title. How had she not known his full name? She'd Seen his whole life, his past and present and future. They traveled together for days, and yet she hadn't known his name. A twisting feeling in her stomach told her it was an omen, and it related to the *other* vision she hadn't understood.

One noble laughed and said, "A...blacksmith? How very...ambitious."

Some of the others snickered.

Aurienne was too surprised at Theo's name revelation to help him.

"Tell me what it's like to make horseshoes all day? Is it very challenging to swing a hammer?" another noble jeered.

Theo said graciously, "I can make shoes. You're right. But I specialize in blades."

The nobles quieted.

"I mostly made swords for my training in the apprenticeship. Swords or bladed tools. There is a science for heating the metal to the precise temperature and folding it and hammering it into shape, and then sharpening it until it could slice a head clean off. It takes hours of...endurance," Theo said and intentionally held the gaze of the young lady next to the noble.

Aurienne grimaced. She did not like that at all. Her fingers itched toward her knife again.

"I swing a ten-pound hammer sometimes for ten hours to get it just right," Theo said. "Then there's the constant sharpening with a wet stone and leather. It's not for the faint-hearted."

Aurienne folded her hands in her lap to keep herself from forming fists. Theo was playing this interaction exactly right. Adonis must have been a thorough tutor. It still heated and twisted her skin in a way that was unexpected.

The ladies seated near the nobles exchanged enthralled glances, and the noblemen's mouths tightened. "It's not the same as running an estate province."

Theo nodded graciously. "No, my lord. I've never had much of a mind for administrative work. Doing math, reading, and all of that is far too tedious for someone like me. We're too lucky to have great men like you for that. I'm far better humbly left to the forge and fire, and hammer and steel."

Theo said the last words with such heat that Aurienne could

almost feel the delicious flames of a forge. He couldn't have said it more graciously and kindly. One woman raised a brow at him, and another batted her lashes. Half of the men looked relieved at Theo admitting his lowly station. The other half caught the veiled insult and stewed. It did weed out those nobles lacking intelligence, which Theo and Aurienne could use to their advantage tomorrow morning.

Pride bubbled in Aurienne's chest. Theo was trying so hard in a situation she knew he hated, and she knew he did it for her. Theo lifted his glass of wine, and from her angle, she saw him swallow before the glass hit his lips, the only sign he was uncomfortable. She looked down and saw his other hand quivering slightly and gripping his pants leg angrily. Aurienne reached over and took his hand. He let her wrap her fingers in his.

Prince Donovan said, "Aurienne, is it? Why did you ask a smith to accompany you? Do you have such an immediate need for a smithy to have one at your call?"

The nobles laughed. Aurienne wondered whether she could find the right place to spill water for the prince to *slip* on.

"She is the High Seer," Theo corrected gently but firmly.

"I Saw he would accompany me," Aurienne said. "The Triple Goddess Saw that he should be here. For what purpose, I do not know. I do know that he has a destiny greater than even I could see. He will do great things."

"Him?"

She said, "I only see what the Triple Goddess shows me."

Donovan glared but leaned back in his chair.

Aurienne leaned toward Theo and brushed her lips against his ear. "Perhaps we can convince the king to attend the summit by charming his court and family. Friends are helpful to have. Watch this."

His skin was hot under her lips, and she had to ignore the impulse to kiss his neck. She leaned back, feeling flushed and almost forgetting what she had been saying. The man was intoxicating. Her heart sped up as she inhaled eucalyptus and pine. She swallowed and took a sip of wine to steady her nerves.

To the table, she said, "I would like to offer a reading to any who are interested tomorrow morning as an extension of friendship."

"I should like that," Princess Arissabett said from the other side of the king.

"Please let me know when you shall be receiving guests in the morning, and I'll come to you," Aurienne said.

Aurienne was looking past the king to speak to the princess when her attention caught on the fork that the king was lifting to his mouth. A vision crashed into her awareness.

The peas glowing green, growing faces to sneer at her.
The king frothing at the mouth.
Prince Donovan donning a crown and locking arms
    with the emperor.
Flames and destruction tearing across the lands.

Aurienne quickly reached forward and grabbed the king's fork just before it touched his mouth. Her palm tightened against the metal as she slipped her soul beyond the veil, Seeing all the possible futures.

"What is the..." the king exclaimed.

"The peas are poisoned," Aurienne whispered. "I just Saw you die."

The king paled and slowly lowered the fork. "Are you sure?"

"I can help you find the culprit, but they cannot know that we know," she whispered.

"Clear this meal and bring the next course," the king commanded.

Wait staff poured out of hidden doorways and whisked the dishes away. Aurienne sifted through the visions, grasping the one she needed.

"Tell the staff you do not want to waste the food and direct them to eat it now. Ensure everyone gets a helping of meat, peas, and pota-toes. Have guards watch to see who refuses to eat the peas. Only your food was poisoned so they will be safe, but the poisoner might not risk it," Aurienne said.

The king hissed, "You can't just see who did it?"

She shook her head. "We must alter circumstances, so they reveal themselves. In none of the current futures are they found out, so their behavior does not reveal them. If you change the present, you change the future. Do this, and the poisoner shall be revealed."

King Jaekob summoned a guard and whispered the instructions. They waited anxiously until the guards returned with two people, a kitchen staffer and a waiter. The guards marched them into the center of the room. A row of guards lined the table in front of the king.

"As you commanded," the guard said.

King Jaekob leaned forward. "I offered you food, and you both spurned it. Why?"

The woman kitchen staffer fell to her hands and knees and began to sob. "I did not mean to offend!"

The man said, "I, too, did as was instructed, my king. What is this about?"

Theo gripped his leg under the table, and Aurienne reached for his hand and gave it a reassuring squeeze. He gazed at her and did not let go of her hand.

"You didn't eat the peas." King Jaekob nodded to a guard carrying two bowls of peas. He handed one to each of the suspects.

"The peas?" the woman squeaked. "Please forgive me."

"Eat," the king said.

Theo squeezed her hand tighter, paling. The woman began shov-eling the peas into her mouth voraciously, sobbing and choking.

"Aren't they poisoned?" Theo whispered to Aurienne, his voice laced with concern.

Aurienne leaned forward, her gaze trailing to the man. Eyes half-closed, she pushed her spectral fingers through the veil, watching all of the futures unfold. In the present, the man held the bowl of peas and cast a sideways glance at the woman. He hesitated and then dropped the bowl to the floor. The porcelain shattered into a thousand tiny pieces, and each reflected a guilty future. In several, he charged the king with a knife. In others, he tried again later. One by one those futures went dark.

"Him," Aurienne said quietly.

The woman froze. "Poison?"

"This was a test," Aurienne answered.

The woman sagged to the floor. A guard helped her stand and escorted her from the room.

"Gods kill the corrupt king!" the man yelled.

Guards swarmed to grab the man, but he moved too quickly. He pulled something from his pocket and tossed it into his mouth before they could stop him.

"He's poisoned himself!" a guard cried.

"Stop him. We need to interrogate him," another ordered.

The guards tried to dig the object from the man's throat. They pinned him against the floor, prying his mouth open with a dagger between his teeth. He started foaming and frothing at the mouth, convulsing as blood poured to the floor and trickled between the stones. The room fell silent. A heaviness settled upon Aurienne. All eyes drifted toward the king.

"Our honored guests have just saved my life, and perhaps all our lives. We owe them a debt of thanks," the king said tightly.

The nobles clapped, and tentative applause filled the room. Aurienne chewed her lip. Feeling heat spread from her nose, she dabbed the napkin, and it came away with blood. Her head throbbed. The visions came too fast these days, and it might all be for naught as the wolf claws and the footsteps never stopped.

"It seems I have matters to attend. Dinner has concluded. A formal audience for our esteemed guests will be held tomorrow." The king stormed out of the room.

Attendants helped the nobles pull back the heavy wooden chairs, and the room slowly emptied. The stunned silence gave way to gossip and suspicion. Whispers filled the hallways. Theo offered Aurienne his arm once more, and she wrapped her fingers around his arm.

"Did you know there wasn't poison?" Theo whispered.

His words crushed her heart. Did he really think she would let an entire castle's worth of staff be poisoned for no reason? She would have put her dagger through the king's throat before allowing innocents to die without cause.

She tried to smile. "Of course."

Adonis and Mathis pushed through the crowd to join them while Aurienne's sentinels worked to keep the crowds from crushing them.

"Are you both alright?" Theo asked.

"Fine," Adonis said.

Aurienne reached out and squeezed Adonis' arm fondly.

"I'll see what the nobles think of this," Adonis said before disappearing.

"I will see what the scholars know," Mathis said.

Aurienne directed Theo the fastest route to their rooms, even if it wasn't the most direct. It avoided the crowds and guards. There was a nagging feeling that still bothered Aurienne. Now that they were alone, she had to ask.

"Why did your Ma name you Atheodoren?"

"She said it suited me. Something about it being an old family name."

Aurienne chewed her lip but stopped when she tasted the paint. "Were you named for King Atheodoren, the first king of Avyllon?"

Theo laughed. "There's probably more than just him in the last thousand or so years."

They reached Aurienne's rooms, and Theo took her hand and kissed it. The kiss was chaste, but spikes of heat gathered where his lips touched her skin.

"Goodnight," he said.

"Goodnight."

She closed the door and leaned against it. She recalled Theo and her kissing in the meadow, deep and intimate and wild. The thought excited her and terrified her because she knew nothing was fated to last.

Aurienne tasted fresh blood on her tongue, trickling down the back of her throat. She swallowed it as her brain pounded inside her skull warning her of the consequences of using too much magic.

HEART'S DESIRE
CHAPTER THIRTEEN

You will get your heart's desire.

*— HIGH SEER AURIENNE AZARRAH, READING
AND CURSE FOR PRINCESS ARISSABETT.*

1152 N.T.C. The city of Wynds, Wyndsel.

Full of unanswered desires the next morning, Aurienne dragged her finger across the top of the spelled box holding her divination cards. "Behave today."

She was answered with inky smoke swirling out of the box in the shape of a skull.

Excellent.

Saryll and Kassia strode inside. Saryll wore the traditional white robe of the seer, and a flower was tucked behind her ear. Her dark hair was wrapped into several long braids, and a smear of gold dust painted her bronzed brown skin. Kassia donned a royal green and bright pink design that looked like she was wearing the garden at the cottage and perfectly complemented her ebony skin. They made a beautiful couple. They entered her room and sat, sipping steamy tea.

"We hear you had an interesting night," Kassia said.

Aurienne sipped the hot tea of honey and elder rose and glared at the turquoise and gold cup. "The poisoners were not expecting our presence, but they were sly. It nearly got past me. They must have decided to go through with it at the last minute."

"How did Theo do?" Saryll asked.

"He did well," Aurienne said. "They did not make it easy, but he kept his temper. I do not know if we managed to make friends, but perhaps Adonis' and Mathis' efforts will aid us."

"When is the audience with the king?" Saryll asked.

"Just before midday. Princess Arissabett will summon us soon for the reading I offered," Aurienne said.

"Do you think you'll learn something from it?" Kassia asked.

"I hope so. It gives you both a chance to practice with your new cards on some of the other girls," Aurienne said.

Kassia's eyes lit up.

Knock. Knock. Knock.

Aurienne smoothed her subdued gown. Where last night's gown intended to draw attention, today's meant to help her disappear. It was black and gray and looked like moving shadows, in stark contrast to her fair skin and dark hair. The sleeves went to her elbows, with the tattooed designs on her arms peeking out from underneath the fabric. The neckline was tall and stiff, with a deep notch cut down the middle, and layers of dreamy fabric floated in the skirts. She opened the door to find Theo waiting outside with a messenger.

"Princess Arissabett requests your presence in her private chambers," the messenger said.

Theo shifted uncomfortably. "I was going to find Adonis. Have you seen him? I...uh...I can walk you to the princess's room and then find him."

Aurienne smiled. "He's probably drunk himself to sleep somewhere. Check the university."

"Good to know." Theo chuckled.

The messenger led them beside open windows that allowed in a salty breeze and the scent of orange blossoms. Fine sea mist lingered on Aurienne's skin, dried by the rising sun. Aurienne's personal guard, Sentinel Kolten, trailed behind the messenger up ahead. Saryll and Kassia chatted merrily about divination card meanings and patterns.

Saryll and Kassia rounded a corner ahead just as Prince Donovan stumbled out of a doorway. Aurienne and Theo stopped as the prince kissed the disheveled red-haired girl inside and turned to leave. After the prince's behavior at the banquet, Aurienne would've seen this coming even without her gift. She pursed her lips.

Prince Donovan froze. He placed his hand upon his jeweled dagger and stormed toward them.

Theo stepped in front of Aurienne, squaring his shoulders. "You go on. I'll handle this."

Aurienne lifted her brow. This side of Theo was...enticing. Glancing between Prince Donovan's and Theo's competing expressions, she acquiesced. Theo would have to face the king in a few hours and must learn to stand on his own. She forced herself to step around the corner and let him handle this. She pressed herself against the wall, listening.

"*Blacksmith Theo*, was it?" The prince said forcefully and with emphasis on the lack of title.

"Prince Donovan, I hope you *slept* well." Theo's tone held the hint of an edge.

"What are you doing in this part of the castle?" Prince Donovan snapped.

"I'm escorting the High Seer and her attendants to the crown princess's private chambers for a reading," Theo said. "I, of course, have no intentions of entering the chambers. The princess is betrothed, after all."

Aurienne could nearly hear the prince's eyes bulge. She could have Seen it if she truly wanted, but the images in her imagination were possibly better. She had to smother a giggle.

Theo murmured something.

"You and that seer will tell her Highness nothing," the prince said. "If you want any chance of the king supporting your little quest, you will keep your mouth shut. I have many friends here and the ear of most of the Council of Wynds. Do you understand?"

"You will address her as the High Seer of Avyllon," Theo said flatly.

Donovan grumbled.

"You won't have many friends if she finds out and refuses to marry you," Theo said so quietly that Aurienne scarcely heard.

"Perhaps, you don't know how things work here. Once I marry Arissabett, I'll be the next king of Wyndsel. You want to stay in my good graces. Do we have an understanding?"

"The High Seer and I saw nothing this morning, your Highness. I haven't seen you since last night," Theo said.

"Good."

Aurienne heard Prince Donovan storm off, and Theo came around the corner. Upon seeing her, he forced his demeanor to change. He softened his fists, pressed his tense shoulders back, and wiped the angry expression away. He offered her his arm, and she accepted, feeling more than a little guilty.

"He's a piece of work," Theo said.

"I See only darkness and pain in his future," Aurienne said.

"Do you see me kicking his ass?" Theo asked.

Aurienne laughed so hard she nearly snorted and had to put her hand against her stomach to steady herself. "Unfortunately, no."

"I'll just have to imagine it," Theo said.

They reached the princess's door, where others waited. Sentinel Kolten posted himself just outside the door with a swiveling gaze. Theo kissed Aurienne's hand and disappeared down the hall in search of her brother.

"Don't think I didn't see you two kissing at the festival," Kassia whispered.

Aurienne saw it also, too often. She traced her skin, feeling the absence of Theo's lips. She lowered her hands.

"And I saw who you were kissing," Aurienne said slyly back and nodded to Saryll. Kassia grinned and blushed.

Inside the crown princess's chambers, more than two dozen girls dressed in gowns of ribbons and sparkles greeted them. Aurienne had to force herself to enter the claustrophobic room, far preferring the quiet of the temple.

"Aurienne! High Seer!" Princess Arissabett said cheerfully and motioned them to sit beside her.

Princess Arissabett's long hair was piled atop her head in an intricate design. Her gown was made entirely of pastel-colored ribbons, bows, and pearls. Aurienne sat beside the princess, who had wide doe-like eyes and fresh brown skin with a wide, bright smile. Aurienne felt twinges of guilt not telling her what her fiancé was up to, but a small part of Arissabett likely already knew.

"Who are your friends?" the princess asked.

"This is Saryll Amydeo, a seer and daughter of the former High Seer. This is Kassia Guara, the witch-in-training for the village of Wildegrove. Both are adept at divination cards and have come to assist me in doing readings for your ladies," Aurienne said.

The girls squealed as Saryll and Kassia found seats in swarms of lace and ribbon.

"Oh good! Everyone was so excited about having their fate read," Princess Arissabett said.

"I Saw that," Aurienne said atop the giggles and whispers. "I have been using my Sight quite extensively for our travels and would not want to tire myself before our departure, so while my companions are ready to read all of your ladies, I shall personally read your Fate."

The other girls exchanged excited looks.

"The High Seer does not give readings often. She must save her gift for matters of state, or for the future queen," Saryll said.

The other ladies wiggled excitedly in their chairs, and the Princess held her chin high.

"The High Seer's readings are never wrong," Saryll said, causing further giggles.

"Tell us our fate!" a lady called out.

Aurienne removed her cards from the spelled box in her lap. She placed them on the table in front of Princess Arissabett.

A red-haired young woman slipped in and sat near the back of the room. Her hair was hastily piled, and her lips had the bruised look of being thoroughly kissed. Aurienne lifted a brow at the prince's dalliance, who refused to meet her eyes.

The seer spoke. "You will have three questions, three answers. Hold the questions in your mind and breathe on the cards."

Arissabett leaned down and breathed on the deck.

Aurienne shuffled the cards until they warmed. "Ask your question."

"Will I find true love?"

Aurienne flipped over a card. The Sea usually meant change, rebirth, and transformation. Aurienne Saw waves, and the seafloor covered in shipwrecks and treasure. The meaning eluded her, yet a word tumbled from her lips as if she knew the answer instinctively.

"Yes."

Princess Arissabett squealed, and the other ladies squealed loudly with her.

"*Of course* you will. You've already found him. Prince Donovan is positively dreamy," a lady cooed.

Aurienne did not believe that for a moment, but she retained her serene mask.

"I'm so jealous!" another squeaked.

The red-haired girl just squirmed.

"Ask," Aurienne said.

"Will I become a powerful queen?"

Aurienne flipped the card. The Siren. Seduction. Painful endings and more painful transformation. Trickery. The card changed—the ink transforming into a sinking crown, then glittering gems, and finally, a burning castle. The ink reformed, showing the princess wearing a glittering golden gown, sinking before reverting. She'd become a queen, but it would cost her everything.

The Siren splashed its tail at Aurienne, spraying ink onto her palm and staining her skin. She glared at the card.

"Yes." Aurienne tried to smile, caught between securing a potential ally for the summit and revealing the full truth of her visions.

More squeals.

"Ask the next question."

"Will I live a long life?"

She flipped the card. The Nightmare. Anxiety, grief, depression. She Saw bruises on the Princess's arms. She Saw the princess being strangled by obsidian flames. She quickly tucked it back into the deck.

"What did it say?"

"It gave no answer," Aurienne lied.

"What does that mean?" the princess asked, concerned.

"I recently received wise advice from a witch," Aurienne said. "Instead of asking a question, I'll let the cards tell me what they want. I will draw six cards. Six is balance. The four cardinal directions plus sky and earth. It is the six-sided star. It is the number of eyes on the faces of the Triple Goddess."

Aurienne shuffled until the cards warmed. She placed six cards on the table and flipped them. A vision came.

Smiling skulls underwater.
Sea serpents and gold on the ocean floor.
Floating corpses.
Ripping teeth. Screams.
Darkness. Spirits. Curses.

Aurienne Saw the princess somehow living forever. She Saw an end and a beginning. It was a fate that could not be changed.

"You will get your heart's desire," Aurienne said.

The girls applauded, and Princess Arissabett blushed. Saryll and Kassia began doing readings for the rest of the girls. The ladies gathered around their cards eagerly, leaving Aurienne alone with the princess.

Aurienne gently took Arissabett's wrist, tasting the blood rolling down the back of her throat from the too-frequent visions. "Your fate is a dark and winding road. When you decide what you want, do not be afraid to take it. It will be yours, but the road to your fate is lined with pain, death, and betrayal. Trust only your own heart."

Arissabett swallowed fearfully.

Wynds of Change

Chapter Fourteen

From tower heights a princess falls,
From murky depths a siren calls.

— High Seer Aurienne Azarrah, prophetic
vision.

1152 N.T.C. The city of Wynds, Wyndsel.

Copper doors separated Theo from the throne room, and he stood fidgeting with the purple velvet cords on his sleeves. It was time to make his request of the king. Sweat pooled under his arms and down his back. His throat constricted, and his stomach flipped. He'd spent half the morning with Adonis practicing his speech. Adonis had only laughed at him twice, so that was hopeful. Theo groaned and took steadying breaths. Even the guild's final exams hadn't been this nerve-wracking.

Aurienne turned the corner, once again looking imposing, intimidating, and divine. Theo's mind drifted back to his first reading in

Avyllon when she was freshly bathed and without paint or jewelry, when she'd licked the blood from his palm. He thought about her dancing wildly under the night sky. She was striking as the High Seer, but underneath the adornments, *Aurienne* was exquisite. Theo pushed those thoughts from his mind. It was never going to happen, and in moments, he would ask the question that all their futures depended on.

The doors opened.

The urge to vomit nearly sent Theo running away, but instead, he and Aurienne strode in together. They stopped in front of the throne, and he bowed. The room was packed full of onlookers. So many people, so many eyes all on him. Hungry for him to embarrass himself.

Coldforges.

"High Seer and regent of Avyllon, you have come to make a request," the king said.

Theo cleared his throat, and every eye landed upon him. "Your Majesty, the High Seer has seen that *I* shall make the request."

"You?" The nobles laughed and tittered.

Prince Donovan chuckled and looked to Princess Arissabett, who was staring out the window at the softly chiming sea glass and did not notice.

Theo's face grew hot. His head felt a little dizzy from the nerves, and the room started to swim. He sweated through his formal clothes —too tight and stuffy. The walls were closing in, but Theo fought it, and spoke in a shaky voice.

"Your Majesty, I am no one. Untitled. Without lands. It is not my place to address kings. You are right," Theo said.

The king's face relaxed slightly.

"If not for the Goddess' will, I would not be here."

"We do not recognize your Goddess," Prince Donovan sneered.

The king cast a glare at the prince.

"But she Sees you." Theo's mouth was full of cotton. His breath felt shaky. He wet his lips and tried to steady his voice. "The Goddess Sees all. Twenty-six years ago, she predicted the Darkling War. She gave us the prophecy as a warning that we might prepare, and She showed our High Seer at the Rite that war would be upon us this year. The time for preparations is over. You are a man of action. I have seen that even just last night. We ask that you join us in a summit at the next full moon in Avyllon. We believe Emperor Rexil of Demorra intends conquest, no matter what he promises. If the nations don't come together, we will all fall."

Silence.

The king began to laugh. It was tinny and rattled in his throat. His shoulders bounced as a thin smile spread.

Theo's stomach flipped into a knot, and he wondered if he might spill the contents of breakfast. His throat constricted, and it was difficult to breathe. Humiliation coated him like heavy mud. He chanced a glance toward Aurienne, who refused to meet his gaze.

"That old prophecy? No one believes it," the king laughed.

"The summit sounds like a trap," Prince Donovan spat.

That weasel. He'd promised to help.

Theo gritted his teeth and stared at the floor. The other nobles were laughing along with their king. He could barely bring himself to lift his head. This was worse than he ever imagined this going. He looked to Adonis. Adonis motioned for Theo to lift his chin.

"I say, is this a joke?" a noble asked.

"The Seven Forests and Titan Cliffs have been closed to outsiders for years. How does he expect to get them to a summit?"

"The Goddess Sees all? Ha!"

"I heard he's a blacksmith and a farmer. What does he know of prophecies and war?"

"I'm surprised he knew all those big words."

"The emperor's demands are fair. Why would we go to war when we could pay a minor tax?"

Each comment stung.

Theo looked to Aurienne once more, who flinched and winced at every comment and refused to meet his gaze. Deep sadness was written all over her painted face.

A surge of anger flared through Theo and reached its boiling point. He was not going to fail her, and he would not subject his family and neighbors to the cursed monsters she'd had seen. This entire trip, he'd endured all manner of humiliation. Blades were pointed at his throat. He had been mocked, jeered, and insulted. He had bowed and scraped and gritted his teeth. He endured it all.

Now, he was done.

He lifted his chin. "The Goddess Saw that I invite you. I have done so. If you decide to ignore her warnings, that will be *your* downfall. Your people will burn and fall to the monsters that come. Your throne room will be soaked in blood. Every single one of you will die horrible deaths as you scream for mercy after watching your families get ripped apart."

The nobles quieted and stared with open mouths. Clinking windchimes filled the silence.

"You all have seen what the Goddess is capable of. She saved your king," Theo said flatly. "Ignore her at your peril. The other leaders of Teridar *will* be at the summit. *I will ensure it.* If you decide not to come, you will be the only leader absent."

The king's face turned purple, and his lips curled into a snarl.

"I imagine you want to be in the room where decisions are made, Your Majesty." Theo bowed low and backed out of the room.

Before Theo left, he heard the king say, "I'll *consider* attending."

Theo stormed down the hall, feeling light-headed and dizzy. He pulled off his velvet jacket and the silk tie contraption around his neck. He leaned against a wall, panting.

What in the world had he just done?

"Good job, man!" Adonis exclaimed and clapped him on the back. "I didn't think you had it in you! But we should probably get on the road before that little outburst gets us a knife in the back."

Mathis passed Theo and said, "It was a calculated risk. Good job."

With the others gone, Aurienne stopped in front of Theo, though he could not bring himself to meet her gaze. He did not want to see what was there in case it broke him.

Aurienne gently took his chin in her fingers and turned his face toward her clouded eyes. Her expression wasn't what he expected. Hope.

"I Saw a thousand futures, but not this one," she said. "There was nothing left for you to do or say. You were trapped, and yet you did. You did it."

Then, Aurienne's lips pressed to Theo's. Her hands wrapped around his neck, and he was consumed by her. He pressed his hands into her vanilla-scented hair and kissed her like they were under a starry sky in the middle of the woods.

Aurienne pulled away and said, "I have asked you to do the impossible. It's not fair, but thank you."

Theo was out of breath and shaken to his core. No words came.

"Adonis is right. We need to leave. Everyone is waiting." Aurienne took Theo's hand.

Sentinels and staff waited by the wagons, their bags packed, and horses saddled. Their bags had been packed earlier that morning and loaded into wagons and onto horses. The travelers changed into suitable traveling attire. Saryll and Kassia were already mounted and waiting. Everyone was eager to leave. Theo helped Aurienne onto her horse before mounting his own.

The caravan made quick time out of the city, not wishing to overstay their welcome. They were soon through the city gates and out onto the road again. Theo glanced back at the cliff-side city and castle.

"Was it enough?" Theo asked Aurienne.

She stared off into the mountains. "We did all we could. I...See the emperor's wolf-faced gold filling King Jaekob's treasury. He has already made a deal. It may be too late, but we did what we could. If the others come, he will."

Wynds fell behind them like a terrible, wonderful dream as they followed the main road to the northern Way. Theo watched the city disappear as they returned to the trees' welcoming embrace and the barking of the fox. It'd been a lifetime since he left this forest.

FORTUNE AND DOOM
CHAPTER FIFTEEN

It's truth that became legend over millennia. All great stories are rooted in history.

— HIGH SEER AURIENNE AZARRAH, PROPHETIC VISION.

1152 N.T.C. The southern road between Avyllon and Wyndsel.

Morning came too quickly, and groans multiplied through their camp as they prepared for a long day's ride. Theo's body rebelled, dreading another day in the saddle after the brief reprieve in Wyndsel. Vines twisted and climbed around foreboding trees. The road weaved, and they passed only a handful of other travelers whose eyes paused on the royal banners of Avyllon and the crest of the temple of the Goddess. They stared in wonder at Aurienne, whispering and gossiping. Theo smiled to himself at their awe, and at Aurienne's kind words and blessings. She never turned a single one away.

Midday arrived, and scouting sentinels located a trail to a stream for the horses. Theo noticed Aurienne staring off into the trees and nudged his horse to catch up with her.

"Aurienne," he said.

She blinked several times and looked at him blankly. A cord of worry wrapped around his chest. This happened a lot.

Theo gave her a gentle smile. "We're stopping to rest and water the horses."

"Oh."

She dabbed a trickle of blood from the corner of her mouth and wiped it on her black sleeves before dismounting and wandering away.

Theo frowned but said nothing. He finished watering and rubbing down the horse, sneaking it a handful of grains and an apple from his personal bags before leaving it to graze. By the time he returned to the camp, their chef had cooked a lunch of spiced rabbit stew over a small campfire, and it melted on Theo's tongue, banishing the hunger.

As Theo shoveled stew into his mouth, he noticed Adonis and Mathis crouching over a fire several feet away. Mathis shaped a marble-sized bit of flame and spun his finger, causing it to orbit. Theo watched, entranced, and a bite of stew slipped from his mouth.

Adonis attempted to copy the skill. He called forth the marble of flame, but as soon as it started to spin, it shot into the trees. Adonis cursed and jumped to put it out. He tried it several more times before finally storming away. As he disappeared into the tree line, Mathis shook his head. Theo approached.

"He would be a fine sorcerer," Mathis said. "I believe he will be one day. He has the gift, but he often lacks the focus. He is more interested in understanding advanced applications rather than mastering basic skills. Even more so, he is interested in doing anything other than studying. But his mind is tuned to magic. He could be great."

"I didn't know sorcerers could control flame like *that*," Theo said.

"Only small amounts," Mathis said. "The erudite tomes provide tutelage to those touched with the gift of sorcery. Controlling flame is a basic skill that assists us in our alchemy, tonics, and other processes."

"Controlling flame is a *basic* skill?"

"Some of us have been able to control as much as a handful, but it is not the main aim of our studies, nor is it where our talents lie. Such tasks must be mastered all the same. I thought that this trip would provide Adonis with more motivation to focus on practical application, but it has not. He has yet to even master making firewater, which is a prerequisite of alchemy. Yet, there are advanced seventh-year tasks he can complete easily, even though he's only in his fifth year."

"It's easy to want to get to the end when you're in the middle of it. What else can alchemy do?" Theo asked.

"Alchemy can make metal stronger than normal. It can create materials that do not exist in nature. It can imbue weapons with magical properties. Alchemy was even the origins of the forge."

Theo's ears immediately perked up at the potential smithing applications.

"We can also make medicinal tonics," Mathis said. "Much of our study into gravity created the aqueducts and plumbing systems for the city and villages. It allowed us to transport vast blocks of stone to build our walls. Many of the advancements we have are due to the studies and efforts of sorcerers."

"I had no idea," Theo said.

"The engineers are working to create long chains of carriages that transport people quickly across the city, powered on steam. They are exploring other methodologies, like magnets, hydraulic power, chemical reactions, and others. A combination of steam and magnets seems the most promising."

"Are they really?"

"They are," the sorcerer continued. "I hear you have recently been admitted into the blacksmith guild. Would you like to discuss metallurgy? Titan ore, perhaps? Sorcerers have been forging it for centuries, taking advantage of its magical properties. It makes the strongest blades and can be imbued with magic runes."

Theo grinned, but his smile faded. "I would love that. But first, could we talk more about royal etiquette?"

Mathis nodded.

Theo learned about forging magic, metallurgy, and royal etiquette until his brain was fit to burst.

The hour of rest passed quickly, and they were soon packing up the horses to ride until nightfall. Fading sunlight glistened off distant lakes, and beyond the mountains, the low sound of waves crashed against the beach. Every so often, the hills flattened, and the sight of the endless ocean filled the horizon. The Wyndsel armada could be seen floating in the bays with warships painted turquoise and black with siren figureheads.

The Way was only another day's ride from the city of Wynds and would reduce their travel to Rodarri by almost a week—thank the Goddess. Theo found himself imagining what the Way looked like and how it worked. He'd heard stories, but the stories were so varied he wasn't sure what to believe.

He hadn't realized how much magic existed in the world, and wondered how much more he'd encounter before the trip was through.

A faint humming drew Aurienne from her meditation. She followed the sound and found Theo rubbing down his horse after another long ride, humming to himself. The tune was familiar yet elusive—a story she had heard before but could not remember.

"Theo, what are you singing?"

He paused his work and tilted his head. "A rope-skipping song I heard at the foretelling. It's from monster stories and fairy tales."

"Can you tell it to me?"

"I don't remember the exact order, but I can try," he said.

As he recited the rhyme, the song filled Aurienne's mind, every line showing her new images.

> *Stars light in cursed blade.*
> *Souls of beasts and monsters weighed.*
> *Evil hides and darkness dies.*
> *Shadows rise as grim falls.*
> *Death to one, death to all.*

Aurienne Saw a figure carrying a vast blade made of starlight. The figure held a scale, weighing the hearts of beasts and judging them. Souls found wanting were destroyed. A sword strike rang out in the abyss, and screaming beasts were destroyed. The wraith held the cards of Life and Death in the scales of justice, which leaned one way and then the other. Echoing footsteps.

Then the cards fell.

"Grimfall," Aurienne whispered.

"Grimfall? The bedtime story?" Theo asked. "It's just a legend. A story that parents tell children to keep them in bed."

She shook her head. "It's not. It's truth that became legend over millennia. All great stories are rooted in history."

Theo's brows shot up. "Did you see the Grimfall?"

Step.

Step.

Step.

Always those steps in her mind leading toward Hallohaim, toward the date they must have the summit.

"Grimfall approaches." The words were only half her own, but she knew the truth of them all the same. The Grimfall legend would somehow tip the scales of fate. She shuddered.

Theo reached out to steady her.

"Wait," she said.

Recollection striking, Aurienne reached into her bag for her cards with shaking hands, then flipped through them until she found the card she was looking for. Grimfall.

Theo peered over her shoulder. The hooded figure on the card faced away, carrying a massive sword half their height that glittered with gold dust and dark ink. The figure turned to look over its shoulder with a glint of fang and stilled.

"I'll never get used to that," Theo said.

Suddenly exhausted, Aurienne slumped from the effort of the readings and vision. She placed her head in her hands and rubbed her pounding temples. Her headache mounted. The visions were coming so fast lately. Theo was like a beacon for them.

"Are you okay?" he asked.

Aurienne pressed her painted fingertips into her temples for a moment longer before standing. She would not let him see her weakness or the toll that the visions were taking on her. She was already asking too much of him by bringing him on this trip and making him stand before kings to request their help. He spent day and night preparing in spite of his fears and doubts, yet never complained. She asked too much and knew in her heart she'd have to ask for much more. The least she could do was be strong for him.

"I'm not used to this much travel," she lied.

"It's taken some getting used to," Theo said lightly.

"I have some matters to settle before we depart again for the day," she said tiredly. "Perhaps you can practice your speech with Mathis again? It does his old heart good to be useful, especially since Adonis does not appreciate him enough."

Theo took the cue and left her alone. Aurienne meandered into the trees to take care of personal needs. Her head throbbed, as it had on and off for days. Feeling something wet on her face, she reached up to find blood coming from her nose. She stared, hands shaking. Just a little while longer. A few more weeks—she could survive it. If her brain was bleeding, at least her deck might benefit from the power. She took her cards from her pack and pressed some of the blood in. Twigs snapped behind her, and she quickly wiped the blood from her face and returned her cards to the spelled box.

She exited the trees and passed Saryll. Saryll's face was pinched, and she blocked the middle of the path.

"Are you alright?" Saryll asked.

Had Saryll noticed her bleeding? No one could know how bad it had gotten. This was her burden alone. And no one could help her anyways.

"A bit of a nosebleed from the air, but it'll be fine. I confess, I'm not used to this much travel," Aurienne lied.

"It is...taxing on us all," Saryll replied hesitantly.

Aurienne tried to keep the grimace off her face. She'd have to be careful that her sister seer would not notice the cost of the constant readings or the smudge on her aura from the necromancy. The moonwater ceremony Theo had stumbled upon earlier had not cleansed her soul as she had hoped. Aurienne wondered whether her stacking lies would stain her soul just like the angry spirits had. Saryll inclined her head respectfully and disappeared into the trees to take care of her own needs.

The caravan departed. Aurienne noticed the red-tipped fox lurking in the shadows and tossed it a piece of bread.

"Don't give away all your secrets," she chided.

It barked and might have grinned.

She stared at the road, head throbbing from hazy visions of danger at their next destination—worse than their last. With unsteady hands, she drew her deck, shuffled, and flipped a card. The Dead Queen. It promised spirits, curses, bloodshed, and betrayal. The queen figure twirled her long skirts and straightened her crown with a coy smile, and then she opened her mouth in a silent scream as her eyes and mouth bled black ink that splashed Aurienne's gown.

Aurienne flinched. She hoped they would all survive Rodarri.

Silver Eyes
Chapter Sixteen

When next we wake, we will not sleep again.

— *Journal of Queen Morgana Margot Lenore, 805 N.T.C.*

1152 N.T.C. Castle Rodarr, Rodarri.

Queensblood Rianne knelt on the worn stone floors before an adorned altar in the late hours of the night before the first touches of dawn warmed the skies.

"Queens be with me," Rianne prayed.

She placed her hands atop the altar among the bloodrose petals, strands of pearls, and loose rubies. She looked imploringly at the fresco of ascended queens. Every Queensblood queen was painted on the walls of this sanctuary and inlaid with pearls, wearing white sacrificial gowns, save for three who wore glittering black diamonds, three who returned to life—so the legends said. Nine hundred and ninety-nine queens ascended in the last thousand years. Three caught Rianne's attention: the three returned queens.

Queen Rebekkah returned in 72 N.T.C.

Queen Samantah returned in 344 N.T.C.

Queen Morgana returned in 802 N.T.C.

No queen had returned for three hundred and fifty years, long enough that some wondered whether they ever had.

"My faith is true. I accept my blessing and duty. I will ascend so that my blood may replenish the land. I've always known what was expected from me, and I do not shy away from it. I understand the importance of our sacrifice," she prayed and prayed.

She folded her hands together and closed her eyes. She pressed her hands against her forehead, pleading with the queens to ease the unrest in her soul.

"Life is precious and beautiful and difficult to let go of, but what comes next is so much better that we cannot mourn what we lose. I shall ascend or I shall return."

Rianne opened her eyes and looked to the paintings for guidance. As she scanned their faces for answers, one depiction caught her attention. Queen Rosalindt was painted in the corner, her likeness half-scratched and wiped away, missing some of her gems.

Still, she wore an angry scowl like armor.

In the painting, Queen Rosalindt screamed and fought against ropes as soldiers held her down and cut off her head. She lost her faith and no longer believed her death would protect Rodarri. She refused her ascension. Weeks later, Rodarri was invaded by the nation of Arryn on the continent of Caedryn. The kings and commanders forced her to ascend, but still, Arryn came. It was not until Queen Marialynn ascended after Rosalindt that Arryn's troops were pushed back across the sea. Rodarri had not been invaded since.

Tears burned in Rianne's eyes. She would not be like Rosalindt.

Rianne bowed her head again. "I will not lose faith. I will not lose conviction. I accept my duty."

Rianne.

Rianne stood. "Who's there?"

There was no answer.

Rianne swallowed and scanned the room. It was nearly empty, save for prayer cushions and candles along a few tables. Icicles of fear settled on her heart, and a weight settled upon her.

She knelt again and clasped her hands together until her knuckles turned white. "Queens be with me. My faith is true. I shall join the other blessed queens in protecting the land for our daughters. We are Queensblood, and our duty is great."

For hours she prayed until her knees were bruised, and her bones and joints ached. She prayed until morning brightened the skies, the sounds of life filled the castle, and light filtered in through the stained-glass windows.

She finally rose. Her legs protested, and she rubbed blood back into them. She chanced a look back at the painted queens, hoping that this terrible nightmare was over.

Later that morning, in a lavish and isolated courtyard surrounded by flowered pools and hanging silks, fear was taking root in the hearts of queens though they feared to show it. Dozens of queens milled about.

Rianne watched the shadows. The hair on the back of her neck prickled, like someone was watching her as well. She looked around from shadow to shadow, searching for monsters and spirits in them all, but saw nothing and no one out of place.

Several teenage cousins lounged beside a pool near Rianne, soaking in the sun. They chatted happily, though she heard only part of what they said.

"What are you going to wear to the banquet?"

"Is there another banquet? We just had one for the full moon a little over a week ago."

"The royal delegation from Avyllon is arriving unexpectedly, so

King Cavendar is throwing a ball for them. Avyllon has not officially visited in many years, so he's eager to show off. It's going to be the biggest party of the year," one exclaimed.

"Ooooo! How exciting!"

"What are we going to *wear*?"

"I want to look like a desert sunset. I want fabric so fine that it looks like sand floating across the dance floor."

"Sand? Ew. I want to look like a flowering pond. I want a blue gown dripping in sapphires and dyed paper flowers."

"I want a gown made from thousands of tiny crystals that looks like armor."

"What noble's eye are you going to catch looking like a warrior? I'm going to wear blood-red sheer fabric to catch a certain noble's eye."

"I want to look like morning mist, purple and white and ethereal."

"My gown will be made entirely of ribbons."

"I'll wear thousands of tiny butterflies."

"Let's hope the dressmakers can get all of this done in time!"

"What will you be wearing, Rianne?" Rianne's sister Jordyn asked.

Rianne tore her attention away from the shadows cast by the lush indoor planters.

"An off-the-shoulder dark blue silk-chiffon gown with purple and pink. It's darker around the heart and fades," Rianne answered.

"Oh! That sounds amazing. You always have the best dresses," the young Ella gushed.

"It's because she's the firstblood. She has to look amazing," Jordyn said dreamily.

"What do you want to look like? What is your inspiration?" Marta asked.

"A dark sunset. The sun sets on all things, especially us queens," Rianne said.

"Dreamy!" Jordyn sighed.

Rianne wondered if it was. The girls giggled and traded jewelry. They discussed hairstyles and shoes and makeup while Rianne warily surveyed the shimmering shadows in the crystalline indoor pools. A silver and red koi fish, imported from Caedryn, flitted away and hid under a bridge. Rianne narrowed her eyes, watching it anxiously. Rainbow birds of paradise flew through an open-air aviary full of lush plants and birdsong.

"Have you heard the rumors, Rianne? Do you know what King Cavendar and his commanders are plotting and scheming?" one of Rianne's younger cousins, Atley, asked conspiratorially.

"There is talk of an early ascension before Queen Vittoria's Day. A second one this year," another cousin finished.

Rianne glanced around the room to ensure that no one could hear this conversation. This was not the type of thing to talk about. Though no secret, it was irreverent.

"Yes, if there is war, an ascension may come. Where did you hear this?" Rianne asked, hiding all emotion.

"A young wife of one of the commanders said that her husband confided it to her," Atley said. "He said that the Emperor Rexil's movements and demands are making them nervous. The emperor conquered the whole continent without anyone realizing. All the nations of Teridar are nervous. War may come from outside or within, and they want to ensure victory. They may agree to the emperor's demands, but they want assurances of protection...from Queensblood."

The eight teenage queens around the circle gave Rianne a keen look.

"War calls for the greatest sacrifice," Jordyn said. "It's always the eldest daughter of the eldest daughter of our line, all the way back to Vittoria. But they cannot have Rianne."

"It's true," Marta said. "If they execute Rianne without a daughter, then the firstblood line ends. She's not an option. It must be someone else."

Rianne tried not to fidget. She took a deep breath and tried to steady herself. She didn't feel so much fear at a future ascension, rather she felt guilty because she couldn't protect them. It should be Rianne ascending, but without any daughters, she could not be the one. Other queens would have to ascend in her place until she bore several daughters to replenish their numbers.

Marta swallowed. "If Rianne won't ascend, who will it be? Who will be executed?"

A voice answered that caused all the girls to jump to their feet. Rianne's elderly Great Aunt Yllicea appeared from behind a dark gray stone pillar, rocking another queen's baby.

"It's not an execution," Yllicea snapped. "It's an honorable sacrifice. The ascension is a queen returning to the land from whence she came and dwelling forever in the land of the dead with the other fallen queens."

"Yes, Yllicea," the girls intoned.

"Yes," Rianne said, more slowly than the rest.

Yllicea frowned, and Rianne knew why. Ordinarily, Rianne would have been the first to defend the rituals. Yllicea nodded dismissal to the girls.

"Too much talk of death," Jordyn said to the others. "Why don't we all go spend some time in the wading pool? I think the peacocks might be awake."

Jordyn took Ella's hand and led the youngest girls over to a heated wading pool full of flower blossoms and fragrant oils.

Yllicea studied Rianne. "Is something wrong?"

Rianne picked at the glitter on her gown. *What could she possibly say? That she dreamed of terrible angry spirits, and she was terrified they were still watching her?*

"I didn't sleep well," she said instead.

"Worried about that Warbringer man of yours?"

"I think his curse is in check, for now."

"Then what troubles you?"

Rianne hesitated. She had never voiced a doubt about their fates.

It was sacrilege. It was disrespectful to the thousand queens who had died for them. She never had a reason to before last night.

"Why is there an ascension every year?" Rianne asked carefully. "Surely, ample ascended queens are protecting the land to not need them so often. We surely cannot require two in a year in any case."

Yllicea frowned. "Who said there would be two?"

"Atley heard the king is going to request a second ascension soon."

"The eldest surviving Queensblood, which would be me, decides who ascends and when. The king has no say."

"He could request a second."

"We can of course decline unless we feel the gods and queens deign it."

Rianne dug her fingers into the glitter. "He will have the support of his commanders. What if we can't say no?"

"If we need to have a second ascension, then we will have a second," Yllicea said. "It is our sacred duty. We bear it so the people don't have to, just like Queen Vittoria and all that followed."

"I bet she didn't die just so that the king could sacrifice her child and her child's child, and her sisters and cousins in the same way years later," Rianne murmured before she realized what she was saying.

Rianne's eyes widened. *What had possessed her?* Those words had tumbled unnaturally in her mouth, as if they came from somewhere else or someone else.

"Rianne!" Yllicea hissed.

Rianne's cheeks burned.

Yllicea quietly said, "If a queen does not believe in her duty when she went to the...to ascend, her blood may not adequately protect the land. You remember the teachings about Queen Rosalindt six hundred years ago?"

"You don't have to tell me," Rianne snapped. "At least you lived well into your seventies before your time came. I'm likely to go after I have my second daughter, so the line continues."

Yllicea looked like she had been slapped. She avoided Rianne's eyes and arranged the blankets around the baby in her arms.

Rianne regretted her words immediately. She was tired. She had not fallen back asleep after the terrible nightmare. Her brain was overfull and hazy, and she did not mean the things she was saying. *Probably.*

"I'll be the next to ascend. I'm the oldest, so it will be my honor to take my place among the queens," Yllicea replied.

Rianne froze as Yllicea's words deflated her arguments. She fiddled with the folds of her gown. "I'm sorry. I don't know what I'm saying."

"Where is this coming from?" Yllicea asked, rocking the sleeping babe.

Rianne sighed. It was pointless. Yllicea was right. They had their duty. Rianne had known this since she was a child. They had a blessed purpose, to protect the entire nation. Keeping it safe was worth the cost. Besides, many queens lived long into their old age, and everyone had to die sometime. It might as well be in service to their land. Rianne knew this. So why was her certainty slipping away?

"You and your Warbringer are trying for a child, aren't you?"

"Yes," Rianne answered.

"Soon enough, you'll have a little one of your own, and it will ease these thoughts," Yllicea said with a gentle pat.

Or root them deeper.

"The withering sickness may have robbed my ability."

"Trust in the Queens." Yllicea handed Rianne the cooing baby.

Rianne's heart melted at the peacefully sleeping babe. She brushed her fingers against her cousin's cheek. The baby made a soft squeaky sleeping noise and nestled into the blankets against her. Rianne pressed a soft kiss to the tender forehead. The spirits whispered to her.

Would you sacrifice this child?

Would you have her head cut from her shoulders and
her body thrown to the pit?
Could you sacrifice your own child?

Rianne swallowed her scream at the last moment. Desperate, she looked around to the other milling queens, but none seemed bothered. They heard nothing. Rianne turned to face the wall so no one would see the tears dampening her cheeks. She choked on a sob and held the precious baby close to her chest.

Rianne waited for the tears to dry, determined to find answers. A hot, fiery ball of rage was building in her chest. She returned the baby to her doting mother and stormed toward the Courtyard of Queens. Guards patrolled the halls outside, as the queens were not allowed out of their wing without an armed escort, but Rianne slipped past unnoticed through a hidden door and passageway.

Suppressing a shudder, she stomped out into the arena, past the executioner's block, and toward the ravine. Dry crimson dust coated her slippers and skirts.

At the edge, Rianne halted and placed her hands on her hips.

"What do you want?" she screamed.

She waited. No response. All was still. All was silent. Not even the wind whistled. Rianne peered into the ravine but saw only darkness, as if the chasm swallowed the sunlight. Rianne angrily kicked a pebble over the edge and waited for the sound. Nothing. She didn't hear the pebble land. It was just as painfully quiet as the dream she remembered; the dream she hoped wasn't real.

"I'm here. I'm listening. Speak now or leave me in peace," Rianne demanded.

Silence met her.

"If you won't tell me what you want, leave me alone," Rianne said.

She waited for any sign of life, any response, anything. She waited for grating whispers. None came. Rianne released a breathy sigh of relief. It was just a bad dream and a tired mind.

"I must be losing my mind," she whispered to herself.

Rianne turned on her heel and retreated out of the courtyard. If she had remained a few seconds more, she would have heard the pebble finally bounce at the bottom of the ravine and come to rest.

Several pairs of silver eyes opened in the dark.

A Warbringer's Curse

Chapter Seventeen

Violence and death will be all you know. You'll kill and kill and kill. It will be as natural as breathing, and one day you'll go mad.

— Grimfall.

1152 N.T.C. Castle Rodarr, Rodarri.

Castle Rodarr's military training ring was in full use. The sands had already devoured offerings of blood from the castle guards and army units stationed at the nearby base. Rhydian Redbrooke swung his wooden practice sword at his opponent with enough force to make the wood creak. He grinned, ducked a thrust from a second opponent, and swung at the third opponent before kicking the first. The three men panted, but they exchanged a glance and lunged for him together.

It's still not a fair fight—for them.

A dozen men armed to the teeth watched the sparring match, hands never leaving their hilts. Another three stood inside the ring in case Rhydian succumbed to his Warbringer curse and lost control, becoming a mindless berserker that destroyed all in his path. Rhydian towered over them, most hardly coming up to his chin. He nearly grinned to himself, feeling his blood sing. The whole lot of them would be hard-pressed to best him.

Parrying a slice, he redirected the momentum into a chopping sweep at his opponent's collarbone. Failing to block, the man's hand burst open, and he lost the sword before falling. The man crawled away as another took his place. Rhydian spun, blocked, and snaked his wooden sword out to spear a man in the leather pads. He stumbled back as a third soldier attacked Rhydian with a complex sequence that Rhydian had memorized when he was eleven. The three men lay in the dust, coughing and holding up their hands in defeat.

Rhydian backed away, stuffing the violent urges down his throat and away from his head. The men dispersed.

The king clapped and approached the ring. "Excellent! Got to keep my Warbringer in fighting shape—and sane! How're you feeling, my boy?"

Rhydian gritted his teeth and forced a pleasant look on his face. The cringing expressions of the other guards told him he failed.

"Fine, sir."

"Good show," the king said. "Nice form. Perhaps I should have you put on a show for the Avyllon delegation."

A snarl curled at Rhydian's mouth, which he fought to keep at bay. The king might as well pat his head like the good dog he was. Rhydian tried to keep his eyes from narrowing and forced his fist to loosen around the sword.

"Avyllon, sir?"

"Yes." The king clasped his hands over his belly. "They should be arriving later today. I received word by raven, and the High Seer is nothing if not punctual. She may have her Sight, but I have you and the Queensblood."

Rhydian clenched his jaw but nodded.

"Be ready for the banquet later," the king said. "I can show off my personal Warbringer. That'll remind them who they're dealing with."

The king strolled away. Rhydian glared at the bloody sand, pacing.

Kingshit coward. Bleeding gods, how long must I put up with that rutting worm?

Snarling, Rhydian slipped into a fighting stance and motioned for four others to come at him. They attacked. He sidestepped the first attack and hit the second soldier once, twice, five times until the man crawled away, spitting out blood. Rhydian narrowly dodged a kick to the knee. He swept the offending man's foot, and the man landed on his back in the dust. Rhydian speared his wooden practice sword down at the man's chest, hard enough to bruise a rib.

His vision began to turn red as an undeniable rage clawed at his mind, begging to be released. If Rhydian succumbed and took a life, there would be no escape. He would go mad within days and be gone —just like every man in his family. It would be so easy to cross that line. Humans were so fragile.

The cold bite of steel nicked his arm.

Tsk. Tsk. Breaking the rules. They're not supposed to use steel unless I lose control.

Rhydian slammed the butt of his sword into the man's face, breaking his nose. He dodged another blow and chopped at the man. He crushed the man against the railing before tossing him out of the ring. Rhydian turned and transitioned into a more fluid style.

Ting. Ting. Ting.

Four more stepped into the ring. Rhydian snarled, grinning. Soon, he'd coat the dirt with their blood and crush their bones beneath his boot. He launched and beat them back. Bodies would pile up in this arena, a mountain of death for him to preside over. His thoughts blurred together in a sea of red. He'd paint the world red, starting with these men.

Time to die.

He bore down on one man who scrambled away in the dirt.

Rhydian's limbs tingled in anticipation of the kill as he basked in the hot sun. Fingers itching for cold steel, he'd abandoned his wooden sword and claimed one of their steel swords to ease the ache in his death-starved hands. Rhydian hunted his prey across the ring and raised his blade to deliver a finishing blow. The first of many.

"Rhydian," a musical voice called from outside the ring.

He slowed his advance on the coughing man, muscles locking as he fought the whispers. A small voice fought through the bubbling wall of bloodlust.

"Rhydian, stop."

Peace like soothing waters rushed down his skin, flooding his heart.

That voice meant flower petals, bubbling wine, and long slow kisses. It meant sunshine and bare feet in clear water. It was disappearing for hours in tall grasses and picnics atop thick wool blankets. It meant love letters and slow dancing under the stars.

Rianne.

The red mist started to clear from his vision. He turned from his opponent with great difficulty, feeling like he was standing waist-deep in thick mud, such was the effort to keep himself from finishing the man. Rhydian's arms shook from the effort, and his face twitched. Tossing his head side to side, he cleared the red fog from his vision. His hammering heart slowed at the sight of her.

Rianne leaned primly against the wooden posts of the training ring. She daintily placed her small hands on the railing and pressed up on her toes to see inside. Her cheeks and lips were rosy, and her glistening blue eyes reflected the afternoon sun.

Rhydian tossed his sword in the rack and smirked at the guards sheathing their steel swords. They watched him warily as he took a long swig of water to finish regaining his composure. *That was too close.*

"The ring is yours," Rhydian spat.

He hopped the fence and picked Rianne up. He swung her around until her full skirts swept a wide circle. His hands touched together around her small waist. She giggled and threw her head back to catch the wind. He swung her in another circle before setting her down lightly.

Her hands pressed against his chest, and she didn't appear to mind the sweat dripping off him. He leaned down to kiss her, feeling her soft skin beneath his lips. She tasted like roses and peaches, and she melted against him. Gods, how he loved her. He leaned over to snatch his shirt off the post and drag it back on. He pushed his hand through his damp, shaggy curls—wrapping it into a short tail atop his head.

"I didn't expect to see you until my guard shift later today," Rhydian said.

"Someone sent for me." She glanced at the pale soldiers. "Apparently, you were having a little too much fun out there."

Rhydian shot a guarded glance back at the other soldiers. The other men averted their eyes and pretended not to see Rhydian and Rianne together. The last man that had commented on Rianne ended up in the hospital for four months, and Rhydian nearly unleashed his curse. Rhydian was been banned from the training ring for three months, but when he was permitted by the king to return, the others were far more careful with their words.

Rianne cupped his chin, drawing his attention back to her. "It's good that someone is watching out for you. I might not always be around to help you. You might need to find another calming measure."

Rhydian kissed her again. "That will never happen. If it does, I'll be long mad and gone, so it won't matter." Rhydian pulled her against his chest and lifted her so their eyes were nearly even. "There is no way I'll live without you."

Rianne's smile dazzled him and made him feel faint. She pressed her lips against his and wound her hands into his hair.

Rianne breathed against his lips, "Should we do that in front of the others?"

"They know better than to say anything," he said. "Besides, what are they going to do? Kill us sooner? They can't. You have your duties, and they're just waiting for me to go mad. The king wants to put that off as long as possible so he can keep me as his secret weapon —as his pet."

Rianne chuckled. "I suppose you're right."

He set her down again and took her hand gently, pulling her toward the gardens. They turned the corner into the gardens, and Rhydian kissed her again.

He murmured, "If my time in the world has to be short, I want every second of it with you."

Rianne dazzled him with another of those smiles. "I'll die happy knowing I spent every second I could loving you. We have some time to kill before the Avyllon delegation arrives, and I could think of a few ways I'd like to spend it." A blush crept into her rosy cheeks.

Her hand was in his dragging him deep into the gardens, and he chased her with a laugh. When he caught her, he kissed her deeply and dragged his rough fingers across her soft skin, pulling giggles from her lips. He unlaced her sapphire gown, and it dropped to the grass. She had unlaced his pants at the same time and clawed his shirt over his head. They rolled in the grass, hardly coming up for air as the sun sank in the sky.

Much later, they lounged on a blanket in the grass surrounded by the high hedges of the floral garden. The lush blooms painted the gardens with splashes of color until every inch burst. Any thought of violence or urges of destruction long fled Rhydian's mind, and his hands were still, no longer itching for steel. His heart thrummed in a slow, steady pace.

Rianne lazily twisted flowers into a flower crown. Rhydian found himself tracing circles on her thigh with his fingertips.

"I love you. I wish all our days were like this," Rianne said.

"Nothing would make me happier than having a future with you," he said.

Rianne played with the dark brown locks of his hair. "Maybe I want a future too."

“You do?”

“If only it could last,” she mused.

Rhydian sat straight up as his heart skipped a beat, then beat twice as fast, then skipped another beat. It might burst with the hope she’d given him. He exhaled a slow breath to combat the nervous jitters racing down his neck.

“What if we left?” he said. “I can bring you home to my mother. We can bring your sister and the other queens. Around you, my curse could stay dormant. Let’s have all our days be like today.”

He licked his lips. It was an argument they had had before—so many times. Rhydian almost knew better than to bring it up again, but if she was at all open to it, he had to try.

“My blood protects the land,” Rianne said quietly.

Rhydian crushed a wildflower in his palm. “Do you really believe that? Do you really think it makes any difference? The land has had its fill of our blood.”

Rianne hesitated—she had never hesitated before. Rhydian held his breath.

“You’ll think about it?” he asked.

Rianne nodded.

“What changed your mind?”

“I don’t want my daughters to grow up afraid. I don’t want them to live like I have, like Jordyn has—like all of them have. And...I saw something,” she said.

His veins filled with ice. “What?”

“I-I had a dream,” she stammered. “But it wasn’t a dream. It was so real, and then I woke up covered in dirt. So much dirt like I had dug myself out of a grave, and it was still there.”

He placed his hands on her shoulders. “Slow down. What happened?”

“I had a dream I was at the Courtyard of Queens. There were angry spirits whispering terrible things. I woke up in my bed, and dirt coated my hands and feet. I thought I heard spirits when I prayed, and then in the chapel, I heard them again.”

"What do you think it means?"

She bit her lip, eyes watering—and he wanted to murder anyone that caused her pain. If she didn't believe in her duty here, he'd have stolen her away long ago.

"I don't know," she said. "There is talk of another ascension soon and talk of war from this new Emperor Rexil. Now the High Seer of Avyllon notifies King Cavendar of a surprise visit, all around the time that I start seeing things. It all seems too much of a coincidence."

"Could it be stress? You've...never heard spirits before."

Rianne nodded.

Rhydian's jaw ticked. "After the Avyllon delegation leaves, I can take you away from here. I can take all of you away. Promise me you'll think about it?"

She nodded. "Maybe...maybe I don't want to ascend. Maybe I want more."

His heart threatened to burst. Perhaps he could beat the odds after all. Maybe he could find a way to keep his curse at bay and have the family and life he never believed he could.

Some hope was better than none.

Mooncursed

Chapter Eighteen

In the times of the Shadow Wars, a shapeshifter killed a wolf and stole its pelt. The moon saw her favorite child murdered and cursed the shapeshifter.

— The Legend of the Mooncursed. Circa 7 N.T.C.

1152 N.T.C. The main road between Wyndsel and Rodarri.

Secrets whispered through the rustling white pine needles. Aurienne kneeled in a circle of candles, holding her hands up to the midday sun, having meditated to a near dream-like state. Indigo forget-me-nots and auburn star poppies swayed lazily underneath the dense canopy of oak trees. Birds chirped as the crimson and black fox crept through the meadow after a finch.

A voice whispered, "You are the great love story I want. I want it with you."

She almost recognized the voice, but it was too quiet and gone too quickly. Fate threads locked around it—someone would say it before the winter. Whoever said it and to whom, whenever it was said, it would surely come to pass. Carefully, she copied it to her journal. She cradled her divination deck and allowed the white candle smoke to waft over the cards to cleanse them. She shuffled and laid out six cards.

The High Seer.

The Dead Queen.

The Warbringer.

The Emperor.

The Wolf.

The Vampire.

The seer waved at the queen, who clawed the skin from her face, leaving only her skull. The Warbringer twirled a large sword, which reached out and gave Aurienne a paper cut, before turning to the queen. The emperor savagely grinned as fangs descended from his wide mouth and a crown of bones grew out of his forehead. The wolf disappeared into an inky smudge as the vampire unfurled its terrible wings on the next card. A third eye opened on the seer's forehead. The cards stilled.

Aurienne's nose started bleeding, and a headache immediately blossomed in her skull. Returning the cards to the box, she wiped the blood away and rubbed her temples. With her eyes half closed, her Sight opened. The stain whirled like a dark specter, always at the periphery of her vision.

They'd reach the Way tomorrow, and Rodarri the next day. After nearly being beset by the emperor's troops, Aurienne couldn't risk remaining on the roads. King Cavendar might be upset, but she'd written ahead—and he could hardly refuse.

Kassia stepped out of the trees just as Aurienne dabbed blood from her mouth. Aurienne quickly slid her hand into her lap. She'd been seen.

Kassia sat beside Aurienne in the toadstool clusters and handed her a steaming tea. "The headaches are worsening. Drink this. It will help. Is it the overuse of your gift, or something else that's causing the headaches and bleeding?"

"I don't know," Aurienne said. "But it doesn't matter. I know how to give us our best chance at salvation, and I must stay the course. Theo is the key."

Aurienne blew out the candles and began collecting them.

Kassia placed her hand on Aurienne's arm. "Your gift is taking too much from you."

Aurienne met her gaze, reading the words that Kassia dared not say. *You could die.*

Aurienne said, "I know, but I don't have a choice."

"Be careful," Kassia said.

"I would if I knew how. I can't stop the visions now," Aurienne said. "The events of the next three weeks will change the world forever. We are in the midst of a great transformation. These events are the ones that they will tell stories and sing songs about. These are the choices that will be remembered...if anyone is around to remember them."

Theo rode beside Adonis and Mathis as the caravan made quick time away from Wyndsel to Rodarri. They nearly reached the border of Wyndsel, where the Way would take them to just outside the main city of Rodarr. He was exhausted; even thinking about making a request of another king filled him with dread, but he dutifully prepared to keep his mind distracted.

"In Rodarri, King Edmunton Cavendar is called King Cavendar," Adonis said.

"But in Wyndsel, King Jaekob Juri is called King Jaekob," Theo said. "Why does one go by the last name and the other go by the first name?"

"Wyndsel values individual achievement, whereas Rodarri values bloodlines. The kings and queens of Rodarri have been the direct descendants in the same bloodline since the Shadow War one thousand one hundred fifty-two years ago. They pride themselves on it."

"What's the difference between the kings and the queens, and the Queensblood? They're not married?"

"Oh, gods no," Mathis interjected. "They don't want that crossover. The first King Edwardt Cavendar and first Queen Vittoria Lenore were said to be lovers, though no one can confirm. They could have been siblings or cousins. They might have been married. Or perhaps they did not even know one another. No one knows. The Kingsline are the direct descendants of the first king. The king has the real power and rules. The Queensblood..."

"What?"

"There are some barbaric customs in Rodarri you need to know about," Adonis answered.

"The Rodarri believe that the Queensblood line protects the land. Nearly every year since the Shadow Wars, they have performed an ascension ritual," Mathis said.

"Ascension?" Theo asked.

Mathis nodded. "They execute one of the queens every year by beheading. They believe that the blood of their queens, soaking into the ground from a willing sacrifice, will protect them from invasion."

Theo's stomach rolled. "They execute them? I know people are superstitious—the Rites your sister endures are an example—but that's insane. Why do they let this happen?"

Adonis flinched.

"Why does our seer allow herself to be burned, buried alive, or drowned?" Mathis interjected. "It's the same. The royal line of queens was selected a very long time ago for this responsibility. They not only believe it to be their duty, but that there is a chance one will return."

Theo glanced at the sorcerer. "Return?"

"Ancient stories say that sometimes an executed queen will come back to life," Mathis said.

"Surely the queens don't actually come back to life."

"The stories are pervasive, but they are also very old. It is hard to know what truly happened that long ago," Adonis said.

"They can't still do this," Theo said.

"Every year," Mathis answered. "In times of hardship, they would give the eldest daughter of the eldest daughter going back to the First Queen."

"They do it on Vittoria's Day, so there's no danger of it happening while we are there," Adonis said.

"That's not that comforting," Theo muttered.

"Most of the other customs and etiquette are the same," Mathis said. "Here, there is no Council of Wynds, but there are commanders. The commanders are blood relatives of the king, one or more places removed. The power is vested in the king, but all commanders vote on important matters."

Mathis continued, "There are some differences, though. Wyndsel is a coastal town with influences from the Arryn people. Their power is in their naval might and trade; they value strength. Rodarri is very different."

"How so?" Theo asked.

"Rodarri is...excess." Adonis scratched his head. "Everything is over the top. It's like a giant party there all the time. There's too much food, wine, and entertainment. No one throws a party like Rodarri. The clothes are intricate and unbelievable like they're made from magic. The gardens are immaculate. Everything is...loud and bright and colorful."

Theo grinned. "Sounds like your kind of place."

"I do enjoy a good party, but theirs are almost too much even for me," Adonis said.

"That's enough etiquette training for now, Adonis," Mathis scolded. "Let's get back to some of the alchemic transformations we've been discussing before it's time to go."

Adonis rolled his eyes. "We get to go on this trip once, and you keep making me study the same theorems. Let me enjoy this!"

"If you want to take your exams early, you need to study more," Mathis replied. "The day will come that you wish you'd learned this."

They wandered away until Theo could no longer hear Adonis' complaining.

He nudged his horse up to Aurienne. She tossed apple pieces to that little fox who'd found them once more.

"He likes you," Theo said.

Aurienne smiled and held out her hand to the creature. "He likes free food—if he's even a fox at all."

"What else would he be?"

"I have a sense this fox is more than he seems. Either way, I enjoy the company, and he enjoys a free meal."

Theo shook his head, not sure what to make of that. "We're nearly to Rodarri. Is there anything I should know?"

"There's much history that could prove useful," she said. "King Cavendar was once a great warrior. Though he had little chance to practice in battle during his peaceful reign, he hosted many a knights' tournament. He would always compete anonymously or under a false name to avoid the nobles being too afraid to strike him, or those who would use it as a chance to kill him. King Edmunton Cavendar went on to win dozens of tournaments in all events until the food, drink, and age caught up with him."

Theo considered the sort of man who wanted to be a warrior in times of peace and now had succumbed to opulence. He considered what sort of man cared more about appearance and honor than all else.

"What will we do after we leave Rodarri? The Seven Forests and Titan Cliffs are still closed, and we need them at the summit," Theo said.

"I sense our visit to Rodarri will illuminate our path," Aurienne said.

Theo found himself looking for words. The only thing he wanted to talk about was that second mind-blowing, world-shattering, life-changing kiss in Wynds. Theo knew he probably didn't want to hear what she'd say. Her readings were never wrong. She was not fated to find love in this life. She had told him as much. But then, why could he only think about what her lips would feel like on his? Why did thoughts of her consume every waking moment?

Theo said nothing, and they rode in silence for some time. Aurienne didn't seem to notice or mind the quiet. If she wasn't staring off into the distance, then she was feeding her little red fox friend. It barked at him. Theo caved and tossed it a piece of meat or two along the way.

Night fell, and Aurienne directed them to stop at a tavern. The caravan was thankful to have a night off from cooking and setting up tents, and of course, the town Aurienne selected had room for all of them among the many inns and houses. Everyone was audibly happy to have a real bed, a warm meal, and a cool drink.

They sat at crowded tables in a tavern with regular customers. Everyone had packed inside to get a glimpse of the High Seer of Avyllon, and she didn't disappoint. Aurienne emerged in full regalia, complete with golden jewelry and body paint. Saryll and Kassia had offered to do readings for the townsfolk to give Aurienne a chance to rest, but many people still requested blessings from the Triple Goddess' own hand. Aurienne gave blessings to all who asked, and as the evening wound down, she was finally left alone.

Theo brought her a cold bubbly cider in a large mug.

She gave him a warm smile. "Thank you."

Her fingers brushed his, and he nearly dropped the mug. Blood rushing through his veins prickled his skin and filled his head with indecent thoughts.

He swallowed. "Well, we might not be able to drink ourselves silly, but it's a decent start. Cheers."

He bumped his oversized mug against hers and guzzled half. To his surprise, she downed half right alongside him until both were gasping for air and coughing up cider bubbles. They laughed, cheered again, and then finished the mug. Theo collected two more full mugs, which the pair sipped quietly in the corner.

Live music started up, and some regular customers pulled Adonis up to do magic tricks. Saryll and Kassia swayed side by side in front of the fire. Mathis slept. Captain Laurier and Sentinel Kolten watched the room like hawks from their carefully selected position between the door and Aurienne. Kolten eventually joined a dart throwing competition.

Being this close to Aurienne, Theo nearly forgot the quest and prophecies and war. He wanted cozy nights in front of the fire, fingertips brushing, and quiet laughter. He wanted her.

"I See futures or pasts just like this but never thought I would experience it," she said. "I'm glad to have made this trip."

"Are you okay?" Theo asked.

"I did something, something with a cost, and I'm paying it. I'm getting used to the number of visions and readings, but there are still so many. I should be fine, though, I think." She glanced out a window to the velvet midnight sky.

I can't help her with magic, but maybe I can make her forget for a little while.

He asked, "Would you like to hear a story?"

She smiled. "That would be nice."

"Do you want to hear about the Golden Winged Warriors of the Lost Pass? Or maybe the legend of the Shadow Wars? Or do you want to hear the full story about Grimfall? Maybe about the Shadow of Heartspring again, or the Shadow's Hunter? Or we could hear about the Mooncursed Warriors?" Theo asked.

"Everyone knows the tale of the 'Shadow of Heartspring!'" a drunk passerby answered loudly.

"The man makes a deal to turn into a Shadow and kills his family," the barkeep said.

Another patron stood. "That's not how it ends! My mother was from Heartspring, and she says the Shadows saw their reflection and how monstrous they had become and locked themselves away in the mountain."

"They didn't lock themselves away. That can't be. If so, who did the Shadow's hunter track down and kill? No, the Shadows ran from their families, refusing to kill their own kin, and devoured all around until a hunter with blood of sunlight slayed them."

"Absurd!"

Several men began shoving one another jovially and spilling drink.

"What do you know!"

They were getting too close to Aurienne, so Theo stood and put himself between the men and her. He put his hands up and out calmly. One man lost his balance and fell backward. He bounced off Theo's chest.

"Oh, sorry, friend! Now aren't you just built like a house?" The man grinned and sat back down to continue arguing about the Shadow of Heartspring.

Aurienne sipped from her mug, hiding a grin.

Theo squinted. "You Saw that happen before it did?"

Aurienne smirked and took another slow draught.

"You knew I'd step in the way," he said.

"It was a possibility, and I wanted to give you the option. I try not to change outcomes when I can help it."

"How often does what people might do alter your opinion of them?"

"Sometimes," she said. "One of those men nearly started a fight just now. If I See enough of those potential futures, it could change what I think of a person."

He returned to his seat. "Do my futures change what you think of me?"

"No. So far, you're consistent with what you do. And what you think about doing or want to do."

Theo started to blush. "You See...the things I think about doing?"

"Sometimes." She grinned wider.

He blushed deeper, realizing what she meant. "Oh."

"Only the things that you might act on. It must be a potential choice you would make, not just think about."

"Oh. Okay," he said, feeling marginally better.

"I did enjoy our kiss on the road earlier, though."

"You... Our? What... I... But we didn't..."

"No. But you nearly did, and I Saw it."

"Well...I'm glad you enjoyed it, then? You're welcome."

She laughed. *Gods, that sound. Maybe I should kiss her.*

She chuckled. "It's a shame you can't See the things I thought about doing. Then you would be thanking me."

Her lips curled into a devious grin, and Theo swallowed. He wasn't sure what to say to that. He looked back, and she was staring off into the distance again, Seeing again. Concern rose in his gut.

He reached for her hand. "The visions are coming often?"

She didn't look at him as she replied, "Usually, I would have a handful a day. Many seers have one a month. Even a few a day would be quite a lot. Since the Rite, it's been near constant. It eventually takes a toll. But the visions are only coming because they're important; we have a single chance to succeed."

"Can I help?"

She squeezed his hand. "You are helping."

He squeezed back. She stared into the large crackling fireplace but did not let go of his hand. He refused to move even a fraction. Did she know she was still holding his hand? He hoped so. He hoped she meant to. His heart fluttered before settling into a natural rhythm and a sense of peace settled over him. He could spend every night like this. He was in trouble.

"Could you tell me about the Mooncursed soldiers? I haven't heard that one," Aurienne said distantly.

Theo leaned in. "Many years ago, in the times of the Shadow Wars, a shapeshifter killed a wolf and stole its pelt. The moon saw her favorite child murdered and cursed the shapeshifter..."

Theo told the story of the Mooncursed soldiers late into the night.

He finished, "If you hear a long low whistle, so low your ears bleed, and the stars fade and the fire goes out, run. It means the Mooncursed are upon you. The moon's grief was so strong that the curse spreads to any who are touched by the Mooncursed and survive."

"I See it," Aurienne said. "So many of these stories are rooted in truth."

"The best stories are."

He escorted Aurienne to her room and returned to his, where his sleep was uneasy.

The next morning, they departed the tavern and reached the Way, which looked nothing like what Theo had imagined. It was fifty feet high, like a tall slim doorway four men could easily walk shoulder to shoulder through. It was translucent, but there was an otherworldly iridescent light floating inside the open door.

Theo watched the Way. He'd never seen anything like it before and did not know if he would again. It was *magic*. All the lore, legends, and stories he had grown up hearing seemed plausible if such a structure existed in the world.

Mathis and Adonis worked to open it. Over an hour later, Adonis was still muttering and waving his hands. Theo was starting to pace. Staying in one place too long made him nervous. Images of soldiers in black armor with a howling wolf crest were at the front of his mind.

"Hellsdamn it!" Adonis cursed and kicked at rocks.

"Adonis, just try it again. Repeat the incantations as we practiced," Mathis said.

"It would help if you cleaned the doorway with moonwater and weeping ivy. It will make opening it easier," Kassia said.

"You know how to open Ways?" Mathis asked.

"No, but all energy and magic work better when they are free from interference," Kassia said.

"By all means then, Adonis could use the help," Mathis said.

"Hey!" Adonis protested.

"You just need to focus," Mathis said.

"We've been here for an hour. I've said the stupid incantation a hundred times!" Adonis snapped.

"Try again. This will be required in your apprenticeship test," Mathis said.

"Aurienne, any help?" Adonis insisted.

Aurienne shook her head.

"Saryll? Anything?" Adonis said curtly.

Saryll shook her head as well. Kassia glared at Adonis and squeezed Saryll's hand.

"Adonis..." Aurienne said gently.

Adonis clenched and unclenched his fists. "Sorry, I just... Sorry."

"Try again," Aurienne said.

Adonis shook his arms and began again.

Finally, Adonis managed to get the incantation timed perfectly with the hand gestures, and the door...shimmered. Opened. It was suddenly a clear path to the other side through a curtain of light and magic. Bubbles of light floated inside the Way. The colors inside were so bright that they were painful. Theo struggled to even comprehend what he saw.

"Don't linger in the Way, or you could get trapped," Mathis warned.

One by one, the caravan entered the portal.

Aurienne entered the Way, but before she could exit, a vision caught hold of her. Hordes of enemies surrounded four lonely pillars. The Eastern Pass collapsed in an avalanche. Creatures with leather wings and long fangs screamed through the skies. Major cities crumbled to dust.

A faceless figure picked up Aurienne's crown from the dirt before plunging the Sword of Souls into her heart. Her chest erupted in searing pain that sent her to her knees. Her soul started unraveling, and she no longer knew if she was in a vision or reality.

Aurienne screamed and screamed. The sword drove deeper into her chest, and her ribs cracked as her heart exploded. And then the footsteps returned.

Step. Step. Step.

She screamed again and fumbled around in the dark. The visions retreated, slowly fading to black as her eyes burned. Her fingers reached into the glacial emptiness. She could see nothing. Darkness descended on her, and there was no escape. Sinking into the heavy mire, she tried to run but couldn't lift her feet. She raised her hand, praying to the Goddess that someone would find her.

Someone grabbed her arm and yanked her out. When she finally came tumbling out of the Way, she realized that Mathis and Adonis were shouting frantically for her.

Theo was dragging her from the Way. "Are you okay?"

"Aurienne! Why did you stay in there?" Adonis yelled.

Theo's hand didn't leave her arm. "Aurienne, what happened?"

"A vision," Aurienne said weakly.

Aurienne checked her skin, but it was unmarked. Her insides still burned from the phantom pain. Her nose and mouth were bleeding, and she quickly wiped it away.

"Another vision came to you unbidden?" Saryll's brow pulled together.

Aurienne leaned against Theo to steady herself. She took long breaths before letting him go. She noticed he held on a second more before releasing her.

"That one was sent to me by someone. It was a warning," Aurienne said.

Saryll paled. "Who has the power to interfere with your Sight?"

"I don't know," Aurienne said. "The emperor may have a powerful seer or sorcerer at his disposal. I'm fine, we need to go."

What she didn't say was that she was afraid of whoever could send her such a terrible vision, and without her permission. Strange that it should happen as they entered the Ways. What could that mean?

The red fox dashed through the Way just as Mathis helped Adonis to close it. The fox sat outside Aurienne's reach as she rested until the caravan readied for the trip. Then the animal raced into the forest and disappeared.

Several hours later, the thick walls of the city of Rodarr came into view. In stark contrast to Wynds, the ramparts were draped in long colored banners fluttering in the wind like ribbons on a ballgown. Black thorny vines wrapped around the spires, dotted with blood-roses. These elegant trappings could not hide the dark truth at the root of this city. Aurienne's Sight showed her the blood oozing from the walls.

This was a city built on bones and death.

DEAD QUEENS
CHAPTER NINETEEN

Tell me your deepest secret.

— Journal of the High Seer Aurienne Azarrah.

1152 N.T.C. Castle Rodarr, Rodarri.

Castle Rodarr's spires reached upwards like bloodthirsty spear tips threatening the skies. Where Wynds maintained flat colorful stone blocks and intricately painted tiles, Castle Rodarr possessed stark gray walls that ended in deadly metal spires, overlooking abandoned ramparts and battlements entangled in black bloodrose vines. Stained glass windows, colorful banners, and glittering flags brought vitality to an otherwise ominous architecture. If not for the splash of color, the castle and city would have seemed utterly haunted.

A strangely chilly wind rippled the banners and called gooseflesh to Theo's skin as they entered the castle gates. He scanned the high windows, unable to shake the feeling of being watched.

The weary travelers were escorted through the castle to rooms readied for them in a vacant guest wing. Theo, Adonis, and Mathis were paired in a suite of rooms together, while Aurienne, Saryll, and Kassia took one across the hall. The rest were housed on the floor below.

"Please freshen up and come for an audience directly. Tonight, you may rest. Tomorrow a royal ball will be held in honor of the High Seer's visit," explained a butler in a starched red waistcoat.

The butler glanced at Theo and sighed. "King Cavendar shall receive you in two hours."

The butler left and closed the door. Theo rolled out his shoulders and removed his boots and jacket, then began unpacking his bags.

"Do you need any help?" an older woman asked behind him.

"Rutting moons—coldforges—rat-loving—" Theo exclaimed with a start.

Theo spun around to see the speaker and tripped on the strap of a bag. He tumbled over the luggage and landed hard on the floor. He scrambled to his feet and tried to straighten his rumpled clothing.

Where had she come from?

A woman bent over with age grinned a cunning toothy smile as if she were used to forming her mouth around sharp teeth, though hers were not. Her eyes gleamed like firelight reflected off newly forged knives. She folded her hands in front of her, waiting respectfully.

"Theo, are you okay?" Adonis popped his head out of the adjoining room.

"Hello, sir. I'm Rosalindt. Do you require any assistance unpacking your bags?" Her tone was soft though her expression was wicked.

"Uh, no, thank you," Adonis stuttered.

Unnaturally fast, she gestured around the room. "There are soap and fresh towels in the bathrooms and fresh bedding on the beds. Extra blankets are in the shared closet. Place any clothes you wish laundered in the hampers outside the room, and they shall be returned to you within six hours."

"Thank you," Theo said warily.

"Do let me know if you need anything else. I do hope your stay is...enlightening," she said.

Theo had battled wolves seeking to devour livestock while armed with nothing but a wooden staff, and yet this frail woman unnerved him more than he'd ever experienced in his life. "I will..."

"I have left some books in your room," she said. "A little light reading while you are here. I hope you enjoy. From the moment you walked into the castle, we could tell you looked like a kindred spirit."

"Thank you," Theo said and glanced where she had pointed.

Several very dusty leather-bound books lay in a neat pile on the desk. He turned back to Rosalindt, but she was gone.

"Wait. Where did she..." Theo trailed off.

Adonis's jaw fell open. "She was just here..."

Theo looked around. He had not heard the door open or close, and there was no sign of the housekeeper.

"Maybe there are staff doors we can't see?" Adonis said.

"Maybe." Theo suppressed a shudder.

After searching the room in vain for secret passages, he closed the door between his chamber and the suite's sitting room and peeled the dirty clothes from his sore, aching body. He stood under the hot water in the shower, feeling the miles drip away with the water. The plumbing was cruder than it was in Avyllon or even Wynds as the water pressure only trickled, but a hot shower was a hot shower. The steam rose in the room, and he soaked it into his flesh.

He gazed upward and noticed indoor lights behind glass. The lights pulsed softly, unlike flame. He would have to ask what they used to illuminate the castle. He wondered if Mathis knew.

Focus—it will soon be time to address the king.

Theo practiced what he'd say in the shower over and over until it was scratched into his mind like initials into a tree trunk, and he thought he'd never forget the words as long as he lived. His stomach felt like it was full of firewyrms that gnashed their teeth and lunged at one another. His chest was tight, as if a workhorse was sitting on it.

When he finally exited the shower and dressed, Adonis and Mathis were waiting in the sitting room. Adonis lounged on a chaise, sipping wine with his feet up. Mathis paced slowly, robes brushing the floor and bells jingling in his beard.

"Your speech sounded good," Adonis said with a grin.

Theo fiddled with the buttons on his shirt and glanced at the pulsing lighting fixtures. "What are those?"

"A bioluminescent moss or lichen that grows only here," Mathis said. "They call it Vittoria's Gift. There is a single tree, the Queen's Root, that it originates from. It's been studied at Rodarr University, but they're still not sure how it works. It just needs a little sunlight and occasional water. They lined the light fixtures in the castle and city with the moss, and it mostly eliminated the need for torches."

Adonis opened his mouth, but Mathis cut him off. "And no, they're not willing to share the moss with us even though we would only need a small sample to begin growing our own. It's sacrilege to take it as they believe it to be sacred, punishable by death."

Adonis grimaced and crossed his arms, muttering.

"I didn't even know such things existed," Theo said.

"The University of Avyllon is trying to gather information to share between the nations. It's making progress, but there is still so much more to do," Mathis said.

"Is there anything else I should know? Any final tips?" Theo asked.

"As long as you stay polite, they will," Adonis said.

"Strange for a place that executes its royal women every year," Theo muttered.

"Don't call the ascension an execution. That's about the worst thing you could do," Adonis said.

"Great," Theo said.

"Let's go over what you have to say one more time," Mathis said.

"It'll be fine. What's the worst that could happen?" Adonis smirked.

Aurienne donned the full High Seer regalia and painted her eyes and lips black and gold. She braided golden cords into her hair and placed a chest full of jewelry on her ankles, hands, neck, forearms, and ears. Here, clothing and ornamentation were signs of power. She must maintain her position in a room full of breathtakingly beautiful queens with little more to do than look the perfect picture of royalty.

Finally ready, Aurienne took her cards from her spelled box. Lorayne's advice was at the forefront of her mind. "Ask the cards what they want to tell you."

"Show me what you will," Aurienne said.

She drew six cards.

The Traveler.

The Dead Queen.

The Warbringer.

The Emperor.

The Road.

The Castle.

A drop of blood found her lips, and she quickly wiped it away. She looked in the mirror and fixed her face paint where it'd smudged.

Saryll and Kassia entered Aurienne's chamber. Saryll wore the white gown of a seer, which was covered in pearls and lace. She had darkened her eyes with kohl to highlight her cloudy stare. Kassia wore a green dress covered in real flowers, which she must have just sewn herself considering the freshness.

Aurienne noticed a few rogue flower petals were scattered across Saryll's gown, and Kassia's hair was slightly mussed. Blushing, Saryll noticed Aurienne's grin and quickly brushed the flowers off.

Saryll asked, "Did you See anything?"

"Whatever Wyndsel decides to do, Rodarri will follow. If the Seven Forests and Titan Cliffs attend, Wyndsel and Rodarri will come," Aurienne said.

"May I try a reading?" Kassia asked.

Aurienne nodded. Kassia took out her deck of divination cards and flipped three.

The King.

The Goddess.

The Wolf.

"Strange. Those cards should not go together. Maybe that suit is too new to be accurate," Kassia said.

"Too much is unknown. The Fates are trying to tell us something, but we do not understand," Aurienne said.

"Let me make you a tea. You will feel better," Kassia said.

Her mind wandered to Theo as she sipped Kassia's tea, missing the brush of his hand against hers as she took the cup. She'd grown used to his constant presence while traveling. She needed to create some distance.

I can't do this to him.

Theo, Adonis, and Mathis waited for the three women in the hallway. They strained against their starched shirts and tight pants, but none more than Mathis, who complained constantly about the ridiculousness of the clothing. The three turned as the door to the women's suite opened. Saryll and Kassia looked beautiful, but Theo's eyes were drawn immediately to Aurienne.

Theo forgot to breathe as she stopped in front of him. The dress was airy and cut low down the front, nearly to her navel. The high thigh slit showed the soft curve of her sun-dusted leg. She smiled, and Theo forgot his name.

"Are you ready?" Aurienne asked.

Theo offered her his arm, and his heart sang as she accepted.

Coldforges. He forgot what he was supposed to say to the king and quickly began to mentally repeat it until they approached the tall throne room doors. Two guards pushed open the receiving doors at their arrival.

"Now enters Aurienne Celestina Azarrah, High Seer of Avyllon, Regent and Guardian to the Crown Throne, Chosen Eye and Vassal of the Triple Goddess, Steward of the Temple at Avyllon, Flame-keeper and Historian," an announcer called out.

The Avyllon party entered the throne room with a handful of sentinels. All eyes fixed on Aurienne, who floated over the stone floor, looking more divine than mortal, and Theo now knew that it was by design. Every gown, every braid, and every stroke of paint was carefully selected for such occasions. Awe settled upon every face in the room.

Theo felt it mirrored on his own as he absorbed the opulent throne room. A tall golden throne stood on the elevated dais, covered in fist-sized gemstones. The room's walls were lined with tall columns swathed in luxurious colorful fabrics. Banners and flags covered the remaining walls. Between each column, dazzling stained glass designs reflected the light into rainbow prisms. Near the ceiling, inset light fixtures of clouded Vittoria's Gift glowed. The illuminated moss pulsed behind the fogged glass as if to the beat of a heart, and he wondered if anyone else noticed the faint rhythm.

"Accompanying the High Seer are her brother, the apprentice sorcerer Adonis Zakar Azarrah, Mathis Mivvem Kaster, and her companions Triple Goddess seer Saryll Aymdeo, Kassia Lora Guara, and Atheodoren Willem Thatcher."

The group stopped at the foot of the dais and bowed or curtsied to the elevated king.

"His Majesty, King Edmunton Eduard Cavender III, twenty-second King of Rodarri, Kingsblood and Protector of the Land, Guardian of the Queensblood, direct descendent of the First King Eduardt Arthur Henry Cavendar, and Lord of Castle Rodarr receives the procession of Avyllon with his wife Queen Portia Cavendar. Queensblood Rianne Charlotte Lenore, Queensblood of Rodarri, eldest daughter of the eldest daughter of the first Queen Vittoria also receives the guests," the announcer said.

The courtiers were impossibly even more adorned than the room. The king wore thick, red fur robes covered in heavy gold plates and medals. His crown was tall, golden, and gleamed in the light. His swollen fingers were covered in gem-encrusted rings. Where the king of Wyndsel was thin and lean in his middle age, all hard angles and suspicion, the king of Rodarri was round and thick from indulging in their legendary parties.

Queensblood Rianne stood apart from the king and his wife, wearing an intricate dress that Theo would never have even believed possible. It was dark, regal purple embroidered with silver leaves and roses. A coronet of flowering vines made of hammered silver rested atop her head. A long cape hung from the back of her dress. It was slightly colder here than the warm coastal City of Wynds, explaining the long sleeves she wore. Her eyes and lips were painted the same shade of purple as her gown. She was frighteningly slim and had a delicateness to her as if she might just disappear. Her expression was kind and warm, but just a little bit haunted.

Other Queensblood queens stood beside the dais, each as painfully beautiful as the last, wearing crowns and gowns as elaborate as Rianne's.

"Welcome," King Cavendar said. "It is customary to greet guests with entertainment in Rodarri. I happen to have a Warbringer in my personal castle guard. He has agreed to give a demonstration."

"Thank you, Your Majesty," Aurienne said.

The king motioned to a soldier standing behind the dais. "My Warbringer, Rhydian."

As if anticipating Theo's question, Aurienne whispered, "A Warbringer is the descendent of the Redbrooke line. They're cursed to eventually lose themselves to bloodlust and go on a murderous spree before disappearing. As soon as they take a life, their madness will soon set in. But before they go mad, they're unmatched warriors with battle in their blood. They hardly need to be taught to fight;

they're born knowing how. He wants us to know he has such a weapon at his command."

"Cursed?"

"Yes."

"A real curse?"

"As real as they get."

Theo shifted. His mother had told him that curses were real, though he hardly believed it. Believing in seers and superstitions was one thing. Curses were an entirely different matter, and curses as powerful as the Warbringer's seemed impossible.

Rhydian stepped out from behind Queensblood Rianne. Theo swallowed in spite of himself. Theo was taller than most he encountered, and strong, but next to Rhydian he looked average—small even. Rhydian was built like a stone wall and somehow moved with an athleticism that defied his large frame. His gaze was hard and serious, seeing everyone and everything as an enemy. He gripped the hilt of his sword so tightly that Theo heard the leather creak from a dozen paces away. Who would dare fight such a man?

"If it pleases the High Seer, I shall demonstrate three weapons. The bow, the spear, and the sword," Rhydian said.

Aurienne inclined her head graciously, always seeming to know what to do. Theo envied it just a little when he felt so out of place.

"Who cursed him?" Theo whispered.

She whispered, "His ancestor was cursed by a bloodwitch. Teridar is brimming with magic if you know where to look."

Eyes wide, he leaned back.

The nobles flocked to the edges of the grand room, leaving the center open. Rhydian took a bow from his back as several guards placed a handful of targets across the room. He nocked three arrows simultaneously and fully extended the drawstring, holding it open without so much as a quiver from his arms. Theo glanced at Captain Laurier, and the soldier's mouth was hanging open. Theo looked back to the Warbringer, understanding that the feat he attempted was impossible even by a trained soldier's standard.

Rhydian aimed and released the string. The three arrows struck three separate targets simultaneously, all bullseyes. Theo's heart leapt into his throat before sinking into his gut. He wiped his clammy palms on his pant legs.

Rhydian fired four arrows all at once and struck four bullseyes. Theo blinked. Even the courtiers murmured, glancing at one another furtively.

"Impossible," Mathis whispered.

Then five and again, five bullseyes. He began to draw arrows one after the other. In the space of a single breath, five arrows were drawn, and five found their marks.

What in the names of all the gods?

Polite applause broke out from the court, and Aurienne's entourage joined in the applause. Rhydian gave a shallow bow, anger flashing across his face. Theo took a step closer to Aurienne. Rhydian took a spear from a nearby guard as other guards set up five targets in a long line, one behind the other.

"What is he doing?" Adonis whispered to Saryll.

"He's going to hit them all," Saryll replied, face drawn.

Theo couldn't believe his eyes. Was this some sort of trick? Theo was no soldier, but this looked...too easy.

Rhydian drew back the spear, took three steps forward, and twisted his body—hurling the spear. It crashed all the way through the wood panels of the first target, through the second, third, fourth, and fifth. More applause.

Theo whispered under his breath, "How many targets can a soldier normally go through?"

"A strong spearman would be lucky to break through one," Captain Laurier whispered.

Rhydian was five times stronger than a trained soldier? Theo swallowed. This show of force was having the desired impact. His stomach rolled.

Rhydian drew his steel sword from his hip, and the metal sang. Five archers faced him with bows drawn. They released the arrows.

Zing, zing, zing—the arrows flew. *Ting, Ting, Ting.* Rhydian's sword moved faster than the eye could follow and deflected each in turn. Then two at a time. Then three at a time.

Theo rubbed his eyes. How was this possible? None of the king's court looked worried, except Queensblood Rianne. Her peachy skin had paled to a ghostly hue.

Interesting.

Rhydian pulled a blindfold out from his pocket, and another round of applause echoed through the expansive room. He secured it over his eyes and raised his sword. More arrows flew toward him, and he deflected each. With a roar, four soldiers waiting behind some columns charged him.

The Warbringer lifted the sword to parry the first swing. He spun and dodged the second swing and rolled away from a third. *Ting, ting, ting.* The swords danced with one another, with Rhydian simply defensively parrying each blow. Blindfolded, he risked a killing blow if he took the offense. The four men charged again.

Concern pooled in Theo's stomach. This was incredibly dangerous, Rhydian's abilities aside. This was asking for someone to bleed out on the floor in front of them. It asked to release a curse. Each narrowly missed strike twisted Theo's stomach into knots. He itched to speak up but locked down the urge.

Rhydian roared and ripped off the blindfold when a blade narrowly missed his hand. Theo's jaw dropped to his chest. Rhydian's eyes were fully blood-red. He growled and advanced on the nearest swordsman, who scrambled away in true terror.

"Rhydian," Queensblood Rianne called.

Rhydian stopped his advance, expressions at war with one another. His fist tightened on the sword until the leather squealed. His hand shook, and his shoulders were tight.

"Excellent demonstration, Rhydian, thank you," Queensblood Rianne said.

Rhydian turned tightly to face her, bowed to her and the king, and stalked back against the wall.

Wild applause erupted from the tension. Hoots and whistles rose from the happy crowd. The nobles returned to their positions in the center of the room—a parade of gowns, ribbons, gemstones, silk, and color.

Aurienne stepped forward. "In appreciation of your great hospitality and an impressive show, I shall offer you one truth. If you ask a question, I'll give you the answer."

The queens, commanders, and other noble guests gathered all whispered to one another excitedly.

Aurienne smiled graciously and lightly said, "Be careful, Your Majesty. Some questions you do not want the answers to."

Polite laughs greeted her, and the king failed to hold back a scowl. He joined the laughter, clearly hearing Aurienne's warning and the reminder of her power. From the gazes flicking from King Cavendar to Aurienne, it appeared lost on no one that the High Seer *herself* offered the demonstration of power, where the king relied on the Warbringer.

"I'm honored by your offer. Well, everyone, what question should I ask?" the king asked his court.

"What was the best party in the history of Teridar?"

"Who is the greatest warrior of all time?"

"How quickly could our king defeat King Jaekob?"

"Who is the most beautiful woman alive!"

"Is there treasure hidden in the castle?"

"Are the firewryms of Fangmour real?"

Suggestions roared in until the king held up his hand. The court quieted expectantly. The king's eyes gleamed wickedly. Theo could almost see him rifling through the pros and cons of possible questions.

Theo glanced at Aurienne, who wore a mirroring wicked gleam, though the white seer's cloud swirling atop her eyes would have disguised it from all who didn't know her well. They played a game of wills and strategies, and the king was at a disadvantage. Who could best the seer who knew the future? Theo almost felt bad for the king. Almost.

"Tell me your deepest secret," the king said.

The crowd gasped, with wide eyes at the terrible question they now craved an answer to.

Theo winced, but Aurienne did not react. She must have expected this and been prepared to answer.

"War with Emperor Rexil comes whether there is a summit or not," she said without a hint of emotion. "The summit gives us our only chance at surviving the war. My secret is that not once have I seen my own future extending past the war. I do not expect to survive. I simply wish for others to."

Theo stared as his heart recoiled from her sharp words.

She believed she was going to die?

Goddess, it made sense. Her hyperfocus on her duty while abandoning all else. Her recklessness. To her, it didn't matter. Nothing else mattered because she wouldn't be around to enjoy it.

Beside him, Saryll and Kassia gaped at Aurienne. Adonis paled, and even Mathis recoiled. Captain Laurier shifted, and Sentinel Kolten gripped his sword. King Cavendar studied Aurienne, looking for deception or ulterior meanings in her words, and finally leaned back—apparently finding none.

"That is why we come, Your Majesty." She glanced at Theo.

Theo bowed low and waited for the king to address him, as Mathis had instructed.

"And who is this?" the king said blithely.

That was Theo's cue. "Atheodoren Willem Thatcher, guild-certified blacksmith of the village Karme from the nation of Avyllon. I'm escorting the High Seer Aurienne Azarrah to gather allies for the summit Avyllon will host on the first day of the next full moon—Hallohaim."

Theo folded his hands and waited patiently, with a bland, pleasant smile plastered on his face like they had practiced.

"You're...not nobility," King Cavendar said.

"No, Your Majesty. The High Seer, in her Sight and wisdom, Saw that I was fated to request the assistance of the nations of Teridar for the summit," Theo said. "Emperor Rexil has made demands of Avyllon, as you may have also received, which are little more than agreeing to shackles. The High Seer Saw that should we agree to these terms, the Empire would destroy the entire continent, and none would be left alive. Our only chance is to ally with one another to hold back the empire from Teridar."

The king clicked his large rings against the throne.

"I don't pretend to understand why I was chosen. Perhaps only that my simple life allows me to know the hearts of the simple people, who this will impact the most. Other than that, I have no land, titles, or birthright to call upon. I merely do the bidding of the Fates and the Triple Goddess," Theo said more reverently than he was anticipating. Aurienne's devotion must be contagious.

The king pursed his lips. "I see. This is quite the request to make on such short notice."

Aurienne cut in. "Yes, Your Majesty. I did not receive the vision until just before we received the missive from Emperor Rexil. His decision to make those demands has spurred our actions. We gave you and King Jaekob as much time as we possessed ourselves."

"Of course. Well, if the leaders of Teridar gather, then of course I should attend. I appreciate you extending the invitation and coming all this way to deliver it in person," King Cavendar said in a way that made Theo think he meant not a single word. "The Seven Forests and Titan Cliffs have had closed borders for years though, so I doubt you will persuade them to attend."

Theo ground his teeth. He looked at Aurienne, who simply studied him. He looked to Adonis, who grinned and raised a brow as if reading Theo's mind. Theo took a deep breath and did something that made him entirely uncomfortable. The lie in his next words tasted like rusted metal.

"We're *confident* that they will attend," Theo said as he gave Aurienne a pointed look for the king's benefit.

"You've had a vision then?" the king asked, leaning forward.

"Would we be here if not?" Theo quipped.

The king leaned back against the throne. "I suppose not."

"It is polite to deliver the invitation in person, of course, but we expect their attendance," Theo said smoothly.

"When they have confirmed, do send word. We shall travel by the Ways to Avyllon. We have a sorcerer at the university who is able to open them." The king waved his hand dismissively.

"Thank you, Your Majesty," Aurienne said.

"Tomorrow night, there shall be a ball in honor of your long overdue visit," the king said.

Applause from the court echoed against the austere stone walls.

"We are honored," Aurienne said with a bow.

The rest of the group bowed and backed away three steps before exiting the room. The group returned to their rooms in the guest wing.

Theo stopped Aurienne. "Was that true what you told the king, about dying?"

The eyes of Adonis, Saryll, Kassia, Mathis, Captain Laurier, and the sentinels descended upon her.

"It's true I have not seen my future past the war. I've wondered if that means I won't survive. But there are many explanations for it. A shadow looms over the war, obscuring it. Don't fret. If my death comes, I will See it and avoid it."

The group breathed more easily. Mathis, Saryll, and Kassia entered their respective rooms. The sentinels took up positions along the hall.

Aurienne whispered to Theo, "Good job. As long as we can keep from offending him, the visit will be a success."

"Yeah, Theo, just don't pull any white knight antics or insult *this* king while we're here, and we should be fine," Adonis chortled.

Theo and Adonis reentered their suite. As soon as his door closed, Adonis approached.

"You lied to the king," Adonis said, amused.

"I did not," Theo said.

"You strongly implied that Aurienne Saw they would come," Adonis said. "You chose your words carefully. Sneaky bastard. I think we were meant to be friends all along. My influence has done you well."

Theo reddened. "I wouldn't lie...but Aurienne did say she Saw a future where the summit occurred."

"You twisted the truth like a proper politician." Adonis clapped him on the back.

Theo wondered whether it was a compliment or not. He changed into more comfortable clothing, splashed water on his face, and rubbed his temples. He had just sat down when a knock at the suite door forced him back up.

Groaning, he opened the door, and Rhydian stood in the doorframe, taking up all the space. Theo raised a brow.

What in the world was the Warbringer doing here?

"Atheo—" Rhydian said.

"Theo. Rhydian, right?"

Rhydian laughed, and to Theo's surprise, the warmth of the laughter reached his brown eyes. Theo was just relieved they were no longer red.

"You seem like a decent guy, so I'll be blunt," Rhydian said. "The king wants me to show you around any place I think you would find interesting and try to dig up dirt on you. It's the last thing I want, but it's not really a request. It is a free pass to see whatever you want to see here, as long as you'll tell me something *secret* that I can share with him later?"

Theo blinked. "That...is... Why does he want to find dirt on me? And why would you tell me that?"

"I hate him." Rhydian worked his jaw. "Anything I can do to be a thorn in his fat side is a priority. He wants to know how a lowly blacksmith *really* ended up in the High Seer's court making requests on her behalf. So, you want to help me out?"

Theo laughed. "I can tell you how that happened, but it's probably not what he's looking for."

He shared the tale. "She honestly does not know why it has to be me."

"Hmmm. Well, I can probably spin the savior thing to interest him. It would be even better if you two were in love." Rhydian laughed.

Theo tried to laugh casually but failed miserably.

"Oh, bloodsun, you are?"

"No... Well...I-I can't speak for her," Theo stammered.

Rhydian whistled. "That secret is safe with me. I know too well the dangers of the heart. Is there anything else I can tell him?"

Theo considered this and searched his memory for a tidbit of information the king might find interesting but would not hurt them. "Aurienne believes in her duty more than anything. Nothing will sway her from her path. It won't work to threaten her loved ones. I think she'd let them die."

"That's cold, but I can make that and the savior thing work."

Theo chuckled.

"By the way, you're a terrible liar with the whole 'the other leaders will attend' nonsense. I think you fooled the king and maybe the commanders, but you'll have to practice if you want to fool others."

"I don't plan on making a habit of it," Theo said.

"Well, if you're in her court, you're going to have to. He'll know if I don't take you on a tour, so where do you want to go?"

Theo grinned and followed Rhydian through the halls and many staircases of the castle as well-dressed staff scampered about, staying busy. The plain gray walls were covered nearly ceiling to floor in vivid tapestries, and the stained-glass windows reflected the light.

"They're fairytales." Rhydian gestured to the glass. "The golden flying warriors, the Mooncursed Shadows, the firewyrms, the elven armies, the bloodwitches of the fifth forest, living stone, sinkholes..."

"I haven't heard some of those," Theo said.

"I'm sure you'll hear many at the ball tomorrow as part of the entertainment. The king likes to show off." Rhydian snorted.

"Why do you serve him?"

"I wanted to join the army, so when I lost my mind and went all *murdery,* only soldiers or criminals were nearby," Rhydian said icily. "It's better than being in the middle of a village. He found out I was a Warbringer when my eyes turned red, and he wanted me as his own personal guard. I'm no better than a pet that he shows off when it suits him. But I'm happy with my post, so I'll endure it."

"Can your curse be broken?"

"If there was a way, you think we'd have found it in a thousand or so years."

"It's been in your family that long?"

Rhydian nodded. "Since the Shadow Wars. I didn't know about it until my father went mad and left us, and he didn't tell me nearly enough. I learned what I could at the university. And here we are—the royal gardens."

Theo stopped a gardener to ask questions about Vittoria's Gift. "Could you tell me how long it lasts, and how often must it be changed out. What sort of care does it require?"

The gardener was clearly uncomfortable, but nervous glances at Rhydian loosened her tongue. Theo finally returned to the Warbringer.

"Did you learn what you required?" Rhydian asked.

"I did, thank you. It does not seem to be tied to anything specifically in Rodarri, though research would be required. It would be a great resource if King Cavendar would share it. Perhaps after the summit, we can broker a deal to purchase a starter amount."

"You're sounding more and more like a politician."

Theo grimaced. "Could we see the blacksmith forges? I'm curious to compare techniques."

"It's your tour." Rhydian shrugged.

They wound their way down to the main level through spiral

staircases nestled in circular spires. Theo found himself studying the walls for hints of hidden doorways.

"Are there any secret passages?"

"Why do you ask?"

Theo squinted at a bookshelf. "Our housekeeper seems to appear and disappear. I was wondering how she did it."

Rhydian shifted, avoiding Theo's gaze. "I've heard there are a few very old passages that have been boarded up and are no longer in use, but the staff wouldn't be using them for housekeeping. She must just slip out of sight."

"Yeah, you're probably right." Theo sighed. "Weary eyes and weary travel bodies aren't the most perceptive."

The pair passed a small shrine on the way to the forge, and Theo stopped. "Who do you worship?"

"They worship the first Queensblood, Queen Vittoria."

"Then the queens are seen as goddesses?"

"Only once they die. Their value is in their death." Rhydian's eyes looked a little more red than brown.

Theo flinched. Rhydian's words cut far too closely to the Rite Theo had interrupted, and what tragedy had nearly occurred.

They passed the shrine and soon arrived at the forge. They stayed at the forge for several hours. Theo asked questions and tried to memorize the answers until his mind was swimming. They stayed until Rhydian's guard shift was over. Rhydian escorted Theo back up to his room.

"This wasn't the worst time I've had on an errand for the king," Rhydian said.

"Thanks for the candor. Let me know if you need anything else," Theo replied.

"Will do." Rhydian strolled away.

Theo pushed open the door to his room to find Rosalindt making down the bed, moving quietly as a ghost. Theo nearly jumped out of his skin. She straightened as much as her aged back would allow and folded her hands. Her silver hair was pulled back into a stern braid. Her eyes still possessed a glimmer of anger and youth, and a sliver of liquid silver flashed through her irises.

"You met the king? I hope your visit proves...fruitful," she said with a predatory tone that made Theo's hair stand up on the back of his neck.

"I hope so," he replied warily.

"You have integrity. It's a rare trait around here." Rosalindt leaned in and whispered, "The king has a habit of saying quite a lot and yet not anything at all. He's full of spun sugar and feathers, no substance."

Theo gaped. He wasn't sure if this was a trick or just a very blunt old woman who believed herself to be beyond consequences. Either way, there was no good answer. "Oh, well I..."

"You didn't get an answer from him one way or another."

"Well, no."

"You wouldn't," she said. "The king is old and weak and tired. He relies on the blood of the queens to protect the land since he cannot."

Frigid icicles burned down Theo's back.

"Weak men rely on the sacrifice of women. And the kings of Rodarri *are* weak. The women have been strong. They've forgotten, but they will remember soon," Rosalindt said.

Theo's tilted his head. "What do you mean?"

"You'll see. Your seer is too perceptive, and your heart is too true not to see the injustices here." She cocked her head. "You simply couldn't let them drown *her*, could you?"

"How did you know..."

"I won't take more of your time. Is there anything else you require?"

Theo looked bewildered around his room. "No, I don't think..."

"Do read those books."

She was gone again. Theo blinked. Had he even looked away from her? He whipped his head around to search the room, but there were no doors or panels open. Nothing was out of place. The main door was still closed and too heavy for her to have snuck out so quickly. Rhydian must be wrong—secret passages lurked somewhere. Or he had lied.

Theo started toward the door to tell Aurienne what had transpired, but his hand lingered over his door handle. She couldn't be his first and last thought. He had to let her go; or at least he had to try.

I can't keep doing this.

That night, he slept fitfully with a head full of terrible nightmares about silver eyes, secret passages, and ghosts.

Midnight Kiss

Chapter Twenty

You are the great love story I want. I want it with you.

— *Unknown.*

1152 N.T.C. Castle Rodarr, Rodarri.

Mountains of food overflowed Rodarr's grand banquet hall while loud music and louder laughter echoed against the stained-glass walls. Acrobats spun and twirled on silks hung from the ceiling. Bite-sized rainbow cakes were decorated in colored whipped cream and candies. Strawberries and spun sugar floated in sparkling wine. The entire city could not possibly consume all the food in this room.

Aurienne hardly noticed. She watched with unfocused eyes, searching for any dangers or advantages. She Saw a thousand futures that would never be. As the world of visions and dreams whisked her away, she forgot to remember which future did, in fact, come to pass.

The visions were disobedient tonight, seeking to elude her, and she had to work twice as hard to bend them to her will. Her head throbbed already. Even yesterday's rest and Kassia's tea had not lessened the ache.

Possible scenes played over and over. A man in a burnt red dinner jacket dropped his fork and erupted in laughter from too much wine. The same man looked up to watch an acrobat, and his hand remained steady. The fork did not fall. The man motioned to a server for more sparkling wine, the fork fell, and laughter erupted. The visions blurred together. A server tripped and spilled wine on a guest. But three seconds earlier, the server noticed the bunch in the rug and avoided it. Or did he trip? Aurienne lifted her hand and caught the server's attention. He refilled her glass and did not trip. Or did he?

She no longer knew.

Studying the room, the seer watched for guarded whispers or sentries gathering. She looked far ahead into the night and then back to the present before drifting back into the future, seeing the possibilities of futures, people's deaths, and entire lives.

Acrobats wrapped themselves higher and higher up the silks until they nearly touched the stained-glass ceiling high, high above. They dropped and twirled, the silks catching them at the last second. Another acrobat spun circles and flipped on a metal ring. Dancers leapt and split the air to the music. The room was all color, ribbons, silks, dessert, and wine.

Compared to the restrained grandeur of Wynds, Rodarr was opulence given form. Greed and gluttony peered at Aurienne from the shadows of the wide columns, the lustful glint of a man's gaze eyeing the Queensblood, or sparkling wine dribbling down a woman's chin. It was enticing and sickening, compelling and revolting. The room was one of the most beautiful Aurienne had ever seen, even in her visions. Though it was gilded in magnificent gowns and gold, the pretty trappings could not hide the truth lurking beneath. The parties and festivities concealed a dark truth. Corpses of a thousand dead queens rotted in the ravine just outside the grand hall. Aurienne pushed the images of their deaths away.

She focused on King Cavendar's many futures into the next

month. His fate was intertwined with King Jaekob's fate. Two old men, two old kings blind to the changes coming to the world. They hung onto the familiar as if it would save them. She picked one of the generals and began sifting through his futures.

Theo nudged her arm, snapping her out of her daze, and she blinked the visions away. He gave her the most brilliant smile, and her heart twisted into a knot. His blond locks were combed into some style of the young men, likely by Adonis. His fine nobleman's clothes couldn't conceal his well-earned muscles and the light tan of a man who worked outside. He smelled like the forest—all earthen soil and tree bark and leaves. He tasted like it, too, if she recalled. Remembering their kiss heated her blood, a blush creeping up her neck as other carnal thoughts flickered.

"Are you enjoying yourself?" he asked.

"Yes," she lied.

"You're somewhere else, though."

"Just Seeing," she said absently.

"But not living," Theo said gently.

She stiffened.

He gestured toward the performers. "You're missing the show, and it's quite good."

Aurienne focused on the acrobats, and Theo was right. She was soon caught up in the story of the Siren and the Sailor. The ribbons hung from the ceiling were purple and blue, representing water, and the performers flipped on the ribbons as though swimming. They started the second act, telling about the Golden Warriors of the Lost Pass. Golden paint and feathered wings filled the room as they walked on tightropes and jumped from rope to rope, appearing like they were flying. The third act ended with the performers in rainbow colors jumping and flipping across the floor—like the elves of Etheria. The finale was fire dancers to honor the firewryms of Fangmour.

Aurienne gasped and giggled. She drank the sweet, dark wine Theo poured, falling into his forest green eyes. She bit into a piece of spiced meat and tasted the spices and herbs rubbed into the skin.

When a flaming dessert was served and the dancers performed their final tricks, Aurienne watched flashes of colored veils and flames and spun sugar.

Once more, Theo reminded her to live.

The acrobats concluded their show, and the banquet guests spilled into the gardens. Theo followed the crowds outside. The grounds were lit so brightly with Vittoria's Gift, torches, and candles, it was like walking under an afternoon sun even though it was well after dark. Fire dancers flipped torches and rings of flames along the paths. Lights twinkled in the bushes and flowers. People strolled and danced as queens were chased by dashing young men in velvet suits. Musicians played soft, upbeat music on trellis-covered patios.

Theo and Aurienne paused near a tall tree with branches spreading out in every direction. It was the tallest tree around, with thick flat leaves as big as a person's head. It was covered in green vines and white Vittoria's Gift. The leaves, vines, and lichen all glowed with unknown magic—lighting up the entire garden. Theo noticed the lichen pulsing in a steady rhythm.

"The Queen's Root is beautiful, isn't it?" Queensblood Rianne asked.

She strolled up wearing a daring gown that looked like a sunset spun into fabric. Thousands of tiny glimmering jewels reflected the light of the glowing tree and caught the light of her crown. She was slight and short, as if childhood sickness stole her growth, and had a trace of bags under her eyes against her pale skin. She stopped and joined them in gazing up at the tree.

Rhydian strolled behind her at a respectable distance, his hand never leaving his sword hilt. Theo gave an acknowledging nod to Rhydian, which he returned.

"Yes, Your Majesty, it is quite extraordinary," Aurienne said.

"Please call me Rianne."

Aurienne inclined her head, and Theo knew Aurienne must have known Rianne would say this. She always seemed to know.

"It glows with some unknown magic. The same moss is behind the many connected lighting panels throughout the city," Rianne said.

"Bloodmagic," Aurienne whispered.

Theo blinked.

"Pardon?" Rianne said.

"I See it has been here for quite some time," Aurienne said instead.

"We're told it was planted here in the first year after the Shadow Wars," Rianne said.

Aurienne stared at the tree for long moments, and Theo wondered if he had lost her to the thrall of visions again.

"I hear you are a powerful seer. Do you See its planting?" Rianne asked.

"It was planted one thousand fifty-three years ago, during the Shadow War," Aurienne turned from the tree to Rianne, "by your ancestor Queen Vittoria."

Rianne gasped. "You See her?"

"I See her clutching her newly born babe to her chest, bleeding out from fatal wounds given to her by cursed soldiers and pains of childbirth. She willingly gave her blood to the land to protect her baby. It shielded the child from the soldiers and wolves until her sister arrived—summoned by the land itself. Her blood was spilled in this very spot, and the land drew her in for burial. The tree grew over her final resting place."

Bile rose in Theo's throat at the terrible story.

Rianne paled. "She willingly gave her blood to replenish the land."

"She willingly gave her blood to save her child." Aurienne turned to face Rianne fully. "She didn't choose the people."

Rianne frowned and rolled the folds of her gown between her fingers. "Will you be staying long?"

"We depart in the morning," Aurienne said.

"I hope you found what you came for," Rianne said, staring at the ground beneath the tree.

"That is yet unknown," Aurienne said.

"Does war really come?" Rianne asked.

"Yes. Even if your king signs the accords, war will come," Aurienne said.

"And the summit is the only chance to win the war?" Rhydian asked.

"It simply gives us a chance to survive it."

Theo studied the bark on the tree, doubt and fear filling his mind at this impossible task Aurienne had set for him.

Theo cleared his throat. "Do you know where I might find the housekeeper, Rosalindt? She left some books in my chambers, and I wanted to thank her for them, but no one seemed to know where she could be found."

"Rosalindt?" Rianne's brows pulled into a taut line. "I know everyone in the castle, and there is no one named Rosalindt."

It was Theo's turn to frown. The old woman who had been taking care of them was named Rosalindt, wasn't she? He was nearly positive that that was what she said her name was.

"I must have misheard," Theo finally said.

"Have a nice evening," Rianne said.

"Rianne." Aurienne grasped her wrist and spoke in a voice not her own. "Death is only the beginning. Who you think you must become and who you can choose to be are not the same."

Rianne's eyes widened.

"Be careful," Aurienne whispered.

Rianne left with a sweep of her full skirts, with Rhydian following behind her. As they were about to turn the corner, Theo noticed Rhydian caught up to Rianne and reached for her hand. Theo smiled. *Good for him.*

Theo and Aurienne wandered through the gardens, walking so closely that her fingers brushed against his. Was it his imagination, or were there hints of sapphire blue in her eyes? Theo saw a couple walking arm-in-arm past them. He glanced at her, swallowed, put on a brave face, and offered his arm to her. She took it automatically and gave him a soft smile.

In that brief look, Theo felt like she could read his soul like a book. Every hidden desire and passion, every secret wish, pages that she had scoured. Half of him hoped she Saw what he wanted. Half of him was terrified she would. A grin tried to tear across his face, but he kept it contained behind a controlled smile.

Damn his heart for feeling this way about her.

Damn her fate.

Damn it all to all the hells.

Theo and Aurienne walked underneath glimmering lights through the hedges as the warm night deepened into a velvet shroud. Wildflowers and roses rustled as surrounding conversations quieted.

Theo cleared his throat. "I must admit, there is something to watching the lives of others when they aren't paying attention. These are people living their lives, and you get to see a small bit of it. I suppose you get to do that all the time?"

"I See it all," she said quietly. "I See wonderful things. Births. Marriages. First loves. Last loves. Peaceful deaths for a life well lived. And better than any of it, I see the promise of it all. I think the hope and possibility of those wonderful things is the best thing I see... But I see the bad too. Things no one should have to know."

Theo said nothing. He wasn't sorry and couldn't wish to take it from her, as that would undermine her burden and duty. They were the cards they were each dealt.

Theo said, "I'm glad your visions brought us together."

"What do you mean?"

He chuckled. "If you weren't trying to drown yourself in front of a live audience, I never would have met you."

A wild laugh erupted from her throat, like river fairies, music, and the sun. He had never heard her laugh like *that* even when they were singing dirty ditties. It was Theo's new favorite sound.

"You, however, didn't seem too thrilled to meet me. I'm not sure if I should be offended," he continued the jest.

Another heady laugh filled the air, this one wracking her body.

"I never thought I'd meet a girl who'd throw me in the dungeon for saving her life. And I must be moon-addled, because I think I liked it," he said, leaning close and lowering his voice.

She laughed until tears welled in the corners of her eyes, and she had to wipe them away. *Gods, that sound.*

"I See a lot, but not the good right in front of me," she said. "In my defense, I had just drowned, so forgive my error."

Theo leaned over and picked her a flower, and she allowed him to tuck it into her hair. His fingers brushed her ear and neck, sending fiery jolts of awareness up his arm.

"Error?" he asked.

She held his gaze. "If I would have known what a gentleman you were, or good dancer, or kisser, I would've had you sent straight to my rooms, not the dungeon. Though, I would not have let you out for days all the same."

He laughed. "I did go to your room next, but I recall someone cutting me with a knife and licking the blood from my hand. You had your opportunity but chose violence."

"Well, I can't See everything," she teased.

Sensing an opportunity, Theo steadied himself, hoping and praying to every god and goddess he'd ever heard of for Aurienne not to reject him. He prayed he would not, once again, embarrass himself. His heart hammered against his ribs, trying to escape the bony prison.

Hellsdamn, my traitorous heart. It'll be the death of me.

"Did you See this?"

Theo drew her into a terrace, shielded from view by tall shrubs. He pulled her close until they were nearly touching, and she giggled softly, pressing her pillowy breasts against his chest.

That laugh, Theo thought. Aurienne biting her lip caused fire to reside in his tightening trousers as his gaze filled with fevered desire.

He had imagined this over and over in his mind the past nights, and there was a chance fantasy might become reality.

He asked, "Can I kiss you?"

Aurienne knew she should say no. He was growing too attached, and she would inevitably break his heart. She opened her mouth to refuse, but as she read the hope in his eyes, her resolve weakened. She Saw his vulnerable heart beneath the armor plating. True. Stalwart. Unshakeable. This surprising, full-of-life, mountain of a man who cared deeply and tried incredibly hard. He tried hard for *her*. He was all duty and honor and sensual heat. He was forges and furnaces with roots deeper than trees. She leaned in, and he smelled like forest leaves.

"You don't have to run from me," he whispered. "I don't want to deny this."

She should refuse him, but the thought was unbearable. Hellsdamn her own traitorous heart, the heat pooling between her legs, and gooseflesh peppering her skin.

She kissed him. He tasted like sunlight filtering between the tree canopy, like the forest, and freshly tilled soil. Everything homey and magical at the same time. She took his stubbled jaw in her hands and kissed him deeply, hungrily, until her lips were swollen.

He encircled her waist with his corded arms and pulled her close. She wrapped her fingers in his hair, and he groaned softly. He traced her throat, neck, and shoulder with his calloused fingertips before finding the exposed skin of her spine, calling forth a shiver. His rough hands on her soft flesh sent heat racing into her core. Her fingertips dragged down his muscled back softly before sinking into his flesh.

I should stop him. I shouldn't let this... Hellsdamn it.

She was so tired of denying herself everything she wanted, and she wanted him. She leaned forward, and their tongues met again. His breath was hot on her lips. He brought his hand from her waist to her face and pulled her lip down with his thumb. Their eyes locked. She nipped his thumb before returning to the kiss.

His stubble scraped her neck. "You are the most amazing woman I have ever met."

Aurienne laughed softly. She had taken lovers. She had been kissed and flattered well enough before. No one ever meant it, not like Theo, and it lit a fire in her.

"High Seer?" Sentinel Kolten called out from somewhere across the hedges.

Back to reality.

Their kiss slowed and broke. She bit her swollen lip hungrily. Nearby giggles caused Aurienne's breath to hitch, and she leaned against Theo's chest. He pressed a final kiss to her lips, slow and soft, before pulling away.

Lacing his fingers into hers, he pulled her back onto the walkway. She slipped her arm through his, soaking in the heat of his skin. His quiet, strong presence calmed her ever-racing mind, and his hunger for life drew her back into reality. They strolled under the blooming cerulean sirenbells and amethyst foxgloves.

"Why would you risk feeling something for someone when it can't last?" he asked.

The words bruised her heart.

I should hesitate with us. I should push you as far away as I can, but I can't bring myself to do it. The day will come, but not today. I'll allow myself this happiness for a little while.

"The future sometimes doesn't come true the way you think it does," she said. "I won't give up these fleeting beautiful moments just because they won't last. That makes me want them even more."

Goddess—she wanted *him*.

Ghost Stories
Chapter Twenty-One

She grasped the block, no ropes on her hands,
As executioner's sword made cruel demands.
Too young to die, but her time was consumed.
Her soul held no guilt, but her blood was doomed.

— The Ballad of the Queensblood.

1152 N.T.C. Castle Rodarr, Rodarri.

A strange mist swirled on the floor of Theo's chamber as his mind raced with the events of the evening. It would be impossible to sleep as his heart thundered in his chest, and he was unable to erase the smile from his face. Though the room was sweltering, frost gathered on the window; Theo paid it no mind as his mind raced. He was in trouble. *Hellsdamn it.* He could no more keep away from her than stop breathing.

For her, he'd endure all the nobles' scorn, take their abuse, and sit through those meals. She carried the burden of their futures, so he'd try to take some small share for her—for everyone. Even if he didn't love her, he would have been determined to help. The problem was that he did yet she was not fated to love him back. Theo lifted his chin—he wasn't ready to give up on her just yet. He'd face Fate.

Noticing the tomes on his table, he wondered whether he should read them after learning Rianne didn't know Rosalindt. Theo glanced at the books again. It couldn't hurt to see what they said, and there was nothing else to do. He approached the table and sat at the stout wooden chair. A cloud of dust spiraled from the first ancient tome. He flipped through the ancient journals. Several entries caught his attention.

28, Deca 72

My ascension comes tomorrow. I will not see my twenty and fifth name day. I'm ashamed to even write this, but I'm afraid to die. I'm afraid I'll exist only in the darkness for eternity. I'm afraid there will be nothing there for me or my daughters after me. I hope the land accepts my sacrifice, even as my mind and body are weak. I hope that my ascension protects them all.

Rebekkah

14, Solla 73

Ascension. Return. Life. Death. I hear all the dead queens screaming, screaming, screaming. They do not live, but they do not die, and they are here with me always. We drove the Shadows from our woods. So-called vampires. Now—something comes for me. Something ancient. Angry. Something from another world. The screams never stop. The smiles never end.

Queensblood Rebekkah Faye Lenore

Theo closed the book, feeling uneasy. A weight settled in the air as if he was not alone. The first entries and the last were starkly different. He opened the next tome and began to read.

16, Mars 349

My heart, so full of anger and vengeance, brought me back. I feel nothing now. I should feel sadness or loneliness or uncertainty. Or maybe there is so much rage we feel nothing else. There are so many of us now. I hope that the angry spirits of queens wait for the souls of kings to fly to peace and catch them in haunted claws to devour them. Heartspring has finally, somehow, rid itself of its Shadows. I feel it again. We have been here for too long. Something comes for me that has come before. They whisper Grimfall.

Queensblood Samantah Julietta Lenore

Grimfall? The legend? The fairytale? Grimfall kept coming up, in the cards, in Aurienne's visions, in the skipping song, and now in these journals. Everywhere they looked was Grimfall. Theo opened the third journal and started to read.

28, Deca 802

My ascension is tomorrow. Fear comes, but I resist its claws. I cannot lose my faith like Queen Rosalindt so many years ago. My time has come. I'm the oldest eldest daughter since Vittoria. None have been permitted to live as long as I. I have five daughters who have their own daughters now. I must go so they might live another year.

Morgana

14, Februa 802

The people don't need my blood. They need my blade. The Free Peoples are pushing into our borders. They want farmland, which they claim sits fallow along the tree line. They seek to take what is mine. I shall not allow it. We will take flaming blades and arrows and cut them down. We shall burn the forest back until they flee. No one takes from us.

Queensblood Morgana

22, Hallows 805

Grimfall comes for me. When we next return, we shall kill the kings. We will have vengeance. The kings shall die by blood and flame and claw, the kings of old shall die. The griffon king falls to cursed claw, the sea king drowns in fire, but worst of all is the lion king who dies by blood. I rejoin my sisters, and then we wait for the one who will free us. When next we wake, we shall not sleep again.
Queensblood Morgana Margot Lenore

These were the journals of ancient, executed queens of Rodarri. Except, these three *returned*. Even if they did not overtly say it, the change was evidence. There was an immediate shift in personality, handwriting, and tone. The queen had died, and something else had come back.

The final journal belonged to Queen Rosalindt Lenore, who had refused to ascend. Theo read the final entry.

9, Maia 579
Don't you hear them? All those queens, dead for nothing.
I fear my time will be short. I have heard the whispers of the queens, and they have told me the truth. Queen Vittoria never meant for her descendants to share her fate. Year after year, more of us are murdered and thrown into the terrible ravine. None of those spirits found peace. They wait for their opportunity to end the terrible cycle of skulls, bones, blood, and death. They're waiting for the one to free them all and save us. She must possess the righteous anger of one who wrongly dies. When they are finally freed, their vengeance will have no bounds. Death is only the beginning of her reign.
Queensblood Rosalindt Daniella Lenore

Theo frowned at the tomes—terrible accounts of a sordid and bloody history, not at all the story Mathis and Adonis told him of the noble sacrifice of willing royal blood. This was anguish, terror, anger, and death.

Why would the housekeeper Rosalindt give these to him? Was she related to the queens? Was she a queen in disguise? A dissenter? Something else?

A scraping noise pulled Theo's attention to a painting along the wall in time to see Rosalindt slip behind the painting, holding a stack of linens. Theo shot up. He knew it. He peeled the painting back and slipped into the dust and cobwebs of the secret passageway. A few sets of footprints led down the corridor. Thankfully, the back of the Vittoria's Gift light fixtures illuminated the way. Theo hurried down the narrow passage, seeing other secret doors opening into nearly every room. Rhydian had been right, though; these did not seem to get much use.

A flash of a gray braid turned a corner, and Theo quickly crept behind the housekeeper. He nearly called out to her but was too curious as to what she was doing. Voices filled the rooms, and he realized that this passage gave unfettered access to the entire castle.

Rosalindt slipped out of a door.

Theo stepped from the passage into what could only be described as some abandoned circle of hell. High amphitheater seating rose into the air, capped by gleaming metal spires covered in bloodroses. The center of the arena was empty save for an executioner's block, stained black and red with blood ancient and new. And the silence... The flags atop the ramparts fluttered in the breeze but made no noise. The air was heavy and *wrong*. The feeling of being watched tickled Theo's neck and made him shudder.

A banshee screamed.

A ghastly, unnatural version of Rosalindt flew from nowhere, surrounded by shadows and whipping torn pieces of fabric from a dark cloak caught in a silent and invisible wind. Her face contorted with sharpened teeth and silver, glowing eyes. She floated inches off the ground and pressed a bloody finger against Theo's forehead with a bloodcurdling shriek.

Theo shouted and scrambled away. He tripped on a stone and fell back, covering his face with his hands and waiting, but nothing happened. He stood warily, but Rosalindt was nowhere to be seen.

Queensblood Rianne shuffled toward the ravine.

Rianne? What was she doing out here? What was this place?

"Rianne?" Theo called. "Are you okay?"

She shuffled toward the ravine—motions rigid and unnatural. Her head was bowed low and lolled from side to side. She wore only a nightgown. Her feet were bare and covered in the grave dirt of this terrible place.

"Rianne!"

She didn't turn, and she was close to the edge now. A handful more steps and she'd be there. Fear alighted in Theo's chest. Maybe she was under the same compulsion that afflicted Rosalindt—or something darker. Theo raced to her.

"Rianne! Queensblood Rianne! Rianne! Stop! Rianne, stop!" Theo shouted.

He pumped his legs as fast as they would go, suddenly wishing he had spent more time out of the saddle the past week. She took step after step drawing near to the edge with no motions to slow or stop.

Blood from Rosalindt's touch dripped down Theo's face and opened his eyes to the world beyond the veil. He saw the realms of the dead, and it was terrifying. Angry, desiccated spirits sunk their silver claws into Rianne and dragged her to the edge. Other spirits were pulling her back in a ghostly game of tug-of-war. Even more spirits swirled overhead, screaming terrible and deafening threats.

> *You can't save her. No one can save her. But she will*
> *save the rest.*
> *Rising queens and falling kings, truth unseen and*
> *ghostly rings.*
> *Skulls, bones, blood, death. The cycle never ends. Skulls,*
> *bones, blood, death.*
> *Grimfall. Grimfall. Grimfall. Grimfall. Grimfall.*
> *Rianne. Wake up. Rianne.*

Poor little lost king, poor little king, you can't save her,
    you can't save us.

He tried to ignore the terrible screaming and raced for Rianne. She was nearly at the edge of the bottomless ravine that swallowed all light. It was darkness that was clawing, aware, hungry. Truly hell.

Theo reached Rianne and spun her around. Her eyes were no longer blue but entirely silver. Her face contorted like Rosalindt's, and she screamed. She clawed at him with elongated fingernails and raked across his chest. Theo stumbled back, and she lunged for the ravine. Theo dove for her and barely caught her around the waist before she fell.

"Rianne? What are you doing? Snap out of it. Rianne, it's Theo, remember? Rianne!" He struggled to drag her away from the edge.

The spirits screamed.

We will have vengeance.
The screams never stop. The smiles never end. The
    screams never stop.
Atheodoren. Atheodoren. Run from this place before
    we never let you leave.
Crowns dipped in blood. Crowns steeped in death.
    Crowns falling down.
The kings shall die by blood and flame and claw. The
    kings of old shall die!

Theo dragged Rianne from the edge, swatting the spirits away that dove at his face. She clawed and fought him the entire way. She smashed a bony elbow into his temple, leaving him seeing stars, and scrambled back for the edge.

He caught her heel. "Rianne, let me help you."

She kicked out and slammed her heel against his cheek, but Theo refused to let go. Theo dove, grabbed her waist again, and dragged her down on top of him. She squirmed to escape his grasp, but he turned to drag her as far away as he could.

"Rianne, wake up," he demanded.

"Fate won't let her live." The lips belonged to Rianne, but the voice did not.

Angry spirits clawed for him and her, diving and screaming more terrible lies and truths. Theo dodged the claws he could, but others bit into his flesh and caused him to cry out. Rianne struggled, kicking, headbutting, and trying to bite him.

"Rianne, I'm trying to help you."

"Let me go," she screamed.

"Hey! What in the moonless sky is going on here?" Rhydian bellowed and charged.

Rhydian never looked at the wraiths in the sky.

He can't see them.

"Help. She's sleepwalking. She's trying to jump," Theo hollered.

Rianne hissed in his face again and clawed at him. Theo dodged her blackened claws and dragged her, kicking, fighting, and screaming farther from the edge. Rhydian did not slow his charge, but his face changed. Anger turned to confusion as he saw Theo fighting to keep Rianne from the ravine.

Rhydian reached them, looked into Rianne's soulless silver eyes, and flinched. "Rianne?"

"*We'll have her. We'll have her. You can't stop us,*" she hissed in a grating voice.

Rhydian tossed her over his shoulder and hurried to the arena wall, far from the lure of the ravine. Theo followed. Rhydian put her down, and he and Theo stood shoulder to shoulder, blocking her path. Rianne screamed and fainted. The spirits darted back into the ravine and were gone. Rhydian barely caught Rianne's head before it struck the stone.

"You have about one second to tell me what is going on," Rhydian demanded, cradling Rianne's head.

Theo searched for words that did not make him sound crazy.

Angry invisible spirits, a possessed housekeeper that floated and pressed blood against his face, the doorway to hell opened in the ravine...it all made him sound insane.

"Well?" Rhydian snarled.

"The housekeeper Rosalindt was sneaking down a secret passageway, and I followed her because Rianne said she didn't work here. The passage ended here, and Rianne was shuffling toward the ravine like she was sleepwalking. She wouldn't wake when I called to her. I tried to drag her away from it, but she fought me. I have no idea what she's doing out here," Theo said somewhat truthfully.

Rianne stirred and reached for Rhydian. "What's going on?"

"I think you were sleepwalking," the Warbringer said. "What do you remember?"

"I...was dreaming. There were angry spirits of dead Rodarri Queens. They pulled me from my bed and..." Rianne met eyes with Theo as if suddenly remembering the whirlwind of spirits clawing into her and screaming. She said, "I must have been sleepwalking. I just remember nightmares."

Rianne looked at Theo and asked, "Why did you come?"

"I followed the housekeeper Rosalindt and found you here. She... left with the others," Theo said quietly.

Rianne's eyes widened, understanding. "Rosalindt, that's the name of the only queen in the history of Rodarri to refuse the ascension," Rianne said pointedly in a conversation with Theo that only the two of them understood.

"She brought me here to help you. She helped me to See," Theo said.

Tears streaked Rianne's face.

"What is the meaning of this!" King Cavendar boomed as guards threw open the main doors.

The king stumbled out, walking as quickly as his girth would allow, garbed only in his nightclothes.

"Rianne was sleepwalking, and Theo saved her," Rhydian said.

"Is that what he told you? Or did he come here to assassinate the Queensblood!" the king boomed.

Theo's eyes widened. His heart raced. There was more than one way a king could eliminate a threat. Perhaps the kings of Wyndsel and Rodarri had worked together to bring the emperor's troops to attack the caravan, and when that failed, they merely waited for an opportunity to thwart them in other ways.

Aurienne pushed past the king to stand in front of Theo.

"No one came here to assassinate anyone," she snapped. "Your own Warbringer said Theo saved her life."

To Theo, she said, "Something has been interfering with my Sight."

Rianne stood on wobbly legs. "I must have been sleepwalking. When I woke, Theo and Rhydian were bringing me to safety."

"Unless he first brought you to the edge until the Warbringer caught him," the king snapped.

"I didn't hurt her," Theo stated firmly.

"Search his rooms!" the king ordered.

Theo paled, nausea rising. They would find the journals of the ascended Queens, and if Rosalindt was a spirit, there would be no explaining their presence. He was suddenly sure he shouldn't have those cursed tomes.

The minutes ticked by as they waited in the courtyard of death for the guards to search the rooms. Theo wiped his hands on his pants, dreading what they might find—or worse—plant in the rooms. The guards marched into the courtyard.

"We found something," a guard said.

Aurienne cocked her head to Theo, and the color ran from his face.

"They've stolen Vittoria's Gift," the guard announced.

Theo felt both relieved that the journals were gone and confused at the finding.

"What?" Theo murmured.

Adonis, Mathis, Saryll, and Kassia poured into the courtyard behind the Rodarri guards, with the Avyllon sentinels just behind them. Unfortunately, their sentinels were too far to help.

Aurienne cast a damning look at Theo, but he silently shook his head. He hadn't touched the lichen. He glanced at Adonis, who was paler than a ghost.

Oh no. He didn't.

Aurienne tracked Theo's gaze to Adonis, and Theo could almost hear her heart fall. She balled her fists by her sides and swallowed.

"Well, do you admit to stealing Vittoria's Gift?" the king demanded.

"The penalty for attempted murder and stealing royal treasure is death!" a guard announced.

Theo swore beneath his breath. Adonis was shaking like a leaf in a gale as his eyes welled with tears. He swallowed and stepped forward shamefully to accept his fate.

"It was me. I apologize," Theo quickly said.

"What?" Adonis mouthed.

Mathis pushed Adonis behind him with a curt swat.

"What?" Aurienne said, studying Theo as if seeing him for the first time.

"I wondered whether your *guest* would attempt to steal from me," King Cavendar said. "Rhydian, tell us all where Theo asked to go for the tour you gave him yesterday."

"He wanted to go to the university gardens to learn about Vittoria's Gift and then to the royal forge," Rhydian said tightly, gaze shifting from Rianne to Theo.

"What did he ask you about?" the king pressed.

Rhydian's gaze darkened. "Secret passageways."

Well, that was damning.

"Do you deny it?" the king demanded.

Theo looked down. "No."

"Then we have our proof," the king said.

"Wait," Aurienne said. "He is owed a trial where his guilt is in doubt."

King Cavendar glared but glanced at the nobles gathering behind him. He narrowed his gaze. "Trial in Rodarri is trial by combat. He shall face Rodarri's champion. If he is innocent, then he will prevail."

Theo had a sinking feeling he already knew who Rodarri's champion was—a hellsdamned Warbringer. Icy dread sluiced down his veins. He squeezed his eyes shut.

"At dawn, Rhydian Redbrooke shall serve as the king's champion to determine Theo's guilt," the king said.

Moonless skies.

The king snapped his fingers, and guards took Theo's arms, escorting him out. Theo glanced to Aurienne, who stood frozen in the courtyard. Theo didn't even have a chance to say a proper goodbye.

Guards brought him to his rooms to prepare for combat. Heart sinking, he prepared for a trial he couldn't possibly hope to win.

The Trial of the Warbringer and the Traveler
Chapter Twenty-Two

The sun never felt as cold as the day the red moon rose.

— *Journal of the Seer Rheia, date unknown.*

1152 N.T.C. Castle Rodarr, Rodarri.

Nearly seeing scarlet and cursing colorfully enough to make a Wyndsel sailor blush, Rhydian kicked a rack of swords, and the steel went flying across the armory.

"I'm fine," Rianne said for the hundredth time.

"What really happened, Rianne?" Rhydian said.

"I don't know," she said quietly. "I've been having terrible dreams. I thought it was the upcoming ascension, but I don't know anymore. These nightmares—I think the spirits of the queens are trying to tell me something."

Rhydian overturned a rack of spears, and they went rolling across the floor. He punched a stone wall, and the stone shattered into dust. He paced before leaning against a table and staring at the ceiling.

"Did you see him look at the seer's young brother? Adonis, I think? Theo didn't even steal the hellsdamned lichen. He admitted it to save the kid, and the king won't care. He just wants to weaken Avyllon. Now I'm going to have to fight Theo, and you know my curse won't allow me to lose. What am I supposed to do? He saved your life. I can't let him die for something he didn't do." Rhydian brushed his fingers against her cheek.

She squeezed his hand. "What choice do you have?"

"I should've Seen this coming!" Aurienne shrieked.

Saryll and Kassia flinched as Aurienne hurled a tray of teacups at the walls of their suite. Tea splashed on the wall as porcelain rained to the floor.

"Theo going on tours with the Warbringer, following ghostly housekeepers through secret passages... Adonis *stealing* from the king? Queensblood Rianne nearly jumping to her death by some... Why didn't I See any of this?"

Saryll watched Aurienne with fearful eyes, cowering and shaking near the wall with her arms wrapped around herself. Aurienne knew Saryll had never seen her angry before, as it did not suit the *High Seer,* but Aurienne didn't care. Theo would be put to death, and she had failed to See it. She could not let them kill him. She could *not.* He couldn't die. Not Theo, who tasted of forests, campfires, and mountain air. Theo, who smelled like forest leaves. Theo, who felt like home. Panic rose in her throat, and she forced it down.

You can figure this out.

Aurienne forced calm into her veins and knelt to pick up the pieces of the teacup. A faint aroma wafted from the spilt tea. It smelled like purple rain. Aurienne searched her mind for that smell. Lavendiir palm. The plant that they gave younger seers to impede their Sight until they gained control. This would have blocked her

Sight... Aurienne stood, holding a piece of a teacup, and faced Kassia, who had been silent.

Kassia looked away and confirmed Aurienne's suspicion.

"Kassia," Aurienne whispered. "You didn't."

Kassia shamefully met Aurienne's gaze. "I'm sorry. I didn't know they would—"

"You poisoned me with lavendiir palm? You robbed me of my Sight?" Aurienne demanded.

"Your Sight was overpowering you. I had to dim it so you would survive," Kassia replied.

"Kassia," Saryll whispered.

"You had no right, and now, because of you, my brother Adonis was nearly convicted of a capital crime. And they're going to put Theo to death. This is all your fault," Aurienne said coldly.

Anger heated her blood, and that sinful smudge on her soul stirred from its slumber, bubbling and pressing against her spirit like boiling tar. She knew without looking that her eyes darkened as an unearthly presence—perhaps the Goddess or perhaps something worse—entered her body. Crimes could not go unpunished.

"Stop it." Saryll stepped in front of a shaking Kassia. "She had no right to poison you, but she was trying to keep your head from exploding."

Aurienne blinked, feeling Saryll's calming hands on her arm—which banished the oily impulses lurking within her heart. Aurienne glared and paced like a caged tiger, spitting and hissing at its captors.

"Your eyes bleed. Your nose bleeds. Your ears bleed. Your mind cannot handle much more, and where would we be without you?" Kassia said meekly.

Kassia's words took the heat from Aurienne's anger. The witch was right. Aurienne's mind nearly frayed before arriving in Rodarri, but the bleeding lessened some with the tea. Kassia might have saved her life.

Hagstit shadows.

Aurienne growled. "I know you're trying to help. But I can't have my Sight limited without my knowledge. Swear you won't do it again."

Kassia said, "I shouldn't have given it to you. I'm sorry. I'll ask in the future."

Aurienne said, "I'll try to accept help better, so you won't feel like you must hide it."

"How are we going to help Theo?" Saryll asked.

Glancing at the spilled tea, dozens of futures played out in the puddles and only in a few did he survive.

Aurienne's clouded eyes welled with frustrated tears, which she quickly banished. "I have no idea."

Theo wandered in the armory, lost. He was instructed to select whichever weapons he'd fight the Warbringer with, but he could go out there unarmed and have as much of a chance at besting Rhydian. Theo stared at the racks of weapons, feeling sick as his brain struggled to come to terms with the events of the past few hours.

Rhydian walked by and muttered quietly, "I'm sorry. My curse won't let you win, so you're going to have to win yourself."

"Thanks," Theo muttered back.

"I'm trying to help you because you saved Rianne," Rhydian said. "As soon as my eyes turn red, you need aim an arrow at Rianne. Even cursed, I'll dive in the way, and you can draw blood. I'm trusting you not to hurt her or kill me."

Theo stared, a sliver of hope cracking the shell of his heart. Rhydian was going to help him? Maybe they could all survive this.

Theo whispered, "Won't your cursed self know what I'm doing?"

"Yes. Maybe. So, you'll have to be convincing. And survive."

Theo pretended to inspect a rack of swords. "Rhydian?"

"What?"

"Thanks."

"I still might kill you without meaning to, but it makes us even." Rhydian stomped out, putting on a show for the waiting guards.

Theo grabbed a gladius sword, bow and arrow, and tucked several knives into his clothes. Looking at the racks, he also selected a buckler shield. Thinking of Rhydian's demonstration, Theo swapped it for a much thicker iron shield that weighed Theo's arm down. The weight wouldn't matter because this match would have to end quickly if Theo were to prevail. Or survive.

Theo followed the guards to the Courtyard of Queens and glanced toward the ravine, half expecting the angry spirits to dart out and attack, but none did. Theo knelt, fixed the leather guard on his shin, and slipped a handful of dirt into his pocket. He noticed several cages of chickens stacked just inside the doorway, near a hall which probably led to a royal kitchen. He'd keep that in mind. Any advantage could be useful.

The stands were full of decorated nobles and citizens who cheered as Theo took his position across from Rhydian. Theo removed his bow and quiver and leaned them against a stone.

Rhydian swung his steel sword in wide arcs, which drew erupting cheers from the crowds, though his expression was frozen into a scowl.

"Atheodoren Willem Thatcher, you stand accused of treason, murder, and robbery. How do you plead?" the king asked.

"Not guilty, and justified," Theo said.

The king frowned. Theo had already admitted to the theft so he must be claiming the theft was justified. The king exchanged a look with an advisor before continuing.

"You face trial of guilt by combat," the advisor said. "If you draw blood thrice on the king's champion, then your innocence is proven. If the champion draws thrice blood on you, or if you should perish, your guilt has been proven. Lift your weapons if you agree to the terms."

Not having much of a choice, Theo and Rhydian both lifted their swords, and the crowd erupted again. Theo lifted his sword to where Aurienne was seated beside the king. If he could not manage to trick Rhydian's curse, then this would be his goodbye to her.

He didn't regret taking Adonis' place. Adonis had helped him greatly prepare for the audience and did not know what the consequences of his curiosity would be. He wouldn't allow Aurienne to lose her brother after losing so much already. If this was his time, it was his time. He pressed his fingers to his lips, a farewell kiss.

"Begin," the king announced.

Rhydian charged, and Theo stumbled back. He deflected the onslaught of strikes that went from circles to straight thrusts back into circles before evolving into short chopping strikes designed to tire Theo's shield arm. Theo's arm already burned from the impact, and he fought the urge to panic. He dodged what he could, parried what he could, and absorbed the rest on his heavy shield with sickening clangs. Rhydian hefted his sword before charging again. Theo was driven back across the ring.

"Keep your hands up!" Adonis yelled from the front row.

Ungrateful brat.

Theo blocked again and again, circling the arena. Rhydian's eyes were not red yet and showed no signs of changing. Theo dodged a downward swing but overextended his reach and missed the flick of the wrist that had the sword coming back for him. The sword merely grazed his shoulder, a testament to Rhydian's superb control. It stained his white shirt red.

"First blood!" the king announced.

Theo needed to try to attack Rhydian if he wanted to wake the curse. He batted at Rhydian with his shield and drove the gladius forward in a basic but well-executed thrust. Rhydian easily evaded, but his features hardened. Theo stepped up, spun, and swiped the sword toward Rhydian again. Rhydian parried with his, too, and launched at Theo. Theo was already retreating, doing anything possible to stay out of Rhydian's reach.

Theo had spent considerable time practicing with the swords he made as an apprentice, but he was thoroughly outmatched by the

Warbringer. He just had to piss Rhydian off enough that his curse came out before Rhydian won. Rhydian drove Theo back, cutting, swiping, and lunging. Theo could not possibly block the barrage and missed a slicing circle to his leg. Rhydian's blade nicked Theo's hip.

"Second blood!" the king announced.

The crowd cheered. Theo panted and lunged at Rhydian. If Rhydian cut him one more time, then he'd be found guilty. And Rhydian was holding back as much as he could without drawing attention to it. This was Theo's last chance. He tried to remember Rhydian's barrage and copied it as best he could. He charged a surprised Rhydian with sweeps and cuts and slices. It was clumsy, but Theo didn't stop his forward drive, which forced Rhydian to dance away.

A rosy hue grew in the corners of Rhydian's eyes. *Almost.*

Rhydian slashed, and Theo caught it on his shield. His shield caved inward. Theo threw the shield at Rhydian, who batted it away like it was a firefly. Rhydian's eyes darkened. Theo charged again, this time armed with only a blade. Theo hacked, swung, and kicked at Rhydian, who blocked each easily with a wicked grin.

Just as Rhydian's blade snaked under Theo's arm and nicked his ribs, Rhydian's eyes turned blood red with the Warbringer curse. Theo pinned his arm over the cut and kicked sand at Rhydian's eyes. Rhydian knew it was coming and dodged, but he did not dodge the handful of dirt from Theo's pocket he had grabbed as he entered the arena. He tossed the second handful at Rhydian, and it splashed against his face. Rhydian clawed at his eyes, while Theo took the opportunity and slashed his blade across Rhydian's arm to draw blood.

"First blood for Theo!" Aurienne said.

Rhydian roared and knocked Theo's sword from his hands. Theo dove for the bow, causing most of his arrows to roll away. He drew back the bowstring and aimed at Rhydian. Rhydian grinned. Theo aimed for Rianne, and Rhydian smirked. He must have remembered his warning to Theo and knew Theo would not harm Rianne.

Theo loosed the arrow and prayed his aim was true. The arrow struck inches from Rianne's head, and right on cue, she screamed. Rhydian roared again as Theo drew another arrow and aimed for her. He loosened it as Rhydian dove between them and deflected the arrow with his shoulder. Blood stained Rhydian's white shirt.

"Second blood for Theo," the king announced, sounding displeased.

Theo was out of arrows, so he drew a dagger and kept his arm tight to his ribs, concealing the blood from the small scratch that would have signaled victory for Rhydian. He circled Rhydian, who rose from the dirt and raised his sword. His eyes were so red they nearly bled. The next point would declare the winner.

Theo was out of tricks. What would Aurienne say? She'd tell him to do what Rhydian least expected. He backed away slowly from Rhydian like one might retreat from a wild forest bear, peering around for the unexpected.

Chickens squawked from the doorway not too far away. Theo ran. Rhydian stalked forward, gripping his sword.

"Running won't help you," Rhydian taunted.

Theo grabbed a discarded dagger on the way toward the doorway. He waited until the Warbringer was just behind him and then wrenched the cages opened. Chickens flew toward the Warbringer, clawing and flapping. The Warbringer ducked, and Theo lunged forward with the dagger. Rhydian sliced down toward the sword where he expected Theo to be, but Theo was gone. Theo's dagger sliced along Rhydian's forearm. Theo darted away, putting space between them as chickens wildly darted around.

"Third blood for Theo!" Aurienne announced loudly.

Theo lifted his gaze and grinned, feeling relief wash over him. He won. Somehow. His gaze dropped to the Warbringer standing across the arena, panting and glaring at Theo with eyes that glowed red. Rhydian snarled and lunged across the arena, lost to the bloodlust.

Hellsdamn me.

"Rhydian, it's over!" Theo shouted, sprinting as fast as he could.

Gods of hells, he's going to kill me.

The thundering steps just behind Theo told him that Rhydian was on his heels. Theo ran for the stands. Rhydian was so close Theo could feel the wind of Rhydian's sword. Theo darted toward a set of stairs and ran up into the stands. Rhydian chased, swinging his sword like an axe. The blade bit into the wood railings, and the cheering crowd began to scream. Theo jumped on the backs of the seats and ran across them at speed toward Rianne. Rhydian chased him, hacking and thrusting the entire time. The crowd dispersed.

"Rhydian! No!" Theo shouted.

The sword nearly caught Theo's foot and sunk deeply in the wood. Rhydian abandoned the blade. Theo threw a bottle of wine at Rhydian. Rhydian blocked it with his arm, and half the bottle emptied all over his shirt.

"Rhydian!" Rianne was standing and screaming.

Theo was too slow. Rhydian swung his fist at Theo, connecting with Theo's side. His ribs cracked with a sickening crunch, and Theo stumbled away. Theo couldn't breathe as sharp pains wracked his side. He choked and staggered away. Rhydian punched again, but Theo ducked into the stands. The fist grazed Theo's jaw, but still left him seeing stars. Rhydian's knuckles ripped Theo's cheek open. Half-blind, Theo ran.

Theo was nearly to Rianne, whom he hoped could calm the Warbringer. Theo dove behind Rianne and scrambled away, bleeding and panting. Rhydian stalked forward, but Rianne's small hand pressed against his chest. He stopped.

"Announce the winner, King Cavendar, and we shall take our leave," Aurienne hissed.

"Theo has proven his innocence. The trial is over. The Avyllon guests shall all be permitted to leave," the king announced sourly.

The crowd cheered.

"Rhydian," Rianne whispered. "Rhydian."

Rhydian took deep breaths and then turned away from them and stalked out of the arena. Rianne followed.

Theo held his ribs, mind addled from the blows. He stared at the ravine, feeling eyes upon him. The eyestone from Ma grew hot on his neck. He lifted it and peered through. Shredded glowing souls hovered near the executioner's block and screamed silently while monstrous black hands reached out of the depths.

Aurienne swung her legs over the railing and dropped down next to him. She touched his cheek, his blood coating her hands. Anger and concern warred in her cloudy eyes.

She took his hand and led him from the stadium. "Let's go while we still can."

His head pounded and ribs ached, and he stumbled behind her as quickly as he could manage. He sank to the floor outside his room unable to stand any longer. Aurienne knelt beside him and wrapped her arms around him.

"I'm so glad you're okay," she whispered.

"Rhydian helped me," Theo croaked. "I wouldn't have made it without his help. Even still, he nicked me a third time before I got him. I was very lucky. He hit me only twice, and I feel like I can't breathe."

"Tell me everything," Aurienne said.

Theo did.

"Rosalindt must have been the spirit of the ascended queen. Why would she bring you there?" she asked.

"To save Rianne," Theo said.

"From what? Other queens?"

He nodded.

"We need to leave," she said. "We've long worn out our welcome here. The king will be looking for another excuse to delay our departure."

A tight chuckle escaped his gritted teeth. "I don't want to stay here a minute longer."

She exhaled and pressed her forehead against his. "You scared me."

"I'm sorry." Wrapping his arms around her, he savored the

warmth of her skin against his, and the scent of her vanilla soap. He hadn't thought he'd make it out of that arena. There were so many things he'd wanted to say to her, but they all died in his mouth now.

"Thank you for protecting Adonis."

I'd die for you.

"Anything for you."

CROSSROADS
CHAPTER TWENTY-THREE

Two paths diverge in forest glen,
And may never cross again.

— *Traveler's folk wisdom.*

1152 N.T.C. Castle Rodarr, Rodarri.

Rhydian paced the gardens like a wounded animal, having suffered only a few minor scratches from the trial. His curse suffocated him like a living thing. Its claws dug into him. Its breath was on his neck. It whispered, telling him to let go of his long-held control and end a life to unleash his power. He cursed colorfully and sank his sword to the hilt in a tree.

"Rhydian, are you okay?" Rianne asked quietly.

"I will be. I just got close to losing control. I nearly killed." Rhydian sat in the grass and crossed his legs, taking deep breaths.

Rhydian flexed his hands. The cuts on his knuckles a stinging reminder that he'd struck Theo, nearly murdered him.

The king stormed out into the gardens, and Rhydian had to force himself not to react. He kept his eyes closed and focused on his breathing.

A large purple vein in the king's bulbous forehead pulsed, and spittle formed around his mouth. "You messed that up."

"My apologies. I have no control when my curse takes over. He won fair and square," Rhydian answered.

The king spat. "You've never been bested before until I need you to win. Then suddenly, he knows exactly how to beat you. I wonder where he learned that."

"Fate?"

The king's eyes narrowed. "They're leaving. I want you to go with them."

Rhydian's eyes popped open, and Rianne's hand went to her mouth.

"What?" Rhydian snapped.

"I need to know if the Free People and Titan Cliff dwellers really are attending this summit of hers. It gives you the chance to redeem your failure," King Cavendar said.

Rhydian began to argue, but the king cut him off. "It's not a request. If you refuse to go, I may have to move up the next ascension. Say your goodbyes. They'll be gone soon, and you need to be with them."

Rhydian snapped his mouth shut and glowered as the king left. He worked his jaw and tasted coppery rage.

He turned to Rianne. "He's already angry, and I can't give him a reason to harm any of you."

Rianne stepped in front of him and lightly touched her hands to his chest. He gently took her cheeks in his hands. He was acutely aware of how soft her skin was on his blistered palms. He studied her, committing every feature to memory. Kind blue eyes that sparkled like distant starlight. A generous smile that lit up the room. Rhydian pulled Rianne in and pressed his lips against her forehead, refusing to let go for long moments. He released the kiss and pulled her into a deep hug, careful not to crush her thin frame.

"I'm going to miss you," Rhydian said.

"I'll miss you too," Rianne said softly.

"I'm not sure I can control this curse without you." Rhydian bowed his head. "I think that's what the king wants."

Rianne tilted her head to get a better look at him. "I believe in you, Rhydian." She placed her small hand across his chest and pressed lightly. "You have a good heart."

"They're asking me to go out on the roads where Avyllon has reported everything from emperor's scouts to war talks with wary allies and veiled enemies. Everything about this is full of violence," he said.

"Rhydian, you are not your curse," she said. "Your life is not dictated by something you cannot control. You are so much more."

Rhydian smiled, just a hint. She always knew what to say to chase his demons away. He took a deep breath in and faintly smelled peaches and honey upon her thick light brown hair. It flooded his nose and filled him with peace.

"If it weren't for you, I would have fallen to my curse a long time ago," he said.

Rianne smiled and kissed him gently, standing on her tiptoes. "I don't believe that."

"When I came here, I'd lost my father and beaten some farmhand bully half to death. I was ready to surrender to the curse and become a Warbringer until I met you," he said.

Rianne cupped the stubble of his face in her hand. "After I met you, suddenly, it didn't matter whether I had months or decades left to live. My life was complete."

Tears prickled at the corners of his eyes, but he refused to cry, not when he was about to ride to prevent a war. Not when she could see how it killed him to leave her.

"Every second with you is a gift. I'll take as many as I can get until that time comes when you must ascend," he said.

A tear fell from Rianne's eye.

"When I return, will you leave with me?"

Rianne nodded. "I'll make sure all the queens are ready to leave."

Rhydian grinned and kissed her deeply. "I love you."

Her eyes sparkled, and her smile widened on her pale skin. "I love you too."

Rhydian slowly and carefully released her. His fingers lingered on hers, savoring the last contact. "I'll be back soon."

"I'll be waiting," she said.

Rhydian forced his feet to take him away, glancing back to give her a final wave.

Aurienne pushed between the veil into the futures and fates. In her spectral form, she stepped through the wall of the king's office.

"Why are you sending the Warbringer with the High Seer?" the king's advisor asked.

"King Jaekob wrote that the seer is stirring trouble," the king said. "She intends to resist the emperor's demands and search for allies."

The advisor poured back a dark drink. "We've already agreed to the emperor's demands, though, as has the Wyndsel nation."

No surprise there.

"Yes, we have," the king said. "But she is very loudly and very publicly sharing her visions of doom and destruction. Prophecies and omens hook people in. If she turns popular opinion against us, we'll have a harder time increasing taxes and sending young men off to fight in foreign wars."

"If you and King Jaekob refuse her summit, won't that put an end to it?"

"She intends to visit the Seven Forests and Titan Cliffs as well. If she convinces them to come, then it'll be harder to argue," the king said.

"The borders of Seven Forests and Titan Cliffs have been closed for decades. She won't even get past the forest."

"She has the Sight," the king said. "She can probably See some ferret hole inside. We can't dismiss her. She's powerful, dangerous. When she asks the right questions, she is given the answers by her Goddess herself. I'm sending Rhydian because I need to know what she's up to. If she gets the southern nations to come, then Jaekob and I will have to attend her summit as well."

"Don't you want him here to defend against the coming threats? Don't we need him here now more than ever?" the advisor asked.

"No. Not when we're going to put to death the woman he loves. Soon."

Oh no, Rianne.

"Your Majesty?"

"This is the greatest threat we've ever faced. We need the eldest blood to ascend."

"But sir, she's produced no children. Moving up the ascension will end the firstblood line. She is the first daughter of the first daughter dating back to the first Queensblood."

The king slammed his fist on the desk. "We can't keep waiting for a child that may never come. She's been bedded for several years already and nothing. That withering sickness she had as a child might have taken the ability from her altogether. We need the protection of the firstblood. This is the greatest threat we've faced since the Elven Wars over a thousand years ago. If it ends the line, it ends the line."

Elven Wars? Did he mean the Shadow Wars?

"Surely, there's another option," the advisor pleaded.

The king growled.

"At least until we're sure of the threat," the advisor said quickly.

The king stroked the fur on the hem of his robe, quietly contemplating his advisor's words.

"Fine," the king answered. "If the seer thinks the threat comes at Hallohaim, we'll wait for that. We'll do an ascension per day for a fortnight. That should protect us. I was hoping the Warbringer would do what they all do and create offspring before going on a mad, murderous spree and disappearing. He's still here, and we have no more time to wait for Rianne to bear children. She may ascend, and I want him as far away as possible when we do."

Aurienne listened, feeling herself begin to slip away from the vision. Hate bubbled in her gut at this cowardly little man.

One day, you'll get what's coming to you.

"What if there is no summit?"

"We do the ascension at the next full moon either way. I want Rhydian to keep tabs on the seer and her blacksmith and report back. Even if they know he's spying, they won't refuse our offer if they want us to join."

The advisor wrung his hands. "Won't they know you've given their location to the emperor?"

Aurienne's blood ran cold. They'd been betrayed again. How could she help them if they were determined to bring destruction down on their heads.

"If they suspect, there's nothing they can do," the king said. "With any luck, both the Warbringer and the seer won't survive the rest of the trip. It would be just as convenient if our problems disappeared together. I've heard the roads are...dangerous these days."

A thin smile crept over the king's face.

Aurienne lingered beside her packed bags, reeling from the vision and ready to leave this terrible place. Waiting for the others to join, she closed her eyes and opened herself to the Fates and the Goddess. Whispers of the past, present, and future that she jotted into her journal.

> *Don't you hear them? All those queens, dead for*
>   *nothing.*
> *There is no way I'll live without you.*
> *Some hope was better than none.*
> *Her time was too short, and her duty too great. But no*

one faced it braver than she did. It made me
love her.
This world makes monsters of us all.

Aurienne smelled burning paper. She drew her spelled divination card box, and smoke poured from the cracks. Yelping, she ripped the box open.

The cards burst into flames in her hands, and she dropped them. They burned on the floor for long seconds until the flames extinguished at once. Five cards lay face up on a pile of ash while the others rattled and scattered across the floor like mice before the flames sputtered.

The High Seer.

The Road.

The Castle.

The Emperor.

Life.

The swiftest flash of a vision appeared and was gone just as quickly. An emissary of the Emperor of Demorra stood in the Temple of Avyllon. The temple was adorned in Hallohaim sage bundles, witch's bells, harvest wreaths, and ancestral bones. Aurienne blinked.

"Saryll! Kassia!"

Saryll's door slammed open, and she and Kassia lunged out. "What's wrong?"

"Emperor Rexil sends an emissary to Avyllon. I must return to greet the emissary at once. We need to travel to the nearest Way," Aurienne said.

"I'll let them know of the change in plans," Kassia said.

She crouched, gently coaxing her cards from under the furniture and rugs. After a quick prick of her golden dagger and an offering of blood, several cards drifted back into her spelled box. Once they were all back, she clicked the box closed.

She'd have to leave Theo. The thought of no longer reaching for his arm or stealing kisses under the moonlight made her chest feel hollow. She had come to look forward to his stories and constant presence. How could she return to life before him? Shaking her head, she chided herself. She was fine before him. She'd be fine now—she had to be. Her chest constricted, and the thought made her feel sick. She froze.

Hellsdamn him. What had he done?

Her reading of true love echoed in her mind. Death precedes love. Either she would die before finding true love, or her loving someone was a death sentence. The Fates were clear. If she loved him, he would die. She was dangerously close to falling in love with him, and she'd failed to realize it. She grimaced.

Goddess' blood. He was in danger. If she continued down this path, it would kill him.

She'd never let anything happen to him. Not if she could prevent it. Saving Teridar was her first duty, but after that, she'd protect Theo with all she had. There was only one thing that could be done.

"Can you send Theo in?" she asked.

"Sure." Saryll gently patted her arm.

Moments later, Theo slipped into her room. "You asked for me?"

The words died in her mouth. Her eyes poured over him, committing every detail to memory. Blond hair, stubble a few shades darker. Forest green eyes that sparkled when they rested upon her, broad shoulders settled in an easy posture, hands tucked into his belt. The bright grin that lit up every room. He met her gaze, expectant.

Aurienne had seen that look before. Reverence. Respect. Awe. When Theo looked at her with those soft green eyes, he resembled a man in prayer.

She crossed the room and kissed him. He wrapped his arms around her waist, and she ran her painted fingertips across his jaw. He tasted bright and citrusy, like the rising sun, and he smelled like pine-scented mountain air and hot forges. He kissed her, and hellsdamn it, she realized he was in love. His hands were firm on her back, pulling her against his chest, and his arms fit perfectly around her. He was breathing her in, kissing her in perfect rhythm. Only a man in love kissed like that. The most powerful seer alive, and she'd been blind to it. She kissed him goodbye, feeling like her heart was sundered into shards of glass.

"Theo, I have to tell you something."

He tilted his head and ran his fingers through her hair before tracing them down her back.

Goddess. Anything but this.

"I needed to tell you that I must go through the Way to return to Avyllon to meet an emissary from Emperor Rexil," she said. "You must go on to the Seven Forests and Titan Cliffs without me. We won't have time to delay, and I won't be able to rejoin you. You have two weeks."

Theo stopped breathing. "I have to go alone?"

Aurienne nodded.

"But I-I can't do this without you," he stammered. "I've already managed to mess it up. I need you."

"The Goddess Saw *you* do this. I believe in you," Aurienne said.

Theo released her and began to pace. "The Seven Forests and Titan Cliffs are closed. What am I supposed to do?"

"The Goddess believes you will find a way, as do I," she said.

Theo cursed, and Aurienne clenched her fists, knowing what she must do. She tasted his lips on hers, and her tongue rebelled against the next words.

That reading was so long ago. It might no longer hold the weight it did, the meaning it did. And he was right here. It was worth taking that risk, for him.

"I wa..." Her vocal cords seized into pillars of stone in her throat. She couldn't breathe, couldn't speak, and coughed until her throat loosened.

"Are you alright?" Theo touched her arm, gaze sharp and anxious.

She wiped her eyes, straightening.

What was that?

She tried again. "I..."

Her throat and chest seized again, as though crushed underneath a great weight. Her lips were wrenched shut by golden threads, invisible to all but her. She clawed at her mouth to pry it open, but it wouldn't move. She coughed into her cheeks and fell to her knees. Her head snapped back as a vision poured over her.

A battlefield full of corpses, and crimson mud.

A man wearing the golden griffin of Avyllon held out his hand to her.

The man's green eyes held a depth of love for her she'd never known possible.

A monstrous wolf biting off the man's head.

Her head fell forward, body limp, as the vision released her. The man from the foretelling vision was Theo. She'd watched him die. Finally, the golden threads and weight vanished, and she could breathe. But the warning was clear. She was never to love, or Theo would die.

"Aurienne?" His voice was sharp, his touch firm.

She wiped her mouth, finding blood springing from her gums and the back of her throat.

"Was there something you wanted to say?"

Yes.

"I don't remember."

I'm sorry.

She took his hands in hers.

"Theo, I've enjoyed traveling with you," she said. "These weeks have given me some of the happiest memories of my life, but I fear that our time grows short. When I return to Avyllon, this will be over. *Us.* It's...I can't."

He stared as the heavy weight of betrayal and heartbreak filled the room. His hands dropped to his sides as his shoulders slumped. He tucked his hands into his pockets and swallowed before clenching his jaw and looking away.

"She never loves them back," he muttered.

His words were too sharp to face, and she looked away.

"I understand." The tone was clipped and tense.

Fiery rage and frigid sorrow clashed in Aurienne's heart, making it feel both too large and too small for her chest. Her hand raised to press against the physical pain growing in her chest.

She hated herself for the lie. "I'm sorry if...I...told you I could never fall in love. I have my duty to return to, and there's no place for you in my life there."

Theo flinched.

Hagsteeth.

"I..." she began.

"There's nothing else to say," he said quietly. "We always knew what this was—a distraction. You told me your fate, so I was well warned."

Aurienne looked away.

"I'm going to finish packing. I'll see you at the stable." Theo slipped out of her room.

She drummed her palm against her chest in case her heart forgot to beat, cursing the gods.

Standing at the shimmering Way, waiting for Adonis to open it under Mathis' careful instruction, Theo was heartsick. Aurienne would soon be gone. She was his rock, his anchor, his foundation in all of this. He was lost and adrift, crumbling without her. How could he convince two lost leaders to join when he'd already failed with the first two?

More than that, Theo knew this was an ending. He sensed it over the past day, with Aurienne pulling away in conversation. She was distant, and not because of her visions. She was returning home, leaving *him*. Whatever they had been was over. Their brief retreat from reality expired. It had been a dream, but it was time to wake.

Theo *knew*. He knew it couldn't last, and the whole time, he knew it was never meant to. He cursed his heart for running away from him. Theo was hopelessly in love with Aurienne, but Aurienne did not—could not—love him. Even as he knew this, he could not help but seek her out for their final stolen conversations the past days. He yearned to hear her laugh and see her smile just once more.

Standing before the open Way, it was now truly over. Some of the caravan went through the Way as Aurienne stood silently beside Theo. A small part of him hoped she wanted to prolong her departure.

Aurienne turned to Theo. "It's time for me to go."

"I know."

"You know my fate. Love with me doesn't last." She smiled sadly.

"I know. But I won't give up these fleeting, beautiful moments just because they may not last," Theo said her own words from the gardens back to her.

"I-I'm sorry."

"I don't regret it, not even a second," he said.

Aurienne planted a gentle kiss on his cheek and then stepped through the Way. It closed behind her, and she was gone, leaving only a whispered farewell against his skin.

Interlude

Never step into a shadow atop dark, still water when the moon is gone, or you could lose your soul.

> — *Warning given to shepherds, sentinels, and spies.*

1152 N.T.C. The city of Rexila, the heart of the Demorran Empire, named for the Grand Imperial Emperor Jhames Edwyrd Alexandir Rexil, the Wolf, Moon-blessed, conqueror of seventeen kingdoms, and favorite son of the Lunar Goddess Niamh.

Across the seas, Avyllon's nameless spy was surrounded by enemies, and he was running out of time to find information for the High Seer. The spy nearly stepped into the inky, swirling shadow near an onyx puddle but froze. The water was still as glass and reflected no light. A strange buzzing noise, one he might have imagined, emanated from the puddle. He glanced up to check if the moon or stars shone, and they were covered by clouds.

Stepping around that shadow, he remembered his father's warning. He wasn't about to lose his soul that day. His father and grandfather, both spies to the former king and High Seer, remained nameless their entire lives—a feat all spies aspired to. His father was a clever and careful man and if he said to avoid something, there existed good reason.

He chose another hiding place in the alcove and waited. Since arriving in Rexila, he learned the fate of the three nations that denied the emperor. Those lost nations had refused his demands, and he erased them from the map. Literally. The rest fell into line soon after. Weeks of searching had only turned up a single old map naming three massacred countries. How many more tribes or cities had the emperor destroyed?

The silver temple of the Lunar Goddess Niamh stood adjacent to the emperor's golden palace, surrounded by overflowing amethyst offering bowls. Priestesses with silver burning rings branded into their foreheads filled the temple. Hulking guards with too-long strides and hunched postures marched lines of supplicants into the temple. The supplicants never emerged. He knew better than to join one of those groups. Instead, he climbed and found a loose window high in the temple rafters and slipped inside.

The spy crept through the attic. He wrapped a stolen white cloak of the believer around his shoulders and dropped into the main temple. Creeping to the doors, he tried all the handles, but they didn't move. With a frustrated grunt, he inspected the layered locks. He was about to leave when he caught the pungent whiff of a familiar smell.

Death.

The nameless one froze, whispering a prayer to Dhagaos and X'era—the god of death and goddess of shadows.

He followed the smell to an underground warehouse in the temple. He turned his cloak inside out so that he was garbed in black and slipped inside. Corpses littered the floor. Gagging, he brought the scarf over his nose, recoiling. At the end of the room, a large furnace consumed the blood and bodies. He slunk to the closest body and inspected it. Its heart was ripped out, a gaping hole where the organ ought to be.

The spy crawled to another body. He rolled it over and stifled a shout—pressing his face mask into his mouth. The body was covered in patches of fur and bone ridges. The skull cracked and elongated with the maw of a wolf and rows of teeth sticking out at odd angles. The skin stretched too tight over the bones.

What were these things? Magical experiments gone wrong? Who was doing this? For what purpose? Had they been successful? What did it have to do with the goddess Niamh?

He backed out of the room, avoiding notice, and followed a group of worshippers outside and back to the streets of Rexila, where he disappeared.

Once back to his apartment, the one without a name wrote the High Seer a coded message. He knew he had to find more information if they were to defeat the emperor. Time was running out.

Part Three

Knots of Fate
Chapter Twenty-Four

This cannot be undone.

— *High Seer Aurienne Azarrah, prophetic*
vision.

1152 N.T.C. The namesake capital city of Avyllon.

Nothing lasted forever. Change was the only constant in life. Aurienne knew this truth but wished her time with Theo could have been longer. Having returned to Avyllon, she felt as though she had woken from a dream and was thrust back into the harsh light of reality. More than anything, she wanted to dance underneath the moon and relive a kiss tasting of forests and mountains. Nothing lasted, though, especially not for her. Affection would only ever be fleeting; the Fates made sure of that. Though she yearned for comfortable fireside conversation with a certain blacksmith, she stared at a stack of papers requiring her attention.

Hours passed as Aurienne made her way through the stack. She signed approvals of temporary taxation waivers, building permit requests for new structures, university expenditures, temple maintenance costs, and a thousand other administrative tasks. Left only with the most complicated matters requiring foresight, she turned to her runes.

"Should I sign this?" she asked her bone runes.

She grasped the top paper with one hand and with the other rolled her carved runes across the altar. *Yes.* Aurienne signed the paper and picked up the second.

"Should I sign this?"

Over and over, Aurienne repeated the process. She signed documents the runes rolled yes, and made a stack of those rolled no. In the morning, she'd use the divination cards for those more complicated matters on those documents. If that did not work, Aurienne would meditate and seek visions for answers. If that yielded nothing, it meant hours in the archives.

She was nearly done when hot liquid rolled down her painted lips. She touched it. Blood. Her hands shook, and she swallowed her fear. She left the papers where they were and fell into bed.

The next morning, she did the same. The stack had mysteriously grown during the night with new requests and matters to attend. She barely finished the work as afternoon set on the grand city. Crossing the room toward the windows, she watched the sun set.

Her mind drifted toward Theo as she lingered before her altar. She held up her hand and summoned her deck from their spelled box.

Holding the divination cards representing her companions—the Traveler, the Magician, the Seer, and the Witch—her soul found Theo, Adonis, Saryll, Kassia, and the caravan in her vision. She watched them travel the road to the Seven Forests, safe and continuing the quest. *Thank the Goddess.* Letting them go, her soul returned.

She contemplated the upcoming visit from Emperor Rexil's emissary. She'd directed some of the temple attendants to prepare rooms for the emissary, but strangely, though Aurienne Saw his arrival in her visions so clearly, there were no messages received indicating his journey. Either he wanted to surprise her, or he was intending to visit someone else. Her nameless spy had yet to write, so she had no other information to go on. She closed her eyes to call forth a vision, but blood dripped from her mouth once more. Eyelids heavy, she abandoned her efforts for now. She needed rest, but first a bath.

Scalding water gushed forth to fill the tub. Avyllon was powered by water from the large dam, which meant the entire city always had heat, running water, and hot baths.

Alone in the tub, she slipped into a dreamlike meditation. As her spirit passed beyond the veil to receive any messages from the Goddess, Aurienne was acutely aware of a dark smudge on her soul, suffocating and crackling. The mark of necromancy remained. She was still unsure whether the necromancy or the increasing demands on her gift were to blame for the headaches and nosebleeds—unsure what it meant for her gift or her life.

Not meaning to, she walked through one of the lands beyond the veil. She didn't know how many lands there were or which this was.

> *A red sky.*
> *Stones stacked as tall and narrow as trees.*
> *A large wave filled the sky.*

She ran. A tidal wave of crushing stone and water buried her. Aurienne screamed and choked. She'd slipped below her bath water. She threw herself over the side of the tub as she fought to catch her breath. Water poured from her nose and mouth. She caught her breath and stared at the bloody water on the floor with wide eyes. She touched her mouth, and her fingers came away crimson.

A vision came—she was standing on the balcony of the temple, addressing the crowd. A celestial calendar marked the day. Today. A crown fell from her hands to the floor. Hallohaim lanterns.

The summit. Someone was crowned at the summit.

A faceless person was lit up by starlight. Aurienne picked up the crown and placed it on the figure's head. She thought that for a moment she could see the face. The figure picked up a gleaming sword and lifted it high. The other nations of Teridar lifted their weapons in response.

"Are you sure?" Aurienne whispered to her Goddess. "You want me to give up the crown? You want me to step down as regent? Today?"

She received no answer, but she did not need one. The Goddess had given Aurienne a command.

Aurienne caught her reflection in the mirror, looking back at her. She had thought for a second it was smiling wickedly, but she saw only herself now. Wet, naked, bleeding through her teeth, and bewildered. She pulled herself from the tub and kneeled on the wet floor. She pressed her hands together in prayer.

"Please be sure. I will follow your command. I will do as you ask, but please be sure. This cannot be undone."

One more vision. A crown fell to the floor, shattering into hundred pieces that bounced and shattered into dust that blew away on the wind.

She bowed her head. "Yes, Goddess."

Aurienne slowly dried off and dressed. She donned a regal black gown stitched with spun gold thread and painted her skin with celestial designs before gilding herself in jewelry. Her hands shook the entire time, and she had to repaint the designs several times. She would not admit it, but she was terrified. What could be coming that would require her to step down? How bad were things going to get?

Another vision slipped over Aurienne, like spider silk upon her skin. Aurienne Saw the Guild Masters gathering in the temple. They clawed for the crown upon her head and scratched out her eyes. She heard their whispers—their pleas, begging, guilting, threatening, deceiving. She heard the entire conversation that was coming.

"Thank you, Goddess."

Aurienne summoned a sister seer, Evani, who had recently finished her training. "Gather the people. I have an announcement just before dusk. Make sure the fires are lit."

"What is the announcement?" Evani asked.

Aurienne's stomach tightened, and she suddenly felt sick. Her throat tightened, and she nearly doubled over, barely able to utter any words.

"I intend to lead prayers," Aurienne lied. The words came out of her mouth without her control.

As Evani left, General Kane entered.

"The Obermeister and other Guild Masters have requested an audience," General Kane said.

Aurienne had already braced herself for that. "I'll receive them in the meeting room outside of the announcement balcony."

"They seek to grab power," General Kane said.

"They're not the only ones," Aurienne replied quietly.

General Kane had the decency to look guilty as he straightened his uniform. "I never sought to unseat you as regent, even if I do believe that military power should remain with those experienced in it."

"You're a peacetime general." She chuckled mirthlessly. "You've resolved neighbor disputes, investigated murders, and provided event security functions. You know war about as much as I do. And you forget the peace you enjoyed was because of me." She rubbed her tired eyes.

General Kane flinched. "We may not agree on some things, but I have never undermined you. I have never worked against you and tried to take power. I was upfront with you."

Aurienne paused. "You're right. You never did. Though I'm not sure it matters now."

"What has happened? Are you okay?"

"The burden grows heavy," Aurienne said.

"You Saw something. You know what the Guilds are demanding?"

"Our enemies are numerous," she said. "They all want the same thing. They want to devour us. They want the crown. They don't realize that if they take the crown, they'll rule over a burning pile of ash by the year's end."

Aurienne squared her shoulders and stared him down. The familiar divine presence of the Goddess settled upon her, and by the general's expression, he felt something too.

"I have seen Avyllon, and Teridar, burn in a thousand ways, and each I have fought against," she said. "We have one chance to survive, Kane. One. The leaders of Teridar *must* attend the summit. They *must* agree to stand against the emperor. Theo is the only one who can get them here. I *know* this. It is not a chance or suggestion. If the Guild Masters take power, they will not heed my visions, and the city and its people will burn."

He frowned.

"Did you know what the Guild Masters were doing?"

"They have always wanted power," he said. "They have always spoken of taking power in quiet rooms after a few too many drinks. I did not know they had taken steps toward it. None of my men have heard such a thing. They must have recently decided."

She shook her head. "They must have been contacted by the emperor. Either they had not made the decision until a few hours ago, or the emperor's actions are shielded from my Sight by something...or both perhaps."

"They were just bragging that they have been gathering signatures. They have five hundred thousand, nearly all the members of all the Guilds."

She quickly did the math. "That's only one third of the adult population. It is not enough to require a monarch to step down by our laws. They would need a three-fourths vote."

"No, but you're not a monarch. You're regent. It only takes half the population to require a regent to step down."

Her lips curled and twisted. "They don't have half. Let's see what they have to say."

Aurienne arrived at the meeting room outside the grand balcony, with General Kane shadowing her at a respectful distance. She entered a room packed full of Guild Masters.

The Obermeister stood in the middle of the room, wearing the pin of the position, with his hands folded in front of himself. "I'm Obermeister Gotrik. I do not believe we have been formally introduced."

Aurienne took slow, careful steps into the center of the room, stopping before him. Obermeister Gotrik was a tall man of about forty years with the lean muscles of a life lived in pursuit of a noble trade. He must have been a woodworker, for his smell of sawdust and the numerous scars marring his hands. She eyed him before walking past him to the doors leading out to the balcony. She climbed several stairs and turned to face the group from her elevated position.

"We have not been formally introduced," she replied. "The Guild Masters voted for you to speak on their behalf. What, a year ago now? It seems we have not yet had a chance to do business in the short time of your term."

He glowered.

"You have brought me a petition to step down as regent with signatures, have you not? May I see it?" Aurienne held out her hand.

The Obermeister Gotrik's hands dropped from the clasped position to hang limply at his sides. The letter was clutched in one fist. He was angry. Good. Angry men made mistakes. He handed her the letter. Aurienne took it and pretended to read it.

"Forty-seven years is too long without a king," Gotrik said. "High Seers have been competent regents, but we are faced with war. It is time that men of knowledge and experience take the lead."

Aurienne noticed General Kane shift uncomfortably at the back of the crowd. They had approached him, then. General Kane didn't look down or away, though. Interesting. He had refused, at least for the time being.

"You think experience is better than Sight? Ruling based on experience is guesswork. Ruling based on actual knowledge of the future seems more reliable, does it not?" Aurienne said absently.

She tracked the floor's shadows. It was nearly dusk and time to make an announcement that would render this conversation moot.

"We are not here to argue the merits with you—"

"That is exactly what you are here to do," she interrupted. "If you wanted to deliver sufficient votes, you would have them. You do not. You are here to convince me to step down voluntarily to save face."

The Obermeister's jaw grew slack. The others shifted and exchanged wary glances. They were used to dealing with her sister seers. They were not used to the power of the High Seer. Aurienne almost felt bad for them. It was no fair contest, not with the might of the Goddess guiding Aurienne.

Obermeister Gotrik glared. "We can get the rest of the signatures, but you'll lose the people's support."

"Yes, yes." She waved her hand. "I'll be expelled from the temple and lose the title of High Seer and be relegated to telling fortunes out of the back of a wagon on the crossroads. Though I realize it is the first time for you, I have had this conversation before in a vision. If you feel the need to continue to waste my time, know that it is what you are doing."

"You couldn't possibly have Seen—"

"No?" She smiled wolfishly. "You'll demand I give up the crown. First, you will try to convince me of the need of a true king—which I just cut you short, so my apologies. You will try to guilt me into doing what is best for Avyllon. You will also threaten me with all the terrible things that will happen to me. I'll continue to refuse, and then you will storm out of here to try to get the signatures. You'll bribe, buy, cheat, steal, and forge whatever signatures you need.

You'll get them, eventually, after tearing the city in half with your foolishness."

Gotrik's face now turned a dangerous crimson as he sputtered, "We will get the votes!"

"Perhaps," she said. "But *you* will then have to get the votes to become king. I assume you want the title yourself. Your fellow Guild Masters may support you speaking for them, but will they give up a chance at the crown? Likely not. You will be contested. And it will not just be the Guild Masters. It will be non-Guild citizens. And then the real scheming and exchanges of promises begins. Ultimately, the worthiest among you will not be chosen. It will be the one best at tricking, betraying, flattering, and making empty promises."

"You can try to confuse the issue with pretty words, false visions, and fear, but you cannot control us," Obermeister Gotrik said. "You have no right to rule us, and we do not worship your Goddess. We have decided we want a king. We will have one. We are happy to get the votes, but it would be easier if you just stepped down."

"All the while, the emperor will sweep through Teridar and destroy us all. You will keep everyone busy with your trivial distractions while our destruction draws near," Aurienne finished.

Obermeister Gotrik glared. "With your support, a new king could be selected without delay. One who would know how to deal with the emperor."

The shadows crossed the flowering tree in the hammered copper pot. It was time. She took a deep breath to steady herself for what came.

"You are right on one thing," Aurienne said.

"What?"

"Avyllon will have a monarch."

Aurienne pushed open the doors to the balcony and stepped out to a quietly waiting crowd. Obermeister Gotrik and the Guild Masters stepped out onto the balcony and recoiled when they saw the solemn, expectant crowd below.

"People of Avyllon, the Goddess has seen fit to grant me a vision of our future," Aurienne announced. "For forty-seven years, Avyllon has been without a monarch. The chosen High Seers have faithfully served you through that time. However, the red eclipse showed us war is upon us. Today, the Goddess showed me that the rightful monarch of Avyllon will return at the next full moon."

The crowd murmured excitedly. The Guild Masters were hissing at Aurienne to stop, but she ignored those foolish tiny-minded men.

"A descendant of the first king of Avyllon will arrive," she said. "The descendant's bloodline will be proven by awakening the Sword of Souls, which will be needed in the days to come. In two weeks, you will not have a regent. You will have a true king or queen."

The crowd cheered and hollered.

"The wise Guild Masters have come to me today with exactly this request. They, too, have seen the need for a king and have requested one be crowned. Little did they know the Goddess had already identified the true heir. These are happy times!"

Aurienne returned to the meeting room, away from the excited crowd. As she passed Obermeister Gotrik, she said, "If the Goddess wanted one of you to rule, you would. She does not, so she will not allow it."

"You're bluffing," he sputtered. "In two weeks, you will be seen to be a fraud. And then one of us will become king."

She crossed her arms. "It's no bluff. You think you can be king? How many aqueducts are in the city?"

He stammered.

"Do you even know how many guilds, which you personally oversee?"

"Well, it's about…"

"What are taxes set to? What's the annual budget for the temple and university? What is the maintenance on the steam power? How much hydropower does the dam generate? How much food must be set aside for winter?"

He pursed his lips.

"I could go on, but you get my point. You're not fit to rule. You want an empty title, a grand chair, and a job you aren't qualified to do. You want a job you wouldn't be *able* to do."

"The new king won't know either."

"I tire of this. Go back to your woodshop."

He stepped closer. "This isn't over."

"That is the difference between the two of us," she said. "Everything you do, you do for yourself. Everything I do is for the Goddess. I obey all her commands, even giving up a throne. She cares for all, but you only care for yourself."

The Obermeister clenched his fists. Aurienne Saw him take a wild swing to slap her, and she stepped beside General Kane. General Kane's hand slowly slipped to his sword hilt.

Obermeister Gotrik glared again. "In two weeks, you will have lost power to us or to this new monarch. The time of the seers is past."

The Obermeister grinned viciously at her and exited the room, followed by the rest of the Guild Masters.

When they left, General Kane exclaimed, "Aurienne! What did you do?"

"What the Goddess told me to," she said tiredly. "She promised royal blood. Someone picks up the crown."

"The Guild Masters won't stop."

"Perhaps not, but they are delayed. Until the full moon, they can't very well demand a throne that may rightfully belong to another."

"You gave them the motivation to cast doubt upon you and your Goddess. If they undermine the people's faith in Her, then Her commands will no longer matter. And now they know there's a deadline. They have two weeks to make the people lose all faith in you."

Aurienne's glassy clouded eyes met the general's gaze. "Do you think I wanted to do this? I obey my Goddess, no matter the cost."

She watched General Kane stomp out, knowing betrayal lurked

in every shadow. Schemes twirled around her, tightening like a noose. Breathing deeply, she prayed to the Goddess to protect her so she could save them.

THE SHADOW WOOD
CHAPTER TWENTY-FIVE

The forest was full of regrets,
Forgotten, forsaken secrets.

— *MARKER TO THE SHADOW WOOD.*

1152 N.T.C. The road to the Seven Forests.

More lost than he had ever been, Theo led the remaining caravan toward the border of the Seven Forests. He took the main road with no attempt at subterfuge. He was sick of politics, deception, plots, and schemes. Without the heart to make traveling conversation, he rode in silence. He failed to formulate a plan, with Aurienne occupying his thoughts, building an ache in his chest.

As Rhydian rode up beside Theo, he side-eyed Rhydian warily, rubbing his cracked ribs. He could almost feel the bruised cut on his jaw aching in the Warbringer's presence.

"I never thanked you for saving Rianne. Thank you," Rhydian said.

"You saved my life by not killing me in the trial, so I think we can call it even."

"You didn't tell the king that I told you how to defeat me, so I also need to thank you for that," Rhydian said with a chuckle.

Theo smiled, despite his gloomy mood. "I think you knew Adonis actually stole Vittoria's Gift, not me, so thank you for not telling the king. Adonis would've died."

"You didn't tell the king I told you I was supposed to dig up dirt on you," Rhydian countered.

"You didn't tell anyone about the ghosts."

"The what?"

Theo chuckled nervously. "Nothing. Just... The ravine... Nothing."

"I suppose it makes us even on the gratitude," Rhydian said. "I did chase you through the stadium, wielding a sword. And I punched you. So, I think I must also apologize."

"You hit me *twice*, but I should also apologize. I threw things at you. Wine. Food. Racks of swords. Wine cups."

"I remember a few other things flying at my head."

"The chickens?"

"The chickens."

Theo snorted. "Anything for a victory."

"I'm pretty sure I got the third cut first, cheater," Rhydian joked.

Theo laughed. "Not if no one saw it."

"I'm glad you managed to win. The king wanted to put you to death. He knew he might not get another excuse. But he's waiting for the opportunity. I'm supposed to spy on you."

Theo groaned. "Great."

"Unlucky for him, I happen to be the worst spy in the history of Rodarri."

They shared a laugh, but Theo's dark mood returned as the miles went by. He stared at the road sourly. Even the fox was nowhere to be seen. He would be talking to Aurienne, but she was gone, back at Avyllon receiving the emissary and trying to buy them time. The problem was, time for what? The borders to the Seven Forests and Titan Cliffs were closed. What was Theo supposed to do? He wished Aurienne was here.

Rhydian said, "You too, eh?"

"What?"

"Homesick already for your woman."

"She's not... Well... I don't know. She's..."

"It's complicated. I get that."

"We're not together."

"You sure looked together."

Theo took a sip from his canteen. "Things change."

"How'd it happen? The blacksmith and the High Seer."

Theo snorted out water all over his shirt. When he finally spit it all out and wiped his mouth, he said, "What about the murdery, cursed Warbringer and the Queensblood of Rodarri?"

"Probably the same as you. Luck. Fate. Destiny. Whatever it was, I'm not complaining." Rhydian winked.

"I'm sorry you had to leave her."

"I'm hoping to be back soon."

"Nothing cuts like being separated from the one who holds your heart," Theo said acridly.

"She is...everything," Rhydian trailed off. "I know she will one day die. I know that her time would be short. I know that her time is too short and her duty too great. But no one faces it braver than she does. It made me love her, still does."

Theo knew what that was like.

Rhydian blinked. "As for how we met, the king found out what I was. My eyes go red when I get, as you say, 'murdery,' and he or some advisor knew what it meant. I got assigned to guard the queens, his most precious asset," he said bitterly. "And that's where I met Rianne. I never wanted much out of life. I always knew that I would one day lose my mind and start killing and disappear. She reminded me that even a short life is worth living..."

Theo studied Rhydian's determined expression. "Sounds like you've got a plan."

"I wouldn't say that."

Theo chuckled. "I know what it's like to not be able to be with the woman you love. If you want to kidnap her and all the other queens, I'll be right there with you. The whole thing is barbaric."

Rhydian looked at Theo with respect. He held out his fist and forearm and bumped it against Theo's. "Same."

Theo grimaced. "If only fate was as easy to overcome as some old, frightened kings."

"Fate?"

"Aurienne read her fate, and she's not destined to find love in this life. She won't ever love me." Theo stared ahead, willing his heart not to break again.

Goddess—it hurt too badly the first time. He couldn't keep reliving this.

Rhydian shifted in the saddle. "Didn't she say to the king that her visions about you changed everything? It changed our fate in the war. Maybe you changed more than just that. I wouldn't count yourself out yet."

If only.

"Thanks. And I mean it about Rianne. After the summit, I'll help you."

"I'll hold you to it." Rhydian's tone possessed a serious edge.

"I need something from you too," Theo said. "I won't fail Aurienne. I *need* to convince the nations to come."

"I'll do whatever I can," Rhydian said. "I swear it."

Adonis guided his horse up to Theo and Rhydian. "What are you two talking about?" More quietly, Adonis mouthed, "Please save me."

"Adonis, do you want to run through the theorems again?" Mathis called out.

Adonis looked pleadingly at Rhydian and Theo, and they exchanged an amused look.

Rhydian answered, "Mathis, he's been helping us map our path to the Seven Forests border. The roads have been closed so long we need someone with expertise and training in maps."

"Oh, well, yes, quite. Carry on then." Mathis reined in his horse farther back alongside Kassia and Saryll.

"Thank you," Adonis breathed.

"There may come a day when you wished you'd appreciated him. They're not keen to help you after the apprenticeship ends. You're on your own," Theo said.

"I've been studying non-stop. I'll pick it up tomorrow. What are you talking about?" Adonis pressed.

Theo tried to cut Rhydian off, but Rhydian said, "Women."

"Oh, because Mr. Thatcher is in love with my sister?"

Theo ground his teeth.

"He doesn't hide it well, does he?" Rhydian jested.

"Nor does she."

Theo lifted his head. "What do you mean?"

"You're the only one who makes her laugh. Even I don't make her laugh, and I'm her favorite person." Adonis snorted.

"Well, she still left."

"She does that. Two weeks will pass by like that." Adonis snapped.

"I don't think you're talking about maps up there!" Mathis scolded.

Adonis sheepishly waved at his mentor. "Everyone keeps going on about the borders being closed. What does that even mean?"

They turned the corner and came across the main road into the Seven Forests, wide enough for ten mounted riders with room to spare. And the entire road was blocked with a large wooden barrier and signs in all five languages stating that the borders were closed. If that wasn't enough, there were some cleverly detailed pictograms describing what happened to intruders, and it entailed the creative use of a spear, fishing hooks, and a very angry-looking badger. Another picture showed an intruder strung up upside down over a fire with their feet cut off, being nibbled by feral squirrels. Several skulls rested on pikes along each side of the barrier, but Theo had helped with enough burials at Karme to know those skulls were too weathered to be recent.

"You were saying..." Theo said.

The entire caravan gawked silently at the barrier, reading the descriptive warnings and the more descriptive pictures.

"The roads are blocked. How do you propose we get in?" Rhydian said.

"I don't think they'd appreciate us sneaking. I think that's how you get an arrow in the back. I think we go in through the main road and unblock it as we go. I'm tired of games," Theo said.

They stared at the enormous logs piled well over a rider's height and spanning the entire road's width, too tall and deep to see over.

Rhydian cracked his knuckles. "We'll have our work cut out for us."

Several hours later, Rhydian brought down an axe with a thunderous crack, going a third of the way through one of the dense logs. He swung it around and struck again.

A handful of guards watched Rhydian between their own toils as they cleared a narrow pathway out of the road. Theo watched Rhydian, too, between swings of his own axe. Rhydian was into the third layer of logs while Theo just finished his first.

"Would you train me to fight?" Theo asked.

Rhydian paused and leaned on his axe.

"It seems like something I'll have to do more of, and I might as well learn from the best."

Rhydian laughed. He cleaved through another log, and it went tumbling into the underbrush. "Sure, as long as you don't throw things at me. You left some bruises. And I still have a few scratches from that hellsdamned fowl."

"If your eyes go red, I'll run and throw things. I may not have a castle to hide in, but I'm decent at climbing trees." Theo laughed.

Rhydian snorted. "We'll stick to drills instead of free sparring. That should keep you from running up a tree like a little bear."

Theo brought down his axe, cracking one of the logs. He swung and brought it down in the same place, and the log rolled into the underbrush where soldiers waited to stack logs. He had to stop to wipe off a sticky tar substance that kept the logs together on the ground. It smelled terrible, and he was careful to use an old rag rather than touching it.

Theo said, "I'm not above dunking you in a stream to cool off before running away. We used to have a bull we had to do that with, and it worked on him. He would be steaming mad, but by the time he escaped the stream, he'd be tired enough to go eat grass."

"If you see me ever eating grass, you'll know my mind is truly gone." Rhydian laughed.

"It's weird. Days ago, I barely believed in curses," Theo said.

"Curses, ghosts, monsters—they can sneak up on you. Before you know it, they're just a part of life."

"Can you train me too?" Adonis asked, shaking his hands to try to get off the sticky tar. He flapped his hands and wiped the tar on a nearby bush. Scratching the back of his hands absently, he popped a few purple berries into his mouth.

"Sure. But don't you need to study for the exams?" Rhydian said.

Adonis groaned. "I'm so sick of studying all the time."

"It'll be over before you know it," Theo said.

"You just finished your apprenticeship. I'm not sure you can give that advice just yet." Adonis scratched his hand rigorously.

"I've been learning even on the trip," Theo said. "There's so much more to know. I feel like it's a wide world of learning awaiting me. When I return home to Karme, I'll start experimenting in the winter."

Saryll cut in, "Water anyone?"

"Thanks," Theo said.

Kassia inspected the tar. "They have nails and wedges. With all this weight, they couldn't have needed a mortar for this wall. Why would they use this?"

"Because they're devious," Adonis answered, scratching his arms and neck.

"How much longer will it take to clear?" Saryll asked.

"We should be through by tomorrow. If the old maps are right, their settlement is right in the center of the seven forests. It's a day's ride through the forest. But the map is over a hundred years old. We don't know whether they're still there," Rhydian said, bringing his axe down again with a grunt.

Kassia leaned in to inspect the tar. She collected some of it in a tiny glass jar and held it up to the light. "What in the world?" she muttered.

Adonis scratched his arm hard enough to begin to leave bright red marks. Theo gave Adonis a wry look, which Rhydian joined in on.

Kassia said, "Everyone stop! Freeze! Stay back!"

Everyone froze.

"The tar is made out of maple tree sap, pine resin, burned honey, and toxic purple algae. The bushes planted nearby are red poison ivy vines. The berries are hallucinogenic."

"What does that mean?" Adonis demanded.

"The tar and bushes are meant to poison. It'll probably give anyone who touches it a terrible rash," Kassia said.

"What?" Adonis demanded.

"Did you touch it?"

"Yes."

"Oh."

"Oh? What do you mean *oh*? Why is it itchy? Oh gods, why does it itch? Is it in my mind? Does it really itch? I can't handle itching," Adonis cried, scratching all over as fast as he could.

"Come with me. Let's put a salve on it," Kassia said.

"What if I ate a berry? Or a few berries?" Adonis asked guiltily.

"Adonis...you didn't..." Kassia's eyes widened.

"Oh Goddess, am I going to die? I'm going to die," Adonis shouted.

"Adonis, no! Stop that. Now, come with me. You're in for an unpleasant night. I'll give you something to be sick and get the berries up. Quickly now," Kassia gestured.

"What happened?" Mathis demanded, stomping out of the trees.

"Adonis is going to be sick, but he'll be fine. Come now. We need you to be sick and then wrap your hands in gauze," Kassia said.

"I'll start boiling gauze," Saryll volunteered.

"We'll need some aloe, honey, mynt leaf, moonwater, oat powder, and cider," Kassia said.

Saryll already collected vials from Kassia's pack and poured them into a mortar before grinding them down with the pestle.

Rhydian and Theo exchanged scowls and checked their hands and clothes for the tar. Somehow, they had avoided touching it.

The caravan continued their work—carefully—until night fell. They made quick work of the wall and managed to break through to the other side. The opening was wide enough for one horse to carefully walk through.

Captain Laurier sat beside them with his bowl of stew perched on his knee. "When do you want to set off tomorrow?"

Theo choked on the stew. There had been too many questions for which he had no answers. Had Aurienne really decided everything like this? Did she decide what road they took, when they left in the morning, how long they rode, and how they announced themselves to their hosts? Theo remembered their travels and nearly cursed. She had. How could she manage all of that on top of everything else?

"The usual time," Theo replied.

"An hour after dawn," Rhydian said.

Captain Laurier nodded and resumed eating. Theo shot Rhydian an appreciative look, and they resumed shoveling stew into their mouths.

Adonis moaned and squirmed across the fire. He was wrapped

from head to toe in poultice-soaked gauze, wrapped in a blanket, and pale from being sick all evening. He stared at a tree, one particular tree, and waved at it.

"Hi. Hello. Hi," Adonis exclaimed.

Theo looked at Kassia, and she shrugged. "The berries will wear off in a day."

"Why, hello. Good day. Or good evening," Adonis said.

"Adonis, I'll be angry if you ruined that mind of yours with those berries. We're doing double lessons tomorrow," Mathis fumed.

"Hi, you're quite tall. How did you get so tall? You're as tall as a tree," Adonis said to a tree.

"Why don't you try to sleep," Saryll coaxed.

Adonis cocooned himself in a blanket and shivered while he sipped hot broth. Saryll and Kassia sat sympathetically beside him. No one sang. No one told stories. They all found their bedrolls and went quietly to sleep.

The next morning, they prepared to depart. Adonis had turned a sickly shade of green that Theo had never seen in human skin before.

Saryll pulled Theo aside. "He's not well enough to ride."

Theo scowled as Adonis vomited broth into a nearby bush. "I'm..." Adonis hurled again. "I'm fine!" he said weakly.

"We'll meet with the Thrymr. If the old maps are right, we should come across their settlements tonight. We will return after that," Theo said.

"No, I want to come with you," Adonis argued.

"Adonis, if they think you're sick instead of berry poisoned, they may not take kindly to Theo bringing sickness to their doors," Mathis said.

"We will try to return after meeting with the Thrymr. Depending on where their settlement is, if it is quicker, then we will go to the Titan Cliffs next. If we can, we will return for you before traveling on to them," Rhydian said, tugging a strap tight on the saddle.

Captain Laurier glanced between Theo and Adonis.

Theo solved the captain's problem. "Aurienne would want you to stay with the caravan. If we haven't returned in a week, we aren't going to."

The captain shifted his weight, and a heavy silence passed before he relented.

"Theo and I will go," Rhydian said.

With a final wave, Theo and Rhydian set off to find the lost people of the Seven Forests. They rode through the hole in the wall across the border and onto the unused road. The abandoned road was full of animal holes and deep muddy wheel tracks. Felled trees littered the road, and grasses and shrubs grew across.

They rode for hours, often having to dismount to clear the road from felled trees and shrubs. The progress was slow for fear of laming a horse. The roads were winding, splitting and coming back together. Some roads ended abruptly, and the pair were forced to turn back.

"This makes no sense. The roads that were here when the last maps were drawn do not match the roads we're on. I swear I'm not holding the map upside down, but it would make more sense. Argh!" Rhydian grumbled.

"Wait," Theo said.

He hopped down from his horse and inspected a tree lying on the side of the dirt road.

"What is it?"

"We've been here before," Theo said.

"What?" Rhydian exclaimed, joining him.

"We were here an hour ago, just before we watered the horses that way. I remember because I cut my hand on this tree. See? There's my blood."

Rhydian released a string of curses involving a donkey, a rat, and fornication. Theo stared at him before bursting out laughing. Rhydian's glare turned to mirth, and he joined his friend.

"We're horribly lost, aren't we?" Theo asked.

"Seems so. They really didn't want anyone getting in. They must have laid new roads to disguise the real ones," Rhydian mused.

"Let's eat and discuss how to start marking our paths," Theo suggested.

After they tended the horses and sat down on the dirt to eat, the fluffy red and black fox appeared.

"Hello there, friend," Theo said. "I haven't seen you since before we entered Rodarri. I wondered where you had gone. I thought you might have gone with Aurienne, or back to the Avyllon forests. Here's a treat."

The fox cocked its head and blinked its bright yellow eyes at him. It pranced through the undergrowth nearby, and Theo found himself tossing it sweetmeats and fruit. A pang of loneliness for Aurienne speared his chest as memories of her feeding their friend plagued him.

"Do you know where to go?" Theo asked it absently.

The fox blinked and hopped across the road. It turned back to look at him. Theo stood and followed the fox. The fox pranced down the road before stopping and turning to peer back. Theo followed, but then the fox jumped into a thicket and was gone.

Theo furrowed his brows. "Rhydian?"

"You should know better than to follow strange animals into the forest." Rhydian chortled.

"Is that what I think it is?"

"That's the red poison ivy vines they planted near the border wall."

Theo found a large branch and pushed at the thicket. It moved as if the whole thing was rooted to the side, and the bush had been flopped to where it now lay—blocking something.

"Help me with this," Theo said.

Rhydian found a branch large enough that it could have easily been confused for a small tree and helped Theo push. The thicket moved, and finally, the two men pushed it into the trees. Hidden under carefully planted bushes, grass, and other undergrowth—was a road.

Theo examined the road they had been traveling and compared it to this hidden one. It was wider and set with stones. It was overgrown, but past the bushes was a straight wide paved road.

"They covered the original road."

"Why would they do that?"

"We're about to find out. I have a feeling we won't like the answer."

"You haven't heard anything weird about these forests, have you?" Rhydian asked.

"As in?"

"Them being haunted," Rhydian whispered. "People disappearing and never returning. Or returning decades later having not aged a day."

They both looked at the concealed trail leading who knew where. A sign was placed haphazardly along the side of the road. *Beware the Shadow Wood.*

"Do those trees look darker to you? The bark and leaves are almost black," Rhydian observed.

"There are seven forests here," Theo said. "Maybe this is just one of the forests?"

"Yeah. A haunted one."

Theo chuckled nervously. "No. There are no haunted forests. It's just stories."

"Like there are just stories about the seriously powerful magic that the seers do? Or the rituals that the witches do? Or stories about ghosts and Warbringers?" Rhydian swallowed.

Theo blinked. How many of those fairytales and monster stories were true? All of them?

He shook his head. "We've wasted enough time. Let's see what they're hiding."

"Let's hope they're not all dead."

They led the horses down the treacherous path. The road was

lined with red poison ivy vines. Every few miles, they were forced to remove temporary barriers of shrubs and branches blocking the road. The tree bark was dark, the leaves were dark, and the shadows darker.

"Stop," Theo said.

He knelt to retrieve a black feather. Ma's words echoed in his head. *Remember to avoid a black feather in the road.* Theo dropped the feather.

"Rhydian, we need to get out of here!" Theo scrambled atop his horse and spurred it into a trot.

Rhydian caught up to him. "What?"

A loud booming collection of screeches and caws filled the trees. Thousands of ravens swept over Theo and Rhydian's heads. Blinded by a flurry of feathers, they dismounted and guided their horses to shelter by the trunks of ancient trees. They covered the horses' heads as a storm of birds descended.

Then the birds disappeared. Rhydian and Theo stared at one another. Theo glanced over Rhydian's shoulder at the tree. Purple moss.

"For the love of the Core god," Theo said.

"What?"

"We need to go."

"It's hallucinogenic moss."

"What?"

"Ma always said purple moss was dangerous, and we saw what happened to Adonis," Theo said.

"Hallucinogenic..." Rhydian smacked his lips around his tongue.

"They—they don't want us to, us to find them," Theo said.

Theo began to see things not long after. The trees grew blinking yellow eyes, and their branches reached out to taste his blood. Rhydian dodged branches as if he might be seeing something similar. Tiny fairies danced in the sunlight with oversized fangs. Theo shook his head, and the illusions were gone. They were replaced by more terrible sights of corpses rising from the ground and spirits splitting through the veil with claws dripping black ichor.

Rhydian started laughing and laughing, holding his stomach while tears streamed down his eyes. Theo saw blue-skinned ballerinas dancing and leaping on the treetops. A horde of menacing troll soldiers stood in front of them, but Theo pushed ahead and rode right through them.

"Don't believe the visions," Theo said to his companion.

Rhydian nodded very solemnly before leaning forward to sniff his horse. He leaned back and nodded, as if he had completed some bizarre pact. "Eyes lie."

Theo saw impossible sights. Elephants stamped through the forest, ridden by talking orange tigers. The red poison ivy turned to snakes that slithered up the sides of trees.

The visions turned into dreams. Theo was carrying an armful of firewood toward a modest cottage. Aurienne and a small toddler, their child, played in the garden. The child ran for him, and he dropped the firewood to spin her around. Aurienne smiled brightly at them. Her eyes were clear. They chased each other around the garden until it was time to eat. They ate hearty stew before telling fairytales in front of the roaring fire. They fell asleep in a single large bed. The child was nestled between them, a furnace of love. Theo leaned over and kissed Aurienne. He blinked, and the cottage was gone—he felt as if it ripped a piece of his heart out.

The dreams turned to nightmares. Theo danced with Aurienne at Wildegrove. He leaned in to kiss her but tasted blood. Her throat was slit, and blood bubbled between her lips. Shadows reached out from the grounds, and the earth swallowed her whole. Then, he was standing in front of his own house. Ma and Pa came outside and waved to him before the house burst into flames and devoured them. Ma and Pa held his hand as his fingers turned to claws and ripped them apart.

Aurienne danced with Theo at the city of Rodarr. He held her in his arms, drove a sword through her stomach, and she died in his arms. He was underwater with her in the foretelling ceremony. She was chained to the bottom of the pool and staring into his eyes for help. Bubbles slipped out of her mouth, and she began to spasm. He tried to help her but couldn't. Refusing to leave, he drowned with her. He saw her strangled by a criminal's noose.

She whispered, "I will never love you."

She kissed his lips. "I could never love you."

He kissed her again, knowing she would never change her mind.

The Will of the Goddess

Chapter Twenty-Six

We believed her to be a god.

— *Journal of Maddelena, bound priestess
of the Lunar Goddess Niamh.*

1152 N.T.C. The namesake capital city of Avyllon.

Sleep evaded Aurienne as she stared off into the night. The events of the past weeks since the foretelling replayed in her mind again and again. She reviewed the visions, omens, and readings—trying to piece together the pattern. Searching for anything she had missed. She wrote much of it in her journal, at least the important parts.

A weight of dread smothered her, and queasiness crept in. The room spun. Her head ached. She was out of breath. Sharp pains cut into her ribs. Something wasn't right.

She stumbled to her secret compartment behind her altar and removed her cards. She sliced her finger and dripped blood onto the back of the cards. They devoured the blood. She touched the deck to her forehead, lips, and heart. She shuffled them until they were warm and flipped over three cards.

The River, water, ill omens.

The Emperor, deceit and lies.

The Black Feather, an omen of danger.

Aurienne tried to summon a vision, but a blinding headache slammed her soul back into her body. She collapsed on her bed, having stepped beyond the veil too many times that day. She glanced at the compartment—at Rheia's journal but averted her eyes, vowing never to do necromancy again. But...she looked again...that journal contained another old ritual, drawing upon the land to increase a seer's power. Drawing upon nature and the power of witches to enhance the Goddess-given gift. Though the Darkling War eluded her due to interfering forces, it was not a question of being powerful enough. It was a question of too many ever-changing fates. Her magic reserves oft exceeded her needs, but perhaps this would provide what was needed.

She collected a handful of tall crystals, blue, purple, and black from her compartment. Selecting a dozen candles from the shelf near her altar, she placed them around the circle carved into the floor of her ritual room before lighting them. She arranged the crystals in a smaller circle just around the center. Rings and rings of circles amplified magic—so the journal said. She took a polished skull of a seer long dead with spell runes painted on it and placed it in the center.

Collecting the last of her moonwater, she dowsed the crystals with it. She sprinkled herbs and plants that she had collected with Lorayne and Kassia over the candle flames. The flames turned purple and remained so. Stepping inside the circle, she closed it with salt.

Aurienne sat in the inner circle of crystals. She sliced her finger and painted the skull with her blood, as she chanted softly. Power rose from inside the circle and filled her blood. The pain behind her eyes lessened, and her exhaustion slipped away. Her breaths came easier. Her muscles relaxed. She picked up the skull and pressed its forehead to hers.

"Show me what I need to know," she whispered.

In a dream, Aurienne stood in a grassy field facing the mountains. Everything was slow, as if she stepped through the time between heartbeats. The wind whispered to the blades of grass and flowers. Fresh water thundered through the city's main aqueduct, carrying it down from the dammed lake.

The aqueduct cracked, and water seeped out. The crack opened wider and wider until it finally split. Never-ending water poured out, flooding the lower streets.

People drowned.

The lake drained.

Without clean water, people died.

Aurienne gasped as she returned to her body. She reached for her cloak to warn the people when something stopped her. Some darkly squirmy feeling ordered her to wait. It told her to think. To be smart. Could this work in her favor? She hesitated. The dark stain at the edges of her vision grew.

Aurienne turned to her wall-length mirror and studied her reflection, looking for answers. She wore none of her finery or regalia. Her feet were bare, and her long brown wavy hair hung loose down to her hips. Dark circles pooled underneath her clouded eyes. Blood trickled down from her nose. She wiped it away.

"I See that the aqueduct will fail," she said. "It will wash over the Obermeister's house, and many of the Guild Masters'. It would be so easy to say nothing. It would be so easy to let it happen and be done with them, but I just don't think I can do it. Hundreds of innocents would die. Thousands."

Her spelled box chattered as her divination cards threatened to escape, but she slammed her hand down on the lid.

A vision came. On the other side of the veil, her skin sparkled like a thousand tiny diamonds, and her eyes glowed like the sun. She felt the dark smudge, like smoke, slithering around her arms. It was a stain that would never leave. The cost of devouring angry spirits remained, whispering.

"Obtain victory at any cost," it whispered.

In the vision, Aurienne scratched at her skin but could not tear the taint from her flesh. The vision departed.

"No!" Aurienne shouted. Her bloody fingertips gripped the sides of the mirror. "Goddess, tell me your will."

Her reflection stared back at her, but it changed. Her eyes bled black. Her features grew a little sharper, a little angrier. It was her face, but it was not her.

"Goddess?" Aurienne whispered.

Her reflection pressed a hand against the glass.

Aurienne fell to her knees before the mirror and bowed her head, but her reflection remained standing. She looked up. Her reflection glared for long moments until smoke poured from her mouth.

"Goddess, forgive me," she whispered.

Crack.

The mirror cracked from the center out, shattering. Aurienne gasped. If ever she were to cry, it would have been then. The Goddess appeared to her, in this world, for the first time. The Goddess' instructions were clear. She could not betray her principles. The Goddess would not allow the gift to be used in such a way.

"I'll do my best," she promised.

Quickly slipping on shoes and a cloak, she did not even bother to change from her nightclothes and flung open her door to the sentinels.

She said, "Gather all the temple guards. Gather all the masons, blacksmiths, woodworkers, engineers, and sorcerers. Meet me at the northern junction of the Aradey aqueduct. It's going to fail. We don't have much time. Hurry!"

Three sentinels sprinted down the hall and were gone. Aurienne sealed the spell lock to her room and raced after them. Two sentinels, Kolten and Edran, remained with her.

Evani, her sister seer, was walking past when Aurienne ran down the hall. "Summon the seers, send them to the aqueducts," Aurienne commanded.

Evani scurried away.

As she ran, Aurienne slashed her hand on the ceremonial blade she always wore, even slept with. She reached the door to the temple bells and pressed her blood against the lock. Only the High Seer could enter the room. The lock clicked open. She slammed open the doors and pulled the rope. Bells tolled into the night.

She left the temple and ran into the evening. Not even bothering with a horse, she ran the mile to General Kane's house with Kolten and Edran sprinting behind her. By the time she reached it, she had blisters on her feet. Rain had begun to fall, drenching her through the heavy cloak and making her lightweight clothes stick to her body. She knocked on his door. The general answered the door in full armor as if already on his way out.

"I heard the bells. What is it?"

"The Aradey aqueduct is going to fail at the northern junction," she panted.

"That's the outskirts of the city. Saddle up," he said.

They raced to the stables and quickly tacked up the horses. Kolten offered Aurienne a hand and boosted her onto a fiery mare who was not amused at being woken at this hour. General Kane jumped onto his own horse, the stallion bucking and kicking. Aurienne's sentinels bridled their own horses and mounted.

The general nudged his horse into a trot, a canter, and then a full gallop. Aurienne steered her horse after him, allowing her eyesight to un-focus and tapping into the vestiges of her gift. She overtook the general and led the group galloping toward the aqueduct. She ignored the blood trickling from her gums.

The general and sentinels quickly noticed what Aurienne was doing and followed her route. Aurienne avoided potholes, uneven steps, and loose stones. Left around a broken wagon wheel. Right over a broken ale mug. She turned down a street and galloped fast. She took another turn and pulled her mount hard right to avoid broken stones. They raced through the night like phantoms.

Sentinels yelled, "Wake up! Wake up! All hands to the northern junction. Emergency! Everyone up! Aqueduct."

The bells had woken many. They were peering through windows and standing in doorways. Upon seeing the seer, General Kane, and several sentinels flying through the night, they quickly followed.

Aurienne reached the aqueduct and ran down its length, full of millions of gallons of frigid water cascading into the city from the mountain. It would flood whole districts, and the flow would not stop for days as the dam emptied. Her heart twinged with guilt that she had even considered doing nothing.

They reached the site of the imminent failure. Water leaked from a small hole, but cracks were spreading through the stonework. A deep groaning noise rumbled inside. Something cracked, and a small geyser sprayed them and the horses. They backed away quickly.

General Kane shouted over the din. "What do we do? This is the main channel into the city. There's no valve or diversion."

Aurienne jumped off her horse and ran to the flow of water. She fought through the spray. Slipping in the mud, she was sent spinning away from the aqueduct. The pressure left stinging welts on her skin. A small pool had already formed on the ground. She stood and eased around the water.

She pressed her hands against the stone and Saw. Her Sight flew up the length of the aqueduct to the dammed lake. She searched for anything to help them. An emergency diversion, plugged with stones. By-pass channels were already full. Canals were full of barriers. The lake was partially drained for dock repair. There were no options...as if it was planned. Beyond the veil, her soul raced across the aqueduct, searching.

There.

An ancient emergency diversion never used and long forgotten.

Turning from the aqueduct, she slipped in the mud again as more water poured from the tiny break and rained down on her head. If the hole got much bigger, it would fail completely. It would be beyond repair. Many would drown, and the entire city would be without water. She fought through the pooling water and mud to reach her horse.

The temple sentinels arrived with soldiers, firefighters, and medics. Blacksmiths, masons, and woodworkers gathered behind her, waiting. A few sorcerers arrived with wild hair. Their wide-eyed apprentices carried large packs of chemicals and tools. They stood half-dressed in their robes, clasping books to their chests. Men and women held buckets and tools, watching her fearfully.

"This way!" she shouted.

With a gentle kick, she urged her horse on. She rode as quickly as she could without losing the crowd. They ran behind her, holding the tools of their trades.

She reached the location of the forgotten diversion. She paled. Ample centuries had left it underground. The lever was halfway down the side of the secondary aqueduct. She slid off her horse and pressed her hands into the dirt.

"What is she doing?" a dubious guildmember asked.

General Kane shushed him.

Aurienne crawled through the dirt, searching for the diversion tunnel.

Aurienne said, "Here. We have to dig here. It's about ten feet down. Hurry!"

The crowd hesitated, glancing at one another. Aurienne hissed and started to dig on her knees with her hands. She dug handfuls out, throwing the dirt to the side like an angry badger. It took only seconds before shovels stomped into the ground beside her. More shovels joined. Others used trowels and buckets to dig.

"Dig toward those trees and up a third of the way toward that group of rocks," Aurienne instructed.

Aurienne continued to dig on her hands and knees. Her long fingernails were chipped, and her hands were coated in so much dirt that she thought they would never get clean, but still she dug. Several feet down, she had to move for the builders to use their picks and tools to break the hardened earth. She climbed out of the pit.

"Form two lines to carry the buckets of dirt away from the dig," Aurienne gestured.

A miner drove his pick into the earth, and it pinged off a buried stone.

"Hit there," she told the miner, pointing.

The miner moved five inches to the left and slammed down his pick again. It gained more depth, and he grunted his appreciation.

Two hundred people dug a deep hole, wide enough to fit at least a carriage. Aurienne pressed her hands into the dirt again, grasping the lever.

"The lever will be rusty. We need something to break up the rust," Aurienne said to the sorcerers.

They sat in the dirt and flipped frantically through their tomes. Page after page fluttered as they speed-read the contents. Books were tossed down, and more were picked up. A faint glow circled a book —the Goddess' light. She picked it up and handed it to an apprentice. He skimmed it feverishly.

"Got it!" the apprentice called.

The sorcerers gathered around the tome, nodding. They separated, unpacking brightly colored liquids and mixing them in beakers. The liquids began to smoke and bubble.

The diggers had reached the top of the aqueduct. They were already halfway to the lever and picking up the pace. Aurienne felt the eyes of guildmembers and Guild Masters upon her.

A young woman yelled, "High Seer? High Seer? Where is the High Seer?"

"Here," Aurienne called.

"The aqueduct is failing below. What do we do?" she asked.

Aurienne chewed her lip. She closed her eyes and prayed. A vision came. Her eyes snapped open.

"I need five master woodworkers and five master stonemasons," Aurienne demanded.

Ten men came to stand before her.

"Woodworkers, construct a small, sturdy platform just under the hole. Build it and then slide it down to the aqueduct. Have five large boards ready. Masons, plug the hole to reduce the spillage. There is a large stone north of the aqueduct. Use levers to lift the stone above the water and drop it down to the platform. Woodworkers wedge the boards against the stone. You'll have to hold the boards manually, but it'll hold for a while. Masons, try to use tar to address the cracks when you're done. You have ten minutes to do this. Go," Aurienne commanded.

This time, the guildmembers did not hesitate. They ran or rode with their tools toward the failure.

"We got it," a woman called from the hole.

"Dig under the lever. We need space," General Kane said.

The people moved mountains of dirt from the hole. The lever handle was seven feet long and two feet wide, and the impressive gear mechanism was the size of a horse's head and completely rusted.

"That's good. Everyone make room," Aurienne said.

Sorcerers in dazzling robes over nightclothes poured bubbling liquids over the gears of the valve handle. They spread the various concoctions, and the rust fell away. But it was a slow process. Several miners and masons stepped in and hammered at the rust and wiped it away, and the sorcerers resumed their painstaking process.

Aurienne jumped into the hole and placed her hands atop the diversion tunnel. It just might turn.

"Enough. The strongest men, press it upward," she ordered.

A handful of large men from various professions descended the pit. They started to push the level upright to open the diversion. The mechanisms creaked and groaned. Then water erupted out of them. The men panicked and nearly stopped pushing.

"It's alright. As soon as it's open, the aqueduct will seal. It's just overflow pressure. It's designed for this," Aurienne stated.

"Get ropes, help them pull," General Kane ordered.

Ropes slung over the top of the lever were pulled taut as the men pushed up. The lever was moving, but rust on the inside of the mechanism stalled the progress. Millions of gallons of water pressing on the interior diversion valve did not help the matter. Water filled the hole around their ankles.

The lever was two-thirds to its resting point, but the water submerged the men's heads. They finally abandoned their efforts and swam up. The progress halted. More and more hands took up the ropes to pull, but the angle was all wrong. They made no progress. A rope snapped from the pressure.

A bolt of fear cut through Aurienne's chest. Nightmares reminded her of her lungs collapsing and her throat burning from the day she'd died. Aurienne struggled to breathe at the thought of what she must do. Her gaze narrowed. She knew what the Goddess would do.

"Pull as hard as you can," she commanded.

She ripped off her cloak and jumped into the pooling water. She took a deep breath and dove. Bracing her legs against a stone, she pushed. She pushed and pushed, and with the ropes above, it started to move.

Alone in dark water, she felt someone swim alongside her and brace themselves and push. Another joined them, and another. The lever slowly started to grind open. Click. It hit the end.

Aurienne fled to the surface and took in long deep breaths. General Kane, her Sentinels Kolten and Edran, and seven brawny Guild Masters tread water in the muddy pool. Muddy hands hoisted them all out of the water.

Water thundered down the diversion channel. Cheers rose, and people hugged and clasped arms. Aurienne sat in the mud, dripping wet and chilled to the bone. They had done it.

Aurienne stood at the failure of the main Aradey aqueduct. The platform and stone plugging the hole had been removed, and master craftsmen from various trades discussed how best to seal it.

"How bad is the flooding?" she asked General Kane.

"Several neighborhoods flooded, but no one died," he said. "The houses are intact, but they lost the majority of their food and trade goods. Several looms were destroyed. They're calculating the damage now and working to drain the water."

Could I have saved them if I didn't hesitate to act?

Guilt bubbled in her throat. She studied the damage in the aftermath of the near breach. She chewed her lip, looking at the long scratches she knew to be hesitation marks along the stone.

Tool marks.

She pointed them out to General Kane. "Do those look accidental to you?"

"No. They were made by man."

"Why would someone do that? Water is free to all, and breaching an aqueduct wouldn't allow you to siphon anyways. Nothing is to be gained."

"Sabotaging you."

"Ah. The Guild Masters. If I didn't see it coming, then I don't deserve to be regent. If I do See it and do nothing to harm a rival, I don't deserve to be regent. And if I allow them to gain power, I'll be overthrown anyways. There is no winning," she mused.

A vision came. The Guild Masters snuck through the tall grass, driving a knife into Aurienne's back. General Kane stepped in front of her, but it was too late. Her blood pooled in the grass, and her strength left her. She died.

Aurienne gasped as the vision left, feeling the knife sliding between her ribs as if it truly happened. She quickly stepped into a shadowy clump of tall grasses and slipped away. A guild member passed, holding a knife. She slipped toward the next shadow, tracking their movements and staying out of the light. Parting the tall grouping of downed grass, she crouched.

"Where is she?" a guild member demanded of General Kane.

"You just missed her." General Kane's eyes narrowed. "Why? What did you want with her?"

The general looked around for her, but she was well hidden now.

He appeared shaken as if he had not heard her slip away or expected them to approach. He hid it well, but Aurienne saw the crinkling of his forehead that gave him away.

"We wish to...talk to her."

"Talking is all it better be." General Kane's hand drifted to his sword.

The man crossed his arms. "You will need to pick a side."

"I will not undermine her," General Kane said coolly. "I won't betray her. I won't allow you to harm her. If I hear or see or even suspect you are planning something outside of the political and legal arenas, I'll arrest you. Gather your signatures. Vote her out. I won't stop you. If you try to harm her, I'll throw you into a dark cell, and they'll never allow you to go free."

The Guild Masters' plan had not worked as hoped, but she knew their schemes were not yet done.

Aurienne left. She didn't need to hear more. It was enough to know where they stood, and they would soon search for her—that they'd risk killing. She needed to be back at the temple before they came across her. She had no desire to take a knife to the ribs *again*.

She quietly returned to her room, managing to avoid the other seers, sentinels, crowds, and patrolling guild members.

At her door, she froze. Faint scratches marred the lock. Handprints smudged the doorframe. Someone had been in her room. Aurienne took her bone runes from a bag in her gown.

"Is anyone inside?" She rolled the runes. No.

She entered the room tentatively, seeing it was empty, she locked the door behind her. Most everything appeared to be in place. The effects on her altar lay scattered.

The journals. The cards.

She nearly ran. She cut her finger on a sharp stone and smeared the blood across the hidden compartment behind the altar. It clicked open. She frantically dug through the contents, and everything was there. The lock appeared intact. Aurienne closed the compartment and searched her altar. Her journal and Rheia's ancient journal were all safe. Her cards were safe.

Aurienne closed her eyes to See the past. A hooded figure slipped into her room and searched her room for something before slipping out. They spent much time at her altar before leaving, and she had a sinking feeling she knew who it was—someone close to her.

Opening her eyes, Aurienne felt warmth dripping from her ears. More blood. She swallowed. It was getting worse. She just had to hold on a little while longer. Theo would return with the leaders. He had to.

She could hold on.

THE SEVEN FORESTS
CHAPTER TWENTY-SEVEN

Seven forests and seven streams,
Giants rooted and forgotten kings.
Seven forests and seven streams,
Desperate deals and desperate pleas.

— *HIGH SEER AURIENNE AZARRAH, PROPHETIC*
VISION.

1152 N.T.C. The Shadow Wood in the Seven Forests.

Lifetimes later, the visions retreated as heavy tears rolled down Theo's cheeks from watching every one of his darkest secret hopes and fears. The long day was ending, and they were nowhere near the settlement site. While searching for a campsite, they came across a stream of inky water full of croaking toads with beady eyes.

Rhydian started to pull his horse toward the stream. The horse dug in its hooves and refused. Rhydian pulled and pulled, but the horse whinnied and backed away.

"It won't come," Rhydian said, his broad shoulders slumped.

"Ma always said never to cross dark water. Maybe we should wait for a bridge or cross downstream," Theo said.

"Did your Ma have a warning for everything?" Rhydian groaned.

"Apparently, just everything in these woods. I think you might have been right about them being haunted. There's the presence of magic here." Theo backed away from the stream. The hairs on the back of his neck rose like he was being watched.

Retracing their steps, they followed the road farther into the Shadow Wood. There were no more temporary barriers or red poison ivy vines. The purple moss was nowhere to be seen, and the trees appeared moderately less dark. Perhaps they were nearly out of the Shadow Wood.

Rhydian stopped and pointed to a thick black line across the road. "I suppose your Ma would have something to say about this?"

"Sinkhole. Quicksand."

"Great."

"We can backtrack and take the other fork..."

"Shh. Do you hear that?"

Theo quieted. A gentle breeze rustled the boughs of the mossy trees, which creaked and crackled. Then he heard it. It was a soft thud, like giant footsteps.

Boom.

Boom.

Boom.

They grew closer.

Theo and Rhydian exchanged a glance.

"Run," Rhydian whispered.

Turning their horses, they fled, tearing down the path, barely avoiding all the dangers they had identified earlier. Branches whipped Theo's arms as the thundering of hooves filled his ears. They reached the dark stream and galloped across it. Dark spectral hands shot out of the stream, reaching for hooves that flew just out of reach. Frigid fingers grazed Theo's ankle.

"Go!" Theo shouted.

They urged the horses on, but the booming noise kept coming. Bark cracked, branches groaned, and grass crunched beneath whatever chased them. They charged down unfamiliar roads, jumping felled trees and traveling rocks. Reaching the end of the road, their horses reared. Theo looked down and noticed that the trees were growing right out of the road, but they'd just been here. The dirt was disturbed, as if the trees had *moved*. Theo jerked the reins toward a narrower path.

They galloped for long minutes, and finally, the booming noises fell away. Slowing to a walk, Theo craned his head for any noises over the panting of horses and his own beating heart. Hunting cries of dozens of warriors reverberated through the trees along with the crashing of underbrush. Theo exchanged a wide glance with Rhydian. *We're being tracked.* They dismounted and led their horses off the road. Theo leaned against the wide trunk of an ancient tree.

The shouts quieted.

"Are they gone?" Theo asked.

The tree opened its eyes.

If you were to ask him later, Theo would never admit to the fragile scream that parted his lips. Nor would Rhydian betray his friend and speak of such things. But at that moment, Theo yelped, and Rhydian scrambled away in the dirt like an undignified crab.

"Here," the tree cried.

Out of the woods stepped bona fide giants. They towered over Theo and Rhydian at over nine feet tall. Their skin was more like bark than flesh, rough and textured. Branches stuck out of their hair and leaves grew in their beards.

"Grind their bones and feed them to the saplings," a giant growled.

"No. We're here to help you," Theo sputtered, backing away.

"What do you want?" the giant snapped.

Whoops and hoots from human warriors surrounded them. Theo turned and found a spear pointed at his throat. He lifted his hands in surrender as his heart hammered relentlessly. He glanced at his friend and saw the Warbringer's eyes begin to turn red.

Bleeding moon.

He kicked Rhydian in the shin hard and motioned him to surrender. Rhydian grimaced and lifted his hands as well.

"We are here to bring a message from Avyllon, that is all. We mean no harm. We just want to bring information," Theo said.

"No talking until we get you before the elders," a warrior said.

The warriors had dark skin, darkened further by the ink tattoos covering them. They wore leathers, animal skins, and some furs over their impressive muscles. They had proud noses and jaws and long foreheads. Their eyes were a deep and dark brown, like the trunks of the shaded trees. Feathers were wound into their long hair. The warriors weren't as tall as the giants, closer to seven feet tall instead of nine—but both were formidable.

The warriors bound their hands. The rope cut into Theo's wrists, and he looked up at the impossibly tall humans. Theo was tall by Avyllon standards at over six feet. Rhydian was taller yet, a giant by Rodarri standards. Both were dwarfed by these warriors and the giants. The warriors dragged Theo and Rhydian back the way they came, winding through roads and paths, over bridges and around hills. Theo's chest tightened. They'd never find the way back through these shifting mazes.

The giants followed with booming steps. They came to an unbroken wall of trees.

The giant lifted his hands. The trees *parted*, sliding through the ground. Theo's mouth fell open as his eyes were drawn up to the rustling canopies. They passed the magic gates and entered a sprawling forest city. Treehouses nestled in the treetops, connected by rope bridges. Houses were built into the trunks of trees, with stair steps cut into the exterior tree trunks. Glowing stones hung from tree branches, illuminating the settlement for what looked like miles. These woods were alive with magic. No wonder they'd closed their borders, that they'd wanted to hide away from the world.

Giants and tall warriors stopped milling about as they noticed the outsiders.

"Gather the elders. We have *visitors*," their captor said.

Theo and Rhydian followed the giant and forest warriors to a large sunken meeting area in the center of the settlement. Their hands were unbound, and they were given their packs back.

People gathered in the houses surrounding the space. High above, people hung out of treehouses, watching. Soon, the elders assembled.

A tall man stood; his long dark braids wrapped in leather. "The tribes have gathered. I speak for the elders of the Free Peoples to gather information before they vote on a course of action. My name is Dharek ThadeElason. My son Thaen DharekElletason and his hunting party found you with the assistance of the giant Allesan Alegry."

The giant grunted, and Theo swallowed. Rhydian pressed his hands flat against his legs.

Theo cleared his throat. "I'm Theo Thatcher, from Karme in Avyllon."

There was a murmur of approval from those assembled, and Theo silently thanked Mathis and Adonis for their tutelage. Decorum and impeccable manners really did go as far as the old sorcerer said.

"I was tasked with escorting the High Seer Aurienne Azarrah, regent of Avyllon, to gather allies for the summit Avyllon will host on Hallohaim. Our High Seer is blessed with prophetic visions from the Triple Goddess and Saw great danger to the entire continent. Forgive us for intruding. There was no way to send word to you, and the information is imperative to your safety, as well as ours," Theo said.

The elders exchanged looks. "Then you knew our borders were closed."

"We saw the barriers," Theo said. "We heard that the borders were closed. We had to get word to you anyway."

"You have traveled the most dangerous roads to speak. So, speak," Dharek said.

"Our High Seer has Seen war coming to the continent this year. She has Seen unending armies. She has Seen every town and village, including yours, burning. The emperor from across the Terre Isthmus has made demands of Avyllon, Wyndsel, and Rodarri. He demands warriors, gold, livestock, and food. He will ask and ask until it is too much, and we will starve. Eventually, he will come here, and everyone will die. Our High Seer Saw that if all five leaders of Teridar meet at a summit at the full moon, we have a chance to keep him at bay."

"She is not here?"

"She intended to come herself, but the emperor sent a surprise emissary to Avyllon."

"Do you have proof of this threat other than the word of an absent seer?"

Theo blinked. Aurienne had always provided the proof. She stopped the poison in Wynds and knew things she should not have been able to in Rodarri. Without her...

Theo bowed his head. "I have no proof."

"Our laws demand proof."

"We only invite you to a summit," Theo pressed. "We only invite you to hear what is said. No decision must be made until you hear her. She can give you proof. We invited the other leaders as well."

"And what did they say?" Dharek's expression told Theo that he already knew the answer.

"We do not know."

"The other leaders refused to go when they had proof?"

"The emperor's gold is a difficult opponent."

"But they did not believe her either?"

"I think they did."

"My king is a drunken, cowardly fool," Rhydian said.

The assembled elders, warriors, and people above them all snickered.

"Let me explain our dilemma," Dharek said. "We have closed our borders for a reason. Ever since the magic of the Seven Forests began to change us, we have been isolated from the world. Greedy men have always sought to control any power they could find. If they learned what we could do, what we were becoming, what would they do with us?"

"The same thing the emperor will, but he has the means to accomplish it," Theo shot back.

Dharek narrowed his hickory-brown eyes.

"I want the same thing for you that you want for yourselves," Theo said. "Survival. Aurienne Saw the continent—and your forests—burn. Demorra has already sent scouts and letters to the other nations. We have seen them and narrowly evaded their blades. They are already here."

"If he hasn't found us yet, he may not," Dharek said. "This emperor will have to come into the Seven Forests. They do not take kindly to outsiders."

"But he will come."

"Did your seer tell you that? Why do you believe her?" The warrior Thaen asked from the sidelines.

"You are not permitted to speak here without an invitation," Dharek chastised Thaen.

How could he describe Aurienne?

Theo finally said, "I could tell you of the things she has known or Seen. I could tell you the thousand times she has been right. I know to my soul that she's telling the truth. If she were here, you would see."

"But she's not here."

"Go to the summit and hear what she has to say. That is all I ask."

"Going to the summit requires revealing ourselves—our magic. It endangers everything we have here. We will vote. All who wish to attend the summit cast your vote."

Not one tribal elder's decorated cane rose.

"Those who wish to remain as we are?"

Over a hundred canes rose into the air. Feathers, colored ropes, knotted cords, and sparkling beads occupied the arena.

Theo's heart sank.

Another denial.

Another failure.

Why could no one see the danger?

"The elders have spoken. This meeting is adjourned," Dharek said.

That was it—it was over.

Theo opened his mouth to speak, but the elders had already filed out of the small arena.

"Please listen," Theo said.

"The meeting is over. Their minds won't be changed. Our laws require proof," Dharek interjected.

"No, you...you don't understand. We're all going to die," Theo whispered helplessly.

The giant Allesan looked over Dharek's head. "What will we do with them? I still say we feed them to the saplings. They could use the protein."

Eyes wide and mind full of images of carnivorous trees, Theo leaned away from the giant.

Dharek scratched his beard thoughtfully whilst studying Theo. "We can trust them. Even if the messenger lacks proof, his heart is true. The trees whisper of his bravery and earnestness. They are never wrong. Come this way."

Theo and Rhydian sidestepped the giant and followed the elder out of the arena. Dharek paused to speak with another elder for a few minutes while Theo and Rhydian readied their now-returned horses.

Thaen, Dharek's son, leaned against a tree outside of the sunken arena. He pushed off the tree and approached. "None have made it as far as you. You were nearly upon our doorstep before we found you."

"I'm not sure if that makes us brave or foolish. Perhaps just a little too stubborn," Theo said.

"You truly believe in this threat?" Thaen asked.

Theo nodded. "I trust Aurienne with my life. She says that if we stand together, we can survive. Otherwise, one by one, we will all fall."

"If you can bring proof, they may stand with you," Thaen said.

Theo's heart plummeted.

Thaen glanced around. "I suggest you don't return here. But if you do, take the path from the north or south. The safe paths are marked with yellow wildflowers. You may have to...find the roads that have been hidden, but the flowers will lead the way."

"Thank you," Theo said to Thaen.

Dharek approached with a wary eye on his son, and Thaen sauntered off, whistling. Dharek turned to the newcomers.

"Avoid the Shadow Woods. Dark things still lurk there," Dharek warned. "Do not return, or you may not be permitted to leave."

I'll be back. Count on it.

Theo and Rhydian kicked their horses forward, and the wall of living trees slid into place behind them with a deafening boom.

LIVING STONE
CHAPTER TWENTY-EIGHT

Spikes of bone, flesh of stone, men of root and bark and home.

— High Seer Aurienne Azarrah, prophetic vision.

1152 N.T.C. The abandoned city near the Titan Cliffs.

Abandoned houses sprawled across the rolling foothills, surrounding Theo and Rhydian with alien silence and overwhelming emptiness. After following the yellow flowers out of the Seven Forests safely, they made quick time to the southern Titan Cliffs. The main roads were blocked by haphazardly arranged boulders, and they'd had to travel through the hills. Only two days had passed since they left their friends. Having taken the southern road out of the Seven Forests, they were not able to return to collect the rest of the caravan before pressing on to find the cliff dwellers. They kicked their horses on into the heart of the main city.

No one was there.

"Where is everyone?" Theo asked.

Rhydian lifted an upturned bowl and dragged his finger through the dust. Stepping into a doorway, Theo peered inside. Rock-hard spoiled food lingered on plates and in stew pots. Even the mold had solidified, it'd been here so long. The bowls smelled musty and rotten. Blankets lay unmade on dusty beds.

"There are no signs of a struggle," Rhydian said. "Nothing is broken. There is no blood. There are no bodies."

"They didn't even bother to pack, though?" Theo observed.

"It's like they all just woke up and decided to leave one day. It looks like they left most everything here."

There was no one. Nothing.

"You hear that?" Rhydian asked.

Theo listened. "The silence?"

"There are no animals," Rhydian said. "Even when someone is hiding, the air feels full. You can almost sense that things are breathing around you. Here, it's just quiet. I would think that the well went bad and killed them all, but there are no bodies."

Theo leaned his forehead against a stone wall and smacked his head against it a few times. "I can't fail again. This is the last place to go. This is the last nation—our last chance."

"We'll keep looking." Rhydian peered inside another house. "Maybe there's another way to get them to the summit. Aurienne says her visions change all the time."

"Not this one. Not ever. I have to get them there, and I can't even find them. We only have two weeks left." Theo kicked a large rock, and it went bouncing down a deserted alleyway.

"You found the Free People when it seemed impossible."

"They turned me down because Aurienne wasn't with us. If she had been there, they would have agreed."

"She said it has to be you asking."

"I've just made a mess of it."

The rumble of an avalanche echoed from the tall mountains.

Sounds like thunder followed, but the skies were blue and clear. Booms and cracks crashed through the mountains.

"That doesn't sound natural," Rhydian said.

"You don't think that it's..." Theo trailed off.

"Monsters? Maybe. I guess we'll have to see what's up there."

"Maybe it's where the people went?"

"This place has been abandoned for years." Rhydian gestured to the thick dirt and dust coating everything. "Decades maybe. Wherever they went, they never came back."

Theo sighed. "Let's go investigate the creepy monster sounds in the desolate cliffs outside of an abandoned city. What could go wrong?"

Rhydian clapped Theo on the back. "That's the spirit."

They led their horses out of the city and toward the booming cliffs. They climbed the mountain all day and stopped to rest the horses. Theo took the opportunity to train with his sword.

"That's it, keep your weight centered," Rhydian coached. "Shoulders back and relaxed. Let's try the eight pattern with your left hand. Side slice, slice, drop, drop, lift, lift, stab, slash. Now backward. Good. With the right hand, and faster."

Theo had worked up a steamy sweat but kept at the drills for an hour. He was a dedicated pupil, following every one of Rhydian's instructions.

"Parry, parry, slash, thrust," Rhydian said. "Good. Now double it. Advance with the combo. Now retreat with the combo. Good. Put it together. That's it. Now add the eight to the four."

As their sweat cooled, they ate a cold dinner and wrapped up in their bedrolls. Neither slept, and they roused before first light.

The thunder only intensified as they neared the Titan Cliffs—aptly named for the titan ore deposits found within, which Theo always coveted. They walked their horses through the narrow paths until they turned the corner, and the Cliffs came into view.

"Duck," Rhydian shouted.

Theo ducked, and a rock crashed into where his head had been. They backtracked around the corner and waited, but the booming continued. Theo crouched and peered around the corner at the massive ravine splitting the cliffside. Boulders flew from one side to the other, hurling over a gargantuan stone bridge.

Theo watched the stones and realized that it was no rockslide. He squinted. Human-shaped statues hurled stones at one another across the chasm. He could now hear distant taunts. Theo stood.

"They're throwing rocks at each other," Theo said.

"Who?"

Theo pointed.

Rhydian froze. "What. Are. They?"

"No idea, but they don't look like monsters."

"How would you know? You meet some giants and one Warbringer and suddenly you're an expert on monsters? As *the* Warbringer, I can tell you those things could easily be monsters."

"We won't find out by standing here."

They led the horses closer, shouting and waving their hands the entire way. Finally, one of the stone people noticed them and called a ceasefire. The warring stone people still held rocks over their heads, waiting to launch them at one another as Theo and Rhydian crept forward.

"We have visitors. Can we agree on a temporary ceasefire? It would be rude to the guests to continue," a stone man said.

A stone man across the ravine, covered in large metal spikes, hurled his boulder into the ravine. The boulder, as large as a horse, exploded in a cloud of dust and pebbles.

Theo and Rhydian picked their way down the mountain path, leading their horses through the trails. To their left, the Titan Cliffs dropped straight to the crashing ocean waves below. Theo peered out over the horizon. He had never seen the ocean before. Nothing but endless waves as far as the eye could see. Somewhere that way across the ocean was the nation of Arryn, but the water stretched on forever.

The pair passed stone people. Men, women, and children completely formed from stone. Thousands of them watched from the mountains, as if the cliffs below did not drop off to certain death.

"Leave the horses there to graze." The first stone man pointed to a short path leading to a grassy meadow.

Rhydian led the horses to the meadow to graze, leaving them saddled but untethered.

"Come to the bridge," the man said, his voice low and gravelly.

Theo followed the stone man to the bridge, and Rhydian jogged to catch up. The bridge was enormous, carved straight from the mountain itself. On either side, the dark cliffs were a sheer drop to crashing waves. The high peaks were snow-capped and kissed the clouds. The mountain was peppered with caves.

The stone man, and other stone warriors met the waiting spiked stone man with his own warriors. Men and women both held stone weapons with set expressions.

Theo studied them, now seeing the differences. The people on the east side of the ravine were all smooth stone, like armor made of rocks and metal ore. The people on the west side of the ravine were covered in gleaming polished metal spikes, like stalactites or stalagmites growing straight from their stony skin or like spiked lizards.

The smooth-stone man said, "You interrupted our debate. Where do you hail from?"

Theo remembered what Mathis had said. Match your host's speech patterns and formality. "I'm Theo from the northern nation of Avyllon. Our leader, the High Seer, sent me here with a message and invitation for the Titan Cliffs dwellers."

The ravine and mountains exploded with shouting and yelling. Small rocks rained down from above, and Theo and Rhydian covered their heads with their hands.

"What did you say?" Rhydian hissed.

"I have no idea," Theo whispered harshly. To the stone people, he shouted, "I meant no offense. Forgive me."

The stone man lifted his hand, and the pebbles ceased to rain down. He gave a challenging look to the spiked man, and the spiked man lifted his hand as well. His side of the ravine also ceased to drop pebbles.

"We are no longer cave dwellers. We do not live in the darkness of the mines for the profit of others. Not for a long time," the stone man said.

"That is the only thing we can agree on," the spiked man grated.

"What can I call you?" Theo asked, putting his hand to his heart in universal apology—another trick from the sorcerers.

It must have placated the stone people since they quieted and leaned back against the mountainside. He owed the sorcerer a gift, maybe a really nice forged alchemical stirring stylus or cauldron. He would have to ask.

"Well, we haven't figured that out yet," the stone man admitted.

Theo offered, "People of Living Stone?"

"Mm. Yes. I am Stone'ward for the warded titan ore stones I chewed as a child, which gives me power over the stones," the stone man said.

"I am called Ore'spike for the titan ore stalactites I consumed, that granted me the first spikes," the spiked man said.

"You consume stone and metal?" Theo asked.

Stone'ward and Ore'spike exchanged a hostile glare that told Theo they were all about to start throwing boulders again.

"I just mean to understand," Theo said. "So much has changed here."

"You know nothing of the Titan Cliffs because we closed our borders a few months ago," Ore'spike said.

"You closed your borders over fifty years ago when the Free Peoples of the Seven Forests did," Rhydian said.

"Impossible. It has not been so long," Stone'ward said.

"Yes," Rhydian said. "I'm Rhydian Redbrooke. I hail from Rodarri, your neighbors. Your borders have been closed for over fifty years—that we know of. Perhaps longer. We never knew what caused you to close them."

"Why did you close them?" Theo asked.

"They have already seen us. We may as well tell," Stone'ward said.

Ore'spike nodded.

Stone'ward clasped his hands causing dust to rain down. "We were miners. We lived in the city below and sent our strong to the mines deep beneath the mountains. We stumbled upon a vein of stone unlike any other. If it is as you say, that was one hundred years ago. The dust settled upon our miners, and their skin began to change. It got into their lungs, and their blood and bones mutated as well. They stopped aging. We began feeding small amounts to the children to strengthen them as well. Over time, we all began to change. The children born to those changed by the ore were fully stone."

"Later, we closed our borders," Ore'spike said. "We had been hiding our changing nature for years, but finally, merchants and traders began to notice. They brought stories back to their lands and more people visited. We closed our borders to keep us safe."

"That's when our disagreement began," Stone'ward said. "We could not agree on whether to open the borders or keep them closed. We want to open the borders, so we are not so isolated here."

"And we want to keep them closed to keep us safe," Ore'spike said.

"You've been arguing about this for fifty years?" Theo asked in disbelief.

"It didn't seem so long. I quite enjoy our battles," Stone'ward said.

"As do I," Ore'spike agreed.

Theo concealed a grin. In becoming stone, their minds had changed as well.

"Well, we're here to bring news from Avyllon," Theo said. "The emperor of the nations across the Terre Isthmus has made demands of Avyllon, Wyndsel, and Rodarri. He demands men, sorcerers, seers, healers, livestock, gold, and food. He demands we swear fealty to him, or he will invade. We have seen his troops here in Teridar. If we found you, they will. He will take and take until he invades anyways and burns Teridar to the ground—including you."

Ore'spike bristled. "Those first people who saw us after the change treated us like spectacles. They tried to take our children. We're no longer human. Why would we help them?"

"We agreed long ago that we won't fight for the humans. We won't fight for those who would hate and hunt us," Stone'ward said.

"I'm sorry," Theo said. "What they did was terrible and wrong, but the threat that's coming isn't human either. Our seer says it's dark magic. It will come for you, too."

"Then you humans can stand together," Ore'spike said.

"Come to the summit. Hear what is said by the others," Theo pleaded.

"If we go, we will reveal ourselves to the world and bring danger to the Cliffs. We must first decide what to do," Ore'spike said. "They have already seen us. They know our secrets. I say we lock them underground until we decide."

"Agreed," Stone'ward said.

"What?" Theo sputtered.

The stone and spiked people began to corral them off the bridge toward the mountainside. The pair tried to run, but there were too many. There was no escape. They grabbed Theo and Rhydian and dragged them toward their earthen prison.

"No, wait. We won't tell anyone," Theo said.

"Let go," Rhydian demanded.

Theo struggled against their grip, but it was truly as strong as stone. The grasp bruised his arm—much more, and it could crush it. Even Rhydian could not get free.

"Ore'spike, Stone'ward, please, no," Theo said.

Stone'ward waved his hand at the sheer mountain face, and the mountain opened. The stone people shoved Theo and Rhydian inside a wide cave. Theo's hands and knees scraped against the rough shale.

"No, wait!" Theo shouted.

"We will return for you when a decision is made," Stone'ward said.

"No!"

Stone'ward waved his hand, and the mountain swallowed them in crushing darkness.

Political Machinations

Chapter Twenty-Nine

The time of the seers has passed.

— Journal of the High Seer Aurienne Azarrah.

1152 N.T.C. The namesake capital city of Avyllon.

High Seer Aurienne stood in full regalia before a notice posted on the temple front wall, wearing a scowl that threatened to light the stones ablaze. Two lines from her birth prophecy had never been released to the public after the Goddess directed the High Seer Syaoran Amydeo to lock it away in the seer's library. Always guarded, only seers were permitted to enter the library. The journal itself could be only opened by seer's tears.

Yet here it was posted for the world to see.

THE TWO-FACED HIGH SEER MUST GIVE UP THE CROWN.
SHE DOOMS US ALL.

One thousand stars fly as souls unearthed.
The monsters of old roam the earth.
Seer's visions condemn the Darkling War,
Against the enemy from distant shore.
Four pillars lost and the fifth lost by Fate.
Darkened skies fill with howling hate.
The fate of the world hangs by moon's light.
Darkling Souls fight, Darkling Souls die.

Birth Prophecy Read by the High Seer Syaoran Amydeo for the High Seer-in-Waiting Aurienne Azarrah, 1126 N.T.C.

The High Seer drew a Death card at the Foretelling and lied. The High Seer brought the red eclipse upon us and then ran. The High Seer cannot be trusted. Unseat the High Seer.

Aurienne's eyes narrowed furiously. Only a seer could open the journal. What should have been a celebration of the Goddess' victory and power in saving Avyllon from the aqueduct failure was tainted by rumors and schemes. A seer had broken divine law and disobeyed the will of the Goddess. Aurienne's heart hammered against her breastbone like a wild, untamed thing railing to escape a menagerie. How dare one of the chosen, gifted priestesses betray their Goddess? Who could be so ungrateful of the gift they received and place their own interests above the Goddess?

Her lips curled into a snarl as her hands shook with rage. She never would have thought one of the faithful would betray her and in doing so, betray the Goddess. Foolish traitor, inviting destruction into their front gates without realizing it.

Aurienne ripped the paper off the wall and crumpled it in her fist, but it was too late. They were posted throughout the city, and already crowds had gathered.

"Is this true? Will your visions doom us?"

"Has the Goddess abandoned us?"

"The masters were right."

"You doom us."

"If you can't tell us the truth, we can't trust you."

"Step down."

The clamor of the crowd grew to a dull roar. They were becoming incensed, and she was the last person that they wanted to see in that moment.

They began to chant "step down" over and over.

Ungrateful recreants, they would be drowning in a sea of frigid water if not for the Goddess. They could question Aurienne, they could expose her secrets, but that they now dared defy the will of the Goddess was inexcusable. Unforgivable.

Aurienne retreated inside the temple behind a line of sentinels. The other seers followed her and waited quietly. She searched for Syaoran, the former High Seer who had given her birth reading. Aurienne spotted her and approached.

"Was it Her will that the prophecy be released?" Aurienne asked, forcing her voice to remain even when she wanted to scream.

"No," Syaoran replied.

Syaoran was a remarkable-looking woman. She shared the same olive skin as her daughter, Saryll, but her hair had turned silver. Aurienne had heard the younger seers tittering that Syaoran had recently run Avyllon's Solla month marathon this year. Her body was covered in dark tattoos that wove together into a single complex story, marred by deep scars on one arm she never spoke of. Most incredible was that the former High Seer's eyes were completely clear, having simply woken up with clear eyes one day, her gift gone. That day, Aurienne became High Seer at only thirteen years old.

"What was your instruction from Her?" Aurienne steadied her voice.

"That it is never read. Ever. The instruction was placed on the prophecy page."

Aurienne and Syaoran shared a silent look. They both knew what this meant. Impossible as it sounded, one of their own had betrayed them. And there were consequences.

"It's the law," Aurienne said.

Syaoran nodded. An entire conversation passed between the former High Seer and current High Seer, which went unnoticed by the others. All seers knew the law, but it was the High Seer who was tasked with bringing the offenders to the Goddess for justice.

"If you are all-seeing, how did they post this without your knowledge?" Evani, one of the newest seers, asked.

The other younger seers all whispered to one another. The prophecy's release was having the desired effect, not only on the public but on the seers as well.

"They decided to do this last night after the aqueduct nearly failed. I was busy saving the city, but you're asking the wrong question," Aurienne answered.

"You still might have Seen it, unless your gift weakens?" Evani pressed.

Aurienne caught Syaoran's gaze again. Syaoran pursed her lips but nodded.

"Summon all seers and apprentices to the inner sanctum. I want everyone there in less than ten minutes," Aurienne ordered.

The seers gaped. The inner sanctum had not been opened since Aurienne took her vows as High Seer thirteen years ago, and many had never seen inside the fabled room.

"Now," Aurienne stated firmly.

The seers scattered. The sound of pattering feet faded away as Aurienne and Syaoran faced each other.

"It's Her law," Aurienne said resolutely.

"Yes," Syaoran replied.

"We have a traitor among our ranks. Not only this but the aqueduct. And someone broke into my room to steal my journal."

"These are perilous times to invoke Her law."

Aurienne exhaled. "I know. It is not for me to decide when Her law may be broken."

"This may be what pushes them over the edge to unseat you. And you've already promised a new king or queen."

"I know."

"Mmm. I hope you know what you're doing, then."

I hope She knows what she's doing.

Aurienne glanced into a temple mirror. Her own eyes darkened for a split second, and her reflection nodded almost imperceptibly.

Aurienne held eye contact with her reflection. "I'm doing her bidding."

Every step of the walk to the inner sanctum was torturous as Aurienne's stomach twisted into knots. She'd have to bring the seer before the Goddess, and it would look like revenge for leaking the birth prophecy. Aurienne could not delay justice or risk the Goddess' wrath herself. The strings of fate wove a trap for her that she could not escape. This might be the Guild Masters' ultimate goal to turn the people against her. Yet, there was nothing she could do. She trembled. Perhaps the emperor already had agents at work in Avyllon.

Aurienne reached the inner sanctum doors with Syaoran walking beside her. The doors reached to the ceiling, as tall as four men standing on each other's shoulders, and as wide as four horses. The stone was sealed by spelled interlocking gears, and only the High Seer's tears and blood could open them.

The last of the seers arrived. Aurienne rubbed her finger against the inside of her eye and pressed the tears into the golden rune lock. She sliced her finger on her ceremonial blade and pressed her blood against the lock.

It opened with a click. Gears whirled and cascaded outward from the lunar keyhole in a starburst. Crescent moons flipped, and metal star shapes expanded. The doors swung open.

The statue of the Goddess was as tall as the room, sixty paces or more. To each side of the Goddess, eternal flames burned in stone bowls that were three paces wide and fed by flammable natural gasses from beneath the temple. In one corner of the room, a bottomless pool was fed by an underground river. Though there were no windows, giant pillars held up a ceiling dotted with thousands of tiny glass pinpricks, illuminating the room with a soft glow of the sun.

The walls were carved with runes to protect from intruders and painted with stories of the Goddess, the Shadow War, monsters, gods, legends, and prophecies so ancient they had been forgotten.

Aurienne entered the room. Four dozen seers followed her inside. The room could have easily fit twenty times their number. When the last seer entered, Aurienne touched a golden plate, and the doors swung shut. The mechanism wound back, and the great doors locked with a click—closing them in. Their faces melted from awestruck to uneasy.

Aurienne climbed the raised dais. She stopped in front of the altar that lay at the feet of the great statue of the Goddess.

"The law of the Goddess has been broken," Aurienne said. "As High Seer, I am tasked with bringing the faithless to trial. Justice is found in this room."

The seers exchanged puzzled looks.

"What is the law of the Goddess?" Aurienne asked.

"Obey her commands," a seer answered. "Follow her faithfully. Tell all visions truthfully."

"Obey her commands," Aurienne repeated. "Syaoran, what commands might those be?"

"Commands in a vision, reading, from the High Seer, or those written in a journal. *Commands noted on a birth prophecy*," Syaoran intoned.

Aurienne noticed Evani shift uncomfortably near several younger seers. "What was written in your journal, Syaoran?"

"The cover and your birth prophecy page were marked as confidential, High Seer. It said not to share them by the will of the Goddess under pain of death."

Many of the seers exchanged puzzled glances. Evani paled.

"The Goddess instructed Syaoran not to share the full reading," Aurienne said. "It was a directive from the Goddess herself in a vision. The only ones who know of the prophecy are seers. Only they have access to the library of journals and prophecies. Only our tears can open the journal. One of *us* had to share it."

Understanding dawned upon four dozen anxious faces.

"One of us shared the prophecy in violation of the Goddess' command and has broken Her law, betraying us all," Aurienne said.

Gasps echoed across the room. Anger, fear, confusion, outrage, and a whole host of other emotions flashed across their faces. Their clouded eyes swirled wildly.

Aurienne gripped the altar, silently begging the Goddess for the strength to do what must be done. "In this room, there is only one law. The law of the Triple Goddess. There is only one will, Hers. We were blessed at birth with the gift of divine Sight. We were given a gift we did not deserve and can never pay back. We swore to serve Her. We swore to uphold Her will. We swore to obey Her. We were trusted with great power. One of us has broken this trust."

She felt her heart breaking. The Goddess was knowledge, love, and light. She was their mother, sister, and daughter. She was wisdom and love and hope, and all things noble and good. How could one of her blessed sisters betray Her?

"One of us has told the Guild Masters that the foretelling pulled a Death card." Aurienne cast a pointed gaze upon the gathered. "The Guild Masters would not share that information without a source. The only people who Saw the cards are in this room. The Guild Masters are using this to create panic so that they might usurp power from the seers—and from the foretold rightful monarch. They wish to ignore the will of the Goddess."

Some of the younger seers squirmed under her unrelenting gaze.

"The aqueduct failed from due to sabotage from the Guild Masters," she continued. "They wanted to see if I would save them or if I would allow them to drown. If I allowed them to drown, they could say I was corrupt and power-hungry. Or that I wasn't powerful enough to protect the people."

She paced, studying them all. "Later that night, someone broke into my room to try and steal my journal. They hoped I was too preoccupied with the aqueduct that I did not See the thief. Only a seer could use her tears to open my room lock."

The tension in the somber room paralyzed the seers in place as her words sunk in.

"You have forgotten I'm not one of you. I'm the High Seer, the Goddess' vassal in this world. You are not trying to outsmart me; you are trying to outsmart a Goddess."

"None of us would do that," a timid seer said quietly, appalled.

"We will see. The second thing that the Guild Masters, and at least one of you, have forgotten is that the ultimate arbiter of justice is our Goddess. If I was doing something against her will, she would punish me, take my Sight, or smite me. If I disobeyed her, she would kill me."

Aurienne stopped pacing. "To prove it, I'll submit to her judgment. I have served her faithfully my entire life. I have always obeyed her and served her. I'm not afraid. If she smites me, it is her will, and I accept it."

Aurienne squeezed the cut on her finger and dripped blood onto the altar. The blood filled the runic carvings before the stone absorbed it.

She kneeled in front of the altar and lifted her hands in supplication. "Goddess. I come before you to seek your judgment. I seek justice. Judge me. If I'm found wanting, strike me down. I accept your will."

The dim lights in the room flickered. The eternal flames sparked and flared. The room was bathed in starlight. Lightning erupted from the eyes of the Goddess statute. The lighting struck hot and white right beside Aurienne, but it did not harm her. The seers screamed and jumped back.

The lightning struck again, and when the flash ended, it was as if they all had stepped through the veil into one of the lands beyond theirs. Their souls laid bare. Aurienne was bathed in light, glowing like a burning white star. She was light and fire, wisdom, and love. She wore a crown of white flames and a gown of burning white flowers.

"My soul has been judged pure. All of you step forward," Aurienne said.

One by one, the other seers were judged. They were illuminated. They were themselves, and yet not. Some sprouted flickering fairy wings. Others erupted in glimmering iridescent scales. One shimmered in and out of the form of a fox. Syaoran stood in renewed vigor and youth, and purple fireflies danced around her head.

Evani finally stepped forward, and Aurienne's suspicions were confirmed. Where others were bathed in light, Evani remained in the gloomy mist. Darkness slithered underneath her skin.

The veil departed, and the seers plunged back into their corporeal forms in the grand room. The room was a little less impressive than it had been after having stepped bodily beyond the veil. Nothing could compare with those colors, with the magic of that place.

Aurienne said quietly but firmly, "The Goddess has uncovered our traitor."

Evani blurted out, "I saw you draw the Death card and lie. You broke Her law. It's why I went to the guilds in the first place."

"I have been judged and absolved. *You* have been found guilty," Aurienne replied.

Evani was right about the lie, but the poor girl did not have enough faith to know the depth of Aurienne's devotion and gift. If she believed Aurienne could betray the Goddess and get away with it, Evani did not know the Goddess.

Aurienne pulled a sacrificial blade and motioned the other seers to push her forward. The girl screamed and cried as six of her sisters surged forward and grabbed her arms. She dug her feet into the stone, but they dragged her.

Aurienne commanded, "Tell your sisters why you betrayed them."

"I'm sorry." Evani sobbed. "The Guild Masters said you were leading us to destruction, and then I remembered your birth prophecy. I just thought that the Goddess was telling me to act. I know better now. Forgive me."

"You did this out of concern for our Goddess? I do not believe you. She Sees all. She has found you wanting. Did they promise you no wealth? No position?"

The girl paled.

"They said you would be High Seer," Aurienne guessed.

"Please forgive me."

"It is not my forgiveness you need. It was Hers, and she did not give it."

"Please," she sobbed.

Aurienne motioned to the seers holding her. "Bring her to the altar."

Dark tendrils of shadow slithered beneath Aurienne's skin, visible only to her, and whispered violent thoughts in her mind. Aurienne hated what she had to do next and hated that a small, corrupted part of her relished this. Her stomach roiled and convulsed as the dark stain on her aura slithered across her soul like oil, eager for what came next.

What am I becoming?

Aurienne swallowed a sob. She was a monster. That's what the others would always see her as after this. That's how everyone would see her. She'd ruined Theo's life, both by asking him to go on this quest and then by allowing herself to get too close to him. She nearly didn't warn the city of the aqueduct sabotage. Now she was about to do something else that could not be undone.

They'd be right to see me as a monster, but it's what I must become.

The seers dragged the whimpering girl to the altar. They held down her arms as Aurienne carved a shallow *X* each across her brow, lips, and chest for the mother, maiden, crone.

"You have no wisdom, no love, no hope. You are banished from our order. Let the Goddess purify your blood of her gift." Aurienne collected water from the bottomless pool and dumped it on the writhing girl.

Evani screamed.

Aurienne saw her blood bubble from her bleeding wounds. "Bring her to the flame."

The seers dragged her to kneeling in front of the flame. Sick at what she must do, Aurienne grabbed Evani's hair and held her head back.

Aurienne hissed through teeth gritted against her turmoil. "Look into the flames."

Though the flames did not touch Evani's skin, and the heat hardly reached her, she screamed and screamed. When they released her, she fell to the floor in a heap. She touched her face, sat up, and screamed. Her eyes were now scarred empty sockets, as if gouged or burned out by the flames.

Horrified seers looked to Aurienne.

Aurienne folded her arms. "The Goddess has taken back your gift."

Evani screamed and sobbed. She flung herself on the floor at Aurienne's feet. "Please, kill me. I don't want to live without it," she pleaded.

"May the Goddess grant you a long life," Aurienne whispered.

"No," Evani screamed.

Aurienne stepped around her, unlocked the doors, and directed several younger seers to lead the blind girl out. Word had spread of the seer's enclave, and a crowd gathered in the temple's great hall. Many Guild Masters waited eagerly.

Aurienne pushed forward the seer. Everyone gasped. Several people screamed. A few vomited. A handful cried. Mothers covered the eyes of their children. Even the sentinels looked queasy.

Aurienne lifted her hands. "The Goddess saw fit to punish Evani for disobeying Her. The Goddess' word is law. Her will is our own. The words from Evani's lips from this day forward shall be deemed false. She will be banished from our temple tonight."

The seers guided Evani away from the crowd. Horrified looks from the crowd settled on her. Where before they were boisterous, now they were silent. Afraid.

Aurienne left the hall, Syaoran following closely. When they were alone, Syaoran stopped her just outside of one of the chambers.

Syaoran pursed her lips. "You have not won their love today."

"I know," Aurienne sighed. "The Goddess showed me a traitor, and I obeyed Her call, even if it was at great cost to myself. My life is Hers."

"This is an ending," Syaoran snapped. "Foreign enemies seek to invade. You put all our hope into the hands of a simple farmer barely out of the apprentice smock, who has no training or education in matters of state. The other kings, not surprisingly, refuse the call to aid. You gave up your rule and promised them a monarch that may never come. The guilds have turned against you, you just lost the support of the seers because they fear you, and you've lost the love of the people too."

Aurienne threw up her hands. "Each of those decisions was not mine."

"For each? That means you're having multiple visions per day." Syaoran cocked her brow and scoffed.

Aurienne nodded.

The glimmer in Syaoran's eyes faded. "If you have visions as often as you say, your body cannot handle it."

"The visions are coming without my seeking them," Aurienne said quietly.

"How can that be? Visions do not come without being called. You need to rest. You need to refuse the visions, or it will kill you. You never Saw that much before. Even if you lived half beyond the veil before, this is too much."

"I have visions by the hour, by the minute. I live fully beyond the veil now. I do not record many. They are constant," Aurienne said. "I saw Her, Syaoran."

Syaoran's breath came shallow, and the whites of her eyes took over her expression. "You must stop. It will kill you."

"It's not my choice, Syaoran. These are the Goddess' decisions."

"I served as High Seer. I know how many of my choices were mine and how many were hers," Syaoran said.

"Every decision I make is Hers. If you made decisions without Her input, then perhaps you did not love Her as I do. Or, perhaps, the Goddess did not love you as she loves me. Maybe it's why She took back your gift," Aurienne replied.

Syaoran glared. "I never would have believed that you, the greatest among us, would bring forth the end of the time of the seers. I always believed you would be our salvation. I should have known better. The prophecy I read at your birth told me otherwise. You truly are our downfall."

The two women stared each other down. Words that could never be taken back had already been uttered.

"You won't even be here to see us through the war. The time of the seers has passed," Syaoran said, her eyes unfocused and hazy.

The other woman stormed off, leaving Aurienne alone.

Each word struck Aurienne's chest like a forcefully hurled stone. They sounded like prophecy. If Syaoran still possessed her gift, Aurienne would have believed it to be a prediction, but she knew better. Prophetic or not, they hurt deeply. Tears nearly welled in Aurienne's eyes, but she refused to allow them to come. She'd endure this too.

"My life is Hers," Aurienne whispered to no one.

Broken Depths
Chapter Thirty

Eyes of stars and heart of stone.
Once remembered, forever alone.

— Book of the Triple Goddess, article IV,
verse 81.

1152 N.T.C. The heart of the Titan Cliffs, caves.

Darkness consumed every surface, stripping all light from the cave. Theo stumbled to the wall, tripping on unseen stones and uneven surfaces. Rhydian was somewhere behind him in the dark. Panic threatened to drown Theo as the crushing darkness coiled around his heart. He pounded his fists against the wall, but twenty feet of solid mountain separated them from the outside.

Theo whispered, "The summit will come and go before they finish. We're going to run out of time."

Rhydian slammed what sounded like his shoulder against the

wall. "They went fifty years without making a decision about the borders. They're going to open this cave up and find our bones."

"How much air do you think we have?"

"Depends on how many caves are connected to this one. The cave system looked big when they tossed us in, so our real problem will be starving or running out of water."

Theo squinted, but the pitch-black prison obscured even the faintest outline of the cave's mouth. He tried to remember what of their surroundings he'd seen before the mountain closed.

We're going to die.

He pushed the thought away. If he gave in now, they would have no hope. He had seen what happened to shepherds who got lost in the mountains or forest at night without a torch. The ones who panicked often made rash choices that got them injured or worse.

You failed her, his traitorous mind said.

I know, he replied silently.

He shook his head again. *Focus. You can get back to her.*

Get back to the caravan, write to Aurienne, and learn what to do next. She had to know what to do.

A secret part of his mind said: *You'll never see her again.*

Theo clenched his teeth until his jaw hurt. *I will find a way back to her.*

The thought of never seeing Aurienne again made his heart twist inside his chest. He saw her dying in his arms from those wretched visions in the Shadow Wood.

She will never love you.

Theo slammed his fist into the wall several times, shouting out his frustration.

After a long pause, Rhydian asked, "Are you okay?"

"Yep. Just letting out some anger. I'll be okay," Theo lied.

Silence. Then Rhydian said, "You don't sound okay."

Theo pressed his palm into the cavern wall, taking steadying breaths. He would see Aurienne again. Once out of this wretched cave, he'd find her and tell her how he felt. He didn't care if she broke his heart, if she never loved him back. Facing death, he realized it was only Aurienne that he wanted.

Theo clenched his fist. "I'm good now. Let's work on getting out. How are you doing?"

"I don't love tight spaces, so as long as we don't have to crawl through anything that touches my shoulders, I'll be okay."

Great. A claustrophobic Warbringer locked in the bowels of the mountain.

"The cave is about twenty paces wide if I remember. Ow." Theo banged into a protruding ledge. "If this is the—ow—mouth of the cave, it should—ow—be about fifteen or so feet until... Argh." Even with his hands out, Theo walked right into the side of the mountain.

"Where are you? We don't want to get separated. Let me grab your shoulder," Rhydian said.

Feeling something graze his backside, Theo snapped, "That's not my shoulder."

"Sorry. Are you at the side wall?"

Blindly, Theo grasped around. "I think so. It goes a bit farther."

"Is there any opening?"

"Not yet. Do you have any water on you?"

"One flagon. You?"

"Same."

"We'll be dead in three days if we can't find water. Quicker if we exert ourselves."

"Do you think the horses will be okay?" Theo asked.

"They have grass and water up there. The saddles will eventually chafe, but they'll be okay for a while. The caravan will search for them. You told them to go back to Avyllon, but you know they won't."

"I hope they don't go into the Shadow Wood."

Rhydian was quiet.

Theo felt around, and they made their way to the back of the cave. "Wait, this feels like an opening to another cave. Do we try it?"

"I think we have to."

"How do we keep from getting lost?"

"Do I look like I spend much time in caves?"

Theo pinched the bridge of his nose. "Me either. It's nothing like getting lost in the forest, either. Okay, suggestion. We mark the *hells-damned hagsteeth* out of the wall they closed on us so we can feel it if we need to find it again. We'll keep to the left wall always so we can retrace our steps."

"I can find a rock and try to scratch a groove as we go?" Rhydian said.

"Let's go back to the cave mouth and scratch."

"Here, I feel a rock with my foot. Got it. *Bloodsun,* where did you go?"

"That's not my hand, Rhydian."

"Keep your butt cheeks to yourself, man. There is such a thing as too many squats. In all the names of all the gods..."

They slowly made their way to where they thought the mouth of the cave was.

"Ow. I definitely hit my head there before. About five steps, and we should be near the cave mouth," Theo said.

Rhydian reached out and scratched and scratched and scratched the around wall that had closed on them.

Theo scratched his chin. "Counting our steps also sounds good."

"Yes. This is our starting point. I'll count. One. Two. Three. Four."

They reached the cave opening.

"Twelve, then turn left," Rhydian said to himself.

"One hundred and seventy-four." Theo stopped. "I feel another opening to the left. Wait. It feels tight. I think your shoulders would touch. Let's see if there's another one."

"Twelve. Left. One Seven Four. Small opening," Rhydian murmured.

"There's a wide one here, but it goes... What would that be? North? North into the mountains. Is that... Do we want that?"

"Twelve. Left. One Seven Four. Small cave. Seven. Large cave,"

Rhydian repeated. "I have no idea. Bigger cave sounds better, though."

"Let's try it."

Theo and Rhydian blindly stumbled around in the dark for hours. Rhydian had turned his chant into a song by the end of it, and though it could have been the madness caused by the suffocating dark, it was so catchy that even Theo joined in.

"Twelve. Left. One seven four. Small cave is bad. Seven more. Large cave and four six six. Hit dead end and had to go back to fix. One hundred and one more, then we found the cave door. Took that cave, found the water, kept on going even hotter. One thousand, seven five three. Took a seat. Hope we'll leave," Rhydian chanted.

Stumbling upon a damp wall, they guzzled water and refilled their flagons. The stalactites dripped water slowly and took an hour to refill, but water was precious, and they could not afford to ignore the gift. Rhydian continued to chant his ever-growing song.

"Cave forty-nine was wrong, wrong, wrong. And cave fifty was long, long, long. Two one four four, then we found a rocky floor. One seven four three, it's getting cold. Hope we don't freeze," Rhydian sang with gusto.

"Rhydian?"

"Yes, my fellow cave raider?"

"If we get out of this, I don't think I want to hear you sing ever again."

"I don't want to sing ever again. Maybe for a week. I think I'm getting too good at this."

"Some of your rhymes are suspect."

They walked for hours. Without the sun it was impossible to determine how much time had passed, but it had been, and their nodding heads told them it was nightfall. Rhydian's singing was the only thing keeping Theo sane in the crushing darkness, but doubt crept in nonetheless. He tried not to consider how they'd been wandering alone in the caves for miles with no sense of direction or time. He focused on the rough scrape of the rock under his hand and the way Rhydian's hand quivered on his shoulder—betraying his friend's fear.

"Theo?"

"Yes?"

"If we fall asleep, will I forget the song?"

"Rhydian." Theo traced his hands across the bumpy wall. "You're never going to forget that song until the day you die, and even then, the lyrics will be carved into your bones."

"Okay. I think we need some sleep, or we'll start making mistakes, and it'll all be for nothing."

They slept. For how long, they were not sure. They woke and relieved themselves standing back-to-back, something neither would ever admit to again. They drank small sips of water to parch their thirst, and both their stomachs rumbled. Rhydian took up his song again.

The earth rumbled, and Theo nearly lost his balance.

"Rhydian..."

"What was that..."

Theo thought he saw the wall of a cave in front of them moving. He swallowed as he led Rhydian closer to the rumbling noise and darkness. He reached out his hand and felt the entire wall slithering by. Scales grazed his fingers. Theo took a large step back, legs shaking and blood pumping through his numb fingers.

"Rhydian. It's a snake."

"What? How big?"

"I think...the whole wall?"

"Oh. It's a cavernwyrm?"

"A what?"

"Like a bedtime story. You have the Mooncursed. We have the firewyrms and cavernwyrms and seawyrms. They're sort of like... elemental dragons."

"Dragons? Wonderful. Let's back away very slowly before we become wyrm food."

Rhydian snorted.

They walked all the next day, making several dozen wrong turns. They sat shivering beside one another, the water long used and the food back at the horses.

"It's-it's getting re-really-cold," Theo said. "We-we can't sleep to-tonight, or we won't wake up." His teeth were chattering hard enough it was difficult to get the words out.

"We've been out of...out of water for close to a day." Rhydian's teeth clacked against each other.

"Should we go back?" Theo whispered.

"Maybe...maybe after a rest."

If we don't return, the prophecy won't come true, and hundreds of thousands of people will die. We have to get out of here. But—even if we do...we failed. None of our allies are coming. What does it even matter if we get out? We failed.

Theo blinked, having fallen asleep without meaning to. Rhydian was quiet. Theo hit him to wake him, and Rhydian stirred but grumbled and turned over. Theo's fingers grew colder, and his mind slowed. He was so cold. So cold. He had to stay awake. He had to. And then he drifted to sleep.

Nightmares drowned him. The horrible hallucinations from the Shadow Wood played in his mind. The terrible unfulfilled promises of a life he could have had with Aurienne. Her dying in his arms. Knives danced on castle ramparts as sickly green poison oozed from the mortar. Elongated shadowy hands reached from the depths of a ravine, dragging him down. Aurienne kissed him until he suffocated and died. Dread and hopelessness burrowed into his chest, whispering to him to let go. It would be so easy to slip into the darkness.

Something warm and furry dragged across his face. He leaned into it before his eyes popped open and he yelled loudly. He scrambled away and tripped over Rhydian, falling on his face. Rhydian shouted and batted at him in the dark.

"There's something in here," Theo exclaimed.

Rhydian slowly dragged himself up to sitting. "What are you yelling about?"

Theo's breaths came fast. He put his hands out, searching. The furry thing crawled beneath his frigid fingers. He froze. It was small. A cold nose bumped his hand. He patted it cautiously and ran his fingers through its fur. It barked.

"It's the fox," Theo said, dumbfounded.

Realization dawned. "The fox!" they both exclaimed.

"We have to be close to the surface," Theo said.

"Hey, little buddy, can you tell us where the exit is? Where did you come from?"

The fox made a barking noise and nosed Theo's nearly numb face. Theo put the fox down. A rumbling noise from deeper in the cave shot bolts of fear into Theo's chest. A cavernwyrm was headed this way. The fox took off into the dark.

"This way. Damn it, Rhydian. That is not my shoulder."

"Argh—it's not on purpose. It's just so hellsdamned dark. Next time, I'll lead, and we'll see if you do any better. Maybe your ass is—"

"It's getting away."

They jogged as quickly as they dared in the dark, following the echoing barks. They walked for an hour, suffering many a bruise and stubbed toe in pursuit of the fox. The fox stopped, yipping excitedly while clicking its claws against the shale.

They followed the fox until dim light flooded the caves. The entrance must have been nearby. The fox stopped and looked at them solemnly before it took off running. It raced along the cavern, and broke free into the sunlight.

Theo and Rhydian hurried to follow and stumbled outside. The light was blinding after spending days in the dark, and Theo fought to see anything at all. His eyes watered and refused to open more than a sliver. Blinking against the burning light, Theo felt like he was being born again. He had not realized how crushing the darkness had been until he could see again. The fox darted around them in a circle. Theo knelt and patted its red and black fluffy head.

"I don't know how you knew to come here. I don't know how you found us or why, but thank you," Theo said.

The fox wrapped its tail around its paws and blinked its yellow eyes, eyes with far more intelligence than any animal ought to have. It darted toward the horses and leapt into the saddle.

The horses? They should have been miles away?

Theo clambered to get into the saddle. Beside him, Rhydian pulled himself up. They urged the horses away, with the fluffy fox standing on Theo's saddle and its little paws on the horse's neck.

"How did you bring the horses here?" Theo asked the fox.

The fox hopped off the horse's back and trotted beside them. Theo dug out a choice strip of meat and threw it to their savior. The fox devoured it in a gulp and pranced along the road in front of them.

"That's not a fox," Rhydian observed.

Theo gave his friend an exasperated shrug.

The fox pranced in front of them for miles through the forest, regally accepting offerings of whatever morsels remained. Theo made sure to feed the fox a bite before every bite he took in reverence. It had saved them from sure death—thanks to Aurienne. He would never question her again.

They turned the corner to see the caravan. The fox, looking pleased with itself, pranced away into the forest. The travelers immediately stood. Theo thought he might cry or fall at the sight of their friends. He choked out a breath and dismounted to approach. He wanted to hug each and every one, even Captain Laurier.

Saryll rose. "You're back."

"How did it go?" Kassia asked.

"Did you find them?" Adonis jumped before Theo.

Captain Laurier stood. "What happened?"

Theo's face fell. His relief at finding them again flew away on swift wings. His heart sank deep into his stomach.

"Do we need to go to the Titan Cliffs next? Did you already go? We've been waiting nearly a week. Where to?" Mathis asked.

"I'm all better from the tar, poison ivy, berries, and algae. I learned my lesson. If you don't know what it is, then don't touch it," Adonis said earnestly.

Theo looked to his friend, and Rhydian's face twisted into a scowl.

Tired.

Weary.

Defeated.

They shared the tales and watched every face drop as the group realized that it was all for nothing. Not one nation agreed to the summit.

They had failed.

DARKLING SOULS

CHAPTER THIRTY-ONE

This is the story of how monsters saved their corner of the world. Whether they deserved to be saved is another story.

— A PROPHECY OF MONSTERS.

1152 N.T.C. The namesake capital city of Avyllon.

Dripping in sweat, Aurienne dreamed in a fitful sleep of past visions and nightmares. She stood on a raging battlefield where monsters battled monsters for the soul of the continent. Nightmarish creatures faced off against the monsters of legend. In a trance, she watched the battle rage on.

She whispered a prophecy.

"This is not a story of heroes saving the world from evil. Here the champions are just as dark as the villains they fight, and their deeds as terrible. This is about curses, sacrifices, and hellsdamned souls losing the fight against corruption yet refusing to give up the last of their humanity. This story tells how monsters saved their corner of the world. Whether they deserved to be saved is another story."

Everywhere she looked were Mooncursed soldiers—wolves, mutated men, and all other manner of beasts raging across Teridar and clashing with their armies at every turn. Golden knots of Fate wrapped around them all, binding them to unknown, inescapable destinies.

> *Divination cards fell from the sky like rain.*
> *A man wearing the skulls of wolves as a crown.*
> *A shadow, filled with cracks of sunlight, bore a chain*
>   *around its neck attached to its own heart.*
> *A faceless young girl screamed as she burned at the*
>   *stake.*
> *A castle was swallowed by the sea.*

Monsters battled monsters. Death reigned. Footsteps were growing ever closer, approaching on the winds of death.

Step.

Step.

Step.

Aurienne turned, and a faceless man ran his sword through her ribs. In her dream, she coughed up blood. She tried to see the man's face, but her vision blurred. She'd died a dozen times since the Rite. Always this vision. Always this faceless man. Her Fate.

The High Seer woke in a pool of sweat with blood dripping from her eyes, ears, and mouth. With shaky hands, she wrote the vision in her seer's journal. Crimson and golden droplets spotted the page. She froze at the sight of the three golden beads shimmering in the candle-light. With her magic depleted, the visions searched for sustenance from the only remaining source—her soul.

Bones and blood of the Goddess, my soul is unraveling.

Fighting to breathe, she touched her cheeks, finding only crimson. She clenched her fist atop the altar to steady herself.

Goddess, save me.

A knock struck her door. "High Seer?" General Kane asked.

What now?

"Yes?"

"The emissary has arrived and is asking to see you."

Aurienne nearly groaned. Since returning, she'd found no time to prepare to receive the emissary. His timing was impossibly terrible. The emissary had been working his political machinations from the shadows, waiting for the wrong time to arrive.

"Where is he?"

"In the grand receiving room."

She forced herself to stand, steeling her limbs, and strode out of her room. General Kane followed her to the receiving room.

She paused at the door. "Permit no one to enter this room on pain of punishment from the Goddess. Do not risk her wrath."

General Kane positioned himself at the door, and she closed it behind her. She braced herself and turned to face the emissary, stopping before him. The two studied one another.

The emissary wore layers upon layers of gray and gold robes trimmed in indigo borders. He wore indigo pants underneath the long, split robes. The outfit was embroidered in dazzling gold thread designs. A snarling gold wolf was stitched on his chest, and more wolf images adorned long panel that hung down from his belt. He wore golden shoes stitched with indigo triangles that resembled teeth. A thick gold chain that held a gold plate hung from his neck. His hands were folded in front of his waistband, but Aurienne noticed deep purple scars. She had seen those scars before—on her brother and the sorcerers.

The emissary was a sorcerer.

The emissary had close-set, hooded eyes that saw everything. An almost invisible smile rested upon the corners of his thin lips. He believed he had already won. It confirmed Aurienne's suspicions that he had been involved in some of the troubles. He could have been in the city for days or longer.

As Aurienne studied the emissary, he studied her. His gaze traveled to her cloudy white eyes. He studied her face paint, body paint, and tattoos. He gazed intently as if looking for mistakes in the designs. He spent long moments looking at her sleeve. He was learning as much as he could about his opponent before they even spoke, the same as Aurienne.

Let the games begin.

"Aurienne Celestina Azarrah, High Seer of Avyllon, Regent and Guardian to the Crown Throne, Chosen Eye and Vassal of the Triple Goddess, Steward of the Temple at Avyllon, Flamekeeper and Historian receives the emissary of the emperor," Aurienne said.

"I'm Emissary Seiko, the Emissary of the Emperor Jhames Edwyrd Alexandir Rexil, Divine Emperor of Demorra and favorite son of the Lunar Goddess Niamh, including the seventeen protectorate states. I speak with his voice in these matters today," Emissary Seiko said.

Niamh. She'd heard that name whispered before. Could that be who inhibited her Sight?

Seiko glanced at her sleeve again, his face resembling a cat who'd killed a mouse. "Apparently, I have missed quite the excitement. The announcement of an expected monarch. A near disaster of a major aqueduct, riots, and the divine punishment of a Goddess-blessed seer."

Aurienne clasped her hands. "And your visit was unexpected."

"I hear you have made a few unexpected visits yourself of late," the emissary replied. "How did you return from Rodarri so quickly?"

He didn't know about the Ways. Good. She ignored his question and answered with one of her own. "If you believed I was in Rodarri, who did you expect to receive you?"

His self-satisfied mask shifted. Surprise. Guilt.

He intended to meet with the Guild Masters.

He said, "I would wait for your return of course."

Aurienne did not believe that for even a second.

She counted down.

Three.

Two.

One.

"We demand entry to speak with the emissary." Guild Masters were yelling from the other side of the door.

There they were, right on time.

The emissary's eyes gleamed. "It sounds like we have additional participants."

Aurienne met his smile. "I've asked not to be interrupted. Would you like to join me on the balcony?" She gestured to the seats.

The yelling faded as they stepped outside. The emissary hesitated but followed.

He perched on the chair. "You received the emperor's missive from his soldiers?"

"We did."

"You have not answered."

Aurienne sipped tea. "No."

"The emperor requested your prompt response."

"We intend to provide it."

"It's been two weeks."

"The demands are great, and the consequences and considerations greater. You ask us to change a thousand years of history. Requiring a response in two weeks is beyond prompt. The Goddess has shown me a vision. You will have your answer after the Hallohaim full moon, in two more weeks. A month is prompt to a Goddess who lives eternal. A month is not so long to wait to acquire a country. And let's not pretend this is anything other than it is. It is a threat of invasion and demand to submit to new rule," Aurienne replied.

"I hear that you believe your new king will be revealed in two weeks."

Aurienne allowed herself a small smile. The Goddess worked in mysterious and wonderful ways. Aurienne had never questioned the Goddess, but seeing all the pieces fit together so beautifully made her want to kneel in prayer right there. The Goddess was protecting them.

"Yes. Our *monarch* shall be revealed," Aurienne said carefully.

"*Might* be revealed."

"It is the Goddess' will that a descendent of the first king will be revealed and take the throne. Are you questioning the will of the Goddess?"

"I do not worship your Goddess."

Her gaze narrowed, and she tasted ash. "We do."

"Less of Avyllon every day, from what I hear," he said.

"I thought you just arrived?"

His eyes narrowed, and his lips pulled up. "What is your answer?"

"You will have your answer promptly after the next full moon, as requested."

"The emperor expects an answer today."

"He shall not have it."

"He *demands* it."

"Then he is welcome to come here to stand before the Goddess and make demands." She gestured over the balcony. "He is welcome to bring his armies here, though I surmise that an army cannot cross the Terre Isthmus in two weeks. He shall have his answer soon enough."

She stood to leave. Emissary Seiko grabbed her arm hard enough to bruise. "I *will* have an answer today."

She ripped her arm away, smearing the paint and nearly pulling him from his chair. She glared, and whatever he saw in her eyes in that moment caused him to lean back.

"Place your hands on me again, and I'll bring you before the Goddess for her judgment. You saw how she judged her beloved daughter. How do you think you would fare?"

She stormed to the doors, where the yelling intensified. She directed the sentinels inside to open them, and Guild Masters came spilling in, surrounded by more sentinels. General Kane followed them in, stony-faced.

"We demand to be present for the negotiations," Obermeister Gotrik said.

Aurienne's temper snapped. She'd tried so hard to maintain patience, but she could no longer. She had been plotted against, betrayed, threatened, assaulted, and forced to take actions she detested. Her soul bled as her body failed, and she'd had enough.

Aurienne lifted her hand as icy darkness entered her eyes. Her voice grew harsh and low.

She whirled on the Obermeister. "You have no *right* to be here. Now leave this place of worship before you're thrown out or brought before the Goddess."

"You won't get away with this. We saw what you did to Evani," Gotrik snarled.

A vision tore Aurienne's attention. She Saw Obermeister Gotrik with Evani when she was a child. His niece. He'd manipulated a family member for his own gains. These men angled and fought for power without any thought to the consequence of others. One day she'd make them pay.

"The people know you're covering your own mistakes and fate. You're hiding from them. You can claim the Goddess deemed you worthy, but maybe we should not follow your Goddess," another Guild Master said.

"Choose your next words carefully in Her house," Aurienne warned, fingers itching toward her golden blade.

The Obermeister glared, but he was silent—a credit to his mild intelligence.

Aurienne looked to the sentinels and motioned for the Guild Masters to be removed. The sentinels hesitated. General Kane nodded to them, and they led the Guild Masters away. One Guild Master wore a dark and murderous expression directed right at Aurienne. He had long blond hair and the build of a mason.

"When you submit, the emperor will help you get your house in order," Emissary Seiko said.

She ignored him. "The attendant will show you to the quarters for honored guests, and after you have rested, a sorcerer apprentice will give you a tour of the temple and university."

"The university?"

"You're a sorcerer, are you not?"

Emissary Seiko sharply inhaled. His eyes widened, and the whites were on full display. His jaw slackened, and his usually sharp lips deflated.

"This conversation is not over."

"It is for now," she dismissed him.

Aurienne left the emissary standing with the attendant.

She hurried back to her room, closed and locked the door, and leaned against it. She crossed the room and fell into a chair. She rubbed her pounding temples and controlled her breathing. Suffocating, she ripped her jewelry off and tossed it on the floor.

She touched her lips to find them bleeding. Her mouth hurt. Her gums were bleeding crimson as well. She closed her eyes and leaned back, trying to calm her pounding heart and head. So tired, she would cry if she allowed herself to.

Aurienne whispered, "Theo, please. We really need you to get them here. It's all falling apart. I can't do this forever. Please come back."

SACRIFICES
CHAPTER THIRTY-TWO

All queens ascend, but not all return.

> — *SAYING OF THE QUEENSBLOOD OF RODARRI.*

1152 N.T.C. Castle Rodarr, Rodarri.

Glittering dresses, twirling, twirling, twirling, never stopped twirling. Queensblood Rianne watched the parade of fabric with a sickening feeling. Another banquet tonight. Another ball. Another night of pointless revelry. Did it matter that they filled their nights with dancing if they would all lose their heads? Rianne touched her neck.

What if her soul became trapped at the bottom of the ravine with her bones?

What if she became one of those angry spirits that whispered to her?

Rianne swallowed, hands still upon her neck. Queens giggled and chattered, choosing opulent fabrics and gemstones for another ball. Final fittings wrapped the queens in beautiful perfect packages for the commanders and their noble sons to rip open. They'd never be wives, never marry. The girls loved the attention, and the nobles were more than willing to perform the required nighttime duties to create more queens. More queens. More fodder for the ravine. More bones.

Her younger sister Jordyn dropped beside Rianne in a whirlwind of ruffles and feathers. "You're not ordering a dress for next week?"

"I told the seamstress to surprise me."

Jordyn gasped. "This is why you're always the best dressed. You're just a step ahead."

Rianne rolled her eyes. "If you say so."

"What are you wearing tonight?"

"Red."

Jordyn's wide gaze caught Rianne's. "What's wrong?"

"Nothing."

"Tell me! I'm your sister."

Rianne tossed a bloodrose flower petal into the crystalline pool where it was quickly gobbled up by a spotted koi fish. "I'm bored."

Jordyn's brows pulled together. "But it's dress ordering day. How can you be bored? You love today."

"It never changes. They keep us distracted with parties and gowns, so we won't fight the fact that they intend to murder us for some *kingshit* magic that probably isn't real. We're just waiting around to die."

Jordyn's mouth hung open.

"Close your mouth."

"But you... You just said... You..."

"I know."

"Rianne..."

Rianne sighed louder. "I've been seeing things, and I don't know if they're dreams or visions—or if I'm going insane—but I'm starting to question everything."

Jordyn's voice was hardly a whisper. "Those questions make you a traitor, Rianne, like Queen Rosalindt."

"I would like to see the Kingsblood kneel before the block for a change," Rianne hissed. "There is nothing special about our blood. We're just too stupid to question it and too weak to fight back."

"Why are you saying these things?"

"The rumors of the second ascension got me thinking, and I visited the Courtyard of Queens and saw something...bad."

Jordyn toyed with the sequins on her gown. "You always told me this was our duty. You said it was sacred, and the people would be in danger without us. We bear it so they don't have to."

"I might have been wrong. I don't know." Rianne rubbed her temples.

"What are we going to do?"

Rianne cast her sister a sideways glance. "We?"

"If you don't believe, then I don't." Jordyn's naïve eyes were too kind and trusting. "Show me the spirits."

"You don't want to see them. Trust me." She lowered her voice. "Rhydian said he could get us out of here. All of us. We just have to be ready when he returns from accompanying the Avyllon caravan."

"How long will he be gone?"

"I...don't know."

"Then it sounds like we need to spy."

"What?"

"We'll have to convince everyone else to abandon their morals and leave before the ascension, so we need to know if Rhydian will be back in time... Or if we need to make our own plans," Jordyn said.

"Just like that... You're willing to go back on everything you've ever known?"

"I trust you. If you say that the spirits are talking to you and telling you to leave this behind and run, I believe it. I'd much prefer to live than die anyway. If you say it's time to go, I'm with you every step of the way."

"I don't even know if I can believe it yet myself."

"Sounds like you do."

The memory of those haunting ghastly words drifted into Rianne's mind. She heard the whispers waking, sleeping, eating, bathing, walking. The incorporeal claws sank deep and tore at her mind.

> *I never meant my sacrifice to live on. Stop this. Stop.*
> *My darling daughter, I loved you more than life. Save*
>   *yourself and your sister.*
> *Lies and lies and lies. Don't believe their lies.*
> *Grimfall. Grimfall. Grimfall. Grim falls on us all.*
>   *Grimfall murderer.*
> *Don't you hear them? All those queens, dead for*
>   *nothing.*

Rianne picked at her dress. "It couldn't hurt to see if we can hear what King Cavendar is planning, just in case."

Jordyn beamed. "To the secret passage."

"How do you know about it?"

"Please." Jordyn flipped her hair.

Rianne glanced at her sister's gown. "You need to change. You look like an ethereal firebird in that dress."

Jordyn pretended to wipe a tear away. "You've never said anything so kind in my whole life."

Rianne rolled her eyes, but her smile never left.

"Meet you in ten. Make it fifteen. There are a lot of clasps and buttons on this *work of art*." Jordyn twirled her skirts. "It really takes work to be this beautiful."

The orange and red feathers caught the light just right, and Rianne thought she might take flight. Jordyn floated away.

A seamstress rounded the corner. "Queensblood Rianne, would you look at this fabric for your dress?"

The pale blue and pink fabric possessed thousands of tiny flowers sewn in waves. It was beautiful, but Rianne had more important things to do.

"That's fine, thank you."

Rianne hurried to her own room and donned a simple long

gown with a skirt that hugged her hips. It would hopefully not catch on the nails or broken boards in the passage, but she had nothing better. Certainly, no pants would be found in her wardrobe.

When Rianne reached the bookcase concealing the passage, Jordyn was nowhere to be seen. Rianne tried to look as inconspicuous as possible and ended up awkwardly leaning against the wall, squeezing her eyes shut as the whispers scratched at her sanity.

The screams never stop. The smiles never end. The
screams never stop.
Let us out. Let us out. Let us out. Let us out.
A thousand queens, dead for nothing. A thousand
more to die.

Finally, Jordyn appeared wearing a form-fitting gray dress with long sleeves. Rianne noticed a sliver of boots under the dress.

"You have *boots*? Where did you even get those?"

"You never go exploring?"

"Sometimes."

"In what? Dancing slippers?"

Rianne's cheeks heated.

Jordyn laughed. "Is anyone coming?"

Rianne glanced back and forth. "Nope."

Jordyn reached behind an adjacent column and pulled a lever. The bookcase popped open a fraction. Rianne slipped inside with Jordyn on her heels. The bookcase door clicked shut. They crept quietly through the shadowy passageway, soon reaching the king's office. They crouched behind a peephole.

"What do we do now?" Jordyn whispered.

"I don't know. I've never spied before. I guess we wait?"

A single minute passed.

"We should have brought snacks," Jordyn whispered.

Rianne rubbed her temples.

Four hours later, the two queens still waited. Rianne's legs cramped several hours ago, and she was no longer sure that she could walk. Jordyn paced quietly. Rianne was hot, thirsty, tired, and sore. Spying was the worst.

"Maybe we should try again later…" Rianne said.

A door in the office opened, and the two queens quickly crouched behind the peephole. They peered inside as King Cavendar and a handful of commanders entered.

The men talked for a long time, and Rianne wanted to take the straw underneath her slippers and stuff it into her ears. Then the conversation changed.

"How did Avyllon escape the scouting party?" a commander asked.

"I have no idea," King Cavendar said. "That seer must have Seen it. I was shocked when King Jaekob informed me of her arrival."

"Will the emperor send another?"

"I expect so."

"What if the blacksmith succeeds in convincing the Free People and Titan Cliff dwellers to attend the summit with Avyllon?"

"He won't. If he does, we'll report it to the emperor."

"And if the seer is right about the emperor's intentions for Teridar?"

The chair underneath the king's considerable backside groaned. "We'll cross that bridge when we come to it. If the rest of the continent stands against the emperor, we have no choice but to consider it. Lucky for us, he has to get through all of them first."

"The seer is causing…complications."

"Careful what you say. She's like a wraith. If you mention her too frequently, she might See." The king crossed himself with some sort of ward.

Foolish old man.

"And of the ascension?" a commander asked.

Rianne clasped her hands to her mouth to stifle a squeal. Her blood froze. If she cracked open her veins, only frozen slush would pour out.

"Should we have one before the summit?"

The king poured a glass of dark wine. "Let's wait and see what happens. We can wait a few weeks."

Rianne mouthed to Jordyn, "*A few weeks?*"

Jordyn's eyes widened.

"We planned to hold an ascension the third day of the next full moon. There's no reason to move it up now."

"Who are we choosing?"

"Queen Yllicea has volunteered."

"Without Rianne to ascend, we require more than one queen. We're going to need ten or more with the war we face. It's really too bad that Queensblood Rianne has taken so long to become with child, or I would send her to the block. I expected a child from her years ago."

Ten queens? It had not been done in hundreds of years.

"She's only eighteen."

"She's had her blood for four. I grow impatient."

"Then why did you send the Warbringer away? You know they've been sneaking around."

"I did want a Warbringer Queensblood. Think of the protection such a babe could provide, but that is taking too long. Besides, I have *plans* for him."

Rianne's skin prickled with needles of ice.

"What of Rianne?"

The king grunted. "For now, we will choose others. If she does not bear a child soon, I'll have to make *other* arrangements."

Rianne's stomach twisted into sickening knots. She crept away from the peephole, first crawling, then scurrying, then running. She vomited at the end of the passageway and collapsed into a sweaty mess.

Jordyn pulled Rianne into a hug and held her tightly as Rianne sobbed. Rianne's head filled with ghostly whispers and dresses twirling and twirling. She realized which of the two was deadlier.

That night at the ball, Queensblood Rianne wore a gown of crimson. Her skirts were made to look like enormous rose petals. Small Rodarri rosebuds were sewn up the bodice and across the dreamy off-the-shoulder sleeves. The fabric was velvety soft, and tiny red gems were sewn into the many layers. The sweetheart neckline pushed up her modest bust into something presentable. Her soft brown hair was curled and swept up into an intricate design and braided with silver strands.

On any other night, she'd have admired herself. She'd have floated through the palace like the queen she was. She would have tilted her chin just so to display the dramatic red paint on her face and stood near the candlelight so that her dress glowed. Tonight, she could not bring herself to do any of it.

It was all so pointless.

Rianne and the other Queensblood gathered in their locked courtyard between the pillars, pools, and hanging chiffon curtains, waiting to be escorted to the ball. The gowns were fabulous, with lace and flowers, dyed patterns, and sparkling jewels. Each queen looked as regal as the next, with thousands of gems adorning their wrists, ears, and necks. Even more were woven into their hair and gowns.

Though, their most powerful accessory lay upon their faces. Polite, empty smiles. The queens chatted as they waited for the last to arrive while Rianne watched them closely. She studied their faces until she noticed what lay beneath the brave duty. It was not quite fear or apprehension. Burden, perhaps? A struggle against resignation? They were trying so hard to do what was expected, but sadness coursed underneath.

Why hadn't she seen it before?

The final queens arrived just as the broad double doors opened, as tall as the ceiling and just as wide. They gracefully floated down the long hallway past murals of the former ascended queens. Soldiers lined the walls, staring straight ahead.

The queens glided into the main ballroom. Two massive double doors opened at the top of a wide, grand staircase. Music played as every eye turned toward them. Three at a time, the queens drifted down the stairs to the great ballroom. Rianne and Jordyn descended last.

Jealous eyes cut into Rianne from the men and women below. She would relish the attention if she didn't know the things she knew. She had all the privileges that a king's money could buy, but she was trapped.

A new tune started up.

A commander's son, Rianne didn't even remember his name, asked her for a dance. It was expected. Declining was never an option, but Rianne could not bring herself to go through the motions.

"Another time."

The young man balked. He hesitated but finally strode away. Rianne perched on a cushioned chair, ignoring the bewildered glances. She sipped red wine and enjoyed the music. Another young man approached. Before he reached her, Rianne shook her head. He stormed off.

Throughout the room, the men approached the queens to ask for a dance. For the first time, the queens were politely declining the invitations—all of them. The music played through the next hour, but none of the queens accepted an offer to dance. Rianne herself turned down half a dozen, and Jordyn turned down three times that.

King Cavendar approached Rianne, and though his expression remained polite, his eyes flamed.

"Why are none of the queens accepting a dance?" he hissed.

"I have no idea. Maybe they don't feel like dancing yet," Rianne said.

"Get them in the mood," King Cavendar said.

Rianne could have shouted or cried. Even refusing a dance was beyond their control.

"No," she said.

King Cavendar glared at her. His eyes might have shot flames. "Excuse me?"

"No. I won't tell them to do anything."

"And why is that?"

"I don't want to."

"I don't give two kingshits what you want," he hissed.

"Am I not a queen?" she challenged.

The king stepped forward to tower over her, and she shrunk away.

"You'll do what you're told, girl."

The exchange attracted the attention of the entire ballroom by this point. The queens watched Rianne carefully to see what she'd do. The commanders and their noble sons scowled and watched the king.

"It's not my job to line up the queens as toys for your commanders and their boys."

Crack.

A slap rang out. Rianne's cheek exploded in heat left behind from the king's fleshy palm. She gasped and held her face. Gasps filled the room. Embarrassment and fear burned in Rianne's chest. The whispers exploded in her ears.

> *A thousand queens, dead for nothing. A thousand*
>   *more to die.*
> *When I am freed, my vengeance will have no bounds.*
>   *The kings will die.*
> *Lies and lies and lies. Don't believe their lies.*
> *Don't you hear them? All those queens, dead for*
>   *nothing.*

She knew she should shut up, but she could no more silence her words than she could stop breathing. Some impossible, unstoppable force urged her on. She felt possessed.

"We already must die for you; we don't have to whore ourselves for you too. Your sons already sow enough wild oats in our ranks. We are not your personal harem. We are not yours," she said loudly.

The music stopped. The king grabbed her arm and roughly jerked her to him.

She spat. "There is no reason to believe that there is anything special about our blood. Perhaps it is your turn, the Kingsblood, to join our ranks in the ravine. If the threat is so great that you are going to order another ascension of *ten* queens, perhaps you should bear some of that burden."

"Watch your mouth," he growled.

"Deny that you will execute ten queens in two weeks' time, then. Deny that you are willing to murder us because you're an old cowardly fool."

Crunch.

She crumbled to the floor as her other cheek exploded in pain from his closed fist.

Tears streamed down her face, and she forced herself up on her wobbly legs. "Hitting a woman? A real man. You can hit me again, but it won't take the truth from my words."

"Commander Jensten, bring one of our watchdogs," the king said.

Rianne recoiled. The watchdogs were vicious, wild, terrible things. The commander returned holding the leash of a barking, snapping dog. It lunged and growled. The strong man could scarcely hold the dog back.

"Remove its muzzle," the king said.

Rianne gaped.

The commander handed the king the muzzle.

No.

She tried to run, but his grip on her arm left her struggling futilely. The king grabbed Rianne by the neck and held her still while he fitted her with a dog muzzle. He pressed the filthy leather against her skin. He was not gentle in tightening the straps and yanked them tight enough to dig into her cheeks. Rianne's eyes burned and tears streamed down her cheeks, but she could not fight. The shame nearly made her collapse.

King Cavendar grabbed her by the hair and jerked her head back. "You will dance if we tell you to, or I'll set the dog on you."

The sight of the barking dog and its gnashing fangs forced Rianne to nod. She looked at the ground, unable to meet his eye.

The king snapped, and one of the noble young men jumped. He took Rianne's slender, frail hands. The king threw up his hands as the music resumed. Rianne danced with the man, dressed like a queen, wearing the muzzle of a dog.

Rianne danced until her feet bled, unable to refuse any request. It was the most humiliating moment of her life. The king sneered, deriving far too much enjoyment from her pain. The commanders chuckled. The noblewomen sneered and laughed.

The worst part was that the queens glanced at her with pity and fear. Jordyn danced with the young man, tears dripping down her smiling face. Rianne's spirit threatened to break, and her pride shriveled.

Hours later, King Cavendar summoned her. He removed the muzzle as tears streamed down her cheeks. He held her chin, forcing her to look at him.

"You are worth only what protection your death provides," the king said. "We can make life as comfortable or miserable as you make it. Remember that. Now smile for me."

Sobs wracking her and tears dripping down her chin, Rianne forced a smile on her face.

"Good girl."

She hissed, "You're lucky Rhydian isn't here."

The king leaned in and whispered, "He's never coming back."

DARK ROADS
CHAPTER THIRTY-THREE

A rising devil and skull-wrought moon
Hiding secrets and untold truths.

— HIGH SEER AURIENNE AZARRAH, HISTORIC
VISION.

1152 N.T.C. The namesake capital city of Avyllon.

Beasts from hell snarled and slashed through Aurienne's mind, hungering for bone and blood and death. Monsters that only resembled wolves raced through the trees, stalking their prey. Thundering paws ripped through the night amidst mournful howls. With misshapen bodies, elongated limbs, blazing hellfire eyes, and broken fangs, they moved like shadows. Nature did not create creatures such as these. Cursed, demon-made things. Twenty or more beasts forged an impossibly straight path over entombed mountains, through grasping rivers, and around angry trees—hunting the Avyllon caravan.

The beasts reached the caravan with a sinister howl and

descended in a frenzy. Saryll and Kassia died in each other's arms, and a distorted paw the size of a dinner plate tore Captain Laurier's head clean from his shoulders. Adonis was ripped in half. Rhydian drove his sword through a wolf's spiked chest plate, and the Warbringer curse exploded from his heart in barbed tendrils of fog. A wolf sprang out of the darkness and sank its broken, jagged fangs into Theo's neck before it flung him into the darkness. Aurienne heard herself, far away, screaming. Feebly fighting to put pressure on a hemorrhaging wound, Theo's blood-speckled lips whispered a single word before he died.

"Aurienne."

She woke screaming. Her ears and neck grew warm and wet. She reached up and stared at her trembling fingers.

No. It can't be...

Golden blood tickled from her ears, eyes, and mouth—her aura, her soul, poured through the veil and from her corporeal form. Her eyes burned with unshed tears. Her strength faded. Much more, and she'd die.

The terrible unearthly howls echoed through her mind. The attack was imminent. No raven would reach them in time. She couldn't warn them. They were all going to die. Her brother was going to die. Theo was going to die. She couldn't breathe. She knelt in bed and prayed.

"Can I save them?" she asked her Goddess.

Golden blood trickling down her face, Aurienne Saw. The beasts tore apart the caravan again.

"I'm sorry, Aurienne," Theo whispered and died.

She screamed again, falling to the floor. "No. Show me! There must be more choices. There must be something we can do. Please."

She watched it again and again. She Saw every single choice in the attack. She Saw Captain Laurier push the sorcerers into a wagon for protection, but a lantern tipped and lit it ablaze. The wagon burned with her brother inside, and she heard his skin sizzle as he screamed. Theo died again.

"Hellsdamn it," she swore.

Sentinels pounded on her door, jostling the lock.

"My lady?" Sentinel Kolten shouted. "High Seer are you alright? Are you hurt?"

"I'm fine. Go away," she screamed.

She chewed her lip and clenched her fists. *Think. Think. What can I change? What can save them?* In every vision, they were caught sleeping. Over and over, wolves jumped on the caravan, and many died before an alarm was raised.

"What if they received warning?" she asked the stars.

Aurienne pushed through the veil, feeling it resist her. Some looming and unfamiliar presence watched her. Opposed her. Aurienne growled and reached spirit claws into her own soul. In her mind, beyond the veil separating worlds—she reached into the part of her that gave her Sight. She reached into that glowing Goddess-touched gift and held it tightly. The invading presence retreated just enough to allow her forward.

She watched the attack again—but this time, they had one minute's warning. Massacre. Then, in one vision, only some of them died. Then some were saved. Aurienne opened her eyes. Some of them could survive. She just had to get through to them fast enough.

I just have to warn them.

She scrambled across the rug and nearly fell onto her altar. Candles and books tumbled across the room. The large stone bowl on her altar tipped onto the floor with a loud boom. She clawed for her runes, crystal ball, and divination cards. She closed her eyes, sinking into that place in her mind. She pushed through the veil again and sought Theo. His soul blinked brightly on the horizon, and her spirit raced for him.

She found him.

Theo slept deeply on the forest floor and didn't stir. She screamed his name into the void over and over. He couldn't hear her. She screamed and screamed for him.

No. No. No. No. No.

Aurienne's eyes snapped open. She flipped through card after card, searching for his. The Traveler. She sliced her hand and pressed the welling blood against his card to try and reach him. The card absorbed the blood eagerly. Aurienne's eyes strayed toward an ancient book detailing the necromancy that she had already fallen to. She averted her gaze. Its presence was already too tempting. She couldn't risk it corrupting her soul, because then she'd be no help to anyone. Her breath caught in her throat, refusing to go down.

Think! How can I warn them?

What would she do if he died? Could she survive knowing she'd killed him? Her heart skipped a beat, and she swallowed. What would she tell his mother if he died?

His mother.

His Ma had given him an eyestone. The stone Saw through the veil, and Aurienne might be able to use that as a portal. She just needed enough power. She had never tried to speak through the veil and wasn't sure if she could do it, especially with how weak she was from the constant drain on her soul.

I have to try.

She held the Traveler in one hand and reached for a dusty black candle sitting high on a shelf. The process was so complex to make even one candle that she'd never made a second—and never would. It was poured on Hallohaim at the witching hour and mixed with grave dust collected by her own hand, moonwater, seer's tears, seer's blood, and other sacred materials, with a wick made of her own hair and cotton from a blessed text.

It might be enough.

She carefully placed the candle on the altar and lit it with a shaking hand before pouring a whole canister of thymewrinkle upon the flame.

The High Seer passed through the veil, holding the candle in one hand and the bloody card in the other. She poured all her remaining power into her voice. She channeled the core of her power, draining every drip of magic. On the verge of collapse, she reached for him, opened the small portal in the eyestone—and screamed.

Theo.

1152 N.T.C. The Shadow Wood.

"Theo," a voice whispered and yelled at the same time.

Theo woke from a deep sleep with a start. The night was quiet and calm, but he had a profound sense of unease reached the core of his bones and made him sick.

Theo shook Rhydian awake. "Do you feel that?"

Rhydian rubbed his eyes, shook off the blankets, and stood, searching the trees. "Yes."

"Captain, get up," Theo whispered.

"What is it?" Captain Laurier asked.

"Something is wrong."

"What?"

"Everyone get up," Theo said.

Mathis stirred and shook his head. Adonis pulled his boots on and opened his sorcerer's pack of clinking bottles. Kassia and Saryll emerged from their cocoon of blankets. Saryll closed her cloud-white eyes in a trance. Seconds later, she quickly opened them.

"Something comes," Saryll said.

The caravan was rousing but not quickly enough. Theo's stomach turned, sensing danger in the foggy mountains.

"Everyone get up now," Theo said.

A long, low whistle rose in the night sky before turning into an unearthly howl. Theo cringed and wiped his fingers against his ear. Blood. Theo stared at it as Ma's warnings filled his head. He looked up to see the stars had darkened.

If you hear a whistle that makes your ears bleed, and even the stars turn away, run.

"Everyone prepare. An attack!" Theo bellowed.

The camp erupted. Soldiers drew the wagons into a protective circle and led the horses away. Cooks and attendants knelt behind wagon wheels, holding makeshift weapons. Soldiers drew their swords or nocked arrows to their bows and waited. Mathis and Adonis mixed vial after vial of deadly potions.

Rhydian fidgeted with his sword handle. He gripped it and released it, clearly torn. Howls filled the sky, and in the distance, something crashed through the trees.

Rhydian's curse.

Theo swallowed. "How much firepower do you have?" he asked the sorcerers.

They looked up from their vials grimly, not even pausing their work.

Theo returned his gaze to the trees. The howls were nearly upon them, and they didn't slow. Branches snapped, leaves rustled, and claws scraped against tree bark. He lifted his eyestone and peered through it. In the distance, he saw the monsters. Flashes of patchy fur amongst protruding bone spikes, jagged fangs, and misshapen bodies. He lowered the eyestone in horror.

Mooncursed.

Theo knew the stories by heart. Hells, he'd just *told* Aurienne that story days ago, but never had he believed that the Mooncursed were real. The blood rushed out of his face. His mind struggled to accept what his eyes saw.

"What'd you see?" Adonis asked.

Theo's throat tightened, and he didn't respond. He shot a look toward Rhydian. Rhydian frowned and gripped the hilt of his sheathed sword. Theo instinctively knew the battle raging in Rhydian's mind. Theo's own mind flashed back to Rhydian's demonstration at Rodarri, and the trial where they'd faced off. He remembered what Aurienne said about his curse. If he took a life, he'd go mad and commit unspeakable atrocities.

"Go," Theo said to his friend.

"What?"

"It's the Mooncursed," Theo whispered.

Rhydian stared. "It can't be."

"You're going to have to kill what's coming if you can," Theo said. "There will be no stopping it without killing it. If what you say about your curse is true, you can't kill. And if you do, you're more of a danger to us and Teridar than they are. Go now. We can't fight you and them."

Rhydian hesitated, casting a look toward the trees. His gaze hardened, and he drew his sword at the approaching howls. "I'll stand with you and hope I keep my sanity long enough to kill myself after."

"You can't save Rianne if you do that," Theo said between gritted teeth, hating himself for saying it.

Rhydian stiffened.

"And you can't help Aurienne either. Go," Theo said.

Rhydian cursed. "I'm sorry," he said before disappearing into the trees.

Theo's meager training did not prepare him for this foe, and even the soldiers couldn't stand against what came. With Rhydian gone, what chance did they stand? Mathis' gaze bored into him. Theo met and held it. Mathis studied his face like one of his ancient tomes.

"Here, Adonis. Take these. Draw as many in as you can and keep them at bay," Mathis said.

"What are you doing?" Adonis asked.

"Preparing another alchemical reaction," Mathis said. "Keep them off me as long as you can."

Kassia and Saryll held hands, tears streaming down both of their faces in silent terror. They gripped vials from the sorcerers and faced the monsters.

"They're here," Captain Laurier shouted.

Theo braced, hands quivering on the hilt. Without armor, his traveling leathers would easily shred.

Bloodsun.

He'd never see Ma and Pa again. They'd never know what happened to him. He'd never see Aurienne.

The beasts that tore out of the trees came straight from hell. Titanium claws clanged against shields and fangs gnashed at the soldiers. Screams followed. One soldier's arm was ripped clean off, and the shoulder spurted arterial blood. Arrows flew into the beasts. Some bounced off, striking plates of bone. Others sank into the fur and flesh. The beasts did not notice. Soldiers hacked at them, but it only delayed the inevitable. More and more of the terrible wolf creatures poured out of the trees, and none were dying.

Theo bellowed and attacked.

Rhydian charged away from the battle through the darkness, hearing the screams. He was both repulsed and drawn to the sounds of battle, and the draw to death told Rhydian he made the right decision to flee. His curse rattled the bars of its corporeal cage, demanding to be let free.

Rhydian stopped to vomit into a bush. He wiped his mouth with his hand and kept running. He had to. If he stopped, he knew he would run back to his friends. His heart sank lower and lower. He heard the death throes of humans and wolves and stopped to vomit again. He punched a tree as hard as he could, and bark went flying. Rhydian kept going.

"You are more than your curse. Do not give in," he remembered Rianne saying.

Rhydian cursed again and continued running. Miles flew behind him, but he kept running. The terrible howls did not stop. The screams did not stop. Death beckoned him back to the camp, but the cost was too high. The curse was too dangerous. It made him feel like the worst kind of friend. He felt like a coward and hated himself.

A Mooncursed crashed out of the brush before him, sliding on metal claws through the grass and roots. It panted, its chest heaving as its muscles bunched. Rhydian dodged, slipping past the beast and drawing his sword. He hesitated. These things looked human enough... As if they once had been. It could wake his curse if they were. He couldn't kill the brute.

Hellsdamn me.

The wolf bared its fangs, and Rhydian thought it might have smiled. Golden eyes burned in the fur and bleached bones of the exposed skull. It charged, but Rhydian parried. His blade sparked against the metal plates as it scrambled past. It turned and clawed at him. Jumping back, he ran again.

Crunching leaves and snapping branches followed him through the trees. Feeling hot breath on his neck, he dove, and the beast sailed over him.

"Damn, you're fast," Rhydian panted.

It bit and raked at him in a flurry of teeth and claws. Parry. Slice. Parry. Block. Slice. Slice.

The Mooncursed was bleeding shallowly from a dozen cuts, but it didn't slow. It clawed for him, tearing his skin and causing him to dive behind a thick trunk. Sword raised, he sliced at it again.

"Stay down!" Rhydian snarled.

It was going to keep coming until it couldn't. He'd have to injure it badly enough that it could no longer give chase. Without killing it. Sweat beaded his brow from apprehension more than effort. He couldn't miss.

It attacked again. Bringing all his strength to bear, he chopped at the beast's hind leg. The beast howled as its leg was lopped from its body. It stumbled, limping on three legs. Blood poured from the cut.

Rhydian swallowed, feeling ice spear the heat in his veins. It was so much blood. More than he expected. If the creature died, he'd go mad.

Three Mooncursed crept from the trees, surrounding him. Throaty snarls filled the trees as claws clicked on stone. He swallowed and settled into his fighting stance.

One slip of the sword, and he'd lose himself forever.

Theo's arm bled from a stinging, jagged gash near the elbow. Wolves dragged soldiers into the trees, screaming and fighting.

One cook was hurled against the side of the wagon, and wood cracked as bones snapped. "Help!"

There were too many. They've never kill them all. A wolf darted in from the trees.

"Now, there." Saryll pointed.

Kassia threw her vial of Adonis' firewater toward a leaping wolf. The vial shattered against its chest plate, and the creature caught flame. The scent of burning flesh filled the air. The wolf screamed and raced into the trees.

"There." Saryll directed.

Kassia threw another vial, but the reaction failed. It darted out of the trees and bit down into Kassia's arm. Kassia screamed as it dragged her away.

"No," Saryll shrieked.

Theo yelled and hacked at a wolf and drove it back, fighting to get to Kassia. Another wolf blocked him. Adonis threw a vial at the wolf in Theo's path, but it dodged and lunged for Theo again. He couldn't reach them.

Saryll looked at her vial and hesitated. Firewater was potent. If Saryll missed, Kassia would burn. *Would she risk it?* Theo was knocked to the ground and scrambled toward them. Saryll's face twisted with rage, and she screamed a war cry, leaping onto the wolf's back. She dug her fingers into its fur. The wolf shook Kassia, and blood oozed out of the wounds. Kassia screamed again, clawing at its eyes. Saryll took her ceremonial blade from her skirts and drove it deep through its eye into its brain. It fell to the ground. Saryll pried the jaws from Kassia's arm and held her tightly.

"There," Saryll cried.

With her good arm, Kassia hurled Saryll's last vial straight into the face of an oncoming wolf. It caught fire and ran off into the trees to die. Even water or dust could not put out a firewater blaze.

Theo reached them and stood guard as Saryll quickly tied a tourniquet around Kassia's wound. With her good arm, Kassia drew a short firewood axe from a barrel. Saryll wielded her ceremonial blade and shouted warnings to the group.

"There," she shouted.

Adonis stopped mixing and hurled a vial of lavender dreamsmoke at a wolf. The blinded wolf snarled and pawed at its eyes. It lunged blindly, searching for prey that it could not see. Adonis palmed another vial and waited.

"There," Saryll cried.

Theo swung his sword around to slice deeply into a lunging wolf. The blade wedged into the bone plates, and Theo fought to reclaim it. The wolf roared and swiped a paw at Theo.

A voice so far away said, "*Duck.*"

Theo released the sword and fell backward to avoid losing his head. The wolf lunged, but Theo dodged. Captain Laurier sent an arrow into the wolf's side, and the wolf turned to growl at the captain. Theo dove toward his sword. He freed it from the beast and swung it again. The wolf dodged and disappeared into the trees.

Five wolves were dead, and nearly twenty were left attacking and prowling at the edges of the caravan. Thirty soldiers had fallen, or nearly so. Only a dozen civilians remained.

Kassia and Saryll huddled together with their pitiful weapons. Adonis was empty-handed and out of vials, swinging a dull steel practice sword at any who got too close to Mathis—who was still huddled over his books and chemicals. Captain Laurier was badly injured and bleeding but loosed arrows at shadows.

Terror hung heavy in the air as the wolves circled. They gnashed their broken, jagged fangs. Screams of the dead and dying filled the air. Several wolves tore into a poor cook, eating him alive. He screamed and screamed, reaching for Theo, but he was too far away to help. Theo vomited. Standing, he stared down the closest wolf, daring him to attack. The cool caress of destiny brushed against his skin. If this was his time, then he would pass into the next world on the wings of valor. He gripped his sword until the leather squeaked.

Standing in front of Adonis, Saryll, and Kassia, Theo braced. The remaining soldiers and caravan members were huddled around them. The wolves circled again and sunk low into the brush, ready to attack. Theo knew they could not withstand another wave. This would be the last stand before they were all devoured by devils.

Mathis straightened, clutching a vial of deep purple liquid. He glanced at Adonis and set his jaw, looking as he ever did. His hair stuck out at all odd angles, and the bells in his beard jingled. His dark blue robe, decorated in swirls and mathematical designs, flapped around him. But his eyes—his eyes were different. Gone was the stern but whimsical old man. He stared down the nightmares with the intensity of a seasoned warrior. The veil of age lifted from his wrinkled face.

Theo knew the meaning of it—the look of someone about to face death. He slashed at the wolves darting in the trees, buying Mathis time. Adonis had lost his sword and was swinging wildly at the Mooncursed with a broken piece of wagon frame. Adonis' face was tear-stained, but he did not falter.

The old sorcerer clutched the vial tightly.

Adonis noticed the vial, and his face went slack. "Mathis? What are you doing?"

"I'm so proud of you," Mathis said. "I believe in you and the man you're going to become."

"Mathis, wait!" Adonis cried.

The sorcerer's gaze hardened. "Run."

The caravan broke ranks and ran for the trees. Wolves caught a soldier and wagon attendant on the way. Theo dragged a struggling Adonis behind him. Captain Laurier limped slowly, falling behind. Theo cursed and returned, holding the soldier up. He half-carried, half-dragged the captain into the trees, shoving Adonis forward, dodging wolves. The Mooncursed descended upon the old sorcerer as if realizing he was the greatest threat.

BOOM.

Dazed, Theo stirred and lifted his face from the dirt. His ears rang and his head throbbed, and it took long moments to push himself to stand. The dust cleared, and one by one, the survivors rose. Blood was splattered everywhere. No one said anything. Theo limped back to the camp. Mathis, or what was left of him, lay in a pile of dead wolves. He had killed them all but sacrificed himself.

Adonis ran to his mentor and dropped to his knees. "No..."

"What did he do?" Theo asked, dumbfounded.

Theo's head pulsed from the pressure, and his heart pounded as fast as a hummingbird's wings from the adrenaline of battle. His hands shook uncontrollably, and he struggled to remain standing. Everywhere he looked, there were dead and dying humans and dead monsters. The wagons and supplies were strewn through the trees in pieces.

"Deathforce. The potion takes the sorcerer's death and amplifies the magic to kill all nearby enemies. It's the most difficult alchemic reaction. I...didn't even know he knew how to do it. He never taught me... He's never going to teach me." Adonis began to sob.

Theo placed a hand on Adonis' shoulder.

"I never listened to him. I should have listened. I thought he'd always be around to teach me, but he's gone. He's gone. He's gone, and he's not coming back. I never told him how much I appreciated him. I never told him how much I looked up to him. I never told him..." Adonis wept.

"He knew," Theo said gently.

Theo surveyed the camp. Only six soldiers had survived, along with Captain Laurier, who had a badly injured leg and was being tended to by Kassia. Seven staff members crawled out of their hiding places.

Another attendant was groaning loudly. Saryll sat next to the woman and held her hand. Theo gave Saryll a questioning look, and Saryll shook her head. The attendant would soon be gone from this world.

Theo stared at the creatures and the dead. His brain fought to make sense of what he saw. It was impossible. A trick or a hallucination. Monsters weren't real. He blinked, but the terrible images remained. Theo turned and vomited until his stomach emptied fully. He wiped his mouth on his hand as he soaked up carnage.

I have to do something.

"Does anyone need help?" Theo called.

Silence. He searched for other survivors for hours but found none. He kept his eyes sharp for lurking wolves, but he found their corpses half a mile from the campsite. Theo returned to camp as his emotions emptied, leaving him feeling only shock.

Adonis laid Mathis' burnt cloak over his broken body. Saryll laid a torn blanket over the attendant, now dead. They looked to Theo for survivors, but he shook his head.

"How many are dead?" Theo asked.

"Ninety-seven in all." Captain Laurier's voice cracked.

"What were those things?" Kassia asked, cradling her arm against her body while she and Saryll tended to the injured.

"Mooncursed," Theo said.

Theo approached a wolf's corpse. A brand peeked out from the burned skin. Theo wiped the char off to reveal the horned howling wolf crest of the emperor seared into the wolf's shoulder. Fear and revulsion washed over Theo as he recognized it.

"They bear Emperor Rexil's mark," Theo said.

Everyone froze. Not a single survivor moved. No one breathed.

Finally, Adonis said, "If these are what we're facing, if this is what his army is made of, we don't stand a chance."

Suddenly weary, Theo sank to the bloodstained dirt and leaned against a tree. "This is what Aurienne Saw."

Gods, if these were the images that filled her mind all hours of the day—if she was forced to bear witness to massacres such as this one on an even grander scale, it was a wonder she hadn't gone mad.

The caravan sat for a long time. Hours passed. Theo wasn't sure how many as time bled together. The survivors stared at the destruction and grappled with it in their own ways. Some cried or screamed. Some lay down and did not move. One cook stabbed the corpse of a wolf over and over and over again until he passed out. Theo could only stare at Mathis' death shroud, and at some point, tears streaked his face.

Silently, Rhydian walked out of the forest and paused to survey the damage. As he looked around, his expression spoke of guilt, and anger. He took calculated steps and paused at every dead wolf, every dead body as if committing them to memory. His jaw worked, and his lips pulled back into a snarl as if he could see the attack unfolding in his mind. Maybe he could. He was a Warbringer. Rhydian sat in the dirt beside Theo.

Rhydian mumbled, "I'm glad you're alive."

"Thanks." It was all Theo could manage.

Theo noticed the blood on Rhydian's sleeve and tiredly lifted his head.

Rhydian glanced at the stain. "I didn't kill anything. The magic killed them first."

Kassia and Saryll held hands and stared at the ground quietly. Adonis sat near Mathis' body and placed his hand atop the black death shroud, staring off into the distant mountains.

Theo stood. "We should bury them."

Theo grabbed a shovel. The end of the handle was missing, but it would do. He found a quiet grouping of shady tamarack trees and began to dig. Rhydian joined him, along with the remaining six soldiers and a bandaged Captain Laurier. Six of the seven surviving attendants were whole enough to help and began carrying bodies to the graves. Kassia and Saryll prepared the bodies.

It took hours, but finally, their dead were laid side by side in a long grave and returned to the earth. Adonis marked Mathis' grave with a large stone that only Rhydian and Theo together could move. Kassia planted hellebore lily seeds at the head of each grave, and Saryll whispered prayers to the Goddess. The captain poured a measure of alcohol at the foot of each. They piled the wolves atop a pyre built from the wagons too broken to salvage.

Exhausted, they sat and waited for nightfall to light the pyre. Rhydian left to retrieve the surviving horses from the hills and returned with half the surviving horses. Theo and Rhydian calmed the horses, watered them, and led them to the long grasses one by one. Silently, the soldiers set to repairing the wagons while the attendants sought what supplies they could salvage. A heavy weight settled on the survivors. They didn't speak. What was there to say?

A white raven found them sometime later. A shaky letter written by Aurienne was attached to its foot. Theo took it from the bird.

> *I Saw the attack and tried to warn you. You are alive, so you must have woken up in time. I'm so sorry. I Saw that there are survivors, and I thank the Goddess. Is everyone okay? Are you okay?*
>
> *Take the Hunger's Teeth Mountain Road.*
> *– Aurienne*

Theo stared at the words, fingering the crimson and gold stains on the parchment.

Was he okay?

He didn't think so. They were something out of a legend or monster story. How could they be real? How could they exist? What else lurked in the darkness? What else did he not know about? Theo had always believed in minor superstitions. He planted the red acorn in the fields in spring and avoided black feathers and lines in the road.

He'd rubbed scarlet clay into wounds and gathered flowers to weave into the bride and groom's hair for blessings. Never had he picked up a face-down coin, and he'd planned to keep his first horseshoe hammered at his forge as a token of luck. Superstitions were part of life, but now there were real curses, ghosts, and monsters. They were all real. Monsters were real.

Was he okay?

He relived friends and companions ripped to pieces as wretched wolves descended upon the nearly dead and devoured them. He saw his friends fighting for one another, willing to die for one another.

When had life become so complicated?

In his mind's eye, Mathis died again and again. The soldiers died. They sacrificed their lives so the few survivors might have a chance. *Did he even deserve a chance?* He had failed at bringing together the nations of Teridar for the summit. The summit was in one week and none of the leaders would come. He failed them all.

If those things were what the emperor wielded, did they even have a chance? Nothing could stand before those monsters. How many did the emperor have at his command? Were there others more terrible than these? How did he make them? They were all going to die.

Saryll broke the silence. "Is *your* arm alright?" she asked her nature witch.

"I need to cleanse it with weeping ivy and moonwater to keep it from becoming infected. But there will be no permanent damage, just a few scars," Kassia replied.

"You need to do it before the next full moon. The legends say that the bitten will turn into a beast if bitten by a Mooncursed," Theo said absently.

"I'll search for the supplies now. We'll need to cleanse everyone," Saryll said.

"I'll help. We don't need any more of these beasts to fight. We don't want to become monsters," Rhydian said.

A realization hit Theo. An idea.

Theo seized a sword from the blood and carnage and approached the dead monster. He lifted the sword high above his head and brought it down deep into the monster's neck. Theo tried to free it from the protruding neck bones, but it was stuck on a wide band of metal wrapped around its neck and concealed by fur—a collar. He placed his boot against the monster's mutated face and freed the blade with a wet crunch. He lifted it up and brought it down again. It took five swings before the head rolled away. Theo gripped a tuft of hair and lifted the decapitated monster's head. He stuffed it into a burlap sack. He freed another two wolf heads the same way.

Horror and disgust painted every surviving face.

"What are you doing?" Saryll whispered.

"The Free Peoples and People of Living Stone wanted proof of the threat," Theo said coldly. "Here's my proof. They cannot deny *this*. It will make them join us or bring these beasts to their door. I'll do whatever it takes."

Gold and clear sparkles caught the light from the black metal collar, catching Theo's attention. "This is titan ore." He glanced at the pile of bodies. "Search them. Collect all you can find."

Queasy soldiers searched the bodies and loaded a stack of over twenty collars into a wagon.

Rhydian singled one corpse out to Theo. "This one's mostly human. He must have been controlling or guiding them. He has a titan ore dagger."

Theo inspected the dagger, studying runes inscribed on the side that matched the collars before he placed it into his saddle bag with the heads.

"Light the fires," Theo gestured.

Captain Laurier directed the remaining handful of soldiers to set flame to the pile of corpses. They watched as fur and flesh burned for hours, until nothing remained of their attackers but ash.

Rhydian asked, "What are you going to do?"

Theo's lip curled. "I'm done asking nicely."

HEARTSPRING
CHAPTER THIRTY-FOUR

No one knows how, but rumor says they were imprisoned in the heart of a mountain outside of a heart spring. They remained imprisoned for almost a thousand years, waiting to inflict their hunger upon the world again.

— TALE OF THE SHADOWS OF HEARTSPRING.

1152 N.T.C. The mountain town of Heartspring, Hunger's Teeth Mountains, Avyllon.

The darkness growing in Theo's heart hungered for destruction and misery as he nursed his third large mug. They'd stopped at a tavern in a town tucked away between the mountains, off the desolate road. The nineteen survivors slouched in wooden chairs, drinking to fill bottomless holes in their hearts. Mathis was dead. Ninety-seven of their friends had been ripped apart. The leaders of Wyndsel, Rodarri, the Seven Forests, and the Titan Cliffs had all turned them down. Theo was going to return to the Seven Forests with the heads, but even that might not be enough. And they were running out of time. Only ten days remained until the summit. Their task was too great and the costs too high. At this moment, it seemed as though there was no chance of success, so they drank.

The pain of his failures and guilt for the loss of their companions were shards of glass in Theo's lungs, and he struggled to breathe. Dejected but angry. Full of rage and somehow empty. With every fiber of his being, he fought the call of desperation, despair, and hopelessness. Memories of magic and monsters, the dire reality of their situation, slapped him in the face. Everyone was irrevocably broken, and he had nothing to offer them.

Breathing took every bit of strength.

Theo glanced shamefully at the people he'd failed. Adonis had not spoken a word since they left the massacred grove. He downed two tankards of ale and sat with his nose lodged in a book, failing to hide the tears that poured down his ashen face to smear the ink.

Adonis mumbled. "Mix two parts alchemical firewater with one part dreamsmoke, add corpseroot and vetiver with black wolf spider web, and boil..."

Saryll gazed off with unfocused clouded eyes, gripping the table until her fingernails left crescent moon marks in the wood. Guilt darkened her translucent eyes.

"I'm sorry," Saryll whispered for the thousandth time. "Aurienne would have Seen the attack. She did See it, and from thousands of miles away still saved us. If only I had Seen it too..."

Theo knew that the noose of guilt wrapping around her neck was the same that strangled him, and no one could remove it from either of them. He opened his mouth to say something, but no words came.

What could he say? Saryll was right. Instead, he took another long sip that burned his throat. It was difficult to comfort someone when the thing that bothered them was the truth. He knew.

"We're lucky any of us survived. You did what you could. We all did." Kassia quietly held Saryll's hand and sipped her own tall mug of amber liquid while tears rolled down her onyx skin.

"I didn't do all I could," Rhydian murmured.

Guilt at not being able to help his friends hung over Rhydian like a wet blanket, and his shoulders sagged. Theo did not fault him for leaving, and if Rhydian were honest, Theo knew he probably didn't regret it. Not if the choice would have cost him Rianne. Theo would've done the same for Aurienne.

Theo marveled at thinking about curses as if they were commonplace, *real*. Theo nearly said something to his friend but wondered if he might be getting close to being drunk, so he let the impulse die on his tongue.

Curses were real.

Monsters were real.

Magic was real.

More than they knew. A strange feeling washed over Theo, making him straighten. It could be the shock or trauma, but something tugged at his awareness. His skin itched and prickled—just like the day he'd gotten his reading. Aurienne might have called it fate or the whispers of the Goddess. He now knew better than to ignore it and allowed his eyes to scan the room for the source of discomfort.

"What brings you all to Heartspring?" the waitress asked Theo.

Theo shook the cobwebs of sorrow from his mind with a blink. "We're from Avyllon, just passing through."

"Are you all...okay?" The waitress glanced over their dour party.

"Animal attack on the road. We lost some friends," he murmured.

"Sorry to hear that," she said. "We've had some problems with animal attacks this week. We lost a few people. We haven't recovered the bodies yet, and all the livestock are gone as well. What sort of animal did you see?"

"Wolves." Theo spat the word like it was coated in venom.

"This is a bit out of the way to get to anywhere. Where are you heading?"

"The Seven Forests."

Her lips twisted, and she folded her arms across her apron. "You know the borders are closed? They have barriers on all the roads."

"We know." Theo tapped the table. "We carry a missive from the regent of Avyllon. I'm hoping they see reason."

Under the table, he bumped his foot against the wrapped severed wolf head. Wrapped in seven layers of burlap to conceal the smell of rot, Theo refused to let the vile thing out of his sight.

"The regent? You mean the High Seer? You carry a missive from the High Seer...herself?" The waitress's eyes sparkled.

"We do."

The young woman rolled forward onto the balls of her feet as if she wanted to bounce in excitement. "Have you met her?"

Theo nodded, pressing his tongue against his teeth.

"They say she Sees all futures, that she is touched by the Triple Goddess herself. We worship the Harvest God here, but I have always wondered what it would be like to See the future. I heard she looks like a goddess and that her power is unrivaled. She took over as High Seer at thirteen years old because she was already the most powerful seer to live. Is she really what they say?"

The familiar aching in his heart returned with the waitress's questions about Aurienne. *Aurienne.* Determined, strong, selfless. She would've known what to do and saved them all from the Moon-cursed. She would've convinced the Free Peoples and People of Living Stone to join. His stomach rolled, and he swallowed. She must be so disappointed in him.

Theo smiled despite his misery. "All that and more."

She sighed wistfully.

Theo looked up from his mug to study the waitress. In her early twenties, she wore a clean apron about her hips, and her sleeves were rolled up to the elbow. He noticed kitchen burns and scars across her arms and hands. Her dark hair was long and clean but not pulled back into a working plait. He looked down and noticed her boots were well-made and clean from mud.

"Your family owns the tavern?" he guessed.

"How did you know?"

"Lucky guess."

"I don't mean to bother you with questions. We don't get a lot of visitors here. Refill?"

He nodded. Ale sounded like just the poisonous cure he needed right now. He might regret it later, but for now, his heart was as dark as the starless mountain skies.

A necklace, a heart carved from red heartwood swung out from underneath her shirt when she leaned down. Well-oiled, the pendant was worn smooth, almost like a stone. It must be hundreds of years old. Maybe a thousand. There was something strange about the young woman. An inkling of suspicion whispered into Theo's ear, and he'd experienced too much to ignore it. Theo had heard of one such necklace in the stories—the heart of Heartspring.

"What is your name?" he asked.

"Miella Rothbain," she replied.

"Theo Thatcher, nice to meet you," he said with a terse nod.

"Well, the shepherd's pies will be out of the oven shortly. Can I get you anything else?"

Theo glanced around the large tavern, paying closer attention to the diners. Recognition tingled at the edges of Theo's mind. There was something about this town that triggered his suspicion. He tried to remember where they were exactly. They were in the Hunger's Teeth Mountain range, near the border of Avyllon.

"What is this town called?" he asked.

"You don't know? This is Heartspring."

Unblinking, Theo stared long enough that the waitress shifted uncomfortably. His slack grip dropped his mug with a thump that caught Rhydian and the captain's attention. Icy prickles filled his blood.

It couldn't be.

"Heartspring? Like the fairytale, the Shadow of Heartspring? As in, 'Rumor says they were imprisoned in the heart of a mountain outside of a heart spring.' That Heartspring?"

She laughed too quickly and too loudly. "It's just a story."

That strange awareness tickled his ears. "Thanks."

She sauntered away, checking on diners and refilling mugs.

"What's wrong?" Rhydian asked.

"The name of this place is Heartspring. I haven't seen it on any maps, but Aurienne told us to come this way. Maybe she knew something..." Theo trailed off.

"Okay, so the legend is named after this place. Or this town is named after the legend. Or a thousand years ago, someone from here told a monster story and it stuck around. Why do you look like you struck gold tilling your father's field?"

"There's more to everything than we knew." Theo gestured. "Look around you. You are a Warbringer. I didn't even know what that was until two weeks ago. We are surrounded by seers and witches, curses, and ghosts. We've seen giants and people of stone. We just were nearly eaten by the Mooncursed beasts from the stories. Is it so hard to believe that all of those stories are real, but the story about the Shadows is not? What if they are here?"

"Are you saying we should leave?" Rhydian asked.

Images flashed in his mind from the last three weeks. All the humiliating things he had endured to save the people he loved. Failure after failure all for a prophecy that doomed them all. A thought danced around the edges of his mind, the same that had troubled him for a day and a half. How were they going to defeat those monsters with armies of men? They couldn't.

Only monsters could defeat monsters. The Shadows of Heartspring were monsters.

Theo took a large gulp of his drink. "No."

"Then what?"

Theo rolled his next words around his tongue, testing to see how they tasted. Mind full of drink, he was sober enough to know the consequences of these next words. Words that couldn't be taken back. When the silence stretched too long, Theo finally met Rhydian's gaze with a harder one.

"I want to find the Shadows and convince them to fight for us."

"How many drinks have you had?" Rhydian chuckled.

"You didn't see what they did to us. You didn't watch them tear us apart." Theo immediately winced, not intending the tone. He'd snapped at Rhydian like a whip.

Rhydian hunched his head, suddenly finding something incredibly interesting in the bottom of his mug. He worked his jaw before downing the rest of the ale. He put the mug back on the table with a thump.

More gently, Theo said, "You didn't see what they did to trained soldiers. With a seer who could See their attacks, two sorcerers, and a hundred soldiers, we killed five. Five of twenty. They killed nearly a hundred of us in minutes. And those who survived only remained alive for so long because they took breaks to *eat*. If not for Mathis' sacrifice, we would have all died. Even you, with all your skills and curse, would have struggled to best them, and it would have cost you your mind. We have nothing that could stand against them."

Rhydian's expression remained dark. "If you could even find the Shadows. They were locked up for a reason."

"I think I know who can." Theo nodded toward the waitress, Miella. "She's wearing the necklace from the story. She's related to the Shadows; she's got to be. If anyone knows where they are, it's her."

"You're really going to do this?"

"Here are those shepherd's pies," Miella said, setting down the overfilled bowls of steaming meat pie.

"What did you say your family name was?" Theo asked.

"Rothbain."

"It sounds familiar. How long has your family lived here?"

"We settled here before the Shadow Wars." Miella beamed.

"Thank you." Theo shot a pointed glance at Rhydian.

She nodded, with a bright smile full of pride, and left to bring out the rest of their dinners to the caravan.

Theo faced Rhydian. "If I can find the Shadows, I'll offer to free them. Humans can't stand against the Mooncursed and any other horrors the emperor might have. I'm a bloodsun failure. I was rejected at every nation. Every single one. We might not have even been there to be attacked if not for me. I'm supposed to... I don't even know anymore. I know I couldn't save all those people when it mattered. I won't let that happen again."

"Theo..."

"I'm going. You don't have to come. I won't hold you to your promise to help me if this is asking too much, but it's something I must do. Until the attack, the Mooncursed were just stories too. Legends are coming back, and monsters are coming to life. We need something to turn the tides."

Rhydian scratched his beard. "Do you really believe they're up there in the mountains somewhere?"

"That's what the stories say," Theo said. "Ever since we got here, I've had a weird feeling. Maybe it's the magic I'm sensing. Aurienne said I would gather the armies for a reason. Maybe that's why she told us to go this way. It's worth trying. If the Free People and Living Stones don't change their minds, we can't go back empty-handed."

"Before you go all monster hunter on me, you should ask our seer," Rhydian said.

Theo leaned toward Saryll. "Can you read the cards for me?"

Saryll blinked away her tears and freed her cards from her spelled box. "Ask three questions."

Theo watched Miella meander between the patron's tables. "Are the Shadows of Heartspring real?"

Saryll turned over the top card. Night. "Yes."

Gooseflesh exploded on his skin. They were real. Gods.

"Is Miella descended from the First Shadow's family?"

The Vines. "Yes."

"Whoah," Rhydian whispered.

"Are the Shadows still..." Theo stopped. He considered his words. Words mattered. Alive was perhaps not the best word. Did Shadows even live? Did they breathe? "Do the Shadows still exist here?"

Saryll turned the final card. The Curse. "Yes."

Rhydian cursed quietly. As Theo stared at the card, his cheeks warmed. A mirthless grin spread across his face.

"Can I ask another question?" Theo said.

Saryll shuffled the cards again. "They're warm. I think they will permit one more question."

"Should I free the Shadows?"

Saryll turned the card. The Owl. "Maybe."

Maybe was better than no.

"What if they refuse to help us and instead eat us?" Rhydian asked.

"Then we'll die a little bit sooner than we thought," Theo said. "As it stands, we have no hope anyways. If it looks like they're going to eat us, you run back and save that queen of yours."

"And if you manage to free the monsters, and they tear across the land?"

Theo tapped his fingers and chewed his lip. Images of the Moon-cursed creatures tearing through the caravan assailed him. Bodies buried in a long grave. The corpses of wolves burned all night. The blood had deeply soaked the dirt. Could the Shadows be that bad? Maybe. But he knew the wolves were coming, and he knew what *they* would do.

Aurienne flashed into his mind—her smile, her distant gazes where her mind wandered beyond the veil, the blood leaking from her mouth and ears when she used her gift too often. What about her? She'd told him the emperor must be defeated at any cost. But would she free a monster? She had trusted him to do this, and every fiber of his being told him to find the Shadows.

Theo shrugged. "Then you kill them and curse my name. Aurienne said the emperor destroys the continent. Nothing is worse than that."

"If they did the things the stories say, they could be."

Theo worked his jaw, remembering the werewolves tearing his friends apart. A wolf chewed upon the leg bone of a cook he had gotten to know. A royal staff member who had repaired his clothing screamed as her head was ripped off. Mathis looked mournfully at Adonis one last time before blowing himself to pieces.

"At least they'll be *our* monsters. You won't change my mind, Rhydian. Help me or don't."

"Hellsdamned moonless skies and Shadow's teeth," Rhydian cursed. He pressed his hand to his head and sighed. "I promised to help you. Hagstit. I'll climb that gods' hellsdamned mountain and free monsters with you."

Theo's heart fell to the depths of his core. He closed his eyes, pushing away the guilt and anger under a numb veil. If he did this, people would die. But his heart told him that if he climbed that mountain, he would find what he sought. *Could he do this? Yes, he could.*

Theo waved Miella over.

"Is everything okay with the pie?"

"It's great. I had something else I wanted to ask you."

"Look, you're good looking, you and your friend, and I appreciate the offer, but I'm not interested in warming your beds tonight," Miella said blandly.

Theo shook his head like he'd stuck his nose into an old boot. "What? No. That's... No. Not what I was going to ask."

Her eyebrows shot up like mid-Solla summer rockets. Her lips parted, and she stared at him for long moments. Her brows sank and twisted into a frown.

"We've all heard the legend of the Shadows of Heartspring," he began.

Miella rolled her eyes. "It's just a story."

"The High Seer is interested in all lore and legends," he said—taking a chance. "We would like to see for ourselves."

"The High Seer?"

Theo nearly smiled. She had been too interested earlier in the High Seer to refuse what she thought would be a request of their regent. He nodded seriously.

"I don't know what you would want to see. There's nothing here." Miella crossed her arms.

"But you know where the Shadows are."

She shifted like she had a pebble in her boot. It was all the confirmation Theo needed. She knew.

"Surely you know where the legends say they're locked away?" Theo asked. "A place children taunt one another to go? Somewhere no one dares to venture? We had one growing up. It was an old barn that burned to the ground. We used to make bets on who could spend the whole night there, but none were brave enough to last. The creaking sounds sent even the most courageous running home. You must have such a place? The High Seer wants us to hunt down any legends that could be helpful to her."

She glanced around and whispered, "There's a place that the locals refuse to go. But it's forbidden, with good cause. The path is treacherous and difficult to traverse."

"It sounds like exactly the place that the High Seer would want us to go."

She frowned. "Why?"

"She had a vision that foretold a great threat to Avyllon. She needs to find anything she can to fight it. Even if it's just information or the basis of old stories, it might help her piece together the puzzle."

Miella tapped her finger on her arm.

Theo fought to steady his voice. "Can you take us there?"

"Me?" she sputtered.

"You said the path was treacherous," Rhydian piped up. "It

doesn't sound like we would find it without a guide. We can pay you if that's what you would require."

"It's not about money. We're not supposed to go there," Miella said.

"You could be saving a lot of lives," Theo pressed.

She hesitated.

"It'll be an adventure."

Miella breathed out. "I'll take you there tomorrow once you've slept off the drink. We should leave early, to be there before nightfall."

"Thank you," Theo said.

She gave him a curt nod before striding away.

Rhydian lifted his mug. "You lied to her. I never took you for the lying type."

"I didn't lie. We want to find the Shadows. I just didn't tell her the whole truth."

"Is there a difference?"

Theo wondered whether his friend was right. His stomach twisted. When had lies and deceit started to slip off his tongue so easily? Why didn't it bother him more?

The growing darkness in Theo had its fill of misery that night.

Broken Chains

Chapter Thirty-Five

1152 N.T.C. The mountain town of Heartspring, Hunger's Teeth Mountains, Avyllon.

Bright morning sun and the accompanying clearer head, unfortunately, did nothing to dissuade Theo from his decision. He almost wished it had. The caravan roused late the next morning.

Theo told Captain Laurier of their plan to visit the Shadows, and the captain spent half the morning trying to talk Theo out of it. "This is a terrible idea."

"I won't ask you to agree," Theo said. "I won't even ask you to come. But I'm going."

Rhydian stood beside Theo. "We're going, Captain."

Adonis' face was drawn, and heavy bags settled under his eyes. "I don't know if Mathis would have wanted this, but he gave his life to the Mooncursed. If the Shadows have a chance at defeating those things when I couldn't... When we couldn't... Let's do it." Something hard glinted in Adonis' eye that had never been there before.

"Aurienne believes in you. I'll go," Saryll said.

"Shadowcursed seers," Captain Laurier mumbled.

Kassia fidgeted. "What if they're worse than the Mooncursed?"

"The Goddess bid Aurienne trust Theo," Saryll said. "I can't imagine anything worse than the Mooncursed."

"Someone locked them away for a reason," Kassia replied.

Theo grimaced. "Or they locked themselves away."

"Is that better?" Kassia threw up her hands.

Theo glanced around for Miella. She'd be here soon and couldn't hear their plans.

"You don't have to come," Theo said.

"Sorry, Kassia. I'm going," Saryll said.

Kassia squeezed her hand. "Then I'm coming too."

Theo nearly argued, but the set of Saryll's jaw and the glint in her eyes told him that she Saw how the argument would turn out and it wouldn't be in his favor.

"You don't need to do this. We have the heads," Captain Laurier hissed.

Theo's heart twisted. "They turned me down before. What if the heads aren't enough? We're running out of time. I can't fail again."

"You can't take this choice back."

Theo grimaced. "I know."

"At least take three soldiers with you," Captain Laurier said.

"Fine, and I'll take a wolf head," Theo said. "We may need it. You keep the other ones safe. Our lives may depend on it."

The captain grunted acknowledgment and limped away, keeping the sack close to his chest and a dangerous expression keen upon his brow.

"We're going with you," Saryll said from a nearby booth.

Theo asked, "Do you See anything?"

"I See only that you are right, and we should go. The cards are in favor of your mission, but the outcome is still uncertain."

"Adonis, are you up for this?" Theo glanced toward the solemn sorcerer.

"I'm fine. Stop asking," Adonis grumbled.

After Adonis left, Rhydian said, "He doesn't mean it."

Theo scrubbed his neck. "I know. He lost his mentor, who was like a father to him. It's tough. I don't mind him beating up on me for a while if he needs it."

"I'm sure your seer would appreciate that," Rhydian said.

Miella strolled outside, dressed in leathers, fingerless gloves, and thick-treaded climbing boots. A rope hung across her chest.

"Are you ready?"

"Ready," Theo said.

Miella gave them all a long look, pausing briefly upon Theo before nodding. "You have rope, water, food, and medical supplies?"

"Always."

"It's a long trip for simple curiosity."

Theo shrugged. "We'll do whatever we can to help the High Seer prevent the foretold omen and the prophecy."

She straightened. "We best be off, then."

The adventurers followed her into the woods towards the looming mountain peaks. The dense trees gave way to open spaces as they began to climb. They climbed for several hours, winding their way across the mountain's face, over the foothills, and higher and higher.

Theo fought his conscience. Was he really willing to do this? Was this the right thing to do?

Gods.

They were soon out of the forest and scaling steep shale cliffs on the goat trail, which was only wide enough to trek up single file. Ancient rope bridges spanned daring ravines and whipped side to side in the high winds. Their little fox companion darted in and out of the rocks, receiving offerings of meat before it decided to take shelter in the denser woods.

The air grew thin as the group neared the tall peaks. Theo's lungs burned already, and they were only halfway up the steep mountain. Saryll and Kassia were beginning to trip on small stones, and even Rhydian worked up a sweat.

"Let's rest here for a quarter hour," Theo said.

"Sure, but we need to keep moving or we will be caught out here after dark," Miella replied.

Theo pulled his boots off and emptied the dirt and small rocks. Beside him, Rhydian did the same. Saryll sat near Kassia on a large flat boulder, sharing dried fruit.

Theo leaned toward Saryll. "Do you See anything?"

"I See we're on the right path," she whispered.

Theo leaned back and chewed dried meats before taking a long swig of water. Saryll's visions comforted him. It was as close to having Aurienne around as he could manage for now.

Miella studied her traveling companions. Rhydian, the Warbringer walked a tightrope, fighting to keep from falling into oblivion. Kassia carefully collected herbs in pockets in her tunic and pack—a witch then. Adonis had his head in a large book and carried liquids and vials. He must be a sorcerer of some nature.

Theo, on the other hand, was an enigma. He spoke well, though his comfort outdoors told her he didn't spend his days inside reading or in leisure. He looked like a farmer, or perhaps a woodworker, builder, or blacksmith, someone who was used to hard work with their hands. What was a tradesman doing as an official emissary to the High Seer, regent of all Avyllon? Miella wrapped the end of her braid around her finger, lost in thought. He was handsome and wore no wedding markings, band, or necklace. Theo was one who would take some time to puzzle out.

Saryll's eyes gave her away as a seer of the Triple Goddess. Miella would have to talk with her, perhaps request a reading. Miella wondered whether it was rude to ask such a thing. She might not get another opportunity though, so she took a breath and approached the seer.

"Seer?" Miella said.

"Yes?" Saryll replied kindly.

"Is it rude to ask for a reading? I've never been to the city, so I've never had one," Miella said.

"I would be happy to do a reading for you. You get three questions. Touch the back of the deck and hold the questions in your mind. Do you have them?"

Miella nodded.

Saryll shuffled the cards. "Ask your first question."

"Will I travel?"

The Road. "Yes."

Excitement rushed through Miella. She loved her little slice of heaven, but she always wanted to see more of the world. Perhaps it was why she agreed to this poorly conceived trip to the top of the mountain with strangers.

"Will I fall in love?"

The Lovers, reversed. "Perhaps. There are too many futures to know."

Miella smiled. "Have I found my calling in running the tavern?"

The Wings. "Another great fate awaits."

Miella nodded, frowning. "Thank you."

"Of course. We serve the Goddess," Saryll said.

Miella sat on a rock alongside Adonis, who had his nose buried in a book. She sat by him for long minutes, thinking about her reading and the possible meanings. Adonis flipped page after page and did not look up or eat to drink water. His silence was unnerving. The rest of the group conversed quietly, with a laugh filling the mountain air every so often, but he simply read as if he needed to read to breathe.

She couldn't take it any longer. "What are you doing?"

"Studying," he said. "I won't be caught unable to defend myself again."

"Against what?"

Adonis snorted humorlessly, his eyes weighed down by bags. "The emperor and his Mooncursed wolf beasts and whatever other monstrosities are out there."

"The threat that the High Seer foresaw?"

Adonis nodded.

"This is a rather strange traveling party. How did you all come together?"

"The High Seer sent a caravan of soldiers and staff, along with me, Theo, Saryll, and…" He cleared his throat. "Kassia and Rhydian joined along the way."

"I see. Theo isn't married?" Miella asked.

Adonis snorted and answered without even looking up from his book. "No, but he might as well be. He has his heart set on someone."

Disappointment coursed through Miella. "Who?"

Adonis looked like he was going to say something and stopped himself. Instead, he said, "Someone he wants to marry if we survive this."

"Survive? What do you mean?"

"The threat Theo mentioned that my sister foresaw."

Miella blinked. "Your sister is the High Seer?"

Adonis let out a giant huff of air and looked at her over the top of his worn leather tome. "Yes."

Miella wrapped her long brown braid around her fingers nervously. "If what Theo says about the threat is true, is Heartspring in danger?"

"My sister says that not a single heart will be left beating in Teridar if the emperor invades. This year, she Saw war. She sent Theo and the rest of us to summon the other leaders to a summit. They refused, but Theo is going to ask again nicely with that severed head he's been carrying around," Adonis said blandly.

She choked. "The *what*?"

"Miella, have you asked why we stabled forty-odd horses when there are eighteen of us? Did you ask why an official caravan of the regent High Seer of Avyllon had so few of us?" Adonis swallowed. Softly he said, "Did you ask why we're injured? Clothes torn? It's because we met the threat, and they killed nearly a hundred of us. Those monsters *ate* our friends. Only the sacrifice of a sorcerer saved us. We would have all died."

Fear tingled at the back of Miella's neck.

"Theo is bringing the head of a beast to the leaders to prove what we face. Do you really think he was just curious about local lore? You're a fool if you bought that."

"Then why are you here in the middle of the mountains?"

Adonis pursed his lips and jutted his chin toward Theo. "Ask him. But if you don't mind, I would like to focus on a particularly difficult alchemical reaction for controlling fireballs." Adonis lowered his nose back into his book without sparing her a second glance.

Anger sparked in Miella's chest at being misled. She stomped over to Theo, who was conversing quietly with Rhydian. At her approach, they quieted.

"You lied to me," she snapped. "What are we really doing up here?"

Theo cast an annoyed look at Adonis. "What did he tell you?"

"He's the High Seer's brother."

"Yes. I didn't lie about that, and I told you there was danger that Aurienne seeks to defeat. And I told you we'd been attacked by animals."

Miella froze. *Aurienne?* Miella hadn't even known the High Seer's name. How close were Theo and the High Seer?

Miella shook her head. "You downplayed it a bit."

"I told you what I know. There is a threat we seek to stop. It could destroy us all, but we're doing all we can to prevent it. That is the truth." Theo's expression darkened. "I've found that people don't believe me when I say that. But if you want to know, I'll show you."

Theo worked his jaw before he nodded to Rhydian. The behemoth of a man unknotted a hefty burlap sack. He reached in and pulled out the severed head of a monster. She gasped. It had long patchy fur and the snout of a wolf that must have been six feet tall—if wolves had deformed bone plates and broken, jagged fangs. Revulsion twisted Miella's stomach, and she stumbled away from it.

Theo grimaced. "That is what attacked us. And this is probably what attacked your villagers. That's what's coming for us, and worse. We can't kill them, not enough of them. And we don't know what else the emperor has. Think about if they were hunting you instead of passing through. Think of the destruction."

"So why are you *here*?" Miella whispered, revulsion coursing through her.

Rhydian put the head back into the bag.

Theo said, "We need monsters to fight monsters. The Mooncursed were just a story, like your Shadows, but ended up being real. We need to see if your Shadows are real too."

Miella said nothing. She stared at the mountain rising above them. The fog and mist peeked out from the snow-capped peaks. The black and gray stones were peppered with clusters of tall grass.

"They're just stories," she whispered.

"Your necklace makes me think it's more than that," he said. "The stories we tell say that the First Shadow carved that as a promise to return to his family before he sold his soul. And you're wearing it. You're probably his descendant."

Miella choked and looked away as she gripped the necklace. "I-it's a thousand-year-old story," she stammered. "Who knows what happened."

"If the Shadows are there, we need their help. We need monsters to defeat monsters."

"You want to *free* them?"

Nothing could be worse than letting those things out if they were real. She'd visited the cave mouth—felt the eyes on her. She'd grown up with the stories... But glancing at the burlap sack, she wondered whether the Mooncursed might be worse than the Shadows.

Theo growled. "The emperor's creations are worse."

Miella glared. "I won't help you free them to murder people."

"I think we can make a deal with them."

Her heart hammered. "Why would you want to?"

"Because we have to, or we all die, Miella," he yelled at her, veins bulging in his forehead.

Miella froze, her breath catching. "It's hard to imagine that the emperor's soldiers are as bad as you say. My entire life I've believed the Shadows to be nothing more than bloodthirsty monsters, the worst of the worst."

"Why did they imprison themselves? Why did they make the deal at all? I think family matters to them. If they'll fight for anyone, it's you." Theo crossed his arms, staring her down. "If you don't help, then your family will die. Your village will be overrun with Mooncursed, and there will be no one left to help you and nowhere left to hide. Aurienne Saw it, and Saryll's cards say the Shadows are still there."

All her life, Miella had been told the Shadows were bloodthirsty monsters that ought never to be freed. *Avoid the cave. Don't walk in the forest at night. Wear the necklace.* Was she really considering freeing them? She'd heard of the High Seer's power. Everyone in Avyllon had. If the High Seer believed this was necessary to save them all, should Miella not listen? Could she believe Theo?

She gripped her necklace, tracing her fingers over the familiar grooves. She glanced at the Mooncursed's head again, swallowing. Villagers were already missing. If what Theo and the others said was true, the bloodshed had already begun. Maybe they needed help. The kind of help mortals could not provide. A whisper in her heart told her to trust Theo. And the alternative was living out the rest of her life in a quiet mountain town, hoping not to get eaten by Moon-cursed werewolves.

Unable to face him, she spat, "We better keep moving. We're wasting daylight. There's no use dawdling when we are going to face monsters."

Miella pushed past Theo and led them up the side of the mountain toward a cursed and forbidden cave, feeling as though this was a mistake that she couldn't abandon.

The mouth of the cave resembled what Theo would have imagined as the entrance to one of the more terrible hells. All light fled from the inside of this cursed cave as though a wall of darkness descended. Stalactites and stalagmites formed a fanged maw around the entrance, jutting out in every direction. One rock formation resembled a human skull, and Theo was all too aware that the silence of this place was far too similar to Courtyard of Queens until he heard the quiet scraping—distant but deliberate.

Theo forced his unwilling limbs to approach. He brushed vines from a stone plaque carved into the mountain near the cave mouth. Painstakingly carved letters read:

Only death exists here.

His neck prickled with the sensation of a thousand eyes watching him, and from the nervous looks the others shared, they sensed it too. Theo swallowed.

Was this a horrible idea?

"Now you know why we avoid this cave," Miella whispered.

"I thought you said it was just a story." Theo side-eyed her.

A hot, damp breeze slithered out of the cave's mouth as if it was breathing sickly air toward them in warning. Maybe it was. With the silence of the Queensblood ravine and the breathing of this cave, Theo was starting to realize that Teridar had magic unto itself and was a land that made monsters.

He clenched and unclenched his fists. "You all stay back. I'll try to find them and talk to them. Hopefully, they're more human than the stories say."

Striding toward the cave entrance, he stepped toward the shadows, pausing when he noticed a large smear of blood just inside the mouth of the cave. He lifted his hand and touched an invisible barrier that reminded him vaguely of the Ways.

Theo cleared his throat. "The stories say you once fought a threat that endangered ten thousand villages. We face the same threat. We seek your assistance."

Silence.

"I know you're there. The Triple Goddess told us," Theo said.

"Leave this place before it consumes you," a voice grated from the gloom.

Theo's heart dropped right to his gut, and a thousand needles prickled his skin as icy fear washed over him in a wave. He took a step back, tried to remember how to breathe, and ended up coughing. Fear squeezed his heart. Scanning the dark, he saw nothing.

He glanced over his shoulder to see the rest of his companions edging away from the cave with pale faces.

"Please help us," Theo said.

The voice was oil on broken glass. "We do not wish to join your fight. If your stories are true, you know what happened to us."

Theo stepped closer to the barrier. "I've come to free you."

"You are a fool."

"I've heard your histories."

The voice cackled. "And what do you think you know?"

"I know that you were cursed to save your homes. I know that you made a deal to defeat your enemies, and it cost you everything."

"Our *souls*. It cost us our souls."

Theo swallowed. "You didn't lose your humanity, no matter what you thought it did. You were cursed."

A human-like silhouette crept toward the mouth of the cave, still bathed in shadows. "Yes. We were."

The words pouring out of Theo's mouth were only partially his, and he wondered if Aurienne's Goddess or another spoke through him. "I think that you fought off the hunger for years, decades. I think that you fought alongside your loved ones even as they cut you down in fear and finally locked yourselves away to protect the world. You were heroes. The kind of heroes that we need now. Another enemy is here, and it is one we cannot defeat without your strength."

Silhouettes shifted in the shadows behind the speaker. The scraping grew louder, and Theo recognized the sound as claws on stone. Wings rustled.

Theo said, "This war determines the fate of our world."

"What keeps us from feeding upon the towns and villages your armies leave unguarded?"

"Because the one who allowed himself to be cursed, who slaughtered his own cursed kin, and who built his own prison would not do that."

"And what if you're wrong?"

Everything Theo had ever known tipped upside down, and nothing was real anymore. This was their last chance. Without allies, they would fall.

"Then come kill me now." He lifted his arms. "Or join me. My fate is set."

The Shadow drew near enough that Theo could just make out the outline. The figure was tall, as tall as Rhydian, but emaciated to where Theo could see the edges of a skeleton.

"I'll do anything to protect this world and my people," Theo said. "I would give up my humanity, my soul, to protect their lives."

"I said that once, too."

Theo squinted to try to see the monster within. "I'll bear that burden for them. We need...monsters to win this. I Saw what came for us, and we cannot defeat them."

"And if they hate you for what you've done? There is anger and death lingering about your soul. I had the same darkness when I made my deal. Beware of it."

"Will you help us?"

Hundreds of glinting eyes caught the sunlight behind the figure. Fear crept up Theo's spine. There were hundreds of the Shadows locked away. Thousands. It was too late to turn back now.

"No."

Theo stepped closer. "Come back. We need the Shadows of Heartspring."

"I am no Shadow. We fought the Shadows with their own corrupted magic. *We* became vampires, and there is a reason we locked ourselves away. We're worse. Go home, boy. Leave this place before you never do."

The vampire was gone in an instant.

Theo controlled his breathing, pacing and glaring at the formless dark. It was time to gamble. He didn't come all this way to fail again.

Theo goaded the vampire. "I never thought you'd turn on your family."

The vampire lunged, and his terrible claws slammed into an invisible wall. The soft light now illuminated the vampire's features, and it took every ounce of willpower for Theo to only flinch and not run away screaming. His hands started shaking as panic roiled in his veins.

The vampire was well over six feet tall, and his emaciated state showed every hard edge. Spiked bone protruded from the skin on his shoulders, elbows, and knees. His fingers doubled the length they should be, with jagged ridges of bone down the knuckles and long claws where fingernails should be.

Decrepit skin stretched across the sharp ridges of bones on his face, and tattered hair hung past elongated, bat-like ears. His deformed jaw hung to accommodate the oversized fangs, and paper-thin lips stretched around extra teeth. The four upper canines extended nearly to his chin, and the four lower pressed against his lip. Every tooth was sharp and dripping saliva.

Most terrifying were the vampire's eyes. They burned with a hateful fury, soulless and black as a moonless night. Death lurked in those eyes. The vampire unfurled wings with sharp bone spikes that filled the mouth of the cave.

The vampire snarled, "I never harmed my family. I would have died first."

"I know," Theo said, lifting his hands. "Someone who gave their soul to protect their loved ones would not turn on them for anything. Help them now."

The vampire raked his claws down the sides of the invisible cage, creating a terrible squealing sound though his dark gaze did not waver. His tongue ran across the edges of his terrifying teeth, and drool dripped down his chin. His eyes dropped toward Theo's throat, and Theo's hands came up to touch his neck without his permission.

"You should leave before you never leave," the vampire said.

The vampire retreated into the shadows again.

"Then your last descendants will die," Theo called.

Silence.

"She's here," Theo said. "The monsters that are coming will devour her the same as everyone else while you rot in here."

Theo nodded to Rhydian, who took the head from the sack and lifted it high.

Silence.

Theo clenched his fists. "The High Seer Saw the destruction of all of us, including the last of your family. If she dies, then your sacrifice was for nothing."

Miella stepped forward. "Please help."

The vampire slipped back into view, a monster coming to the surface of dark waters. His expression, bony and rigid, softened.

"You look just like my daughter," he whispered.

Miella did not retreat from the nightmarish visage before her. She stuck out her chin and lifted the necklace. Her bravery was impressive.

The vampire inclined his head, and his sunken features pulled together mournfully. "I gave that to my wife before we left."

"We've passed it down in our family for generations. My mother gave it to me a few years ago," Miella said.

"Then you are the last of us?"

"I think so," Miella said.

"What is your name?"

"Miella Rothbain."

The vampire looked at the severed head intently for long moments. Rhydian lowered the wolf's head into the sack again.

"The High Seer Saw that our continent would be destroyed by those things," Miella said.

At her side, Saryll stepped forward. "It's true. We have all Seen that danger comes."

"Do you know what those things are?" the vampire asked.

"Mooncursed?"

"They're the same cursed creatures from the Shadow War, a thousand years ago. It is the same dark magic in their blood that we fought all those years ago," the vampire said, tongue struggling around words that he had not spoken in who knew how long. "That ancient taint lives in that beast."

"Where does it come from?" Theo asked.

"Not this world," the vampire answered. "If those beasts have returned, there is no hope for this land."

"Please help us," Miella begged.

"We swore to stay imprisoned here until we died. I cannot break that vow."

"That was when your family was safe," Theo said. "Didn't you vow to protect your family until your last breath? Doesn't that vow supersede all?"

Miella crept closer. "Please help us. I have worn this necklace my entire life because I believe in the goodness of our family. I believed in forgiveness."

The vampire's expression looked pained. He looked back to the lurking shadows and then back at Miella. He clicked his jaw. A growl rumbled in his throat. Then he tore his teeth into his wrist, and he dropped precious blood to the land.

"This I swear to you, none of us shall spill a single drop of innocent or unwilling human blood from you or your allies, or the vampires shall die by my hand. We shall fight and drink only your enemies. We will protect you," the vampire swore.

Miella took a utility knife from her belt and cut her own hand. "I accept and free you," she said.

Her blood dripped to the line of blood running across the mouth of the cave.

"How did you know your blood would free us?" the vampire asked.

"There is only one thing you would use," she said.

"Call me Stellan Rothbain, the first vampire," he said.

Theo reached out to find the invisible barrier had disappeared. The vampires were free. Theo's blood ran cold, and he wondered again if he'd made a horrible mistake.

"We'll find you tomorrow evening after we have regained our faculties. First, we must feed," the vampire said.

The sun dipped over the horizon and a horde of shadows flashed out of the cave, too fast for Theo's eyes to track. The force of their wings knocked him to the dirt, and he covered his head as an unending stream poured from the cave. And then they were gone. Theo and the others slowly stood, watching a black cloud of vampires disappear over the mountains.

The gravity of Theo's decision crushed his heart with fear and doubt.

INTERLUDE

— HIGH SEER SYAORAN AMYDEO, PROPHETIC
VISION RECORDED IN THE YEAR 1133 N.T.C.

1152 N.T.C. Hunger's Teeth Mountains, southwest Avyllon.

The night embraced the beasts prowling the starless sky as fangs pierced human flesh, and hot, fresh blood flowed down ravenous throats. Stellan glided through the trees on leathery wings that blocked the waxing moonlight. Over a thousand vampires flew beside him, cruel predators all. Having agreed to only devour the willing or the sinful, they followed the scent of guilt across the lands.

Delicious.

They descended into a sleepy little town ripe with depravity. The vampire knocked on the door of a woman whose animals suffered horrid neglect.

"Who is it?" A woman opened the door dressed only in a night-gown and shawl, wielding a wooden broom handle.

Seeing him, she nearly screamed, but her gaze locked with his, and her face relaxed, eyes losing focus. He willed serenity into her mind, dragging her resistance from her in lapping waves. The stick slipped from her fingers, bounced against the floor, and rolled away.

"Invite me in," the vampire crooned.

"Please come in," she said dreamily.

The vampire's smile was all fangs. Suppressing a satisfied shudder, he stepped across the threshold and closed the door. Inside, he took her into his arms in a lover's embrace and tore out her throat like a wild beast. She did not even struggle. Her eyes grew glassy, and he sighed as her fresh blood melted on his decrepit tongue. He drank her dry and licked her blood off the floor. Then he slipped out a window like a wraith.

Seven more vampires spilled from dwellings. A horrible rot of the soul had taken over that place, so they fell upon the guilty and were gone. Another sleepy town. Another set of victims. Town after town, they culled the wickedness—root and stem.

Murderers, rapists, abusers, thieves, liars—all slain. The vampires drank deeply from the guilty, savoring each drop of life. Once the edge of their thirst was sated, they began to play with their food.

The first vampire, Stellan, stalked a man with sin so black it permeated his scent, and his garden was lined with lonely graves. His dark intentions were an aphrodisiac for the ravenous vampire. Stellan snapped a branch in his long, clawed fingers, watching the man spin around in the night. Another vampire, Julietta, smirked and dragged her claws through leaves across the path. The man whirled again, demanding that they show themselves. A vampire flitted across the path in the man's peripheral, and he started to run. Stellan howled and flew after him, catching him by the throat. The man yelled and tried to fight, but before he could, Julietta sank her fangs into his throat. Stellan did not hypnotize him—he wanted the man afraid. He sank fangs into the man's wrist, draining him. They flew again.

Stellan landed just outside a house where a man was beating his wife. Screams filled the night, but none of the nearby houses came to her aid. Stellan lifted a wheelbarrow, hefted it several times, and then hurled it through the front door. The man, wielding a club, stumbled out the door, his pants unlaced. Stellan sank his black claws into the man's shoulder until the man cried out and dropped his club. The vampire dragged the man away from the house, nearly ripping the man's arm from its socket.

"Please, no," the man whimpered.

Stellan's fangs dripped acidic saliva as he rolled his long tongue across blood-stained lips. "My dear," he called to the woman, "come out if you want to live."

The woman crept out of the house, battered, bruised, and naked. Suppressing a sob, she stood shaking before the vampire with only a blanket draped over her shoulders. Tears streamed down the bruises on her face.

"Julietta, bring her neighbors," Stellan murmured.

"With pleasure," the vampire snarled.

"Are you going to kill me?" the woman asked.

"You have a chance to save your life. Do you want that?" he asked.

"Yes," she answered without hesitation. "And my children?"

"They will be safe too."

"What do I have to do?" she asked, standing taller.

"Kill your husband with that club."

The man squirmed in the vampire's grip and roared at his wife. "Don't you do it, you hagsteeth whore. Don't listen to him."

Her throat bobbed, and her eyes flickered from her husband to the vampire. Her neighbors were herded like cattle, terrified, mesmerized, and silent—forced to watch the scene unfolding.

"Don't fail," Stellan whispered to the woman, his eyes burning with hellfire.

Hands shaking, she bent down and clutched the club. Stellan could not suppress the grin spreading across his fanged mouth. He thought the woman might beg or cry or refuse, but she did not hesitate. Such was her love for her children. Stellan remembered love that true, long ago, when he bargained away his soul. She made him proud.

The man squirmed in his grip, and Stellan squeezed his shoulder until dark blood oozed out.

"What are you doing?" the man shouted.

Hate and fear on her face, she gripped it with both hands and swung. It smashed against his cheek, tearing the flesh, causing blood to pour down his chest.

"Stop, please." The man's voice was drowned by wet crunches.

He shouted, but she lifted the club and swung again, cracking his skull. He feebly lifted his arm up to block, and she crushed the bone. She sobbed.

Guttural roars erupted from her throat. "I hate you."

The vampire watched the victim get her revenge without even a hint of remorse. Strength could be taught to those who earned it. Wickedness could be stamped out.

The man screamed, and his blood sprayed her naked body as she swung again and again. The woman swung the club like her life depended upon it, and it did.

Bones broke, blood ran, flesh tore, and the man hardly looked human anymore—as she beat him to a bloody mess.

Finally, Stellan said, "He's dead. You may go inside to your children, and no one here will ever hurt you again."

The woman dropped the club with a sob and darted inside. The neighbors, released from their trance, sprinted screaming back into their houses, locking their doors as if it would protect.

Julietta prowled closer. "No sense in wasting warm blood." She sank her fangs into his neck and sucked the corpse dry.

The vampires disappeared into the night, like phantoms in the fog.

1152 N.T.C. Warden's Watch Mountains, northeast Avyllon.

A cursed hunter sat alone in a dark cave. He had been there, alone, for centuries. While the hunter waited, he slept. The burning sunfire in his veins told him that his task had not yet ended. Terrible monsters yet remained. He sensed their hunger but could not find them. They had been dormant for so long that he wondered if they really existed at all. He wondered whether they would ever return to the world.

While he waited, he dreamed. He dreamed of a loved one's betrayal, of vampire fangs ripping into his throat, and the poison threading through his blood, seeking to turn him into the beast he hated. He dreamed of a waterfall made of sunlight that burned the corruption out of him, giving him the means to destroy these terrors of the night.

If those monsters ever rose again, if they were ever freed from whatever prison they found themselves in, he would wake and finish what he started. Across the distant lands, he heard a scream.

His eyes flicked open.

Somewhere deep in the faraway mountains, a vampire fed. The hunter stood, and centuries of dust and cobwebs fell from his clothes. His head turned toward his prey, and he took up his hunt.

PART FOUR

BEASTS IN THE DARK
CHAPTER THIRTY-SIX

Blood and bone, and curses wrought.
Life now ends as death is bought.

— HIGH SEER AURIENNE AZARRAH, PROPHETIC
VISION.

1152 N.T.C. The namesake city of Avyllon.

Exhausted, Aurienne clutched Theo's note in her hand. She'd read it over and over, dedicating it to memory, and once memorized, she read it again to be sure. He was safe.

To our High Seer Aurienne Azarrah,
We live. Mathis saved us with his alchemical works, but it cost
his life. Adonis is alive but grieving. Saryll and Kassia live.
Captain Laurier lives. Seven soldiers and six staff survived.
Rhydian escaped the attack and his curse, thankfully. Ninety-
seven of us are gone. We buried them by a grouping of tamarack
trees near a stream. We'll take a wolf's head to the Free Peoples

*and the People of Living Stone to beg them to reconsider attending
the summit. I haven't given up. Thank you for the warning. The
Mooncursed wear the emperor's brand. Please be careful.*
  – Your Emissary, Theo Thatcher

Please be careful.

Aurienne breathed in the note, his hands having touched the
paper. The scent was woodsy, containing the bark of ancient trees
and mountain air. Breathing him in, she could almost hear what he
meant when he said to be careful.

I love you.

Aurienne wished with every piece of her heart that she could say
it back, but she knew better. Fate did not destine her for love. It was
not hers to claim. Instead, she pressed the paper to her lips, imagining
the life they might have had together.

I haven't given up.

Her heart twinged with guilt. He was trying so hard for her to
accomplish an impossible task that would leave scars on his soul and
body to match her own. It wasn't fair.

I'm so sorry, Theo.

Her seer's effects whispered, and the spelled box of divination
cards vibrated, but she was so tired. Checking on the caravan
survivors had drained the last of her magic. She laid her head on her
altar—ignoring the cards and wanting to slip into a deep, dreamless
sleep. Opening her eyes, she glanced at the cracked mirror in her
chambers, a reminder the Goddess was always watching. She tucked
the note into the folds of her gown near the ceremonial blade.

See.

So tired. Lifting her head, she reached for the Sight, and nothing
came, only a trickle of crimson blood from her nose. At least it
wasn't golden soulblood. She gathered her bone runes, but they
remained cold in her hand. Her magic stores were too low.

See.

The Fates wanted to show her something now, and she had

nothing left. It would take more effort than usual. From the secret compartment behind her altar, Aurienne set a small dusty handheld mirror in the middle of the double pentagram carved into the stone floor. She placed a bowl of moonwater at true west, the ceremonial black candle at true east, a large crystal and bowl of grave dirt at true south, and a glass crystal ball containing a seer's last breath at true north.

With a flick of her wrist, she summoned her divination cards. They flew from their spelled box to form a perfect circle around her. The figures on the arcane suit cards grimaced, paced, or bled.

She lit a dozen candles and dropped nightrose petals between the four elements. Sprinkling salt, she drew an unbroken line around the carving. Finally, she pricked her finger and drew a smaller circle on the floor around the mirror. Leaning forward, she touched her forehead to the mirror, chanting prayers to the Goddess. She breathed on the mirror and pressed her lips to it in a sacred kiss.

Head. Heart. Lips.

Crone. Mother. Maiden.

Wisdom. Love. Hope.

The mirror gave way, and Aurienne's head plunged through the surface as if submerging in a pool. She opened her eyes to see a hooded wraith. Footsteps approached.

Step.

Step.

Step.

Something came. Something dark, ancient, and powerful. Something came closer every day. Someone. The vision changed. She Saw enemies. Guild Masters. Danger. Poison dribbling into the city's water supply. Fire burning through the city's food stores. Deceit. Lies. Betrayal. Blood on her hands. Death. Aurienne pulled her head out of the mirror with a gasp. Every candle in the room blew out. Every silently screaming figure on her cards reached for her with ink-bleeding hands.

The Guild Masters were sabotaging the city again.

"No," she gritted.

Aurienne swiftly stowed her ceremonial effects. "Those bastards. Are they really willing to kill half the city to gain a crown?"

Aurienne dressed and tied a dark cloak about her shoulders. "Sentinels," she summoned.

Her door opened as three sentinels stepped inside.

"Summon General Kane to the eastern granary," she ordered.

"They're going to set it on fire. I'll be going to the northwestern well and aqueduct water testing access point to stop the poisoners. Send soldiers behind me. Be quick but be quiet. We need to find who is doing this."

"Yes, High Seer," Kolten answered.

Minutes later, she was upon a horse riding with Sentinels Kolten and Edran toward the access. Warning bells rang in her mind as this all seemed vaguely too similar to the aqueduct sabotage, but she pushed it away. She'd catch the poisoner, the sentinels would arrest them, and then she could slip into a deep herb-assisted sleep and recharge her magics.

They slowed the horses at the access point. The doorframe was kicked in, and the lock was broken.

"One of you stay," she whispered. "The other with me."

The pair slipped into the shack. There were two separate access points behind barely ajar iron doors. Aurienne nodded to Sentinel Kolten. He stepped into one room, and she the other.

The door snapped shut behind her and locked with the slide of a great iron bolt. Aurienne spun to see the blond Guild Master—the mason. The one who'd glared daggers at her when she refused a joint audience with the emperor's emissary. Murder had glistened in his eyes, but she had not realized how close to the surface those urges lay.

The man chuckled, licking his lips. Two men lurked beside him, masons by the dust all over their clothes. One wielded a large club with nails driven through it. The other fingered a wicked-looking knife. The Guild Master held a short length of rope between his hands and kneaded it.

"I knew you'd show up," the Guild Master said. "I knew you would, because I fully intended to dump the poison if you didn't. Your little Goddess must have known the real threat was here and sent you. I would've done it gladly if it meant getting you here. Without sentinels. Alone."

Shouts rang from the next room. The sentinels were under attack and would be of no help to her, especially not behind the iron door. Her eyes glanced to their weapons and realized that this was an entirely different form of trap. She hadn't known they'd drawn her here to be murdered.

As with the aqueduct, they laid carefully crafted traps just for her. She managed to outsmart them last time, but alone in the dark, facing three armed men, she would die.

Gritting her teeth, she said, "You planned the poison and fire to lure me to remote places to kill me."

"We suspect whoever is at the granary is getting arrested right now, but we all agreed on the risks. Once the Guild Master is crowned king, we will be pardoned," the shorter mason said.

Aurienne backed away, hands raised. "Why do you want to kill me so badly? I have protected and served Avyllon. My readings and omens have saved lives. They kept us safe through winters and drought. I'm frugal with taxes, give to charity, do not indulge in excess. What have I ever done? The Goddess kept you safe for generations."

The two masons exchanged quick glances. They were clearly less comfortable than their Guild Master. But their tight grips on their weapons told her they wouldn't be swayed. Gold was a powerful god, and the emperor promised mountains of it.

"And your time is over. We warned you, but take heart. They'll probably put up a statue in the temple in your honor. You'll be remembered. Martyred. You served well, but it's time for a new reign." He pulled the rope tight between his hands. "This will be over quickly, and then you'll be a saint."

Muffled shouts and death screams echoed from the next room.

Thumps and crashes followed. Heart sinking, she hoped the sentinels made it out. They didn't deserve to die for her failures.

Aurienne retreated toward the water access until her spine brushed the metal pipes and wheels. The men advanced.

She prayed she had enough magic left. "Goddess. I have served you my whole life. I'll serve you until my last day. If that is today, I will go happily beyond the veil and embrace you. If it is not, show me your will."

"Pretty last words," the Guild Master sneered.

Aurienne pushed her back against the enormous pipe in the small room. Rusty clay coated her fingertips. The Guild Master lunged to grab her, and she threw a handful of the sandy clay into his eyes. She dove across the room, and the knife rang against the pipe where she'd been. Rolling through the dirt, she came up near the second mason.

In a vision, the mason's club smashed against Aurienne's head. The nails drove into her skull, and she died. She ducked as the club whooshed by. It hammered into the wall behind her in an explosion of mortar and stone. She spun away, but the first mason yanked her wrist. A vision consumed her sight—he pulled her back against his chest, held the knife to her throat, and slit it while the other two watched.

Aurienne put one hand up against her throat to protect her from the blade and reached into her gown with the other. The knife nicked her, and scarlet blood sprinkled the floor as she struggled with him. She drew her ceremonial blade and stabbed the mason deep in the thigh. He cried out, and she bit down on his wrist until his blood fountained in her mouth. The mason's knife went flying, and he shoved her to the ground.

A foggy future of them threatening to use the poison if she didn't go easily to her death danced across reality. *Not happening.* Aurienne dug in his pocket for the poison. Snatching it from his pants, she broke the vial upon his face. He punched her to the ground but then screamed, clutching his eyes. She scrambled toward her knife, which was still stuck in the man's thigh, and tried desperately to tug it free, but the man's spasming muscles held it tight. He kicked her backward.

"Goddess hellsdamn it," she swore.

"Get her."

Another vision. The second mason's club slammed down on her arm and shattered the bone to pieces. Scrambling away, she pulled her arm back and the club went sailing by. It hit the ground in front of the first mason. She kicked the club, and the nails sank into the club wielder's boot. He shouted and hopped backward.

Darting forward, she reached for her knife again as its victim screamed and writhed on the ground.

An unseen fist punched her hard in the face and sent her flying across the room. She found herself beside the first man's curved dagger. She lifted it and slashed at the Guild Master, but he easily stepped out of her reach. The club wielder had freed his foot and was swinging the club toward her. She couldn't escape it but charging closer would avoid the nails. She lunged toward the club handle, which caught her thunderously in the stomach. Unable to breathe, she dropped to her knees. Another massive fist came for her. She Saw it just in time and scrambled away so that it glanced off her cheek.

Golden blood trickled from her mouth as her magic drained her soul. Her sight faltered as her vision blurred. Her face throbbed, her ribs ached, and her cuts burned. Her breath came shallow.

Would my soul or body give out first?

A dark entity appeared in the center of the cramped room—and her attackers didn't give it so much as a glance. They were unable to see it. It was veiled in shadows, with glowing purple eyes and glowing purple runes. It grew, taking up the entire corner.

"You're so weak," it hissed. "All that power could be mine."

Aurienne stumbled, dodging spirit claws and cornering herself against mthe wall. "You," her voice was barely a whisper. "You've been interfering with my Sight? Who are you?"

A rope corded around her neck and dragged her backward. The

Guild Master lifted Aurienne off the ground with the makeshift noose. She coughed and struggled. The one with the club dropped it, and smashed her hand into the stone wall until broken bones made her release his curved dagger.

The dark entity floated forward and slashed her spirit with its silver claws. Thick golden soulblood dripped from her astral form. Her body drooped, weak from exertion and her bodily and unworldly injuries.

No.

The entity grinned and vanished into amethyst smoke.

Aurienne screamed silently, and though she heard the shouts and loud bangs on the iron door from her sentinels, they wouldn't break into the room in time.

The Guild Master licked her neck before he whispered in her ear, "The time of the seers has passed."

Aurienne's vision danced as her air was stolen. The club wielder held her broken hand against the wall, the Guild Master pulled the rope tight, and the third man advanced with his curved dagger. The third man sank his dagger into the meat of her arm, and scarlet blood poured out.

She tried to scream, but no sound came.

"It has to be done. Stop fighting," he hissed.

Aurienne struggled, but it was no use. Her feet dangled uselessly. She clawed at the man, and though her nails left deep gouges in his arm, he did not release his hold. The rope crushed her neck. Her eyes bulged. She choked on nothing.

I'm going to die.

I never got to tell him...

A voice called to her. "Aurienne?"

Aurienne glanced to her left to a veiled dreamy image of Theo. Her heart leapt even though she knew he was not truly here. He couldn't be—he was hundreds of miles away. But in her final moments, she saw *him*.

"Look at me," Theo said.

Aurienne glanced at him before she clawed at the rope and looked at her attackers. Wicked smiles split their faces as they watched her die.

"Don't look at them," Theo said. "Look at me."

Aurienne complied, knowing that the last thing she saw in this world would be Theo's face.

"Look at me. Look this way. Can you drop your chin near your shoulder under the rope? Tuck your chin, my love," Theo said.

Suddenly, a whisper of air trickled down her throat. She still fought and struggled, but a tiny bit of the pressure was released.

Theo reached for her, but his hands passed through her face. "It's not your time. You haven't fallen in love with me yet."

Aurienne fought weakly. The small gulps of air she managed weren't enough. The mason ripped the blade from her arm, and she would have cried out if she could.

"Your dagger," Theo whispered.

Aurienne kicked at the ceremonial dagger still lodged in the man's leg. She missed. Vision fading, she kicked again, and he fell to the ground screaming.

"The eyes," Theo whispered.

Aurienne reached back and clawed at the Guild Master's eyes. He yelled and released the rope just enough for Aurienne to get a hand inside of the noose. She spun and kneed him between the legs. Than kneed him again. He wheezed and toppled forward. The club wielder reached for her. She grabbed his club from the ground and swung it blindly as hard as she could.

A wet crunch squelched from his head. The club cleaved off the top of his skull, and the nails sank into what remained. His eyes darkened, and he fell to the ground, dead. Aurienne tripped on her gown and landed hard on the ground.

The Guild Master lunged for her and landed on her, pinning her against the ground. Aurienne scrambled and tried to crawl, but the Guild Master's body pressed against her back, pinning her.

"Fight, my love," Theo said, rage shadowing his face.

Aurienne pushed up on her elbows to create some space to breathe. She spun to face him so that he was lying on top of her chest. He pressed his thigh between her legs, blocking her. Aurienne rammed her knee toward his crotch again, but she missed. Before he could pin her further, Aurienne reached up and bit into his neck. The man released an inhuman, guttural scream, but she did not release him. She tore flesh from his neck until he rolled off her. He bled, not enough to kill him, but enough to hurt.

The other man kicked her hard, twice, rolling her away from the screaming Guild Master. He then grabbed her ankle and, limping, dragged her across the room toward the water access. He slammed her against the pipe and opened the access panel. The man clutched the back of her hair and lifted her to her feet. He pushed her face into the raging waters.

Aurienne held her breath as she began to panic. Dark waters assailed her face as she struggled against the man's weight. If she died now, would her soul find peace? Had she damaged it beyond healing with her necromancy? Was there enough of it left, or would she be forced to haunt these lands forever as a tormented ghost? Aurienne screamed under the water.

The hilt of a knife pressed against her leg. Her knife. She reached for it with her broken hand and, with a drowned scream, closed her fingers around the hilt. She gave it a sharp twist and pulled it out of the man's leg. The fingers released her, and she came up for air. She fell to the dirt, wheezing.

The man's leg spurted arterial blood. He tried to put pressure on it but failed as blood pooled beneath him. Aurienne rushed forward. Twisting her fingers in his hair, she pulled back his head and dragged her knife across his throat. He dropped to the ground. Two dead. One left.

Two dead. One left.

A vision hit Aurienne hard, the Guild Master stabbing her to death. She spun, taking a shallow stab to the hip instead of the gut. The Guild Master stabbed for her again and again, and she dodged and twisted. She backpedaled as quickly as she could, avoiding only some of the wild arcs. Sweet, honeyed roses filled her tongue from her golden soulblood, and her legs shook.

"Our Goddess will have vengeance," Theo whispered.

Aurienne's back hit the wall as she ran out of space to flee. Theo's ghost stood behind her attacker. He nudged the length of rope with a ghostly boot.

"I'm going to kill you slowly now," the attacker hissed. "You should have just taken the quick death we offered. It would already be over. But now? Now I'm going to make it hurt."

"Don't make promises you can't keep," Aurienne snarled.

She hurled her fallen cloak at the Guild Master and leapt for the rope. The Guild Master batted at her cloak and charged. She dodged his blade and wrapped the rope around his neck. She danced under his arm and behind him. Crossing it at the back, she wrenched as tightly as she could. The man swiped for her, but his muscled shoulders made it impossible to reach her. He rammed her against the stones. The impact reverberated through her spine. Theo remained at her side.

Aurienne pushed off the wall, and the man sank to his knees, clawing at the rope. She brought her knee up and pressed it against his back. He fell to his side, and she increased the pressure as she drove both knees up. The sounds he made would stay with her until the day she died. He twitched and struggled for far too long before growing still. With a stifled sob, Aurienne scrambled away from the corpse.

Theo pressed his lips to her forehead before the illusion vanished. His phantom kiss tickled her skin as if he'd been there. She wanted nothing more than to feel his arms around her, holding her, but he was halfway across the country dealing with demons of his own.

She limped to the iron door, cradling her hand, and slid open the bolt. Sentinels flooded the room as she collapsed. She surveyed the carnage, fighting back tears.

"My lady, are you alright?" Sentinel Kolten demanded.

"High Seer? What happened?"

"Search the area. Find any conspirators."

Aurienne blinked. "Could you help me to my horse?"

Sentinel Kolten carefully carried her outside and set her beside the horses. He tended to her, wrapping the shallow stab wounds in gauze. His scraped and bleeding hands were gentle on her skin. He cleaned her wounds, cursing the three dead men loudly.

"If they weren't already dead, I'd kill them for this." Blood mixed with sweat and trickled from his brow.

"It was a trap," she said soothingly. "Even I fell for it, but the Goddess' will was done in the end."

"How did you survive? Three of them? That size? They should have killed you," Kolten said. "I struggled to fight off three, and I'm armed."

Her eyes felt empty as she relived the attack. "The Goddess saved me."

Once her wounds were temporarily wrapped, Kolten boosted her onto her horse. He slowly led her horse back through the now-waking city.

General Kane met her at the temple stables. "What happened? You need a healer."

She coughed—and thankfully, the blood was only crimson—and filled him in.

He swore. "We have to increase security if they grow this bold."

Kolten carefully helped her down from her horse. Five sentinels, the general, and Aurienne slowly made their way to the temple doors. They turned the corner and were greeted by an angry mob of guild-members.

"There's the false seer."

"Liar!"

"She killed a sister seer who questioned her."

"Murderer."

"Give up the throne."

Her heart burned. After what she'd endured for them, they still hurled hate her way. She had nothing left to give.

General Kane immediately stepped in front of Aurienne. "Get more soldiers here now."

Two visions sparked in Aurienne's vision. She Saw handfuls of goat shit flying through the air at them. The manure struck her, and the crowd erupted in laughter. Only her pride was injured.

She then Saw herself sidestepping it. The crowd grew enraged and surged forward in an attempt to strike her. Kolten pushed them back and was blindsided with a hammer to the temple. She Saw him go down.

Aurienne's lip pulled back into a snarl.

The steaming manure flew, and Aurienne stopped in its path. It hit her, along with four more handfuls, and the crowd erupted into laughter. Aurienne glared at the road before she limped to the temple doors as the sentinels pushed back the crowd. Her eyes burned with rage.

Inside, General Kane said, "You knew it was coming, so why did you stand in the way?"

Aurienne wiped hot manure from her face. "I already need a bath and a visit to the healer. I would rather take a longer hot bath than I was planning than have Kolten spend two months at the healers."

General Kane's eyes widened.

Kolten gripped his sword tightly. "I would happily spend two months at the healers if it meant teaching those insolent rioters a lesson."

After visit to the healer's hospital, where young master healer Elianna advised her to rest for several weeks, bandaged her cuts, and keep her hand in a splint, General Kane and Sentinel Kolten escorted Aurienne back to her room. Four sentinels were already posted at her doors. Sentinel Kolten took his usual post just beside her door on a chair she'd ordered for him. Tonight, they all were as alert as first-year sentinels.

Aurienne closed her door and left her ruined clothes in a pile.

She slipped into her spirit form, trying to keep the hemorrhaging soulblood from flowing out. Hours later, she managed to stop the flow. Just as sleep reached for her, her thoughts drifted to the caravan and Theo.

Just a glimpse.

She used the last remaining sliver of her gift, and nightmares filled her mind. She shot upright. Theo had released the Shadows of Heartspring from the stories. Vampires. Theo somehow found them and freed an army of mindless, soulless, bloodthirsty things. They drank endless blood to satiate a bottomless thirst.

Aurienne paled. "Goddess, help us. Theo, what have you done?"

BLOOD OF THE LAND
CHAPTER THIRTY-SEVEN

Leave this place before it consumes you.

— *GATES TO ETHERIA.*

1152 N.T.C. Castle Rodarr, Rodarri.

A somber, fearful ambiance possessed the Queensblood chambers. More still than it had ever been, Rianne felt her shame keenly. The other queens quietly whispered, read, or pretended to knit. The traumatic ballroom events left everyone empty and morose, but none so painfully as Rianne. The moment she thought she might possess no tears left to cry, more surfaced. She had not stopped crying in days. Another ball was scheduled in a few nights, and the thought physically sickened Rianne. She could still smell the leather of the dog muzzle.

Her great aunt Yllicea broke the silence. "The king ordered me to give him the names of ten queens for the ascension. Since Rianne revealed his secret, he no longer feels the need to hide his plans. It's probably for the better. This way, we have longer to say goodbye."

Rianne could barely lift her head. She studied the floor as though it held the secrets of an ancient civilization. They couldn't select her, but that reality made her guilt grow to the size of a castle tower.

"I'm sorry," she whispered.

Yllicea clicked her tongue. "You have nothing to be sorry for. I, for one, thought it was very brave of you. You can't control that his fear and cowardice ordered this ascension, and you can't control the ascended queens not yet gifting you a daughter. None of this is your fault."

"If I had a daughter, I could save ten of you."

"But you don't, dear. And we would ascend one year or another. That's not your fault either." Yllicea straightened. "Queensblood, we have a difficult decision to make. We need ten names."

The older women exchanged serious looks. They already knew what was coming. Not a whisper followed. Not a breath. Not the whoosh of a butterfly wing. Pure silence filled the room like smoke.

"The oldest of us shall take her place. It is fitting we all go together now," Yllicea said.

"This is wrong," Marta whispered.

"The first name on the list to ascend shall be mine," Yllicea said.

Rianne felt her heart drop. Yllicea had been like a mother to her since her own mother Charlotte had ascended. Now, she was about to lose her second mother.

"I've had a long and happy life," Yllicea said. "I'm the oldest living Queensblood, and as such, it is my time to return to the earth."

"I'll go," Aunt Tamiira said. "I have five daughters and am the eldest daughter of the second-born daughter. It is my time to go, to give my daughters a longer life."

Rianne looked down. She could not watch these women stand to give their lives when she knew the truth. It was all a lie.

"I'll go," another said, and another, and another.

"I will ascend," the tenth said.

With that, their death warrants were signed.

Jordyn, Rianne's sister, slipped through the crowd to stand beside Rianne. Rianne looked away, feeling tears slide down her face.

"What's wrong?" Jordyn asked.

Rianne slipped her arm around her sister's slight shoulders and exchanged a look with Marta. She felt her blood bubble with frustration. These brave women deserved more than the end of an axe. Her gaze fell on the younger girls around the room. These young girls deserved to live a life without the cloud of death hanging over them. The babes in mother's arms deserved it too.

"We ascend like the queens before us, as is our duty," Yllicea said.

Queens stepped forward to hug the volunteers. The mood was gloomy, though they all tried not to cry. They congratulated one another, spouting lies about joining the other queens and all being together one day. Rianne could see it now as they hugged one another and sat with their loved ones. Fear rippled through the old and guilt hung over the young. The women sat together, holding hands, painting false smiles on their faces, and providing one another with strength where needed.

Rianne looked away, feeling sick. She couldn't bear it. They were lambs being fed to hungry wolves, and they didn't even know it. A terrible execution disguised as an honor. More than anything, she felt helpless. The whispers came again.

Ascension is a lie.
Don't go willingly into the dark.
Run.

"What if we didn't have to?" the words tumbled from Rianne's mouth.

Every eye turned to Rianne.

"All queens ascend, but not all return," she continued. "It's queenshit. We should not shoulder this burden alone. No queens need ascend. We're done."

Yllicea paled. "Rianne...that's heresy."

Rianne pushed her shoulders back. "I'm not sticking around for a fat old man to kill me. I don't think our ancestors would have wanted that either. Queen Vittoria didn't sacrifice herself to save her baby and her people so that her granddaughters would share the same fate." Rianne hesitated. "I've...been seeing things. Hearing things. I think I've been hearing the spirits of the ascended queens, and they're angry. I don't think they want us to do this."

Queens exchanged wild glances.

"I won't wait around for another banquet, another ball, another stupid party while my fellow queens prepare to die. I won't." She shook her head. "I can't."

Jordyn asked, "What choice do we have?"

"I'm leaving. Rhydian and I discussed a plan. There's a village not too far from here. We just have to make it there, and we can hide."

"Through the forest at night?"

"But we have no shoes, no cloaks, no provisions."

"What of the babies?"

Rianne swallowed. "Rhydian told me to take the blanket from my bed as a cloak and to bring as much food as I could carry. We'll wrap our feet with fabric and escape through the secret passages. I'm not staying here any longer. At midnight, I'm leaving. Meet me here if you want to join."

"Rianne," several voices called, but she could not stand to face them.

"I'm not waiting here to die. Not anymore. I'm done with that. Join me or keep believing their lies."

Rianne fled to her room and prepared herself. Her heart ached, and crushing waves of fear filled her bones. She'd made her decision though, and there was no going back from it. She knew their chances of escape were slim, but they had to try. They could hardly afford to wait. The fickle king could turn on them at any moment.

At midnight, she crept to the bookshelf. She waited, but no one came. The clock tolled quietly. She was alone. She was about to leave then Jordyn appeared. Next, Marta tiptoed out. Then a handful more, and another. The room filled with queens. Every single one crept into the courtyard. Yllicea joined last. Rianne's heart filled with pride. They might not make it, but at least they were willing to try.

Rianne opened the secret passage to the gasps of the others. One by one, cloaked in blankets carrying children and towel-wrapped food, they escaped. Hope filled the space where emptiness once existed in their hearts. They might finally be free of this haunted place.

They hurried through the passages until they reached a barred cellar door, which was rusted shut. She stopped short.

No. We can't come this far and fail.

Rianne strained, bringing down her entire weight. Jordyn gripped the wheel and pushed, straining. Two more queens reached pale, thin arms to yank on the door. It creaked. They were so close.

Please. Please.

The door gave way with a groan and opened to the night air outside the castle. To freedom. It was a long run to the tree line over open space. They darted for the trees.

For a blissful, fleeting moment, Rianne thought they might be free.

"Who goes there? Stop," guards called from the high ramparts.

Rianne cursed. The guards weren't supposed to be there. The queens raced for the trees. They tripped on their gowns and slippers. They carried babes, small children, and provisions. They ran as if their lives depended on it.

Alarm bells tolled. Soldiers appeared out of another doorway and gave chase. They were much faster than the slipper-clad queens who hadn't trained for running in their cramped apartments. The soldiers soon overtook them.

The women huddled together, surrounded. They put up no

fight. What would they have done? They were unarmed. Untrained. Helpless. Kept that way for a reason.

The soldiers escorted them to the ballroom. The king, in his nightclothes, waited. The women guiltily stood before him.

"What in the ever-loving hellsdamned moonless nights were you doing?" he demanded.

The queens said nothing. A baby's cries broke the silence.

"I give you everything you could ever want, and this is how you repay me?" he shouted.

They stared at the floor.

The king pointed at Rianne. "You."

Rianne shrunk in fear.

"Escort the ladies back to their quarters and lock the door this time," the king ordered a soldier.

"It was locked."

"Then how did they get out? I said *lock it*." King Cavendar shouted.

The soldier flinched and mumbled his apologies.

The soldiers escorted the women back to their gilded prison. Their fearful glances gave Rianne no comfort. She'd face her punishment alone, but she was eternally grateful to the queens and gods that only she would face it.

Once they were alone, the king paced. "I thought I'd taught you your lesson, but apparently not. What is it going to take, Rianne?"

Rianne swallowed. New sweat rolled down her neck, and she started to tremble. Fear crept into her heart, and her breath came in shallow pants.

"If you ever try to run again, I'll find you and catch you. I'll find them and catch them. And for every day you are gone, I'll kill one of your relatives. It'll be nothing so quick as a beheading. I'll make it slow and terrible. You'll hear their screams from wherever you're hiding."

Rianne sobbed.

"Do you understand me?"

She nodded, trembling.

"Answer me."

"Yes, Your Majesty."

"Good. Now for your punishment."

Rianne collapsed to the floor. Her hands shook uncontrollably. Sobs wracked her shoulders. She whimpered but knew better than to ask for mercy. None would come.

The king bent down beside her. He brushed the hair away from her face as she sobbed. She tried to pull away, but he grabbed her and pulled her so close that she could smell the whiskey on his breath.

"The next time you think about running, I'll cut off your feet, you ungrateful queenshit."

The king drew a dagger and stabbed it deep into her leg.

Rianne screamed.

Wolf's Head
Chapter Thirty-Eight

We don't want to become monsters.

— Rhydian Redbrooke of Oakville,
Warbringer, royal guard to Queensblood
of Rodarri.

1152 N.T.C. The Seven Forests.

During the journey back to the Seven Forests and Titan Cliffs, Theo's veins pumped molten rage. As the miles passed, hot anger chilled into an icy, unending fury. While his anger began as a wet, hot thing full of passionate outbursts and flashbacks at night, his veins now cooled like iron at the forge as they neared their destination.

The initial shock of the Mooncursed werewolf attack wore off, and his memories of the last weeks drifted through his mind. He remembered the sneering disrespect of King Jaekob, and the knife pointed at his throat by Prince Donovan. King Cavendar's wasteful opulence and the unnecessary, violent trial. The ghosts and the curse-crazed Warbringer. All over again, he watched Aurienne leave through the Way and felt the stab of loneliness at her absence. He relived the horrible nightmare where he'd nearly watched her die— the one that felt as though it could have been real.

Rejections.

Schemes.

Lies.

What haunted him most was the attack on the caravan, which he relived over and over. He wondered if he'd spent too long in the Titan Caves, for how his heart hardened to stone. His was the anger that lingered for years, for a lifetime—anger he hadn't known existed.

Was this how Aurienne felt, and what made her so quiet? Did she feel this intense rage? Did her soul rail against despair and hopelessness as she fought for survival? Did she hate herself for failing? If so, Theo understood. He now realized the cost of her terrible choices, having made one of his own. He'd have to live with the consequences of freeing the vampires forever. If she had to see the things haunting his nightmares, if she'd seen worse— how had she retained her empathy? Her kindness? All *he* felt was anger.

Resolve turned his will as cold as winter frost settling upon raw ore. He ground his teeth and glared at the road until they reached the edge of the Seven Forests.

"Find a road with yellow flowers," he said to Rhydian.

Rhydian nodded and kicked his horse into a trot.

"Yellow flowers?" Miella asked.

"A marker," Theo replied.

"To what?"

"To a road that's safe," he said.

"Will Stellan be able to find the way safely to meet us?" Concern laced her voice.

Theo scoffed. "I doubt anything can hurt the vampires. The things in the forest should fear *them*."

"That's probably true... Was it a mistake, freeing them?"

"Only time will tell. Let's hope not." He glanced her at. "Thank you for your help."

She blushed. "What are you going to say to the Free People? They turned you down last time."

Theo grimaced. "Whatever I have to."

"Theo, this way," Rhydian beckoned.

Theo and Rhydian led the caravan and herd of horses through the dense woods, following a trail of yellow flowers. The trail wound through the trees, sometimes ending where the road was hidden. As promised, the paths near the flowers were safe. They never crossed the dark water with reaching hands. No poison ivy or purple moss caught them this time.

Though it took most of the day to clear the barriers, they arrived at the tall gates of living trees without incident.

Theo announced, "It is Theo Thatcher. I return with evidence of the threat of Emperor Rexil."

The trees parted. Dharek stood inside the sprawling settlement carved into living trees with arms raised. Exertion brought sweat to his brow.

The seven-foot-tall man stared down his nose at the travelers. "I warned you not to return."

Theo glanced up at the glowering warrior. "You said I needed proof. I have it."

Dharek and the nine-foot giant Allesan surveyed their group. "There are more of you."

"Last time, some of our party fell to the ivy and moss, so we came alone," Theo said. "We have some other companions who may be joining us shortly. Please hear us."

"Come in, and we'll decide if we should let you leave again."

Miella grabbed Theo's arm. "If they try to keep us here, Stellan will see them as an enemy and attack."

"Then they'd better listen." Theo gently tugged his arm away.

The caravan entered the settlement, and the gates closed behind them with a flourish of Dharek's hand.

"Father, you really should let me do it," Thaen whispered.

"You'll have time enough for that."

Theo's brow pulled together. Why did Thaen want the duty, and why did Dharek want to spare his son from it?

The caravan followed their escorts to the sunken meeting arena in the center of the treehouse causeways.

Dharek said, "Speak."

Theo panned his gaze over the crowd. "Last we were here, we spoke of a dangerous threat. Emperor Rexil will conquer the continent and all who live here. We had no other proof but the visions of our High Seer. Now we do."

"Where is this proof?"

Theo nodded to Rhydian. Rhydian collected a spear from one of the few remaining Avyllon soldiers and strode to the center of the sunken arena. With a single drive, he thrust the spear deep into the earth with all the strength of a Warbringer.

Theo gripped the wolf's head by the fur and freed it from the canvas sack, lifting it above his head and turning slow circles. The head was as large as Allesan's and stank with clotted blood matted in the fur. The white bone of the fangs and unnatural bone ridges were evident. Having been kept in a sack for days, it looked truly monstrous.

Gasps and quiet whispers filled the space and the treehouses above.

"Twenty of these attacked and killed nearly a hundred of us in minutes," Theo said. "They're fast. They're almost as tall as the Free People and stronger than your giants. They're vicious. They kill without hesitation, hunt without tiring, and are singular in focus. They eat their prey, sometimes while they're still alive."

Bile rose in Theo's throat. "And they were just miles from here when they attacked. One day, the emperor will set them on your home, and you won't have a sorcerer willing to sacrifice his life so that some of you may live. What if there were fifty or a hundred Moon-cursed? None would survive."

With a crunching squelch, Theo drove the severed head down on the spear.

Everyone recoiled. Even Theo's own caravan companions flinched. Only Rhydian was unfazed.

"This one's for you. Keep it if you want." The words tasted like acid in Theo's mouth for all the poison his tone carried. "But know this: the threat is real. It's coming. It can't be stopped unless we fight together. Here is your proof."

No one said anything.

Thaen smirked. "You did say to bring proof, Father. Here it is."

Dharek's expression twisted.

Theo crossed his arms. "All I ask is that you come to the summit. You can't stay hidden forever. One day your secret will get out, and this will all have been for nothing. When *they* find you, you'll have no allies alive to stand with you."

Dharek studied Theo for moments that stretched on. He glanced at his son and the people around.

"You've heard his testimony and proof." Dharek lifted his hand to call for a vote.

Now closer to the towering man, Theo noticed that Dharek's arm had a strange texture, one he hadn't noticed the last time he was here. At his last visit, the skin only looked rough. From this angle, it was now completely covered in tree bark.

"We have seen indisputable evidence. We have been asked to attend a summit to decide how to face the threat. It does require revealing ourselves. How vote you?" Dharek asked.

"I know I do not have a vote yet, but as a warrior, I would vote to attend the summit to have all the information," Thaen said.

Warriors in the trees and the sitting stones nearby all cheered and raised their staves and spears. One by one, elders raised their hands.

Nearly all voted yes.

Tears sprang to Theo's eyes, and he quickly wiped at them to avoid them being seen. A weight lifted off his chest.

They agreed to come.

He had finally succeeded. One of four was only a start, but it was something. Theo tuned out the rest of the conversation. His ears rushed with blood. Distant words broke through his trance.

The sun dipped below the horizon. An eerie calm descended upon the settlement. The breeze stilled. The woods grew silent. The Free People looked around at one another and the sky.

"Oh no," Theo groaned.

With a flourish of living shadows, a dozen vampires appeared in the center of the arena. Their faces appeared less creature and more human now. They still had wings, fangs, and bone ridges, but the gaunt skin had a healthy, vibrant hue. Their hunt had filled out their flesh. Theo shuddered. How many people died for the monsters to become so revived?

The vampires set their predatory gaze upon the gathered as if making a mental tally. The monsters stood in the arena with regal poise and predatory grace. More than that, they were terrifyingly beautiful. An unsettling feeling took root in Theo's stomach. He preferred it when they were monstrously ugly. These beautiful creatures possessed a different kind of danger in their eyes and fangs.

"What have you brought to our gates?" a Free Peoples elder demanded.

"Draw your weapons," another elder commanded.

"Hold." Theo put himself in front of the vampires.

"Theo, what is the meaning of this?" Dharek demanded.

"I told you we expected some companions. The vampires have sworn to fight our enemies," Theo said.

"We swore to fight the enemies of our kin, Miella. They just so happen to be your enemies as well," Stellan corrected.

Dharek's meticulous gaze studied Theo, taking his measure. "Theo? These... They are the Shadows. Why are they here?"

"They're not Shadows. They're vampires, and...I freed them."

Dharek's face changed, like he saw something new in Theo—something he did not like. He pursed his lips.

"I would only do so if I truly believed that the threat required it." Theo could not bring himself to meet Dharek's gaze.

Stellan spoke, his voice silky and smooth like chocolate poured over hot cream. "The monsters Theo showed us are like the ones we fought in what you call Shadow War. They were what you now call Mooncursed. We believed them to have been banished back to the realm of the elves, but it appears they have broken free. You are no match for the heroes that defeated them. You won't have the allies they had."

Theo nearly overlooked the reference to elves. His brain struggled to make sense of what that could mean. He was going to ask, but Dharek cut him off.

"You didn't mention these creatures when you made your request," Dharek said.

Stellan snarled, and the other vampires snarled alongside him. The Free People put their hands on their weapons and took a step back. Even Theo's hand drifted to his weapon.

Stellan licked his elongated fangs, and shadows danced around him.

"We've agreed to assist your allies. We ask that you leave our place of peace," Dharek said to Stellan.

Stellan looked to Miella, who gave him a gentle nod, and then to Dharek. "We depart to hunt. We must replenish what was lost. We will find you tomorrow."

The vampires simply vanished. They did not leave, did not fly away. One second, they were there, and the next, they were gone.

We will find you tomorrow. Theo shuddered. Why did that sound so ominous?

"Eletta, my heartwood, would you find our guests a place to sleep for the night," Dharek said to a tall, strong woman waiting with a group of shy children.

"We will bring linens and bedding to the guest quarters." Eletta left with her gaggle of children toward the towering treehouses.

"When is the summit? The full moon?" Dharek said. "That's in a week."

"Yes, but we need to visit the Titan Cliffs first. I'm going to show them their proof as well, and return to Avyllon through a Way," Theo said.

"Then tonight we rest," Dharek said. "In the morning, a few of us shall travel with you."

"Thank you," Theo said.

Dharek crossed his arms. "You brought monsters to our door."

Theo stiffened at the accusation. There was nothing he could say. Without realizing it, Theo *had* endangered everyone here. He only meant to bring them proof, to bolster their armies with beings who could stand against monsters. But he allowed the vampires to come. He had all the best intentions, but Dharek was right.

"I never meant to endanger you," Theo said. "I'm sorry. I only want the continent to be safe."

"That's what makes it worse." Dharek patted Theo on the shoulder gently and walked off toward a group of elders.

Dharek's son, Thaen, approached. "You got what you wanted."

Theo grimaced. "I thought I did."

"Everything's got a cost."

Theo looked to Dharek, and Dharek's bark-skin arm, where it hung by his side near the elders. "Is that what happened to your father?"

Thaen nodded. "Magic always has a cost. This is ours."

"Does it stay like that forever?"

"If we use it too often, yes. If we refrain, it eventually recedes."

"The people of Living Stone know that cost all too well. Their transformation is complete. You'll see."

Thaen whistled. "We heard the rumors, but they've been gone so long we didn't know if they were true. We're all changing."

Theo frowned. "Avyllon doesn't seem to be changing."

Thaen snorted. "You have witches, seers, sorcerers, and legends that come true. You're changing too, just in your own way."

Thaen left Theo alone with those chilling thoughts. Magic cost the Free People and Living Stone people their bodies, but Avyllon's magic...it cost your sanity, your soul.

Rhydian stepped closer to Theo. "Do you think he's right? Do you think the land is changing all of us, and we just didn't know?"

"Maybe, but why now?"

"Maybe it was always this way."

Theo tilted his head to peer at the night sky. "Or maybe something woke it up."

Miella leaned over the treehouse balcony. Glittering firelight lamps and candle-lit torches hung in lines between the trees. Rope bridges connected the houses, stores, and restaurants in a spiderweb. Miella breathed it all in. The air was fresher here. The abundance of magic-touched trees cleaned the air until it nearly burned her nostrils.

Giants walked alongside the Free People. Earlier, Miella passed a handful of trees that opened their eyes to watch her. Heartspring's magic was implied, haunting, but always out of grasp until just days ago. Here, people embraced their magic.

Saryll leaned on the balcony beside her, wearing a white shoulderless gown, washed in the nearby whirlpool. Standing in the waxing moonlight, Saryll looked once more a seer. The breeze ruffled the layers of the gown.

Miella played with the end of her braid. She had a thousand questions. Where to start? How many were rude? Did Saryll already know what she was going to ask? Would she tell her about Aurienne?

"You can ask," Saryll said. "I don't mind."

A blush bloomed on Miella's cheeks. "Sorry, I don't mean to stare. This is just all so new."

"You have the soul of an adventurer, of a warrior," the seer replied. "I Saw your fate. Your soul would have found a way out of

Heartspring eventually. It may not have happened until war came, but you would be forced to find a new home or fight. Or worse."

"What's worse?"

Saryll was quiet.

Miella thought for a moment, answering her own question. "I might have gone to the mountain and asked to be made vampire."

"That's one future."

"Can you See them all? Like her?"

"No one Sees what Aurienne does. She is directly connected to the Goddess."

Miella sighed. "I wish I could see the future. I want to know if I made the right choice."

"No one can answer that but you," Saryll said. "The feast should be served soon. Shall we go?"

They met Kassia, wearing a gorgeous dress of braided vines and flowers, and descended the treehouse stairs to the festivities below. Miella glanced at her own plain tunic and pants, feeling underwhelming. She shook the thought from her head.

Tables lined the paths, allowing them to all eat together before their departure. Drums beat a lively and joyous tune. Miella squeezed into a long wooden table between Saryll and Adonis. Adonis discussed the various plants and their uses with a healer. Saryll and Kassia held hands and laughed.

"Eat well," Kassia said to Miella. "We'll be on the road soon, and I don't expect a warm welcome from what Theo and Rhydian said about the People of Living Stone. If they do eat, we don't want any of it."

Miella shifted on the bench, her feet skimming the ground. The table was tall, and the plate was at her chest. The wooden cup was oversized, requiring both hands. A cook placed a massive, grilled fish onto her plate. She took a bite, and the flavor exploded in her mouth. It was seasoned perfectly and moist. The greens tasted just like the forest. She took another bite of carrots and potatoes from the gardens, and she nearly groaned it was so good.

"It's delicious," Miella said to Thaen, sitting across the table.

"Thank you," Thaen replied. "We honor nature with our cooking. Tell me, what food do you eat in Heartspring?"

"Pastas, wine, meat pies," she said.

"Is it what they eat where we're going? I am keen to try the new food."

"I think they have some in the city, yes. I'm told the city has everything."

"Excellent," Thaen said. "Then after the summit, we will all eat pasta."

Several warriors near him cheered. Miella laughed and raised her glass in a toast.

She glanced down at the table where Theo and Rhydian conversed with Dharek and several elders. They laughed when appropriate, but it didn't reach their eyes. When the conversation stilled, Theo's gaze grew distant as though he'd gone faraway. Haunted by something terrible, Rhydian sat beside his friend, tensing every muscle as if losing one ounce of control was unacceptable.

She frowned. *How horrible was the Mooncursed attack? What else had they seen?*

Diners rose from their seats to mill about under the canopy, sampling deserts, chasing children, and playing games of skill. Rhydian showed off at the darts while Saryll and Kassia read fortunes for wide-eyed children. Adonis took copious notes about something at a quiet table. The others mingled politely.

Miella approached Theo. "Aren't you happy?"

Theo blinked, then chuckled. "I realized that coming here brought the vampires and, in doing so, endangered the people. I didn't even think..." He shook his head. "Yes. I should be happy."

"This isn't your fault, you know."

"What isn't?"

A sliver of guilt wormed into her chest.

"Everything," she said. "But especially the vampires. You didn't let them out. I did. I could've said no, but I didn't. A small part of me wanted them to be free. I wanted the story to be real. I wanted...to be important. I wanted adventure."

Theo smiled. "I understand that all too well. When Aurienne asked for my help, I couldn't say no. Something in me desperately wanted to help her."

"That's how I felt when you asked for my help with the vampires. You said that...Aurienne"—the High Seer's given name was sacrilege on Miella's tongue—"told you that her Goddess showed her the way? Maybe the Goddess is speaking to us too."

Theo's shoulders wilted. "Thank you."

"Let's just try to stay alive, shall we? Your seer said we're all going to need each other."

Miella hoped she wouldn't regret her choices.

The Vampire's Shadow

Chapter Thirty-Nine

The dark king stepped into the sun and grinned.
He burst into flames and sent his ashes to the wind.

— *SARYLL AMYDEO, SEER, PROPHETIC VISION.*

1152 N.T.C. The southern road between Avyllon and the Titan Cliffs.

Monsters surrounded Theo as day gave way to night. The vampire Stellan lingered in the shadows of trees as the sky faded. Having fed the past nights, hopefully only upon criminals, his skin was filled out even more. The vampires were even more beautiful than before. More mortal than monster, even if the bony plates and wings remained. They lurked in the trees, all fanged shadow and sex.

The Free People watched the vampires curiously, and while not appearing as afraid as the rest of the caravan, they kept their distance.

The vampire Stellan cast the Warbringer a dark look. Theo had noticed that the vampires watched Rhydian carefully, not daring to venture too close.

Maybe they've met a Warbringer? Goddess, how bad was Rhydian's curse if even the vampires were afraid?

A vampire drifted too close, and the horses neighed and stamped their hooves.

"They know they are prey, and we are hunters," Stellan said simply.

"Only criminals," Theo warned.

Bleeding suns. What am I going to do if the vampires decide not to listen?

"What about the horses of criminals?" a female vampire quipped from somewhere in the trees.

"No," Theo said. "If you have to hunt wild prey, that's fine, but leave livestock alone. People need them to live."

"Dead criminals don't," a male vampire muttered.

Theo looked up. Hundreds of human-sized shadows lurked about the treetops. *Great.*

"You're asking us to *starve* and then have to fight," a vampire whined, licking their teeth.

Theo turned. "Not starve, but humans need food."

"What about chickens? They crunch wonderfully under the fang." Vampiric murmurs of agreement flooded the trees about the delicacy that was a frenzied, live chicken.

Theo rubbed his temples. This was his actual nightmare that he never knew existed. These murderous, bloodthirsty monsters were going to ask him questions until he died. They'd wear him down until there were no limits on their cruelty.

An echoing battle cry shook the trees, and Theo spun to see their ambusher.

A figure threw off their cloak and lunged at the vampire Stellan with a short sword that glowed as brightly as the sun. The man's skin burned with swirling tattoos of light. He was dressed in hunter's leathers with a longbow across his back.

"Die demon!" the hunter cried.

"You? I knew you were still alive, you traitorous sunworshipper. Come meet your due," Stellan snarled and lunged at the hunter.

Stellan sunk his fangs into the hunter's shoulder but immediately screamed and released his hold. Stellan's mouth and lips smoked with the repulsive scent of burning flesh. Stellan sped away.

The fox leapt onto the attacker's face and clawed and scratched. The man tried to throw the fox to the ground, but his hands passed through the fox as if it were made of smoke. The fox shot away, snarling and hissing.

A vampire darted out of the trees and slashed at the hunter's midsection. The vampire's claws went up in smoke, and the vampire screamed and disappeared.

"Stop," Miella cried.

Theo jumped between the vampire and the hunter but was shoved to his backside in the dirt, knocking over Captain Laurier and Rhydian. Allesan, the giant, and Dharek and Thaen drew their weapons with the other Free People.

The hunter lunged at another attacking vampire and sunk his blade deeply into the vampire's arm. The vampire cradled the nearly amputated limb as it spurted out black, bubbling blood.

"I'll kill every last one of you," the hunter roared and attacked another vampire.

"Marco, you murderous bastard," Stellan roared, swiping at him again from the shadows.

"Go to hells!" the hunter bellowed back.

Stellan darted around a wagon and spun away to avoid Thaen's blade. The hunter drew a dagger and lunged at Julietta, narrowly avoiding a living spear from Dharek's magic. Julietta hissed and disappeared. The hunter faced Stellan.

Theo sat in the dirt, staring at the absolute mayhem unfolding in their camp.

What in the shadowsucking hells was going on?

Stellan ripped a tree, a whole *tree*, out of the ground by its roots and hurled it at the attacker. The hunter didn't dodge quickly enough, and the tree took him from his feet, flinging him into the undergrowth where more screams and smells of burning vampire flesh filled the night.

Theo scrambled to his feet and chased the attacker. He drew his sword with Rhydian, Captain Laurier, and the remaining soldiers at his heels.

The attacker burst out of the now-flaming brush, swinging at a half-dozen vampires that beset him at all sides. The man was bleeding liquid sunlight that splashed on the ground and caught fire. The vampires recoiled like it was alchemical acid. One hurled a knife at Marco, and it struck him deeply in the shoulder. Blood pooled down his ripped shirt.

"Stop," Miella screamed.

"Stop. Everyone stop. Stop," Theo shouted uselessly.

Theo and the others ducked as flaming arrows flew above their heads.

"Kill him," Stellan roared.

High above, vampires ripped branches from the trees and hurled them down at the attacker. Marco was soon nearly covered in a massive pile of branches, but the pile just burned. He burst out of it with a roar like an exploding star.

Dharek and Thaen began using their magic to create a branch cage for the hunter, but the hunter's burning tattoos cut through the branches, leaving only smoke in their wake.

"Who are we fighting?" Thaen demanded.

"Just keep them from killing each other," Theo yelled.

Marco threw a knife at Stellan, which the vampire caught effortlessly. He dropped it, but not before his skin hissed with the poison.

"I knew you were just hiding, you worthless bloodsucking leech," Marco snarled.

"You killed your own brothers, you blood-traitor," Stellan snarled back as he threw another tree at him.

Marco dodged this tree and charged Stellan. Stellan side-stepped at the last minute with a beat of his wings and kicked Marco in the back, sending him sprawling into the dirt. Marco scrambled to his feet and nocked a flaming arrow, pointed right at Stellan's heart. Stellan lifted an entire wagon.

Theo waved his arms before the vampire. "Stop!"

This was entirely out of control.

Adonis muttered to himself as the attack raged, "Just mix the blue lizard spit into the inferno flower and stir seven times, add a pinch of deathwater... I don't have deathwater. But I have corpse-root. Bottle and throw." Adonis looked up from his miniature laboratory. "Throw? Oh, it's done. Okay, Theo, I'm ready."

Oh hells.

"Put that down. You'll kill everyone," Theo snapped.

Theo and Rhydian darted between the vampire and hunter, with Miella, Captain Laurier, Saryll, and Kassia behind them. Adonis tossed a glass vial in the air like a leather ball, ready to lob it...somewhere. The sorcerer didn't even look sure who he intended to attack with the questionable mixture. Dharek, Thaen, and Allesan moved to corner the hunter from one side while the hunter lunged for more vampires.

"Stop. Everyone, stop," Theo demanded.

Miella darted into the fray. "Stop!"

Stellan hesitated and put himself in front of Miella. "Miella, get behind me."

Stellan's words stopped Marco, who looked at Miella, and something clicked in his mind as if recognizing her. He froze.

"Miella?" Marco said. "It's okay. I'm family. You don't know me, but I recognize your blood. I can sense it in my own. You don't know what those things are. Get behind *me*."

"He's a murderous bastard who kills his own family. Stay away from him," Stellan snarled.

"I'm not standing behind anyone," Miella shouted. "Now, put down your weapons, and someone explain to me what the shadow-steeth is going on."

"Can't do that, sweetheart," Marco said. He pulled the arrow back farther as sunlight oozed from his cuts.

Stellan easily hefted the wagon above his head as if it weighed nothing and bared his terrible set of double fangs. "This is personal."

"I'm not moving," Miella said.

Both Stellan and Marco hesitated but didn't put down their weapons. Hate flooded their eyes, with Stellan's eyes black as pitch and Marco's as bright as a midsummer high noon. They were opposites in every way, even if their features were eerily similar.

"They're killers, Miella," Marco said. "They'll suck you dry and leave you to die. I've seen it."

Marco's eyes darted to Miella, and a frown creased his bright features.

Rhydian crept forward, sword in hand. That caught both Stellan's and Marco's attention. *Interesting. Both were wary of the Warbringer.*

"We took on a terrible curse to fight back the Shadows in the Shadow War and returned to hate and fear," Stellan said coldly. "We protected our families and found that they had disowned us. We sacrificed everything, and they turned their backs on us. And then *he* hunted us down."

"You returned as monsters who would devour us all," Marco said.

"A few could not control the hunger," Stellan said. "It was tragic what happened. But the rest of us did, and yet we received no thanks for our sacrifice. We left as demanded, and then you hunted us still."

"Only because you killed," Marco said.

"Some of us. Not all. But you killed without discernment," Stellan said.

"You're related?" Miella asked quietly, in horror.

"He's my brother," Stellan said.

"You *were* my brother. No longer," Marco said.

"And what in Saturn's name happened to you? Did you suck the sun's taint?" Stellan goaded.

"Better than licking the devil's balls like you," Marco snapped.

"We can show you the threat we face," Theo interrupted.

The hunter's sunlight tattoos flared as he directed his ire toward Theo. "You would stand with these soulless demons?"

"To fight the Shadows, yes."

Marco tensed, and the tattoos dimmed. "What did you say?"

"They're back," Stellan said. "They serve an emperor who demands subjugation."

"They're back to finish what they started?" Marco asked.

Stellan licked his fangs. "It appears so."

"The Shadows... They killed so many..."

Stellan cocked his head. "Our true and ancient enemy has reappeared. It is the only reason we allowed ourselves to be freed from our self-imposed prison. We swore to protect my last remaining descendent, Miella."

"She's my blood too." Marco leveled a stare at the vampire.

"It seemed like family didn't matter to you then, Brother."

Marco rolled up his sleeves to display his glowing tattoos. "We haven't been brothers since you sold your soul. I only took up my cause to rid the world of you because you endangered our family. I finally saw you all for what you really were."

"Did you?" Stellan growled. "When you were more child than man, sleeping in your bed safe at night while the rest of us were out killing and dying, you knew why we made the sacrifice we did? You didn't fight the Shadows. We did."

"I saw the aftermath of the destruction you all left behind," Marco snapped. He leveled a stare at Theo. "You'll answer for all their sins."

The vampire hunter slipped into the trees and was gone.

Descent into Madness
Chapter Forty

Be warned: the cost of spiritual necromancy is your own soul. Extensive damage to the soul may prevent the user from finding peace beyond the veil. You may be forced to haunt this world as a wraith in eternal misery.

— Journal of the seer Rheia, 3 B.N.T.C.

1152 N.T.C. The namesake city of Avyllon.

Golden soulblood dripped from Aurienne's nose, and she rubbed her aching temples. No amount of rest could restore her soul as quickly as her visions came. These days, she barely required her scrying crystals, bone runes, or divination cards. Since the blood eclipse, her visions increased daily. Soon, without Theo to ground her, she would no longer reside in reality—if she lived that long.

Everywhere she turned, condemnation always lingered. She glimpsed broken images where the barriers between the worlds grew thin. Visions of the future waited in the beams of sun piercing heavy clouds and in ruddy red and purple sunsets. They passed between the shadows of mountains in the dusk and dawn. They lingered in the morning dew sitting atop a flower in the gardens and in the eye of a stranger across the room.

She tasted it in a stolen kiss at midnight and in the first sip of dark red wine. It echoed in the sad melody of the violin as the harp joined and in the bubbling waters of a cool shady stream. It burrowed into her bones in the warmth of a fire and in a frosty winter breeze.

She Saw Teridar's demise in every reading, vision, and omen.

Year after year, she'd Seen death and war. It burned her eyes until it was nearly all she could see. She Saw her people ripped apart by monsters. Villages razed. Entire forests raged with the infernos of hell until even the skies caught flame. Crows picked at piles of bodies as tall as the ancient trees. Shadows with empty, yellow eyes stared at her. She refused with every fiber of herself to accept that fate, no matter the cost.

She wouldn't allow it.

In her visions, she also saw hope. Young parents chased small children around gardens, laughing and showering them with kisses. They held giggling infants closely, breathing in their love. Families sat in front of fires, wrapped in blankets, telling stories late into the evening. Couples shared passionate embraces under the stars. People fell into earth-shattering, soul-binding, heart-stopping kinds of love. Elderly relatives rocked babies, watched children, offered advice, and peacefully passed after a life well-lived.

It was so beautiful.

Village festivals offered music, food, drink, and bone-deep camaraderie. Farmers tilled rows of wheat with their loyal dogs trotting beside them. Weavers spun colored lengths of wool as cats purred and rubbed against their legs. People lived wonderfully full, genuine, and loved lives.

Aurienne Saw it all, and she'd fight for it. Her recent travels, being among the people, experiencing it with them—made her more determined to save her people, even if they called for her demise.

Outside the temple doors, guild members protested. She did not know whether she heard them truly or in visions. It hardly mattered. Her sister seers avoided her. Syaoran, the former High Seer and Saryll's mother, also avoided her. Saryll was still on the road with Adonis. She'd pushed Theo away. For the first time in her life, she felt utterly alone.

Maybe I've always been this alone and just never noticed before.

Before spending time with Theo, she wouldn't have noticed the silence, but now, it was crushing. She grew too accustomed to their conversations. She relied on his constant presence and easy smile. For the hundredth time, she re-read his last letter.

Aurienne put the letter away and let her head fall into the dusty book on the desk. She'd spent the past days reading about the Moon-cursed and the Shadow War. She read about the Shadows, creatures of nightmares. She read about golden flying warriors and about wraiths that she now knew were called vampires. The ancient books told tales of the ground opening and swallowing armies. They told of mountains coming to life and trees moving. Elementals were fully transformed by the land.

Her visions and Theo's messages told her that it was all happening again. For some reason, magic that had long slumbered was waking and changing people. And it was all connected to Demorra and the Shadow War. Aurienne lifted her head and continued to read. She stopped on a page about the elves.

Elven warriors appeared to fight the Shadows. Etherians were faster, stronger, and more impervious to injury than humans. They lived immortal lives, and only their weapons could kill the Shadows. They raised the four pillars, banished the Shadows, and vanished.

With a loud thump, she closed the book in a cloud of dust. The summit was days away, and Aurienne had no idea what she'd say to them. She prayed to the Goddess every day, but no answers came yet. Something shrouded visions of the coming war, and she was beginning to believe that the entity served the emperor.

Paper moved beneath her fingers. She lifted her head. One of her divination cards had escaped the spelled box and slid under her hand.

Grimfall.

The figure on the card wore a sword of starlight, and the glint of fangs peeked out from under the hood. The bedtime story.

> *Stars light in cursed blade.*
> *Souls of beasts and monsters weighed.*
> *Evil hides and darkness dies.*
> *Shadows rise as grim falls.*
> *Death to one, death to all.*

She glanced at the card, and the figure pushed back its cloak, revealing the long ears of an elf. Her breath caught, and she scrambled to open the history book, but the card flew toward another stack of books—burrowing itself between the pages. Carefully, she flipped through the dusty, crumbling pages and stopped at a passage.

> *Grim steps fall ever closer on the ears of monsters. The elven warrior hunts the darkness, passing judgment on evil, powerful beings. None can escape her. Not even the Shadows. The elves vanished, but the reaper stayed behind to guard the realm.*

The echoing sound of a specter's footsteps clicked on the hallway outside her door.

Step.

Step.

Step.

Coming closer every day. Haunting her, eluding her Sight—they'd be here soon. Chills raced down her back. On the verge of collapse, she dabbed more golden soulblood from her nose.

I can't fail now.

Paid in Blood
Chapter Forty-One

Don't ever forget what I am.

— *Stellan Rothbain, vampire.*

1152 N.T.C. The southern road between Avyllon and the Titan Cliffs.

Under a dusk sky blossoming with stars, Theo and his companions approached a grouping of houses that was far too quiet. No fires crackled in the hearths. No animals neighed or nickered. A door swung ajar on the hinges, battering the frame in time with the breeze. The homes were maintained well-enough that someone ought to be here. His stomach twisted into a heavy ball of knots that sank toward the saddle.

Miella rode beside him, casting furtive glances his way. "What's wrong?"

"You should go wait at the back of the caravan." His grip tightened on the reins. "You don't want to see this."

"See what?" She paled.

Theo motioned for the caravan to stop. "Death." He turned to

Adonis. "Would you go with Dharek and Thaen to find some firewood?"

The tree warriors glanced at the houses and nodded in understanding, leading the boy away.

Theo reined his horse to a stop and dismounted. He kneeled before a dark stain, dabbing his fingers into the liquid. Blood. The drag marks led away from the houses into the woods.

"I'll check the bodies and see what did this," Rhydian said.

The Warbringer followed the smeared blood into the trees. His boots crunched on the dirt and foliage until he slipped into the shadows.

It could be Demorran soldiers, Mooncursed, predators, bandits, or...vampires. Theo swallowed, not sure which would be worse.

While Rhydian searched the trees, Theo scanned the houses. He peered into a paddock, noticing unmoving dark lumps in the grass. His neck prickled as his heart grew heavy. An entire herd slaughtered. Tensing, Theo stepped into the house. He wasn't ready.

He backpedaled out the door, nearly knocking over Miella. He heaved against the house, waiting for his eyes to cease swimming and his stomach to stop churning.

Miella pushed through the door.

"Miella, no." Theo reached for her, but her wrist slipped through his grasp.

She froze in the doorway, taking in the arterial blood that coated the walls. Her shoulders and arms shook, and her knees wobbled. She backed away, more ashen than he'd ever seen a person. She sank to the ground, staring inside with vacant eyes.

Theo pushed off the house and put his hand on her shoulder. She sobbed and clutched his hand. He squeezed her shoulder and re-entered the house. Drying blood coated the walls, while more blood dripped from the ceiling. Two bodies lay twisted in the corner. One of their faces was frozen into an eternal scream, mouth open wide enough that the jaw was askew. The other held a glassy, empty expression. Both necks were ripped open, leaving nothing but gaping holes.

The horrors were just as terrible as the Mooncursed attack. The images burned into his mind.

A bump from the bedroom caught Theo's attention. He drew his sword and crept toward the noise. Taking a steadying breath, preparing for some terrible monster, he slammed the door open and lunged into the room. It was empty. But where...

Bump.

His heart slammed into his throat. The noise came from under the bed. Full of adrenaline, Theo gripped the edge of the bed and tipped it over in a single motion. It went crashing down, and Theo readied to strike whatever leapt for him.

Two children huddled together, tears staining their dirty faces. The girl gasped and clutched the younger boy close to her chest, shielding him with her body. They looked at him as though he was death coming for them.

"It's okay," he murmured, sheathing his sword. "I'm not going to hurt you, I swear. Are you alright?"

They both nodded their heads, shaking.

"What's your name?" he asked.

"Josalin, and my brother is Jamie." Her voice shook. "Where's my Ma?"

Theo grimaced. "She's gone, sweetheart."

Josalin looked down.

She already knew. How could she not know?

"How old are you?" he asked.

"Eight," she said. "And my brother is five."

Theo took off his coat and kneeled beside the children. "I'm going to carry you outside, if that's alright. I don't want you getting hurt on the way out."

He didn't want them seeing what had become of their parents, or the blood soaking the walls. They'd heard the attack; they didn't need the images to accompany it.

"What's outside?" Jamie asked.

"There's some damage to the house," Theo lied. "I'm going to reach for you now, alright? We'll get out of the house and get you some food. I'm sure the chef can put together something warm for you both."

Josalin's dull eyes found a hint of life at the mention of food. "Could he make stew with bread?"

Theo forced himself to smile comfortingly. "I'm sure he can. Let's go outside so you can help him. Do you have any shoes for me to grab?"

They shook their heads.

His heart lurched. "We'll find you some extras."

Theo took both children into his arms and tucked his coat over their little heads. He walked them through the main room, past the corpses of their parents and the blood, and into the night. Miella stumbled after him. He set them down far from the houses beside one of the only remaining wagons.

"Do you have any family in other towns?" Theo asked.

"Our aunt and uncle live that way a few miles," the boy said.

Theo patted the boy's head. "We'll take you there in the morning."

Saryll and Kassia rounded a wagon and froze.

"Could you get them some stew and bread? And find them some shoes?" Theo asked.

A kind expression fell over Kassia's face. "Of course."

Each woman took a child by the shoulder and led them toward a fire.

Saryll cast Theo a grim look. "Let's go dears."

Rhydian came out of the trees. "It wasn't Mooncursed. I found bodies. Mooncursed would have eaten them."

"I found bodies in the house. And two survivors. Both children," Theo replied.

Rhydian frowned. "Everything else is dead, even the animals. What would leave children?"

Dark, liquid anger trickled through Theo's veins. "I'm going to find out."

Theo stalked away from camp. He braced himself and pushed open the door to the second house. He stepped over a dismembered arm. Rhydian and Miella followed him inside. Theo covered his nose with his arm as the smell of blood and shit filled his nostrils. These people died afraid. Three bodies were stacked in the center of the room.

What was left of them.

Weapons were tossed across a table, nicks and dings along their glinting edges. Black masks and hoods sat in a pile beside the dirty knives. A few small bags spilled gold and valuables onto the table. Only one thing explained this odd assortment laid out so casually.

"Highway bandits," Theo murmured.

"It's unlikely one of these groups robbed travelers, and the others didn't know about it. They were probably working together," Rhydian said.

Theo stared at the bodies. Natural predators, even bears or wolves didn't do this. Humans certainly didn't cause this. He shuddered. The fact that bodies remained meant it wasn't the Mooncursed. He crouched beside a corpse, checking the neck. He found fang marks.

Blood draining from his face, he slowly stood, seeing the carnage in new light.

"What did this?" Miella whispered.

"The vampires." His voice was rough. "Mooncursed don't drink blood. They don't leave children alive. But vampires sworn not to hurt innocents would."

"This is what we let out," she whispered. "This is what I freed."

"Because I asked you to," Theo said. "You don't bear this alone."

"Why did they do this?" Miella stared at the bodies.

"They were hungry," Theo replied.

He gathered what supplies he could: gold, extra shoes, blankets, clothes, and food, and then stuffed them into a sack for the children. On the way out, he harvested what he could from the gardens. He'd give them everything he could before he brought them to their family.

Nearing the third house, he noticed bloody drag marks leading out to the woods. He quickly gathered what he could and retreated.

I did this. This is my fault.

"I know what you're thinking," Rhydian said. "Stop."

"This was my choice." Theo met his friend's gaze. "This is what will happen to every house if we don't stop the Mooncursed. I just... hoped the vampires would be better."

The fluttering of wings told Theo the vampires had arrived. Stellan appeared between the houses and the wagons with an unreadable expression. His skin was silvery and even more full, his fangs resting atop his lips. His leathery wings folded against his back.

Theo stormed up to the vampire. Rhydian was hot on his heels, hissing something, but Theo ignored him.

"*You* did this." Theo said.

Stellan lifted his nose to sniff the wind. "Some of us did. I can smell the sin of the departed from here. They were righteous kills and in accord with our bargain."

Theo's face grew hot. "You left children alone!"

The vampire's eyes flickered toward the children sipping soup beside the fire. "We did not harm innocents, that was the deal."

"You killed their parents. What are they supposed to do without anyone to care for them? They would have died if we hadn't found them, and then their deaths would be on your hands." Theo was close enough to the monster he could feel the hot breath licking his face, but he didn't stand down.

"They should not have been left." Stellan tilted his head. "I will speak to the others and ensure no more children have been abandoned. You have my word."

Another vampire, Julietta, was drifting closer to Theo with fangs half-bared.

Theo pointed at her. "Back off." Returning his attention to Stellan, he said, "And how good is your word? Those children are traumatized."

"Yes. They are. But not only by us," Stellan stared down his straight nose at Theo. "Look closely. You don't notice how badly they're taken care of? The girl is how old?"

Theo glanced at Josalin. "Eight."

"She is small for her age is she not?"

All the little details Theo had missed were now so evident. Their gaunt, hollow faces and bare, grimy feet were not signs of well-cared-for children. Their clothes were ratty, covered in holes. Bruises covered their little arms. They had no shoes. These issues far predated the attack. Who was the monster here?

Josalin peered at Theo from behind Saryll, eyes not blinking. Jamie was on his second bowl of soup.

Theo stiffened and took a step back from the vampire. "How often must you feed?"

The vampire laughed. A full, throaty laugh that echoed off the blood-soaked houses and trees where moving shadows revealed hordes of vampires. His teeth reflected the starlight.

"Are you regretting your choice so soon?" Stellan growled. "Don't forget, we would have stayed in our tomb. You begged for this."

Theo stood his ground, not willing to give up a single step until the vampire answered his question. "I want to know how much blood bought our salvation."

The vampire delicately raised a brow. "Now that we are revived, we must kill every other night or every third night to survive. Not always human, but we cannot survive on animals alone."

"Can't you drink their blood and leave them alive?" Theo snapped.

"No. Blood strengthens us, but we need lifeforce. They must die," the vampire said.

Josalin's screams cut the night. A pale vampire grabbed her by the wrist and dragged her closer. She writhed and threw her steaming bowl of soup into his face. He hissed and unhinged his jaws. Staff and soldiers fled, leaving her to her fate. Kassia dove for a blazing stick and swung it at the vampire's face. He dodged, the distance between him and Josalin growing.

Theo was sprinting for her in an instant. His sword appeared in his hand, and he brought it down in a sweeping arc toward the vampire's arm just as Rhydian had showed him. Black blood sprayed the grass. Josalin scrambled away from the severed hand, screaming.

The vampire howled and whirled on Theo. His claws raked toward Theo's chest, and he sprang backwards to avoid the worst of it. Thin streaks of blood darkened his shirt. His chest stung from each shallow slice, and he inhaled sharply. He raised his sword, waiting for the vampire's killing blow.

Before the vampire could strike again, his head rolled from his shoulders. Stellan was standing behind the vampire, claws dripping with blood. He'd taken the vampire's head off.

Stellan glared toward the trees. "Our oath stands. Any who defy it answer to me." The vampire looked to Theo. "Once the sun touches his body he will die. If we keep his head separate from his body until then, he won't be able to heal."

Howls descended upon them in a frenzy. Mooncursed creatures crashed through the brush and toward the fire. Miella screamed. Kassia dove under a wagon with Josalin while Saryll disappeared with Jamie. Theo lifted his sword as Rhydian drew his. Caravan staffers screamed while the remaining handful of soldiers readied their weapons.

They were too slow.

Stellan was gone. Standing beside the beheaded, snarling vampire one minute and colliding with the Mooncursed the next. His long claws raked the Mooncursed's chest, slicing through fur and flesh until it reached the metal plates. The Mooncursed snapped at Stellan, but the vampire wasn't there—appearing behind the beast. He punched through the wolf's bone ridges, and with a sharp tug, ripped its heart from its chest. The beast died howling.

Julietta and another vampire slashed at the other Mooncursed viciously. Long, deep cuts stained the wolf's fur black and red. Over nine feet tall, this beast was the larger of the two. Julietta flew, landing on its deformed shoulders. She snarled and sank her teeth into its neck. It grabbed her and threw her to the ground, but she rolled across the grass and leapt for him again. Her teeth found his neck again. He scratched and batted at her, taking chunks of skin.

Two more vampires sank their teeth into his thick neck. A crunch snapped the wolf's neck, and it fell to the ground. The vampires drank every drop of the beast, slurping and sucking him down. Others fell upon the first wolf.

The rest of the vampires vanished into the night, leaving Stellan and Julietta and the two corpses. Julietta stood primly, dabbing at the corners of her mouth as a rosy hue filled her cheeks. Stellan crouched to inspect the corpses at his feet.

Theo blinked. They'd just killed two Mooncursed in no time at all. They'd fought hard, but they took them both down. His stomach churned. The grass was soaked with blood and adrenaline filled his veins in just minutes. The vampires feeding was horrible, far worse than he'd imagined. The sounds... He shuddered.

Kassia crawled out from under the wagon and pulled Josalin against her chest while Saryll emerged from where she'd carried Jamie.

Theo knelt beside the girl. "We will protect you, see?"

Her watery eyes met his. "We were safe until you all arrived." She glanced at Stellan. "They're your friends. Who will protect us from you?" She buried her face into Kassia's shoulder.

The words physically knocked the wind from Theo's chest. He forced himself to meet eyes with Stellan as his body fought to freeze in place at the sight of the Mooncursed that plagued his nightmares.

"They are as you said," Stellan said. "Made with the same magic that created the Shadows all those years ago, that created us. The Shadows were animals and men corrupted by dark magic from another world, that seem connected somehow to the cycles of the moon. They existed only partially in this world, and partially in another—like smoke or shadows. It was how they got the name. I can hardly believe they're back, even when they're lying at my feet."

Marco stepped out of the forest, removing his dark, thick cloak that had been covering his sunlight tattoos. Theo braced for another fight, but the hunter's weapons remained sheathed as he approached.

"We banished them. I don't know how they returned," Marco said.

"The emperor brings an entire army of them. Hundreds of thousands," Saryll said quietly.

"You've seen this?" Marco asked.

"Our High Seer has," Saryll said.

Theo glanced between the vampire and hunter, realizing the opportunity lingering in the wind. "We are going to a summit of the five nations to convince them to fight the Mooncursed."

"Let's hope it doesn't come to war. Last time it destroyed the continent. Entire civilizations vanished. Monsters were born," the vampire hunter murmured.

"War may come regardless, but this way, we might have a chance to survive," Theo said.

"You say five nations? There used to be more," Stellan said.

Dharek, Thaen, and Adonis returned as the vampire asked the question. The tree warriors stared at the new carnage, but Adonis drew a book from his bag.

Adonis showed Stellan the map, pointing out the cities of Wynds and Rodarr, the Seven Forests, the Titan Cliffs, and the city of Avyllon. He then strode across the grass and showed the map to Marco.

"Much has changed," Stellan commented. "The main city of the nation you call Avyllon used to be farther south. You don't have the pillars marked, either. Seems important to have on a map."

"The pillars?" Theo asked.

"Monuments to the elements that finally defeated the Shadows," Marco said icily.

"Can we defeat the Shadows again?" Miella asked.

Marco's attention turned to his distant kin. "Miella? You really are a descendent of Stellan?"

"That's what he says. And that's what he says this means." She produced the heartspring necklace from her jacket. "It's been in our family for generations."

He studied the necklace. "I recognize it. Stellan gave it to his wife before he left to fight the Shadows. I was there."

The hunter's expression softened, and he took her hands in his. "You can't trust them. They lie as easily as breathing. It's in their nature. Their hunger is so consuming, they'll do anything to sate it. Even if it means hurting those they love."

Miella glanced at the sunlight tattoos peeking out from underneath his leather jacket. "How did you get those tattoos?"

The hunter stood. "I swore I would never believe their lies again. I found a way to ensure they could never harm me again. I found a way to kill them. If you want, I can show you too."

"You can give me tattoos of sunlight?"

"Yes, but then no one can touch you ever again without risking harm. It will burn even a human's skin."

Miella swallowed.

"The vampires will betray you, as they did me. As they did all of us. When that day comes, I'll be waiting."

"Will you help us?" she asked.

The hunter glanced at the children and the Mooncursed corpses. He looked to Stellan. "You have kept your word. Killing the sinners and enemies of our kin while protecting the rest. I will hunt the Shadows. I'll agree to a temporary stalemate as long as you keep the oath."

Marco looked to Miella. Then he drew his dagger across his hand and let liquid flames drip into the ground, starting small fires. "I swear to fight your enemies and defend you from those who intend you harm. I swear not to raise a hand against the vampires unless they break their pact with you."

Stellan nodded to Theo. "We're going to hunt. We'll find you tomorrow."

Marco rolled up his sleeve to show his glowing tattoos. "You drink a single drop of innocent blood, I'll kill you."

Stellan's fanged smile was without any humor. "I have given my word not to hurt innocents, but I do find it entertaining that you think you could stop me should I break my word. You're not been successful yet."

"All it takes is a single touch to send you to hell."

"If it was that easy, you would have done it by now."

"Remember, when you break your oath—and you will—I'll wrap you in chains of living sunlight and drag you into the light to burn," the vampire hunter vowed.

"You better be sure those chains are true because your life will end at the same time as mine. It will be my hand around your neck squeezing the life from you as I burst into flames." The vampire disappeared into nothing.

The fragile truce hung in the air, threatening to rip them all apart.

Heart of Stone
Chapter Forty-Two

Titan ore is the hardest known metal and is exceptionally rare, only found near supernatural landmarks. The hardness makes it difficult to forge, but a superior material for armor and weaponry does not exist. Beware—it displays volatile magical properties.

— The Secrets of Metallurgy, by Tyrilla Duskcut.

1152 N.T.C. The Titan Cliffs.

The road to the Titan Cliffs felt like it took no time at all. After bringing the children to their relatives, Theo directed the caravan straight to the thundering cliffs, knowing exactly where to go. Dharek, Thaen, and a dozen Free Peoples, along with the giant Allesan, rode on borrowed horses. The devious little fox reappeared and trotted happily alongside Theo's horse.

"Do you want a ride, friend?" Theo asked.

The fox leapt higher than it should be able to and landed in the space in front of Theo's saddle. Theo fed it small treats and scratched it between the ears.

"Do you know what that is?" Dharek asked.

Thaen snickered.

Theo scratched the fox's chin. "A forest guardian?"

Dharek shook his head. "I...do not think so."

The fox spun a tight circle on the saddle and glared at Dharek. It released a low bark at the tall warrior.

Theo chuckled. "What is he?"

Dharek grinned, but he lifted his hands and said nothing.

"Are you sure that the Avyllon sorcerer will meet us at the Way in time?" Rhydian asked. "If she doesn't, we won't make it home. We're almost two weeks travel from Avyllon, and the summit is in days."

"Aurienne said she'd already sent the sorcerer through and she's waiting for us," Theo said.

Thunder boomed as rocks smashed against cliffs. They turned the familiar corner to the cliffs. The People of Living Stone, both spiked and armored, remained on their respective sides of the cliff hurling boulders at one another.

Theo dismounted, and the fox darted away. He approached the stone people as shadows from airborne boulders flew over his head.

"Stop. We have visitors," Stone'ward shouted.

The booming stopped. Boulders crashed into the waves below.

"Theo? How did you get out of the cave? We hadn't yet decided on what to do with you," Ore'spike said.

His voice was more gravelly than Theo remembered, like a small landslide of sharp rocks.

Theo rubbed his temples. "Yes, we got out of the cave. You put us in there with no food, water, or blankets. It's been over a week. We'd be dead by now if we hadn't."

"Oh. I'm very sorry. That is true. Next time we will remember."

"There won't be a next time." Rhydian's hand drifted toward his sword, and there was a promise in his steely gaze.

"People of Living Stone," Theo began. "You couldn't decide

what to do before. You refused to show yourselves to the human world. I'm here to show you the monsters we face. They will corrupt the land and you with it. We were attacked by Mooncursed."

Theo lifted the remaining wolf head. It was worse than it'd been at the Seven Forest settlement. Time had not been kind to the deteriorating token. Swollen and oozing, the skin and fur were beginning to slide off the skull.

"Put that disgusting trophy back in your little bag," Ore'spike said.

Theo did. "They bring corruption. They're cursed. You think that won't have an impact on you? They can hurt you. It may just take them longer."

Ore'spike's polished spikes bristled. "We're indestructible. Those things can't hurt us. We've been blessed by the lands and changed by titan ore." He tapped his spike with his fingers, stone clinging against metal.

Titan ore. The same that made indestructible blades. The ore that Mathis explained had alchemical properties. If it transformed the People of Living Stone from human to living statues, perhaps it could be used against them—by the emperor. Mathis said it could be imbued with magic? What if Theo could use it to prove the danger to them. Images of those blood-soaked houses and the huddling children lurked in his thoughts. Torn bodies and limbs. The blood that stained his hands.

He'd come this far and couldn't stop now. He'd have to go a bit farther.

Theo glanced at the saddle bag with a dagger and one of the titan ore Mooncursed collars. His gaze strayed toward Adonis. He motioned for the apprentice sorcerer to approach.

Theo murmured, "What can titan ore be used for?"

Adonis blinked several times. "Um... Strong swords. Wards. Magically imbued weapons. Magic cancelling shackles. Naturally, they can be amplifiers of magic. There are some tomes in the libraries that suggest that negate certain types of unnatural magic..."

Theo raised a hand. "What will the collars we found do to *them*." He jerked his chin toward Stone'ward and Ore'spike.

Adonis' eyes widened. "If it created them... It might speed up the transformation. Or reverse it? Maybe? Or mind-control them?"

"Permanently?" Theo asked.

"It shouldn't. It should wear off." Adonis raked his hand through his shaggy hair.

"Should?" Theo rubbed his hand against his pant leg.

"I don't know what all the runes mean," Adonis said, gaze downcast. "Mathis would have known."

There'd been too much death already. Theo wasn't sure how much more blood on his hands he could bear. He woke from nightmares sweating and swinging at phantoms. He hardly knew himself anymore. But if this was the only way...

"What are you two whispering about? We're not..." Stone'ward began.

Theo strode toward his horse with a grim expression.

"Theo," Dharek hissed. "Don't do whatever you're thinking of doing. You'll regret it."

Theo met the tree warrior's gaze. "I'll try to do better after this."

He reached his hand into the satchel and removed the collar. Palming it, he approached one of the stone warriors standing beside Ore'spike.

Dharek dismounted, chasing on Theo's heels. "There's another way."

As Theo passed, Rhydian asked, "What are you doing?"

"Here's your danger. Here's the proof," Theo announced.

He raised the black titan ore collar, the diamond and gold flecks sparkling in the sunlight. He didn't slow his approach.

"Where did you find that? What is that?" Ore'spike demanded.

Almost there.

Theo swallowed. Was he really going to do this?

"Theo!" Dharek's hand was on his shoulder, but he shrugged it off.

The spiked warrior stepped in front of Ore'spike, and Theo pressed the ore into the warrior's stony neck. The warrior stumbled back, knocking into Stone'ward and Ore'spike, but Theo clicked the collar shut. The man opened his mouth to shout, but no words came out, only garbed angry noises.

Anger and guilt coursed through Theo.

"What are you doing?" Stone'ward demanded.

Stone'ward's carved runes lit up with golden light as Ore'spike's metal spikes rattled. The collared stone warrior clawed at his neck, writhing with jerky motions. The stone people backed away with horror written on their faces.

Theo wanted to look away but forced himself to watch. He wouldn't avoid the consequences of his choices.

"Stop. Can't think. So slow," the warrior's words slurred.

His actions slowed, dust raining from his joints. Then he stopped moving altogether.

Theo cleared his throat, slowly drawing their focus to him. "This collar came from the Demorran Mooncursed beasts that attacked us. They have titan ore forged armor. Titan ore collars and weapons. They have Mooncursed beasts using Shadow War magic. They have knowledge and power we can't even guess at. You are not safe. No one is. Their magic froze your friend to stone temporarily, but what can they do with more? If you don't fight, eventually they'll make their way here and kill you all."

"He will be alright?" Ore'spike asked quietly, concern carved deeply into his stony expression.

Other warriors raised boulders from the cliffside, preparing to launch them at Theo and his companions.

Theo unclicked the collar, and the metal fell to the ground. *Please move, please move.* Theo held his breath. The man didn't move. Theo's heart sank. *Did I just kill someone?* He picked up the collar as though nothing was wrong.

"It'll take some time to wear off, but yes." Theo prayed he wasn't a liar.

"The Demorrans have this magic?" Stone'ward asked.

"Yes."

The People of Living Stone were quiet for long moments. They went so long without moving, Theo wondered whether they'd all frozen into stone. Minutes passed. Theo waited. The air crackled with change.

"We will come to the summit to hear what your High Seer has to say," Stone'ward said.

"I too will come." Ore'spike motioned to Theo.

"You...will come to the summit?"

"Yes," they both said.

A band of iron that'd wrapped around Theo's chest snapped, and relief flooded in. *They would come.* They would come, and if they came, then Wyndsel and Rodarri might come. Almost a week remained before the full moon. There was still a chance Theo could fulfill his potential destiny and bring them all together, but his heart lurched. At what cost would he fulfill his task?

On the way back toward Avyllon, the caravan passed the stone warrior, frozen in eternal screams, who may never wake.

Theo set ink to paper, his final task before returning to Avyllon with his army and his guilt. He wrote to King Jaekob and King Cavendar.

The nations assemble at the summit as promised. Come, or be forgotten as your lands burn.

Underneath the numb exterior Theo's mind created for his sanity, fury pulsed with wicked intent.

SECRETS AND LIES
CHAPTER FORTY-THREE

When I am freed, my vengeance will have no bounds. The kings will all die.

— JOURNAL OF QUEEN ROSALINDT DANIELLA LENORE, 579 N.T.C.

1152 N.T.C. On the main road at the border of Wyndsel and Rodarri.

Queensblood Rianne sat beside Princess Arissabett on wooden traveling chairs on the road to Avyllon for the summit. Rianne watched the kings scheming across the spacious campsite in fading afternoon light. She gripped the arm of the chair hard enough that her manicured nails left crescent dents in the wood.

Dull practice swords thumped where the princess's fiancé, Prince Donovan, trained with a handful of Wyndsel soldiers. Rianne glowered behind the flourish of her lace fan. A soldier pretended to trip and yielded when Donovan's sword came to his throat. Donovan lifted his sword in victory, and Arissabett cheered loudly. Behind his back, the soldiers exchanged an exasperated glance.

Were he and Arissabett the only ones that did not see it?

Prince Donovan glanced from Arissabett to Rianne, and Rianne clapped softly and nodded politely. When he looked away, Rianne's hands immediately dropped to her lap, and she rolled her eyes. These minor rebellions were all she could risk. Rianne had learned her lesson against speaking up, for now. She could still feel the leather of the muzzle digging into her face and could smell the sweat and fur of the hound. Her bandaged leg ached from her punishment after her escape attempt, forcing her to limp. In a place like Rodarri, she'd have to take another approach to get what she wanted. For the time being, she'd have to play by their rules.

She nearly gagged.

"Isn't he marvelous?" Princess Arissabett asked dreamily.

What? Rianne mouthed to the trees.

"An incomparable swordsman," Rianne said aloud, rubbing her temples.

King Jaekob Juri and King Edmunton Cavendar remained deep in quiet conversation. They glanced her way for too long, then glanced again. She swallowed. They returned to their conversation, but she had a sinking feeling she wouldn't like whatever their plans were.

"I yield," a soldier called.

"Another victory," Prince Donovan announced, slicking back his dark hair.

He was handsome. If only he wasn't a royal kingshit.

"My hero," Arissabett cried.

"Queens save me from this hell," Rianne murmured.

"What was that?" Arissabett asked.

The princess's wide brown eyes met Rianne's gaze as she swept her long black hair over her shoulder. Rianne and Arissabett could not have made a more distinct pair. Rianne's pale skin, rosy cheeks, and blue eyes in her ombré blue gown clashed with Arissabett's dark olive skin, sharp nose, and bright pink and white gown. Not so long ago, Rianne might have been as blissfully happy as Arissabett, but she'd learned better. The whispers filled Rianne's ears.

> *The kings shall die by blood and flame and claw. The*
> *kings of old shall die!*
> *Not much longer now.*
> *A kingdom built on bones fears ancient spirits.*

Arissabett waited.

Rianne said absently, "I said that he did splendidly. Perhaps he'd enjoy cool water?"

"What a terrible wife I would make. I have brought him no water," the princess exclaimed.

Arissabett jumped to her feet and collected cool water from a barrel. She brought it to the prince who was laughing loudly with several nobles. She tapped his shoulder and offered him the water with unwavering devotion brimming in her eyes.

"Did I ask for water?" he snarled and knocked the cup out of her hand.

The ceramic cup crashed against the packed dirt and shattered. The princess yelped and recoiled. She dropped to her knees to pick up the pieces, but he hauled her roughly to her feet.

"Don't act like a servant. I want to marry a queen, not a serving girl," he snapped.

"I'm sorry," she whimpered.

Prince Donovan's face softened, and he pushed a curl out of her face, tracing his fingers across her cheek. "I can't stand the thought of you forced to do any work," he said gently. "I love you too much."

The princess leaned up to kiss him. He kissed her briefly before motioning back to her chair. She returned to Rianne and perched on the edge of her chair as tears streamed down her cheeks.

Guilt speared Rianne's chest and moved like sludge through her veins. "I'm sorry," Rianne whispered.

She hadn't meant to cause the princess embarrassment. She had no idea the prince would react like that. Perhaps—she should have.

"It's my fault. He's right, of course. Silly me, just embarrassing him. I can be so stupid," Arissabett replied cheerfully, wiping away the tears streaming down her face.

Rianne knew the falseness of her cheery tone all too well.

"He's not right," Rianne whispered. "It's never right to do that. You can't believe he loves you if he would do that."

"Of course, he loves me," Arissabett said defensively. "He's just..."

Rianne watched him eyeing a servant girl who passed with a tray of ale for the soldiers. He stopped her to take a mug from her tray and leaned to whisper into her ear.

"If you say so."

"He does," Arissabett said too loudly.

The kings peered in their direction.

Rianne painted a regal smile on her face and hissed under her breath, "Be quiet, foolish girl, or we'll both get it."

Arissabett froze like a doe in a hunter's sights. The kings returned to their scheming.

Rianne whirled on Arissabett and snapped, "If you want to survive, you'll learn something quickly. Jealous, powerful, weak-minded people maintain their power by putting others down. Play their games. Do what you're told and bide your time. Plot. Scheme. Plan. But never, never, never be so foolish as to believe their lies."

Arissabett's pretty mouth fell open.

"Has it never occurred to you that you don't have to be what they tell you to be?" Rianne resumed fanning herself to mask her lips. "You've never thought you could be more?"

"I... I'm going to be queen."

"Are you? Or are you going to be Donovan's wife?" Rianne jerked her thumb toward the rowdy prince.

"All I want is to be Donovan's wife."

Rianne sighed. "Then I'm sure you will be."

The pair were quiet for a while. Kings schemed. Prince Donovan pretended to defeat soldiers who knew better than to injure or best him. Across the camp, the wives of the kings worked their needlepoint and politely nodded and smiled like dolls. Bile crawled up her throat, seeing *that hell*.

Then Arissabett surprised Rianne. "She said I would get my heart's desire. The High Seer, Aurienne? That's what she told me. She said my future is lined with pain, death, and betrayal. She told me to trust my heart and not to be afraid to take what I wanted. I thought she meant Donovan."

"Does your heart really want him?"

"I thought so."

"Once you know what you want, do as the seer says."

"The things she said scared me."

"Me too." Rianne picked at her chair. "I'm afraid our kings won't agree to help her. I'm afraid they'll acquiesce to the emperor."

"I'm more afraid of the war she says is coming," the princess said.

Rianne scowled. "Either way, we're all likely to end up dead."

The princess fidgeted with the folds of her gown.

Prince Donovan followed a waitress out of the clearing behind the wagons. Rianne glanced at Arissabett. The princess stared at her gown and said nothing. Either she knew and could not stop it, or she was too naïve to notice. Either way, Rianne decided to remain silent.

Better than being muzzled.

"Do they... Do you really... Are you going to... I mean... Is it true..."

"Yes," Rianne replied. "All Rodarri queens ascend. Not all return."

"Ascend means..."

"That they cut off our heads and throw our bodies into a bottomless ravine."

Arissabett swallowed a squeak. "That can't be true. That's just a story, right?"

"What did you think ascending meant?"

"Being banished."

Rianne snorted, which was very unladylike. "No. Our blood and deaths replenish the magical protection of the land."

"How often are the ascensions?"

"Every year." Rianne scowled at King Cavendar from behind her fan. "This year, more frequently."

"I just thought when they said ascend and return that the queens might...return from banishment."

"It means they return to life."

"With their heads cut off?"

Rianne chuckled in spite of herself. "I don't know how it works either. It's been over three hundred years since it last happened. Over the years, only three queens have returned."

"When will it happen for you?"

"Some queens live to old age. As firstblood, I won't."

"I'm sorry."

"Me, too."

"Why haven't you tried to escape?"

It didn't go so well.

"Why haven't you?" Rianne shot back.

The princess blushed and recoiled. Tears brimmed in her eyes once more.

Rianne sighed. "I'm sorry. I...always believed it was my duty to protect my people. Only recently did I begin to question. I tried to speak up, and the *king* put a dog muzzle on me. I tried to escape, but they caught us." Rianne's words dripped venom.

Arissabett gasped. "No..."

Angry tears prickled Rianne's eyes. "I'm no warrior. I've been frail all my life. I've been stupid. I believed that my only worth was my death. What a pathetic fool. I can't believe I did not see through their lies sooner. Now that I do, it may be too late."

Arissabett picked at her gown. "I'm sorry."

"I'm sorry, too. Our situations are not so different."

"They won't execute me," Arissabett said defensively.

"Maybe not," Rianne said bitterly, nodding toward the two queens. "But that over there is your entire future. It's death all the same."

Arissabett's face fell.

The whispers returned, and only Rianne was haunted by the terrible scratching voices.

> *Death is not the worst thing that can happen to you.*
> *A thousand queens, dead for nothing. A thousand*
>   *more to die.*
> *Your death comes on wings of betrayal. Let us*
>   *avenge you.*

Rianne dug her fingernails into the wood of the chair, fighting to keep her expression soft and serene or risk angering the king or revealing her whispers. "I thought I would be able to escape and have a life with Rhydian. I see now it was never possible. My fate was already sealed. My only solace is that the rest of them are going to die too."

HOMECOMING
CHAPTER FORTY-FOUR

I go where you go. You'll never be alone again.

— A PROMISE OF LOVERS.

1152 N.T.C. The namesake city of Avyllon.

The towering city of Avyllon glinted in the afternoon sun. Elevated, smooth stone buildings sprawled across the valley, nested between the mountains. Avyllon was impossibly imposing, powerful—constant. The fresh, crystalline water bathed the city at every turn, sparkling like diamonds in the pools. Fountains erupted, and waterfalls poured water from the towering aqueducts to the basins below. Just as glorious as before, the city no longer took Theo's breath away.

Theo led his caravan through the pristine, orderly streets. The towering giant Allesan and Free Peoples Dharek and Thaen with patches of bark growing from their skin, and the living statues Stone'ward and Ore'spike walked alongside the humans. People stared and whispered at the foreign guests, not bothering to hide their fascination. Marco's thick, multi-layered cloak managed to conceal most of his radiant tattoos, but he, too, received many a stare.

Nearing the temple, Theo urged his mount faster. His breath was shallow and strained. Warm butterflies raced through his bloodstream. His palms were cold and sweaty.

Why am I nervous?

He had spent many a quiet, intimate moment with Aurienne, but somehow this reunion meant everything to him. He remembered what she told him—it was over—but he could hardly believe it. She kept him going through the depths of despair. He had to see her, praying to the Goddess she was hoping to see him too. His heart beat so hard he thought it might crack open his ribs and escape its prison to find *her*.

At the stable, Theo slid off his horse and pushed through the crowd, leaving his companions behind. Seeing the top of the temple columns and the sealed wooden doors, he broke into a run.

Pushing through the crowd, he reached the temple and stopped. His breath caught.

Aurienne stood on the steps waiting.

The High Seer was everything he remembered. Vibrant. Terrifying. Divine. An impossible sight dripping in gold jewelry from head to toe—white flowing fabric and gold adornments. Her clouded eyes were painted with kohl; gold leaf dusted her cheeks. Her arms were painted with eyes and moons and stars, and high slits showed off soft, curving, painted thighs. The sun framed her like a portrait he never wanted to forget.

Her roving gaze picked him out and settled. From across the courtyard, Theo saw burden in her eyes. There was also an anger that Theo now shared. In a second that lasted for eternity, he let himself look at her. She was here, right in front of him.

With one look, Theo knew without a doubt that he was eternally, deeply, and undeniably in love with Aurienne. He *knew* he'd spend the rest of his life loving her, even if she could not love him back. And then she *smiled* at him.

Theo's heart and resolve cracked open. So rarely she smiled. So rarely she had cause to. Her face lit up when she saw him, and she took several quick steps forward. Then she stopped herself. She hesitated and then dashed, descending the steps toward him, gown fluttering behind her.

Theo ran to meet her.

Aurienne's heart betrayed her. Theo had returned. He pushed out of the crowd, travel weary, battle-worn, triumphant. Was he always so impossibly gorgeous? Rugged and untamed in the best of ways. Stubble covered his jaw, and she wanted to run her fingers across it. She recalled glimpses of his broad chest and muscled arms beneath her hands when they kissed. His gaze had a touch of steel that softened when it fell on her, and he stared at her reverently. His lips parted, and she wanted to cover his mouth with hers.

Hellsdamn her heart.

The hard glint in his eyes, one that never existed before, told a story of pain, resolve, and now anger. She'd Seen some of what he endured these past weeks, but his eyes showed the true toll it took. He'd lived a lifetime since they parted. He did what she had asked and accomplished an impossible task, but it cost him a piece of his soul.

The last time she saw him, she told herself that she had to stay away from him to keep him safe. Telling herself that their parting was for the better.

Never destined to fall in love.

Then the past weeks, she had to live without him. In the quiet moments alone with her haunting thoughts, she missed everything about him—their long conversations, his easy smile, his kind heart, quiet strength, and resolve. She missed how deeply he loved those he cared for. She missed how he dragged her back into the world of the living. When a hallucination of him came to her when she needed it most in that dark and deadly room, she realized she was falling for this traveler.

In spite of herself, she *smiled*. Upon seeing her smile, Theo's face lit up like the sun on Solla. Her heart blazed like a forest fire—wild and hot as hells.

She tried to keep herself from running to Theo, but her feet began moving on their own, racing toward him. It was poor judgment. It was dangerous. She shouldn't let her enemies see he was important to her. Yet, she hurried down the steps. He ran to meet her.

She ran into his arms, hugging him tightly, eyes growing glassy. He wrapped his arms around her and clutched her to his chest, lifting her feet off the ground. Her chest cracked open with relief at seeing him. He held her tightly enough that he must have felt the same, and then he buried his nose in her hair. A single teardrop splashed against her shoulder. He was just as relieved as she was.

"I missed you," he whispered.

"I missed you, too."

Breaking the hug, Aurienne leaned up to kiss him. The kiss was brief but poured life into her soul. Theo tasted warm and woodsy like sunlight filtering between the tree canopies. Everything cozy and magical at the same time.

He tasted like *home*.

Theo's mind struggled to comprehend what had happened. Aurienne smiled at him, ran to him, and kissed him. It couldn't be real. This was just another dream from which he'd wake in disappointment. They ended their kiss before their companions and guests arrived.

"You did it," Aurienne whispered. "Wyndsel and Rodarri will arrive tonight, just in time for the summit tomorrow. You brought the five leaders of the continent together."

Theo breathed deeply and let his head fall forward in triumph. Aurienne turned her gaze to Adonis and opened her arms to give him a hug. Adonis, who had been keeping a tense and straight spine, collapsed against her.

"I'm so sorry." She hugged him tightly for long moments before releasing.

Aurienne reached for Saryll's hand and then for Kassia's. "I'm so happy you're both safe."

"I Saw you had some troubles," Saryll whispered.

Theo's brows pulled together. *What troubles?*

Aurienne replied, "Nothing that could not be handled. Kassia, Saryll, thank you for keeping them all safe."

Aurienne squeezed their hands and let them go, before standing by Rhydian.

He bowed low. "High Seer."

"Thank you." Aurienne's lips twitched. "You saved his life more than once."

"And he mine."

She approached Dharek, Thaen, and Allesan. "Welcome, Free People. Giant Allesan, welcome. Tomorrow at the summit, all will be explained. Tonight, please enjoy yourselves as our guests."

The Free Peoples and People of Living Stone bowed.

Next, Aurienne addressed the vampire hunter. "Hunter of Shadows, welcome. I'm sorry your slumber was disturbed, but I am glad you are here."

Lastly, Aurienne spoke to Miella. "Your fate is important."

"Me?" Miella's rich brown eyes blinked slowly, looking Aurienne up and down in awe.

"You are going to turn the tide of this war."

"I can't..."

Aurienne smiled. "I'm never wrong."

Miella squeaked excitedly and covered her mouth with her hands.

Aurienne turned to Captain Laurier, the soldiers, and the rest of the weary caravan survivors. "I'm sorry I could not protect you or your friends better. My failure haunts me. I'm in your debt. Nothing I can say will make up for the horrors you survived. Know if you need something, ask. I shall provide for the families of the fallen, and I owe each of you a favor."

She turned back to the group. "Please follow me to the palace. I opened it and had guest quarters prepared for all of you."

The caravan neared the palace, a gathering of beings, each as terrifying as the last. Aurienne glanced at Miella and Saw glimmers of fate sparkling around her like fairy dust. Aurienne sensed great destiny and trials coming for the vampire's heart-kin and felt twinges of empathy for the young woman. She remembered what it was to have fate thrust upon you and to feel its teeth sink into your flesh.

Noting that the girl walked slowly, gaping at every tower and spire with wide, nervous eyes darting this way and that, Aurienne reached out to squeeze Miella's hand as they approached the palace.

The moment her fingers touched Miella, a vision crashed into her mind. Theo and Miella locked in an intimate, passionate embrace. Theo's fingertips clawed into Miella's hips, and Miella arched her back in pleasure. Their tongues danced as their naked bodies met. Theo pulled Miella's hair back, and she rode him with rhythmic circular motions of her hips. Sweat rolled down Miella's breasts and splashed against Theo's scarred chest. Theo flipped her over onto her stomach and pressed his hips against the curve of her ass, driving in. She cried out, and he groaned.

With a small gasp, Aurienne's hand grew limp. Miella beamed at Aurienne and squeezed her lifeless hand. Aurienne pushed away her own feelings and forced herself to smile. She released Miella's hand, swallowing bile. Her fingernails dug bleeding crescent moons into her palm. A searing vine of thorns wrapped around her throat and heart, its barbs pricking her with their poison.

It's just a possible future, not a fate. It's nothing.

The palace was only across the courtyard from the temple, but the walk was an eternity as Aurienne banished the haunting images from her mind.

Obermiester Gotrik and several Guild Masters were waiting at the main palace doors.

"You opened the palace. Has the *monarch* returned?" Gotrik jeered.

Goddess, please smite this man.

"Please show our guests inside to the prepared rooms," Aurienne said to a newly hired palace staffer.

The Free Peoples, People of Living Stone, vampire hunter and others filed inside. Rhydian lingered near the door. Theo stood beside Aurienne, glancing from the Obermeister to Aurienne, waiting.

Kolten stepped forward and drew his sword. "I know what you did, and it's only a matter of time before we prove it."

"I have no idea what you're talking about." The Obermeister sneered. "I had nothing to do with any *troubles* you've had."

Fear gripped Aurienne's heart, but she refused to show it.

Kolten raised his chin. "If you take a single step closer, I'll—"

"You'll what?"

Kolten twirled the sword. "I'll run you through without a second's hesitation."

The Obermiester's brows hit his forehead as he took a step back.

Theo stepped in front of Aurienne and drew his own sword, glancing from Kolten to Aurienne. He might not know what was going on, but he would protect her.

The Obermeister said, "I received word your companions were returning, with royal guests. And King Jaekob and Cavendar are coming as well. It seems you're planning something."

Hagsteeth.

She hadn't wanted him to find out.

"I assume it was a last-minute gathering and my invitation would arrive soon. As you know the guilds' Obermiester, University Dean, merchant Trademaster, and bank Custodian must attend all summits with foreign dignitaries." He smiled. "By law."

Aurienne did know; she just didn't care after she'd nearly been murdered and betrayed by the guilds. But now that she'd been found out, she had to play along. For another few days. Then, she'd no longer be regent.

"I'm sure your invitation is arriving soon. It might have inadvertently gone to the prisons, seeing as how I expected you to be there already." She crossed her arms, aware of the ache in her broken hand.

"Not quite." His grin was toothy. "I'll expect those details soon." He strolled away, whistling.

Kolten sheathed his sword, glaring at Gotrik.

"What's his problem?" Theo's voice grated harshly.

"I suspect the emperor's gold weighs his pockets, and now he knows what we've been planning," she said. "Let's hope it doesn't ruin everything."

They'd come too far and sacrificed too much.

THE SUMMIT
CHAPTER FORTY-FIVE

Stars light in cursed blade.
Souls of beasts and monsters weighed.
Evil hides and darkness dies.
Shadows rise as grim falls.
Death to one, death to all.

— *LEGEND OF THE GRIMFALL. CIRCA 4 N.T.C.*

1152 N.T.C. Hallohaim Festival. The namesake city of Avyllon.

Dusk descended on the palace summit room, and the fate of Teridar hung in the balance. Aurienne prepared to convince the leaders to save themselves from the prophecy, but great powers swirled around them and clouded her Sight.

Every seat in the room was filled. Imposing wood carvings of each nation's crest stood guard behind the respective delegation's seating box.

The griffon and sword of Avyllon.

A siren warring a battleship on towering waves for Wyndsel.

The lion and the rose of Rodarri.

The seven trees of the Seven Forests.

A chain-bound multi-headed hydra for the Titan Cliffs.

They were all here. Somehow. Against all the odds, Theo had succeeded. The thought brought a brief smile to Aurienne's lips.

He convinced, threatened, and dragged them here.

Her heart burst with pride. He'd done his part, and now, it was time to do hers.

Aurienne's stomach knotted, and she kept from flexing her broken hand. She refused the urge to chew her painted lips as she still had no idea what words would change the course of fate. Sweat beaded underneath the makeup concealing her bruises. Gilded black lace sheathed the splint on her healing hand. Her ribs ached and the stitches from the stab wounds pulled. She dabbed a droplet of crimson blood from the corner of her mouth, wishing she had more strength to face this.

Behind Aurienne, Theo, General Kane, Saryll and Kassia, Adonis, and Miella were dressed in their finest, tugging their sleeves uncomfortably while watching the other delegations like hawks. Sentinel Kolten shifted along the wall, his ever-vigilant gaze pouring over any threats. Obermeister Gotrik wore lavish clothes, far finer than he ought to be able to afford. He glared at her with a sinister grin, and she forced herself not to flinch. He'd been behind the assassination attempt—she just hadn't been able to prove it yet. She set a returning glare upon him, forcing him to finally look away. The Dean, Custodian, and Trademaster were seated in the back. She continued scanning the room.

The red fox, now wearing gold earrings, crept in through an open window and sat beside Theo on a decorative pillar. It was double the size it had been before, and runes marked its fur.

Not a fox.

It blinked at her with its golden eyes, as if it could read her thoughts. Aurienne had thought it was a forest guardian, but now she wasn't so sure.

King Jaekob, Queen Elissa, Princess Arissabett and her fiancé Prince Donovan waited beneath the Wyndsel crest. The princess batted her thick lashes at her fiancé who surveyed the room down his nose. The king and queen cast furtive glares at Aurienne.

Fate's energy prickled the air in this room, like the buzz before a lightning strike. It was a powder keg, and one spark would send them all to hell.

King and Queen Cavendar, Queensblood Rianne, and a handful of the king's commanders represented Rodarri, dripping in gemstones and fabrics that cost more than the room they sat in. Rianne's black paneled gown with splashes of red Rodarri bloodroses contrasted with her pale skin and rosy cheeks. Relief was painted on Rianne's face when she glanced toward Rhydian. There was also sadness and fear in her eyes that had not existed before, and she winced in pain when she moved.

The ghost Rosalindt shimmered into existence in their box and peered at Aurienne. Aurienne's blood froze. She quickly glanced around the room, but no one else appeared to see their visitor. Rosalindt bared silver fangs.

Goddess—any one of them could be the spark.

From the Seven Forests, Dharek and his son Thaen sat in a box with the giant Allesan and the vampire, Stellan. The Free Peoples and giant had been uncomfortable sitting next to the vampire hunter's gleaming sunlight tattoos with their bark-studded skin. Across the room, Stone'ward, Ore'spike, and the vampire hunter Marco shared a box. The hunter sat with crossed arms, glaring at the vampire. The vampire snarled with fangs that nearly reached his chin, and the hunter pulled back his cloak to reveal tattoos of sunlight.

One spark.

Fate prickled her skin. She took the floor. Her long gown swept the stones as the many delicate chains and bracelets she wore clinked. Every eye was upon her. Her head was a little woozy, and her body felt weak. She needed rest, a reprieve from her gift—but there'd been no time. She lifted her chin, steadying herself for this final battle.

"I invited you here to discuss what Emperor Rexil has to say," she said. "He promises protection in exchange for fealty and tribute. It won't end there. The taxes will increase every year until he bleeds us all dry. When there is nothing left to take and no one left to fight, he will invade anyway. I have *Seen* this. There is no escaping it."

King Jaekob spoke, "We recently learned your own birth prophecy states that your visions can't be trusted."

Aurienne glimpsed the Obermeister's smug grin.

Rat-loving bastard.

"All prophecies are riddles," she replied. "Sometimes their true meaning is not understood. And until it is, we cannot wait around and do nothing. We stand together or we fall on our own. I believe I've proven the value of my visions to you. You would be dead from poison and buried in the cold hard ground right now if not for me."

King Jaekob pursed his lips.

"What is the birth prophecy?" King Cavendar asked.

Saryll spoke before Obermeister Gotrik could, earning her a dark glare from the man. "One thousand stars fly as souls unearthed. The monsters of old roam the earth. Seer's visions condemn the Darkling War, against the enemy from distant shore. Four pillars lost and the fifth lost by Fate. Darkened skies fill with howling hate. The fate of the world hangs by moon's light. Darkling Souls fight, Darkling Souls die."

King Jaekob snorted. "Seer's visions condemn the Darkling War? That's reassuring."

Immediately the delegations broke out into separate side conversations.

Aurienne spoke over the din. "I have a spy in Demorra who confirms that this has happened to nations past. The nations who resisted have been erased. The ones who didn't resist are crushed beneath the demands of the empire."

That silenced the room.

"We have a chance to stop him," she continued. "He intends to take us one by one, to isolate us, but we are stronger together. He has the armies of all Demorra. To defeat him, we must work as one. Or we accept his eventual demands of death. He conquered all of Demorra without anyone knowing it. He won't be stopped unless we stop him."

Nods of agreement circled the room.

Emissary Seiko pushed open the doors, and he strode in, dripping in arrogance. The doors closed behind him, and Aurienne gritted her teeth.

"Where has he been?" Theo whispered behind Aurienne.

"We couldn't find him last night," General Kane replied.

"Wise seer, if you're discussing the imperial emperor's demands, perhaps you should hear from him," the emissary said, words slathered in spite.

King Jaekob and King Cavendar both nodded.

"You shall have your chance to speak at the end," Aurienne said in a clipped tone.

The emissary raised his hands.

Boom.

The room exploded with light. Wind whipped the clothing of the attendees, and they covered their faces with their arms. Aurienne inhaled sharply. A Way opened in the middle of the room.

It shouldn't be possible.

Emperor Rexil stepped through the purple, flame-licked portal. He appeared in his mid-thirties with straight black hair that might have hung to his shoulders if it wasn't tied back. His dark eyes were framed by wide cheekbones set in a flat face. Striking good looks. Regal posture. Easy confidence that showed no fear stepping into a room full of enemies. Aurienne couldn't have painted a more accurate picture of a conqueror.

An entourage of advisors, two dozen armed soldiers, and a handful of priestesses with a ring of light burned into their foreheads followed him through the Way. They fanned out around him.

The Way closed behind the emperor.

Hellsdamn it.

"High Seer, Aurienne Celestina Azarrah, Regent of Avyllon," the emperor said. "I come unarmed and greet you in the spirit of friendship."

Aurienne forced the expected words out. "Your Imperial Majesty, you're welcome in our lands if you come in peace."

His dark gaze weaved through the room, noting everyone. "I see you spent the time gathering all of your allies." His brow lifted. "I didn't expect this."

Something in the way he said it made Aurienne wonder whether he had his own seers—or worse. It could be how he has managed to elude and obscure her sight if he had those who worked to thwart her. Anger bubbled in her throat like a living thing. Not possible. The Goddess wouldn't bestow her gift upon their enemies. It had to be something else... She tried not to think of what it could mean.

She clenched her jaw. "If you are here to make your offer. Make it. We shall discuss our response."

"So be it." Emperor Rexil strode into the center of the room with a sweep of golden robes. "Join the empire, become protectorate states. You adopt our laws and disband your army. You will honor the goddess Niamh. You will send seers and sorcerers, and others with magic to Rexila to share knowledge." He repeated his specific tribute demands of gold and soldiers, enrapturing them all with his smooth voice.

He finished by saying, "Our empire protects its protectorate states. We have laws and punish those that break them. We have the means to provide for nations in their times of famine. We ask only that you join what shall become an empire that stretches across all continents."

"You want to rule the world." Aurienne's voice was flat.

"We shall enforce disputes between nations," he said. "When you abolish your armies, per the terms of the protectorate status, it shall make up for the taxes taken."

A shudder rolled down her spine.

They would never free themselves if their army was disbanded.

Stellan said, "I've lived a long time. Those with power seek more power. Their promises evaporate into mist as soon as they obtain the power they sought. They forget from whom they gained it."

Marco scowled. "Those in power lie. That we can agree on."

"Our people are governed by the rule of law," Dharek cut in. "Checks on power are key. No one person holds power alone. The power is dispersed. It keeps everyone honest. If one man holds all power, everything rests on his heart alone, and one heart can be corrupted."

Allesan grunted his agreement.

"Strength is power. Without armies, the nations have no power," Stone'ward observed.

Adonis piped up. "And what of the demands of sorcerers, witches, seers, and other magical entities being sent to Demorra permanently?"

The emperor's glare traveled the room. "It will be discussed once you sign."

"No," Ore'spike said, his voice gravely as if his mouth were full of rocks. "Nothing will be signed until these questions are answered."

The emperor said, "There are specific provisions for those with magic. Sorcerers, seers, witches. We were unaware of the rest of you."

Adonis crossed his arms. "You required half the seers and sorcerers to travel to the empire indefinitely."

"Half our people must go to Demorra?" Stone'ward asked.

Emperor Rexil's lip twitched.

His emissary stepped forward. "The section was not drafted with an entire people in mind. We shall discuss acceptable terms to mirror what the other nations send."

Stone'ward and Ore'spike exchanged a glance with Dharek. Aurienne's heart sank. They were considering it. By King Jaekob's and King Cavendar's silence, they were too.

Aurienne asked. "What of the things I See? I See that your empire brings destruction and creatures of darkness. What of the death?"

The slow dark smile on his lips told her of her mistake before he even spoke.

Oh no. What have I missed?

"What death?" he asked.

"I've Seen it."

"Do you have proof?" he said wickedly.

Always needing more proof. She could scream. Every face turned to Aurienne and remained. Even the Free Peoples and People of Living Stone looked to Aurienne for answers. Their fate depended upon what she said next. Her heart hammered her breastbone.

Goddess' breath.

"Theo, Rhydian, Adonis, Saryll, and Kassia were attacked by Mooncursed soldiers. Theo brought back a head. It's in a poor state now, but we can fetch it," she said.

Emperor Rexil's gaze settled upon Theo. "You were attacked by the Mooncursed?"

"Yes."

The emperor worked his jaw. "And you survived?"

"Barely, but we took their heads," Theo replied darkly.

Emperor Rexil's jaw clenched. "It is a terrible thing that most monsters roam these woods once more. What fortune that you managed to survive."

Theo stood, slamming his palms on the low dividing wall. "We all know you sent them. Let's not dance with words. We know what you offer and what you threaten." He pointedly looked at everyone in the room. "Our only choice is whether our destruction is slow and compliant, or if we fight like hells."

Aurienne's heart warmed.

"You have no business speaking here, blacksmith. Sit down before I make you," Prince Donovan snarled, shoving Princess Arissabett off his arm unkindly.

Theo pointed at the prince menacingly, the motion full of promise. "Watch your mouth. Much has changed since we last spoke."

The prince scowled angrily, but Theo's glare rivaled the sun. He stepped forward to make his point, and the prince lifted his chin in challenge. Rhydian gripped his sword.

"Silence." The emperor's voice boomed through the room, full of an unknown power. "Accept the terms or fall beneath the might of the empire."

Aurienne knew the voices grew louder but they fell away as though she stood far, far away. She Saw a shadow of herself. Her own reflection watched her with eyes gouged out seeping liquid gold. Then her face split into three others, watching her with unblinking eyes.

The Goddess wanted her to See something.

Aurienne pushed her soul through the veil and reached across the continent for a vision. Her soul flew over the Warden's Watch Mountains and across the Terre Isthmus to the empire of Demorra. Desperate, she called for a vision—the nameless one's report fresh in her mind. She Saw nations fall. Wars waged and lost. Blood seeping into the ground.

Blood.

She followed the blood.

Trails of blood throughout the emperor's city all lead back to a temple. Niamh's temple. The name slithered into her mind as her soul flew toward the source of the pain and death. A vision came to her. The emperor, surrounded by maidens bound in rings of light, kneeled at the foot of the goddess. To her supplicants, she was beautiful, divine, merciful. Aurienne Saw through the mask. Niamh devoured the blood poured upon her altars. Human sacrifices.

The seer's eyes snapped open. "Do you not sacrifice people to your goddess?"

Her words silenced the room.

Emperor Rexil visibly flinched. Her words surprised and alarmed him. At his reactions, people began to whisper to one another.

"How did you..." he trailed off.

It was Aurienne's turn to smile. "I Saw *her*."

He froze.

"Our goddess is powerful and hungry god," he finally replied. "You could see her sacrifices, but the only ones who give blood are the faithful."

"Until you ran out of fodder."

His lip twitched and the polished mask slipped. She pressed on. If she could get him to admit his cruelty, she might sway the others.

Words slipped into her mind. "I know your secret."

The emperor's gaze darkened. "Take my offer or suffer the consequences. I won't ask again."

A feeling of dread flooded Aurienne. She could nearly See their fate, hazy but coming into focus. No one would agree to stand against the emperor. They would accept bondage over war. It would cost everyone their lives. This was the end. They were going to die.

Until...

The winds changed. Aurienne looked up. Footsteps approached —the same from her visions. No one else looked to the door. No one else could hear it but Aurienne.

Step.

Step.

Step.

Each step was measured and purposeful, full of intent. Each step brought the figure closer. Consistent as a heartbeat. It came, bringing with it a wraith of death.

Step.

Step.

Step.

Boots striking the floor. Coming down the hall. Aurienne stared at the door, frozen and unable to move. Her blood spiked with terror. Shivers ran down her spine.

Step.

Step.

Step.

Someone terrible came. Powerful. Deadly. Ancient. Eternal.

Someone that even the gods would not look upon directly. Even the stars fled the dusky sky in the presence of this otherworldly being.

Aurienne's eyes widened. Her breath caught.

Grimfall.

The doors to the summit room opened with a thunderous bang. The wooden doors, twice as tall as the giant Allesan, shuddered and wobbled on the hinges. Opening with enough force that the torches sputtered and threatened to go out. Everyone froze and gazed upon the face of death. It might have been Aurienne's imagination, but a gentle fog crawled across the floor.

Not a single sound echoed in that room. No one even breathed. Several throats swallowed, and the leather grips of swords creaked.

A wraith entered the room, gliding like an apparition, cloak swirling in the fog. An enormous sword, shining like starlight even inside of the scabbard, rested on the figure's back. The figure passed by one of the emperor's priestesses. The back of the figure's hand brushed against the priestess's hand causing the priestess to blink and shake her head.

The figure claimed a place in the center of the room and pushed back her cloak. Aurienne gasped aloud.

An elf.

A living elf stood just paces away. An elf from the ancient stories from before the Shadow War a thousand years ago. The elf's leathers were scratched and marred from conflict. She moved without a sound, but her presence roared. Words whispered through Aurienne's mind.

> *Stars light in cursed blade.*
> *Souls of beasts and monsters weighed.*
> *Evil hides and darkness dies.*
> *Shadows rise as grim falls.*
> *Death to one, death to all.*

The elf's skin was ashy gray, as if all the color had been siphoned from her, and it was patterned with predatory camouflage. Her ears were pointed, and a tattooed gold line ran down the center of her face. Sharp canine teeth gave the elf a feline appearance, and platinum-colored hair hung past her hips, swaying as she walked. Her limbs were long and willowy, ready for battle.

Her too-large eyes flicked from person to person, pausing before moving on. Judging them. Finding them worthy or wanting. When she spoke, a crushing weight washed over the mortals.

"Now *this* is my kind of party," Grimfall said darkly, without emotion.

The elf took a slow, circling lap around the room studying each person. No one moved. No one even turned their head. Few breathed.

"How could I refuse such a gathering?" the elf said. "A Goddess-touched seer, a moon seer, a witch, sorcerers, a vampire and his hunter, living stone, giants, forest wielders, a doomed queen, a ghost, bound priestesses, and...a Warbringer."

The elf's gaze lingered too long on Rhydian. He swallowed and paled. The first to move, he took a slow step back. *Even the Warbringer was afraid.* A terrible realization clicked in place inside Aurienne's mind. Her blood froze at the implications. The elf named off her friends and companions, her intended allies. But on the elf's tongue, they sounded like monsters.

This world makes monsters of us all. The words slipped into Aurienne's mind. They were foreign and ancient, and not her own. She wondered if she was losing her mind or her soul.

Grimfall inclined her head at the red fox. "May your dreams reach the stars, Etherian."

The fox twitched its tail and inclined its head at the elf.

Etherian? That sounds so familiar. Where have I heard that before?

The elf stopped before the emperor and looked him up and down. A dark grin revealed the tips of her pointed canines.

Emperor Rexil turned a painful shade of purple. For the first time, he stumbled over his words. "I extend the offer of peace to the elves."

The elf chuckled mirthlessly. "The elven armies have stood for thousands of years. Empires have risen and fallen, but none have lasted. Keep your promises and offers. The elven armies don't need them."

Elven armies?

Aurienne's blood chilled.

"They say elves could take the measure of a man by looking at them," Kassia whispered to Saryll and Miella.

The emperor swallowed. Aurienne looked from the emperor to the elf. What did he know?

The emperor took another approach. "The elves have sworn not to interfere in the matters of man."

The elf stilled in an unnatural, lifeless way. How did the emperor know anything about the elves? To everyone in the room, the elves were just another myth. Only in the past week had they learned from the vampire and hunter that the elves were once real, but no one had seen an elf in a millennium. At least, no one had seen an elf and lived to tell.

Grimfall's eyes narrowed. "The *elves* do not interfere. *I* am not so bound. My words and my actions are my own."

The emperor tensed.

The elf continued, "My blood-sworn duty is to rid the land of monsters. Beings that grow too powerful, too dark, too destructive. When they threaten the balance, I restore it. When a monster needs killing, I do it. As I have for a thousand years."

The elf's eyes bored into Rhydian before darting to the others. She cast a long look at Stellan and Marco. The vampire and hunter grew wary by the way both tensed every muscle. Recognition flashed across their faces, and they hardly breathed. How could they know her? It would have been...

They all fought in the Shadow War a thousand years ago.

They're all over a thousand years old.

The High Seer of Avyllon suddenly felt small. Insignificant. Powerless. There were forces at play here far beyond her understanding. The emperor making these demands *now* was not an accident. Ancient events returned to haunt this land as the gods and goddesses of old stood against new threats. The land was shaking off its slumber and preparing its people for a war they could not have won as humans. Magic would drown them all and turn them into monsters to protect itself.

This was why her visions of the war were shadowed. This was why she couldn't see past this summit, this war. Her human mind, even touched by the Goddess, could not comprehend the forces at play, and an ancient power beyond measure stood against her Goddess—one working with the emperor.

Chills prickled her skin.

"This doesn't concern you," Emperor Rexil snapped.

"There is a gathering of monsters and beasts here that says otherwise," Grimfall replied with her hunter's teeth on display.

"Hunt these monsters if you must," the emperor said. "Kill them all if you desire. But armies of humans are not your problem."

A thousand futures crashed into Aurienne's mind too quickly to grasp any. Too many futures. The room fell silent again. The elf glowered at the emperor. Aurienne Saw a scale, weighing their hearts with all life hanging in the balance.

The world rested on the edge of the elf's blade.

Swaying one way then the other.

If Grimfall stood with them against the emperor with them, they had a chance. Aurienne swallowed a sob. They had a chance. Theo brought the monsters together, which lured *her* here. Theo's actions brought Grimfall, the only force strong enough to withstand the might of an empire. If the elf turned on Teridar's monsters, they would all die. Aurienne had no idea what to say to bring the elf to their side.

Theo cleared his throat, and all eyes went to him. "They aren't armies of man."

"What?" the elf asked.

"What?" the emperor snapped.

Aurienne's heart slammed into her throat.

Theo swallowed. "You said the armies of man are not your business, but these aren't mortal armies. They're Mooncursed warriors, like those from the Shadow War. Curse-twisted wolves. Vicious and bloodthirsty and unstoppable. Twenty of them killed nearly five times that of our men before the sorcerer Mathis sacrificed himself and killed them. They're...not human. You could help us."

Mouths dropped.

Eyes widened.

The elf turned her heavy gaze to the emperor. She spoke slowly but firmly. Every word a trap laid for him. "An army of the Shadows?"

He opened his mouth but closed it.

"You brought back *the Shadows*?" she demanded, advancing on him with each word as her face twisted in fury.

The emperor's soldiers formed a wall shielding him. The branded priestesses gathered around him, and Emissary Seiko raised his hands in defense. The elf wasn't deterred.

"If you bring an army of Mooncursed beasts and Shadows here," the elf said, "they threaten the balance of life. I will stand against them."

Aurienne gasped.

Grimfall had decided.

With one sentence, the elf changed the fate of Teridar.

One spark.

"We refuse your demands," Aurienne declared.

"Your laws go against our values. We won't be victim to the whims of one man. The Free Peoples stand with Avyllon," Dharek said.

"We stand with Avyllon," Stone'ward said.

King Jaekob and King Cavendar stood. "We shall pay your

offering but give no men. If your army comes to *our* land, we will stand against it," King Jaekob said while King Cavendar nodded.

The rest of the room stood together, rejecting the emperor's demands.

Grimfall prowled forward. "You'll die for your crimes."

With that, the continent declared war on the empire. Monsters and gods stood with humans to fight for the future.

"That's disappointing," the emperor said.

One spark, and the room ignited.

A vision, only seconds ahead of time, slammed into Aurienne hard enough to knock her backwards. She caught herself against the low dividing wall. Strange purple shadows slipped out of the emperor's robes as his skin burned with runes carved into his body. He blasted the room with purple light. Phantom horns sprouted from his head as corrupted magic poured from his mouth—crashing into their allies.

"No!" Aurienne shouted a warning before she collapsed.

The emperor's gaze flickered to her as purple light flared in his hand. Aurienne froze, watching the purple light flare toward her. General Kane stepped in front of her moments before the light reached her. It slammed into him, arching his back hard enough his heels left the floor, shouting out as purple tendrils pierced his body. He fell.

"Kane!" Aurienne cried.

The emperor's eyes narrowed, and he raised his hands again. His purple light slammed into the starlight pouring from Grimfall's sword, forcing the emperor to take two steps backward. The warring beams of light were nearly solid, colliding again.

The emperor reached behind him.

Boom.

A shimmering Way split the air and out poured the Mooncursed and their titan-ore-armored wardens. Sweat poured down the emperor's face as he held the Way open and hurdled purple tendrils of power toward his foes.

Dozens of Mooncursed beasts with titanium claws and mutated bone ridges growled from the shadows of the shimmering portal—eyeing the summit with slitted golden eyes.

Theo slid in front of Aurienne, drawing a sword and standing over her. Aurienne touched her nose and mouth—finding golden soulblood mixing with crimson lifeblood. She'd pushed too hard.

"Are you okay?" Theo demanded, raising his blade.

Her head throbbed and heart fluttered weakly. She shook her head slowly as her strength drained. She wouldn't be able to help. Too many weeks of selling her soul for their salvation left her with nothing to give.

The Mooncursed charged through the Way.

Grimfall caught the first by the throat with her claws. A wet crunch erupted from its throat as she squeezed. It dangled in the air helplessly as she held it up. Then she slammed it into ground—cracking the stone floors. She plunged her sword into its heart, and it stilled. Her blade blurred as she descended upon the monsters.

Howls erupted in the room as steel clanged against metal claws.

Aurienne tried to push her soul through the veil to See anything that would help as more monsters poured through the Way. Blinding pain erupted in her skull, and she had to abandon the effort.

"Aurienne!" Theo shouted as she sagged again.

Mooncursed lunged toward the Avyllon delegation, and she covered her head with her arms. They were nearly upon her. It slammed into a golden shield and slipped off. The fox pushed up on its front legs on the pillar, and its fur now glowed with green and gold spirals. Its eyes shone from within with golden, runed light that swirled into the shield.

Sentinel Kolten slashed at a Mooncursed through the shield, face pale and hands shaking. Kassia scrambled to form protective circles of plants and salt inside the fox's shield. Saryll raced to Kane and checked his pulse. She shook her head as she crawled to Aurienne. Saryll stilled, seeing the golden liquid seep from Aurienne's eyes.

Saryll eyes were pleading. "How can I help?"

Aurienne shook her head.

There was nothing to be done.

The fighting raged on. A mountain of corpses piled up around the Grimfall as she cut them down with wide arcs of her starlight blade. The Wyndsel delegation huddled behind the People of Living Stone. Blood squelched on the floor as Stone'ward crushed the emperor's armored wardens between his fists. Ore'spike lanced Mooncursed wolves with gleaming metal spikes. Even impaled—they fought and clawed until the vampires launched at the Mooncursed, ripping them to pieces and devouring their blood.

The Rodarri delegation cowered behind the Free Peoples. Dharek lifted his hands to call vines crashing through the windows. A warden lunged for Thaen, but Dharek's vine speared him through the exposed throat.

Rianne screamed as a Mooncursed prowled forward.

Thaen lifted his arms.

"Thaen, no!" Dharek shouted.

Thaen too called the vines. A thorned vine wrapped around the Mooncursed's throat and strangled it. It writhed and clawed at its neck, eyes bulging and mouth foaming. Bark sprouted across the younger man's arms.

The Mooncursed was just a poor person or animal who'd been corrupted and now paid the price. It didn't have a choice. Goddess— it was awful.

But where was Rhydian?

Aurienne's lidded gaze searched for him, finding his back pressed against the wall. His eyes burned red, and knuckles grew white. His eyes were locked onto Rianne, as if waiting for anything to get too close. Aurienne could See the crimson vines of his curse wrapping around his heart, the vision fading with her strength.

Rianne cried out. Rosalindt was pushing herself underneath Rianne's skin. Settling inside, Rianne's eyes glowed silver as her fingers extended into claws. She raked at a Mooncursed, and its skin hissed at her ghastly touch.

Theo kneeled beside Saryll at Aurienne's side. "Aurienne? What do we do?"

"Grimfall," she choked, raising a quivering hand. "Help her."

Theo dashed out of the golden shield to stand at the elf's side. She hacked and slashed at the never-ending horde. She made it look easy, but there were so many. Theo kicked the bodies out of her way, cutting down those who tried to circle behind her.

Snarling, Rhydian shoved off the wall and joined Theo. He drew his blade. Aurienne distantly heard Rhydian say, "I'll down them, and you deal the killing blow."

Theo nodded and finished all those who Rhydian felled.

Rhydian was trusting Theo with his life, his soul. Goddess— Rhydian was playing with fire. If Theo missed one, Rhydian would go mad.

Stellan dodged the wardens and gripped one of the Demorran priestesses by her hair. She squirmed and screamed, the glowing brand in her forehead flaring. He yanked her head back and struck. His fangs sank into her throat, tearing flesh. He drank as blood spurted out. The other priestesses screamed as they were surrounded by the grinning vampires.

The priestesses struggled under Stellan and Julietta's grasps. Julietta laughed and ripped the head off the one in her embrace. A warden's arm flew across the room. Stellan clawed into a Mooncursed beast's chest and ripped out its still-beating heart. Stellan bit into the heart, savoring the blood dripping down his chin. The vampires were worse than the Mooncursed.

Stronger.

More bloodthirsty.

And they enjoyed this.

Aurienne paled, and Theo cast dark glances toward the vampires. If they ever broke their oath...

"Help Grimfall," Aurienne croaked to the rest.

Teridar's monsters advanced, following Theo to aid the elf. No longer holding back the horde alone, Grimfall lifted her sword, the light beam coming down toward the emperor. The emperor raised his hands to deflect with his purple light. He was sweating as the starlight bore down on him. Dying Mooncursed howled as wardens were pressed back by blade and claw and magic.

Aurienne dragged herself to standing, leaning on Saryll. She stared down the emperor as he glared back at her. The Way started to flicker as the emperor's strength waned. The Grimfall pressed forward, starlight slashing through his magic.

Emperor Rexil took slow steps backward and pointed to Aurienne. "This isn't over."

"No," Aurienne said quietly.

Emperor Rexil snarled furiously. "I'll bring down the might of my armies upon you. You thought the Mooncursed were terrible? They're nothing. I have creatures of nightmares. I'll crush this continent and grind your bones to dust."

"I won't allow it," Aurienne said quietly, feeling an otherworldly presence stirring in her bones.

The Goddess flooded strength into her waning limbs.

"You made a mistake," he pointed at Grimfall.

The air grew cold around the elf's words as she slashed at him with starlight. "You would not be the first to try to kill me. There is nowhere you can hide from me, and I have all the time in the world to find you."

The Emperor glanced between Aurienne and the elf. "Death comes for you all."

The Demorra delegation backed into the Way and were gone.

The elf growled, the sound rumbling in her chest with ferocity and promise.

With a few words and blood spilled, so began the war of otherworldly and cursed creatures, of ancient and angry powers refusing to surrender to the demands of new gods. So began the Darkling War.

AFTERMATH
CHAPTER FORTY-SIX

"What if I choose wrong?"
"You'll spend your whole life regretting it."

— *JOURNAL OF MIELLA ROTHBAIN, 1152 N.T.C.*

1152 N.T.C. The namesake city of Avyllon.

Dawn followed the night Teridar declared war on Demorra. Scorch marks marred the floors where the Way had opened, a constant reminder of their decision. The weight of what they had done lingered in the smoke and fog, air tingling with magic and fate. Aurienne's heart throbbed as she knelt beside General Kane's body. A sentinel covered him with a sheet. Other sentinels carried the bodies—human and monster—from the summit room. It'd happened so fast.

She glanced around for the fox, but it was already gone.

King Jaekob approached. "We'll return to Wyndsel in the morning. There is much to be done." He avoided Aurienne's gaze as the Wyndsel delegation left.

The Rodarri delegation was just behind them. "Rhydian will stay here as our emissary. We leave now."

The ghost Rosalindt, apparently invisible to all but Aurienne, winked and vanished.

More quietly, King Cavendar said, "Let's hope you haven't doomed us all with your war."

"You don't want me to return with you?" Rhydian asked.

"We will call for you. Come along, Rianne. There's no time for reunions," the king said. "Now. Jordyn will be missing you."

Rianne hesitated, but then followed the king out of the room with a final look over her shoulder. She pressed her fingers against her lips in a sad kiss for Rhydian. Tears dripped down her cheeks, and she forced herself to look away. She limped behind the king, barely able to put weight on one leg. Rhydian bit down on a shout, the sound gurgling in his throat, and he punched a wall. He stormed out of the room and down the hallway opposite the Rodarri guests.

Grimfall's gaze tracked Rhydian like a mountain lion watching a rabbit frolic in a field.

"Nesryn." The name came to Aurienne as if she already knew it.

The elf, Nesryn, the Grimfall, considered her. "Aurienne Celestina Azarrah. Third High Seer of Avyllon. Goddess-touched."

"Thank you for what you did," Aurienne said.

"Don't thank me," Nesryn replied. "What comes for you is darker than you can imagine. Even you cannot know the horrors of war."

Aurienne's soul dragged her consciousness into that magical place in her mind and through the veil. A vision descended on her like a hammer. Nesryn fought side by side with their armies. She stood in a river of blood, holding back the waves of monsters. The elf just needed a reason to stay. A golden braided cord wrapped around her heart and led her away. Aurienne's mind followed the cord. It stretched into the distance, to Rhydian.

In the vision, Nesryn and Rhydian stood in a bloody clearing with swords drawn. Her starlight sword clashed against his blood-soaked blade. Steel rang. The swords shattered, and the pair locked into death's embrace. They each lifted a dagger and plunged it into the other's back.

Aurienne blinked.

Nesryn and Rhydian's fates were linked.

"I saw you coming here before you arrived." Aurienne's brows pulled together. "I heard your footsteps; I heard a prophecy you would come—the Grimfall legend. I didn't know it was you, but Fate has been warning me for weeks. I didn't know if you would help us."

"And do I?" A hint of a smile danced at the elf's lips.

"I Saw the types of beings that will fight in this war. They're your business. Just like the Mooncursed and other creatures from Demorra."

Nesryn chuckled. "Beings?"

Aurienne pursed her lips.

"Monsters," the elf said. "I would know. I am one."

Aurienne looked around the room full of so-called monsters. She Saw their struggles. She Saw their bravery. Her heart ached for them. "What they want to be does not capture their hearts."

The elf smiled without any amusement. "You have not seen their hearts as I have."

Aurienne swallowed. "We need them all the same."

Nesryn rolled out her shoulders. "You're taking a great risk, asking monsters to fight for you. The vampires, and the others."

"The Darkling War will be the bloodiest clash that the world has seen. That I know for sure. And we need them. Even him." Aurienne looked toward the doorway Rhydian had stormed out of."

"Warbringer?" Nesryn hissed.

"I have seen Rhydian fighting in this war. He is needed. Do not kill him until you absolutely must."

"I'll do what I have to."

The elf strode out of the doorway, hunting the Warbringer.

Having bid goodbye to their new allies, Aurienne returned to the Avyllon seating box. She resisted the urge to rub her temples. Down to the marrow of her bones and the essence of her soul, she was weary. There was still too much to do. Now they must fight a war.

"Did we do it?" Theo asked.

Aurienne smiled tiredly. "Yes. We have our chance. You did it. I have one more thing to ask of you."

"Anything."

Saryll approached, hands folded before her. "High Seer...Aurienne...what now?"

"Return to the temple," Aurienne said. "We need all our seers doing readings and seeking visions. We need them scrying and rolling bone dice. And we must understand the events of the Shadow War. Please let them know. Call in people from the towns and villages for a public audience. We must tell them what comes."

"I'll write to my grandmother to warn the witches. Perhaps they can help. I thought I might stay here if that's alright?" Kassia asked.

The witch's glance darted to Saryll. The moon seer, as Nesryn had called her. Aurienne would have to ask the Goddess what that meant. Kassia looked back to Aurienne, smitten. Her expression warmed the seer's heart.

Aurienne squeezed Kassia's shoulder. "We would be honored if you stayed."

Adonis packed up his books and stood. "I'm taking my exam in a few weeks for my guild membership. I can't bear the thought of studying under anyone else, and I'm ready. Will you do a reading for me for my sorcerer's certificate?"

Aurienne nodded slowly, watching her brother leave.

Miella fidgeted in her seat. Sympathy and guilt washed over Aurienne even as dark visions haunted her and poisoned her heart.

"You did wonderfully," the seer said as gently as she could.

Miella's eyes widened. "Really?"

"Yes."

"I felt like I was the least important person here. I can't fight a war. I'm no help to anyone." Her eyes slipped to the floor.

"You are one of the *most* important people here."

"Because of my blood."

"Yes," Aurienne said. "You are the vampire's kin. If vampire loves anything, it's family. You ground him. You are the promise of what they could have. The vampires' love for you is what will keep them in this war and keep them from becoming animals again. He means his oath. You don't realize how important it is. And you also have to keep the hunter at bay."

"Why will the hunter listen to me?"

"You are the promise of what Marco and Stellan are both fighting for. The survival of their kind and humanity. Their family died at the hands of the vampires and Shadows all those years ago. You're a reminder of all that they lost."

"I'm all that one has left, and I'm everything the other lost?"

"It is a heavy burden you carry." Aurienne tried to smile, tried not to hate Miella for the vision she'd seen. "Saryll told me you have a great destiny. You just have to capture it. Your blood ultimately won't be what defines you."

"I don't even know what that destiny is."

"You're going to have to choose one day. That choice is going to determine the course of the rest of your life."

Miella's throat bobbed. "What if I choose wrong?"

"You'll spend your whole life regretting it."

Aurienne returned to Theo. His smile was tired and dim, but the light she'd come to rely on was still underneath the pain.

"We did it," he said. "We have a chance to overcome this threat—to overcome fate."

Aurienne took a steadying breath for what she was about to do next. "We just have to survive a war of monsters without becoming them ourselves."

GRIMFALL

CHAPTER FORTY-SEVEN

I realize now you didn't deserve to be saved.

— JOURNAL OF NESRYN ASHWILDES, 3 B.N.T.C.

1152 N.T.C. The namesake city of Avyllon.

Chaos thrived on war, and war bred new chaos. During the summit, Rhydian waited quietly at the edge of the fray unfolding before his eyes. Anger, hate, and fear filled the room like smoke. His blood roared at the conflict, the pain, the death.

He stormed through the empty palace halls, fighting the urge to tear it down. Watching Rianne limp away ignited rage inside him. What happened to her? Rhydian focused on Rianne. Gentle, kind Rianne. He pictured her face in his mind, smiling at him like she'd done so many times before. Her gentle touch on his arm, steadying him when his blood rushed like now. He could no longer leave her in the hands of that monster, King Cavendar. He had to find a way to free her before it was too late.

What would Rianne tell him?

"You are not your curse."

He could almost hear her delicate voice, like the soft strums of a harp. He said it over and over in his mind, feeling his heart slow as the red fog receded from the edges of his vision. This was a dangerous place to be for one who craved death.

Movement caught Rhydian's eye. A swish of a cloak approached. Footsteps. The Warbringer tried not to stare but could not control his gaze. It was as though he was looking at a storybook picture come to life. Grimfall's skin was ashy, like a wraith or a shadow that had stepped into the light, patterned with subtle stripes and dots of camouflage. Everything about her looked as though the color was drained away. Her pointed ears peeked out from behind her ashy-white hair. A tattooed gold line ran down the center of her face, looking like summer-spun gold. Her storm gray eyes were larger than a human's, and her teeth sharper. She was a creature from another world.

Feeling like cornered prey, Rhydian's breath caught in his throat, and his lungs pressed against the inside of his chest, threatening to crush his heart. His skin prickled with gooseflesh. He nearly stepped to the side, but her eyes froze him in place. The elf headed right toward him, walking with a purpose that seemed out of place on her willowy frame. She wore warrior's leathers of muted browns and greens, and knives were tucked into the leather at her hip, forearms, and ankles. Her dark cloak hung about her sinewy shoulders. The sword on her back gleamed with starlight, peeking out from the scabbard.

As she strode up, she watched him with an expressionless mask. Her eyes seemed to darken as she drew nearer. Those glimmering, iridescent, spectral eyes were full of stilled fury that looked like a liquid mirror—fury directed at him. Rhydian suppressed a shudder deep in the marrow of his bones. The hairs on the back of his neck prickled, warning him of the danger that followed her like a shadow. He pulled his hands out of his pockets and forced himself to breathe.

He averted his gaze for several moments, gathering his resolve before peering up cautiously.

Time slowed, and a dreamy hazy descended.

The elf stopped beside Rhydian's arm. She leaned in and inhaled deeply and inhaled again. She licked the points of her sharpened teeth.

"Warbringer," she said dryly.

Time snapped back into place as a spike of fear and shock pierced Rhydian to the core. How could she know?

"Grimfall?" he whispered, not even meaning to.

"I'm called Nesryn."

He swallowed. "Rhy-Rhyd-Rhydian."

She ignored him. "A Warbringer and nearly fallen to his curse already. What has this world done to deserve another one of you?"

"Another...one...of..." he stammered.

She shook her head as her dimly rose-colored lips curled into a snarl. She looked him up and down and turned to leave.

"I'm no Warbringer," he sputtered.

Nesryn looked at him impatiently and lifted a single pointed brow. She blinked as if it was painful how stupid she thought that he was.

"I—" He wiped his palm on his leg. "I'm no Warbringer, yet. The curse remains dormant."

With cool indifference, Nesryn watched him squirm with the barest flash of a smile.

"How did you know my curse is close to waking?" he said.

He tried to take a step after her, but his heart pounded so hard his legs turned to jelly. His voice was small in his mouth.

She was terrifying. And far too interested in him.

"I can smell it on you," Nesryn said pointedly.

Rhydian's mouth dropped open, and he could not think of anything to say.

"The last one of you that fell to the madness of the curse caused destruction lasting a thousand years. I should kill you now before it takes you." Her voice waivered with a low growl in the back of her throat.

Rhydian forced his mouth closed and took a breath to steady himself. "I'm no Warbringer, yet. I'm fighting the curse."

She chuckled darkly as if finding his resistance amusing. "You? You think you can resist what so many before you have failed to do? What better men have failed to do?"

Rhydian nodded hesitantly.

"The curse is thick on you. Even now, it seeps into your bones and soul. There's not much time before the curse fully consumes you," she said, studying him as though she could see the curse taking root.

Maybe she could.

Rhydian looked to the floor. He knew he was close to losing control. He could feel it in his blood. Every time the red fog surfaced, he knew how close he was to giving in. If this war came, he knew that he'd unleash his curse. Maybe the elf knew a way to help him. If he could defeat the curse, he could return to Rianne with no fear of hurting her.

"There's no way to stop it?" Rhydian asked.

Nesryn pursed her lips. She tilted her head as if considering him carefully. She lifted an ashy brow. "There is. You must avoid all bloodshed and violence for the remainder of your life."

He gaped.

She smiled cruelly. "But I can see it in you. You could no more do that than you could stop breathing. The curse will be upon you all too soon."

Anger rose in his chest. She was determined to doom him and yet offered him no help. She didn't believe he was able. She wouldn't even let him try. He refused to succumb to this fate. People were counting on him to beat it.

"I won't give in," he said.

She paused, and her ethereal eyes studied his features. He could nearly feel the weight of her gaze upon him, threatening to crush him, and he tried to straighten his shoulders to meet it despite the physical chill it produced.

The spite fell away from her voice. "You think it's a choice?"

"If any of my ancestors knew what the curse really was, they never said. All we know is that if we kill anyone, even by accident, we start to go mad. We leave and never come back. I just...have to avoid killing."

"You really know nothing about your own curse?"

He shook his head.

"Being around violence, no matter how small, feeling deep-seated rage, or seeing terrible things will awaken the curse," she said. "Slowly at first. Once it begins, it's impossible to fight. The temptation toward violence will grow and grow until you cannot fight it anymore. Your mind will soon snap. You feel it already, don't you? The draw? That means it's already too late. You will kill, and once you do, the red veil will remain forever. Violence and death will be all you know. You'll kill and kill and kill. It will be as natural as breathing."

"How close is it?"

Nesryn's expression almost looked sad. Maybe it was pity? "You see the red veil?"

He nodded.

"Then it is nearly upon you," she said. "You've seen violence that...stirred it. Any day now, the red veil will descend, and you'll finally take a life, lose yourself, and go mad. You'll go on a killing spree until the curse is well and truly unleashed. You can't stop it. Every time it comes for you, it will be harder to fight."

Rhydian paled. He thought he might be sick. Everything he fought against was for nothing. He truly was doomed. His life with Rianne shattered before his eyes. *He was nothing more than his curse.* The Warbringer leaned against the wall, legs unable to bear his own weight.

She fingered the knives at her hip. "Becoming a true Warbringer does not often occur. A *true* Warbringer's blood sings for violence and death and can cause incomparable destruction. They are fearsome warriors, nearly undefeatable. They gain supernatural powers from the killing. Legends say the very ground shakes, and the skies explode with lightning when they go berserking. They are impossibly fast and wicked strong. Most of your ancestors went mad or died before they gained these powers. It has been a long time since they unleashed the might of the Warbringer curse. And the curse itself isn't what kills you. It's forgetting to eat or foolishness in battle or being hunted down and killed."

He frowned. He'd never heard any of this, but then none of his ancestors stayed around long enough to share much. Most ran off to kill and die before their children were grown, leaving them to deal with the curse on their own.

"I'm immortal?"

Nesryn's mirrored eyes flashed, and Rhydian thought that the edges might have turned black in sharp contrast to her ashy skin and the golden tattoo halving her face. The elf spit on the floor.

"I forget how utterly stupid you humans are. This is why so many of our kind do not believe you're worth saving." she snarled. "As long as there's war and you're fighting it, you won't die. Your curse could allow you to live many lifetimes. As soon as you stop fighting, you start to age. But let me be crystal clear. Once the madness takes you, you're not yourself anymore. It's a different kind of death. You can be cut down in battle the same as any man. I'm telling you that you will go mad—a pale, distorted reflection of yourself—and you don't hear it. You just want the power."

Nesryn shook her head and shrugged her shoulders as if washing the inferior taint from her clothing. She began to walk away. Rhydian took several quick steps and stopped right in front of her, blocking her path. She growled.

"I don't want the power. Is there a cure?"

She rolled her eyes cruelly, and he could feel exasperation rolling off her in waves. "What about you is worth saving? You know nothing."

"My father died when I was just a child. And his father, and his. None of my kin has survived long enough to pass the stories down if they ever knew them. I've never had the chance to learn. You don't even know me. I didn't come here for war. All that this curse offers, I don't want it," he said, growing quieter with each word.

Her eyes flicked away from him, signaling that she had, for the moment, lost interest in him. Rhydian glared at her. She had an infuriating ability to turn all his words back upon him. Her tongue was as sharp as a sword, and her eyes were full of icy daggers. Worse than any of that, she had written him off as just another doomed victim of a millennia-old curse. He knew he was more than that.

"Elves can take the measure of a man by looking into his eyes," he said. "You can see his soul, right?"

Nesryn paused before finally nodding slowly. She inclined her head at him thoughtfully with eyes full of renewed interest. The expression on her face would have resembled a grin if her teeth didn't make it look like such a snarl.

"Look into my eyes, and you tell me if I'm weak," he said.

"You may not like what I see," she said.

Without waiting for his response, she stepped forward until their faces were nearly touching. The gold line on her ashy face drew him in until his gaze came to rest upon hers. He stared into her otherworldly mirrored eyes.

The floor dropped out from under him, and then he was falling. It was like being under cool water or having the wind driven from your chest by a battering ram. She studied him closely for long moments that stretched into eternity. He did not know what she saw but glimpsed what lay beyond her defenses. She broke the gaze and took a slight step back.

"I do not see weakness in you, Warbringer. I just see pain. Heartbreak. Desperation. Anger. All the things that are going to lead to your demise," she said.

Each word tore at Rhydian's chest like the claws of a shadow beast.

Feeling like his soul had been laid bare, he snapped back at her in anger. "Do you know what I see in you? Nothing. You've lived hundreds of years, but you have no purpose in life."

Her face darkened again, and the corners of her lips rose into another snarl. Her nimble fingers closed upon the hilt of her starlight sword.

"You presume much," she said coldly. "And you're wrong."

"Maybe I'm not as stupid or weak as you thought," he said.

"You are whatever I say you are." She backed him up. "And I say you are nothing. Your life is fleeting and over before it even begins. Your curse will take you, body and mind, Warbringer. You will hunt and maim and kill everyone you love until you die, crazed and alone. You will die a slow, lonely, cold death, and you won't even remember your own name. With any luck, your miserable line will end with you, and the world will never see another Warbringer."

His hold on his temper wavered. The floodgates inside his chest groaned under the pressure of the hot fury bubbling up his throat. The edges of his vision turned red, and his skin grew damp.

All emotion left Nesryn's voice as she spoke next. "Maybe you're just some unwanted nobody coming from a line of absent fathers and murderers who deserved to be cursed into oblivion. The only surprise here is that your pathetic bloodline lasted so long. Everyone thought your miserable lineage would have died out by now, but between the whoring and raping, somehow, it's limped on."

The truth of her words was a dagger in his gut.

"Take. That. Back," Rhydian snarled between his teeth. His control on that terrible temper loosened like threads on unraveling fabric.

Nesryn gripped his arm with more strength than he believed possible and marched him out of the hallway and into a small room. He tried to wrench his arm away, but her grip was like hammered iron. She shoved him inside.

He turned, stopping just in front of her. "Why did you do that?"

"If you're going to lose control, it won't be around all those people. You want to lose your temper? You want to kill? You want to finally free that curse of yours?" she said.

"Maybe."

"Then take your best shot. I'm right here, Warbringer." Nesryn drew her sword.

The white blade glittered with a thousand stars and nearly blinded Rhydian. At the sight of that legendary blade and the sound of the whirring of steel, rage like pure white fire boiled from his eyes. He could almost taste blood in his mouth. He was so angry. A wall of red descended over his eyes, and his blood pounded in his ears.

"Ask me what happened to the Warbringers," she snarled. "Ask me what happened to your family."

Red. Everything was red. The walls were red. The floor was red. The elf was red. Her sword was red. The Warbringer would paint the room with her blood.

"What kills the Warbringers?" he hissed.

"I do." She bared her fangs.

Murderer.

Rhydian roared and drew his own sword.

"Show me what a Warbringer is capable of. Show me war," she said between her teeth.

The red fog consumed everything around him. Rhydian's mind started slipping away as he prepared to attack an immortal monster hunter. Her cool eyes studied him intently, and she brandished her sword easily. *She waited.*

A cool realization pierced Rhydian's fiery anger. She was goading him, waiting to see whether he had control or not. This was a test that he was failing.

Oh gods, Rianne.

Rhydian took several steps back and screwed his eyes shut. His sword clanged against the floor as it slipped from his hand. He leaned against the wall and sank to the floor. His knees pulled in tightly toward his chest. He sucked in deep breaths as sweat dripped down his face.

"I won't succumb. I won't be weak like the rest of them. I'll control this," Rhydian said.

No one spoke for long moments. Rhydian was breathing hard, unable to catch his breath on the verge of panicking.

"I'm not sure you can hold back this curse. No one has," Nesryn said quietly.

"I'll be strong enough," Rhydian said.

Nesryn sheathed her starlight sword, and the room darkened.

"You won't be," she said quietly. She looked away, and a cold, metallic edge entered her voice. "This world makes monsters of us all."

"You're wrong," he said.

"You say you are not weak? Prove it, Warbringer. And when you fail, I'll be there to do what must be done," she said bitterly.

Nesryn left Rhydian alone on the floor with a sweep of her cloak. Sweat poured down Rhydian's face as he pulled himself back together. His chest shook with the effort of regaining control.

"I am not my curse," he whispered.

Several angry tears rolled down his face, and he wiped them away with the back of his hand. He refused to be a creature of chaos.

GILDED CAGE
CHAPTER FORTY-EIGHT

— *THE TALE OF THE BLOODROSE.*

1152 N.T.C. The namesake city of Avyllon.

Palms pressing against her temples, Rianne whimpered at the ceaseless shrieking in her mind. Her fingers itched for a blade to drive into King Cavendar's heart—or rather, Rosalindt's fingers did. Rianne glared at her reflection, seeing Rosalindt staring back at her instead. The ghost slithered through her veins.

"Get out!" Rianne's pale fist cracked the mirror.

"The kings, they will all die." Rosalindt's voice trailed through the chambers.

Rianne gripped the vanity, staring into the depths of the mirror. "I have to get to Rhydian. He will help us escape. Can you help me?"

Inside the cracked shards of the mirror, Rosalindt pursed her lips. "It all ends in blood."

"Help me. I know you've been trying to help me. I'm weak and can't get past the guards alone. Please."

The ghost surveyed her, lips curled back and eyes wild. She floated inside the mirror, tracing the cracks with boney fingertips.

Rianne's voice trembled. "Please help me. I want to live."

A silver tear slipped down Rosalindt's face. Her contorted expression softened. She reached through the mirror and brushed a single lock of Rianne's hair from her face, and it faded to platinum. The icy touch stung Rianne's cheek.

Rosalindt pressed against the inside of Rianne's skin. Rianne's spine arched as cold, spectral fingers clawed out of her body. Rosalindt tore from Rianne, floating silently. The ghost's head turned sharply toward the door, and she flew through the wall.

Rianne blinked. Cries and shouts rose from outside her door. Flinging open the doors, she lifted the front of her ball gown and darted down the hall toward the summit room. She glanced over her shoulder to see all three Rodarri guards batting at the air and shouting as their skin bled. Rosalindt circled them, scratching and slicing at any exposed flesh.

Quietly, Rianne slipped through the halls, peeking her head into each room. The living statues were grinding up bricks under their molars, dust sputtering from their mouths. She crept forward, searching for Rhydian. Empty room. Empty room. Staff stripping the bedsheets. Wounded Avyllon soldiers gathering with healers.

Terror prickled her heart. She'd be found any minute. But she had to get to Rhydian. He'd save her and the others. She just had to get him a message.

Rhydian, please be close.

She made it back to the summit room where maids scrubbed at blood and scorch marks from the emperor's Way. Men moved the corpses of humans and nightmarish beasts. Blood thickened between the stones. Matted hair and fur sat in clotted puddles. The fight had been quick but brutal. She shuddered, chills racing across her arms. She rubbed them, trying to coax warmth into her chilled flesh.

Where was Rhydian?

Continuing, she froze, hearing the ringing of steel on steel. She'd been around the practice arenas enough to recognize the sound, and to know when it was in earnest. The fight quieted.

Heart in her throat, she peered into the room. Rhydian leaned against the wall with his head bowed against his knees. His body shuddered.

She hesitated.

Her Warbringer was steady, tough, resolute. He'd always carried the weight of his curse, of everything. But right now, he was broken.

Her heart ached. She couldn't put the weight of her troubles on him. Standing frozen in the doorway, she warred against her conscience. But if he needed to be brought back, if he needed her, then she had to help.

She took a step forward.

A firm, gloved hand clamped down around her mouth. Then she was dragged backward fast enough she nearly lost her slippers. She squirmed and tried to call to Rhydian, but her voice was too muffled.

"Going to your Warbringer for help?" the Rodarri guard hissed in her ear.

She wiggled, but the guard dragged her back to the chambers where the other three waited. The guard continued toward the stairwell where the rest of the Rodarri travelers were departing. No one said a word at her rough escort. Reaching King Cavendar, the guard removed his hand from her mouth, and she coughed and choked for air.

"Escaping again?" His oily breath was hot on her face. "You'll regret that." He gestured to the carriages outside.

The guards hauled her to the grand carriage and pushed her in. Sobbing, Rianne righted herself and climbed onto the seat. Her arms were bruised, but more than anything her heart hurt. She'd nearly been free, and now there was nothing left she could do. They'd declared war, and the king would order ascensions. She swallowed a sob and bit her fist.

Rianne had stopped crying when the king and queen entered the carriage. The queen worked her needlepoint, embroidering a red rose, refusing to look at Rianne. The king glared at her as the carriage started moving.

Rianne brushed her fingers against the window, watching Avyllon shrink to nothing—her last chance at salvation. Rosalindt floated into the carriage, a white wraith, looking out the opposite window. The king didn't move, didn't react. He couldn't see her. Tears slipped down Rianne's face as she wondered whether she was losing her mind. She'd tried everything to escape a fate she never wanted, but it wouldn't let her go.

She'd been born to die, and nothing would keep her from that bloody ravine full of angry ghosts.

THE SWORD OF SOULS
CHAPTER FORTY-NINE

The Avyllon crown sat upon the lost king's head.
The Sword of Souls answered and struck the darkness dead.

— *FIRST HIGH SEER KHIANYA ARRALYN,*
PROPHETIC VISION RECORDED IN THE YEAR 1105
N.T.C.

1152 N.T.C. The namesake city of Avyllon.

Heart aching, Aurienne led Theo through abandoned palace halls toward the royal armory. With a brass key, she unlocked the thick wooden doors carved with golden griffins. Tables and glass cases held every weapon imaginable, and plaques detailed their history. More weapons rested on shelves scaling up to tall, painted ceilings.

Theo's jaw dropped. "All this has been here the whole time? Forgotten?"

Waiting.

She said, "Since King Elemere Aradey died fifty years ago, the palace has been unoccupied. The High Seers reside in the temple, but I had the palace opened for the summit." She hesitated. "And because I made a promise to the people of Avyllon."

"This is amazing." His eyes brightened.

"This isn't what I wanted to show you. This way."

She led Theo down a connecting hallway to tall steel door with a colossal lock. She slid the key into the keyhole and spun the mechanism in a complex series of rotations. The door clicked open, and they entered.

This room was smaller but ornately decorated. A complex configuration of small light holes and mirrors made the room shine like daylight, even through the thick stone walls. Ornamental swords and suits of armor decorated the perimeter of the room.

A large sword waited on a stone pillar atop a raised dais. The sword was black as a moonless night, absorbing the nearby light. A black scabbard leaned against the pillar.

"Kings and queens of Avyllon called this the Sword of Souls," she said. "Legends say that this sword was forged with magic from the blood of a fallen star in the fires of hell and cooled in the icy hidden springs at the summit of a broken mountain."

He chuckled. "That must have been a feat to get to all those places while forging a sword."

"The best we can tell is that it was forged in the crater of an active volcano with the hot molten metal of a fallen star." She smiled. "If it was in the mountains, there may have been natural, pure streams running right by. We don't know who made it, but the forger must have been a master craftsman who likely studied with elves, maybe even giants."

"I kind of like how the stories put it better," he said.

"The sword's creator had magic." She gripped her skirts, hating what she must do.

"How do you know?"

"The sword illuminates the blood of a king."

"You mean it glows when a descendant of a king touches it?"

Not just any king.

"The king for whom it was made," she said. "Atheodoren Avyla Aradey, the first king of Avyllon in the first year. The king's own blood was used in the final stages of the sword's creation, binding it to him and his bloodline. Should anyone not of the blood take up the sword, it is just another hunk of metal, if a strong one. For one with the king's blood, it becomes a powerful weapon that unravels magic and kills monsters."

Aurienne drew Theo into her arms. "What I asked of you was not fair. I asked you to do the impossible, and you did. Thank you."

She knew in her heart that she had already asked too much, and she was about to ask for much, much more. She'd Seen his heart before, but now she *knew* it. He was true, stalwart, unshakeable—surprising and full of life but reliable and unmovable like a mountain. He cared too deeply and tried so hard. He had endured hell for *her*, lost pieces of his soul for *her*.

Now she'd ask him for the rest.

Theo leaned down and kissed her. He tasted like sunlight behind tree leaves—soft eucalyptus and cedarwood. His warm presence felt like sunrises. With an arm forged of steel, he held her. He stood with roots deeper than trees, and yet, she knew in her heart that she'd break him. He loved her, but she was not destined to find enduring love in this life.

"Theo?"

"Yes?"

"I have another request to ask of you." She hesitated. "I'm sorry."

"Why?" His kind, wide expression cut as deep as a blade to the heart.

A familiar pang of guilt returned. She thought she'd changed his life with her first request—to gather the allies of Teridar. Now, though, his life would truly change forever. There was no going back from these words. This would rip away everything he loved. He would never return to that simple, happy life he so desperately wanted.

And his future?

So. Much. Pain.

Aurienne released Theo and approached the dais. "While you were gone, we nearly lost the city. I had a vision of the new monarch returning, a descendant of a long-dead king. I promised the city we would have a king or queen, and I stepped down as regent."

"You did what?" Theo exclaimed. "That can't be. We need you. You've guided us through all this."

She swallowed. "I'll remain High Seer, but the Goddess showed me that the rightful ruler would return, at least until the war is over."

Theo's shoulders sagged just a little before he forced them straight. "You need me to find them?"

A pained smile drew across Aurienne's lips. She reached up for the sword and removed it from the dais. It remained lightless, unstirred by her blood. She allowed the sharp blade to catch and reflect the light from the windows. Tiny white flecks of glimmering metal caught the light.

"Do you want to hold it?" she asked with a smile.

"No...I..." His eyes fastened to the crisp lines of the sword, and he took several steps forward. "Is that titan ore?"

I'm sorry.

She turned it around, holding it by the flat of the blade and offering the hilt to him. He reached for it, and his fingers closed. The sword exploded with dark light.

The light illuminated the room, pouring out. If Nesryn's sword was starlight, this was darkness. The light emanating from the sword was inky, and swirling tendrils took control of every shadow in the room.

"Aurienne?" Theo's eyes remained on the blade, but his voice shook.

"When I first read your fate, there was a great destiny that I did not understand." She tried to keep her voice from cracking. "All the threads of fate tied to you. I learned your Ma named you for Atheodoren, and then the Goddess showed me that the king would return. I thought it *might* be you...and I was right. Somewhere in your lineage is the first King Atheodoren."

"Aurienne..." His eyes met hers. "No... Please don't ask this."

"The sword has now confirmed your heritage. You're the only living descendent of the royal bloodline." She swallowed bile and guilt.

"Do not ask this of me. Anything but this." Theo gripped the sword until the bones of his hands protruded from beneath his skin, and his breath came sharp and fast.

"I'm so sorry, Theo," she whispered. "I wish I could prepare you for everything that would be asked of you. There are such dark days ahead. There is so much pain. For you and for me. Fate does not grant us the luxury of peace until the war is done. I have no choice."

"The past weeks have been hell. I barely survived it. I'm not built for this life. Don't bind me to a duty I don't want. Please."

"Theo...I..."

"Aurienne, if you speak those words, you know I cannot refuse you. So...don't..." His voice was hard and pleading.

Aurienne met his gaze. She didn't know what he saw in her eyes, but she knew what she saw in his. The hardness returned, not even softening for her. The hope disappeared. Fear gave way to excruciating resignation. Defeat. What hurt her the most was that not a trace of blame could be found in his eyes. He couldn't hate her, even if she hated herself. He simply *saw* her now. For what she truly was, what she'd become.

Goddess—that was worse.

The once-blacksmith closed his eyes, steeling himself for what came, bidding farewell to the life he wanted and yet would never have.

I would do anything to save you from this if I could.

Flexing her broken hand, she relished the pain. It was what she deserved. She was a blight on the world, a curse for everyone she cared for. Theo was willing to give up his life because he loved her. And she could offer him nothing in return but more suffering. More than anything, she wanted to flee that room and forget the sword ever responded to his touch, but the words spilled from her lips.

"Atheodoren Willem Thatcher of Karme, son of Willem and Anna Thatcher, will you serve as King of Avyllon? War is coming, and Avyllon needs its king."

Lifting his chin, he clenched his jaw while his eyes raged. His shoulders tensed as if preparing to take on the weight of the world.

"Yes. I will serve as king." His voice was unyielding and unforgiving.

Theo spoke the words, and his future was sealed. The golden, writhing cords of fate stabbed through the veil, wrapping around Theo. He grimaced as they sunk into his skin, his eyes locking on them until they vanished. His words were as binding as any could be. A soul oath. Aurienne knew the gods would never release him from his vow. In so many ways, his life was over. He never had a chance—not after he met her—and this war had only just begun.

"I'd do anything for you," he whispered.

Her heart broke, but she shoved down her guilt and regrets. She would become whatever was necessary to save them.

This world makes monsters of us all.

Afterword

Thank you for reading!

If you enjoyed *The High Seer*, please consider leaving a review on Goodreads or Amazon. Reviews, ratings, and word of mouth are so important for independent authors. Every review helps.

For more information about upcoming works and updates, visit my website www.alexbreewrites.com or follow me on Instagram @alex.bree.writes.

Want to stay up to date? Sign up for my author newsletter for exclusive updates, sneak peeks, and release news.

Alex Bree is a fantasy author and attorney living in Meridian, Idaho, with her husband, son, and dogs.

Acknowledgments

Words cannot express how excited I am to share this story after years of work. It has been more challenging and rewarding than I could have imagined.

I couldn't have done it without the support of my husband Korey who has been my ultimate supporter, first alpha reader, and brainstorm partner. You listen to all my insane musings, first drafts, editing and revising woes, bad poetry attempts, and you never question when the writing process gets weird (and it does). To my children who inspire me every day, I love you! Your story is just beginning. Hopefully, one day, when you're much older, you will read and love this.

Thank you to my writing group partners. I'm so thankful to have found you, and this would not have been possible without all of you. You have been there every step of the way. You have critiqued the earliest drafts of the manuscript, reviewed it many times, edited it, asked hard questions, broken it down and built it up, and helped polish it to where it is today. You're the first ones I go to when I'm deciding on the million things that go into a book—artwork, artists, editors, blurbs, chapter titles, website design, social media posts, fonts, formatting, obscure grammar questions, and everything else. Thank you: Billie Grey, Loren Huxley, Cole Layne, Jaci M. Lunera, Tiffany O'Haro, PC Nottingham, N.C. Scrimgeour, and Kaela Woodruff.

To my cover designer, Lisa Marie Pompilio, thank you for bringing my vision of the book to life in a way I never could have imagined. I'm floored and amazed by the beauty you brought to this story.

Special thanks also go to my wonderful friends who have encouraged and supported me and provided a sounding board when I desperately needed one. Taylor listens to hours of me obsessing over bookish things and always encourages me. Jaime is my litmus test, and her wit is the whetstone that sharpens my mind. Angela always tells me the truth when I need to hear it. Ruth is my cheerleader and the best phone conversation buddy. Thank you to my parents who always encouraged my love of reading and writing, and my brothers for their years of support.

Finally, to all those of you who read and enjoyed this book—I want to thank *you*.